MORE PRAISE FOR
THE SHOOTING GALLERY

"A powerful book that's dark, gritty, occasionally funny and has that street-smart ring of authenticity that Trigoboff does so well."
—T. Jefferson Parker

"THE SHOOTING GALLERY is social observation as seen through the bloody glass eye of a murder victim. As entertaining as a night out with the boys."
—Joe R. Lansdale

"Trigoboff's prose reminds me of Ed McBain's: rich, real witty and tough."
—J. Madison Davis, author of *The Vertigo Murders* and *The Murder of Frau Schutz*

"A gritty, uncompromising and suspenseful police procedural. Joseph Trigoboff has been too long away—welcome back."
—Les Roberts

"Sly, cunning, wise . . . A New York City novel in the best sense. Trigoboff at the top of his very good game."
—John Westerman, author of *Exit Wounds* and *Ladies of the Night*

"By turns hilariously funny, grim, grisly and always true, THE SHOOTING GALLERY hits the bull's-eye." —Barbara D'Amato

"THE SHOOTING GALLERY possesses a raw, sharp realism and a taut, interesting storyline that grabs the reader right from the beginning and propels them right through the final pages. I personally enjoyed the authentic treatment of the streets of New York and the cops that police them. An excellent read." —Hugh Holton

"A fast-moving, compelling and exciting read, full of fast, crisp dialogue and appealing characters. Trigoboff is a master of the hard-boiled genre. THE SHOOTING GALLERY is a winner."

—Gerald Petievich, author of *To Live and Die in L.A.*

ACKNOWLEDGMENTS

THE SHOOTING GALLERY is dedicated to Norman Rosten (1913–1995) and Bob Tramonte (1946–1998). Great writers and friends, they lit the lamps wherever they walked.

I'd like to thank my wife and children for their constant support during the eight years it took to research and write THE SHOOTING GALLERY. Also, special thanks to my agent, Matt Bialer, and his assistant, Cheryl Capitani, of the Trident Media Group, and to Brando Skyhorse, the best editor in town.

Copyright © 2002 A.S.T. Productions

The Lyons Press is an imprint of The Globe Pequot Press.

Printed in the United States of America

Design by Compset

10 9 8 7 6 5 4 3 2 1

Library of Congress Cataloging-in-Publication Data

Trigoboff, Joseph.
  The shooting gallery / Joseph Trigoboff.
    p. cm.
  ISBN 1-58574-547-2
1. Police—New York (State)—New York—Fiction. 2. Manhattan (New York, N.Y.)—Fiction. 3. Journalists—Fiction. I. Title.
  PS3570.R46 S56 2002
  813'.54—dc21
2002000932°

THE SHOOTING GALLERY

A Detective Yablonsky Mystery

Joseph Trigoboff

The Lyons Press
Guilford, Connecticut
An imprint of The Globe Pequot Press

ONE

We ought to legalize murder, Yablonsky. The average murderer serves less than seven years in this country. In effect we've already made it a misdemeanor. Besides, people only like to do what's forbidden. I bet if we made murder legal, the rate'd go down."

It was Withers's job to sit with the corpses until the coroner's van came. Tonight, though, he was off-duty. Detective Yablonsky reached into his coat pocket for a cigarette, an addiction that struck him usually only when he was at a crime scene. He did not feel like dealing with the implications of legalizing murder in New York City.

Ahead the lights of Tavern on the Green beckoned. Inside the large, lit windows, surrounded by huge dark topiaries, celebrities connected to the movie that had just wrapped were determined to dance and drink through the night and into the morning of the New Year.

Although it was winter, the weather had been unseasonably warm lately. The unexpected thaw brought the homeless into the park. Some had camped on the Great Lawn near the restaurant, and their anxiety-provoking presence had compelled the restaurant's owner to request police protection for tonight's party.

Yablonsky and Withers followed a trail that led to the Crystal Room's verandah, joining the other cops under the awning. Rain fell into the restaurant's fountains, rippling the water. A few cops stood under culverts at the great wide windows, peering into the park. Other cops pushed tables under the awning, hoping waiters would emerge and serve them. Some of the cops sitting at the tables were winding up the talking toy parrots the restaurant sold as souvenirs. You spoke into a concealed mike inside the parrot and it recited your words back to you.

"Better than a Naga recorder," Patrolman Androtti, a tall, thin rookie, said. "Merry Christmas, Alvin."

"Hey, Alvin! Happy New Year."

The rain had cleared the verandah of guests. The oversized windows of the Crystal Room revealed the flushed and chattering celebrities inside. Half wore costumes, all carefully designed to reveal their identities.

"Fuck them all," Androtti said. "A bunch of *cazzus*."

Yablonsky didn't respond. Unlike most of the cops there, he only partially resented the wealth and fame of the people he guarded. He knew that despite their complaints, most of these cops were thrilled to be in such close proximity to so many celebrated people. Maybe some of the fame and insularity would rub off on them.

The door to Androtti's left opened and two Hispanic guys came out, carrying a black Hefty bag of garbage toward the Dumpsters. One hand each gripped the garbage bag, the other held a bottle of Dewar's scotch.

"Christ, Alvin," Androtti said. "Even the kitchen help gets comped with liquor. It doesn't pay to be an honest cop in this city."

"You're not an honest cop," Withers said. He was about fifty, thin, with a slight case of palsy. He needed to put on weight and had rheumatoid arthritis. However, a murder scene energized him. He liked being a corpse-sitter. Murder kept him young, he said.

Patrolwoman Debra Trousdale heaved her bulk out of her chair. "The homeless aren't going to riot tonight. They're too stoned on kif and forties. I'm going in."

"So am I."

Withers slowly moved away from the window he'd been leaning against. "Coming, Alvin?" Withers handed a fifty-dollar bill to the doorman. He pointed expansively to the group of officers and patrolmen. "We're all disguised as cops tonight," and with that Yablonsky, along with the others, strolled through the glittering, golden doors.

Before the cops came in, they removed their shields and I.D. tags to prevent identification. Patrolman Goldstein elbowed his way to the front of the squad. "Blend," he said. The cops scattered. Some rushed the liquor bar at one end of the room. Most of the others flooded the bar at the other end.

A few feet away from Yablonsky stood a six-foot-tall woman that the detective recognized from the cover of *Playboy*. She only went by the name Anneka, and she had just graced the cover of *Esquire* in their yearly issue, "Women We'd Love to Love." She stood under a banner that plugged the movie.

Androtti approached the model. "Catchy title."

A glacial stare. "You don't belong here. You're either a cop or a crasher. And I'm gonna call security and have you escorted out."

"Don't drop a dime on me," begged Androtti. "I'm incognito."

She looked flustered, confused. "Oh, yes. The Italian cinematographer. Sorry. I didn't recognize your name."

Martin Wells, the actor, stood by the bar. Yablonsky recognized the other guy, too. His name was Ram and he was six-feet-five, with a lionlike mane of blond hair. He starred in soap operas and was part of a duo that did pregnancy test commercials.

"I just got back from shooting in Italy, where I saw Michelangelos's *Madonna*. She was magnificent."

The lion-haired actor beamed. "I didn't know Madonna was on tour in Italy. Or that she was repped by Michelangelo. Who's he with? CAA or William Morris?"

"Neither," Martin Wells said. "He's with Florence. Of Italy."

The giant nodded and left. Wells and Yablonsky exchanged smiles.

"The most dangerous person in the world," Martin Wells said, "is an actor who believes he has brains."

He spotted Barton McLeash and Roger Lloyd, the film's lead, sitting at a table along with the picture's director.

"Time to do some lines," said McLeash.

Did that mean they were about to rehearse or do cocaine? Yablonsky wondered.

"These lines'll blast your nostrils away," said McLeash.

It was time to leave.

He wasn't alone in the Oak Room. A tall, very thin, blond-haired woman sat at the bar by herself. Julie Benfield. Her family name was one of the great aristocratic names in America. One of those names that over the passage of time comes to resemble a title. No New Year's Eve costume for her. She wore a black evening dress with a simple string of pearls. She looked elegant. Her slender, fine features emphasized her unapproachability. Yablonsky approached anyway.

"Alvin, it's you," she said, tucking back a strand of loose blond hair. "Sit down. Join me. There's no one I'd rather drink in the New Year with."

"I will," Yablonsky said. "But I want to know why you're drinking so much."

"That's the detective in you." The aquiline features of her face narrowed. "I've just learned Dad has cancer."

"I'm sorry," Yablonsky said. Why did wealthy people always say "Dad," as if their dad was the only one in the world? Three months, two weeks, and five days ago he'd lost his own father. He knew he'd be in mourning for the rest of his life. "I understand." He touched her hand in an instinctive, sympathetic gesture. "You must love your father very much."

"Of course." Seeing the disapproval in his eyes, she pushed away her drink. "Pretty soon there won't be much of him left to love."

Yablonsky was embarrassed and felt he was intruding on her grief. "Do you want me to leave?"

"No. Please stay, Alvin. I'll never forget what you did for me that time with Warhol, partying in Studio 54."

"I was only in on the raid to bust Steve Rubell, the owner," he reminded her.

"Yeah, but you saved my O.D.-ing ass. You could've arrested me too, Alvin. Instead you took me to Roosevelt Hospital and made sure I recovered. You didn't even write it up. You're one of the few guys I can count on when I get in a jam."

"I'm sure you can count on Skinny. How come he's not with you tonight?"

"Skinny's weak, unlike you. The holidays remind him of his dysfunctional family. He's up at the country house in Stockbridge, working on an article. Why'd you help me that night, anyway?"

"I had a crush on you, Julie. From the magazines. I also figured, with your brother's death, the way he died—that's why you took the drugs that made you O.D."

"In those days I didn't need excuses to powder my nose." Her face clouded. "Not even Jimmy's death. You quashed 54 so it didn't make the papers. Rubell went to jail. I went home. You gave me another five years as an actress and model, before I tanked." She paused. "The one indispensable guy in my life, and when's the last time we saw each other?"

"A few months ago," Yablonsky said. Eight months ago, to be exact. There'd been a show celebrating models of the past. He'd seen her. On the runway.

"Alvin, I never forgot how I felt about you after that night. Stick around, you might get lucky."

Boy, did he want her. But he also wanted to stay friends with Skinny. "Things have a way of working out, Julie. Your boyfriend managed to save my ass a couple of months ago."

"Knowing the way you cops work, I assume you can't tell me how."

"I can't. You're a reporter."

"So you had a crush on me? If I'd have known that, you would've been able to catch me in between divorces. It might've been nice having a strong, dependable guy around for once."

"My ex-wife thought so too, right up until she dumped me. Complicated women have been the death of me, Julie."

"I always remember how kind you were. Atypical male behavior."

Through the sliding glass door of the Oak Room, then onto the verandah. He was surprised to see Withers, seated by himself under the awning, surrounded by empty tables. Withers stood, and the two men leaned against one of the windows, reverting back to sentry duty.

"Why'd you leave so early?"

A bitter look passed over the usually flippant man from the coroner's office. "I saw you talking to Julie Benfield. The detective and the debutante. The bitch shot you down, right?"

Cops and socialites, princesses and frogs. Yablonsky knew that in history, there were always peasants that, against all sense and logic, and despite past injustice and mistreatment, during troubled times rushed to defend their lords and noblewomen. He knew they were considered traitors to their class, and in times of revolution, they were always the first to be hung. "Of course she shot me down," he said. "But she was nice about it."

"Three cheers for her," Withers said. "Did you see those babes in there? I mean, *marone,* I'd sure like to be sued for sexually harassing some of them. But we ain't never gonna get women like that. Alvin. They're bred for the exclusive use of the men inside."

Flood, short, thin-featured, and balding, but definitely more successful, came out to join them. "I want to commend you both. You're the only ones in the squad who showed any strength of character. The only ones who stayed outside to keep watch. The only ones who didn't try to crash our party."

"Those were your orders, Captain," Yablonsky said.

Inside, the countdown had begun to another new year. Outside, the three men stared at the ice sculptures that flanked the restaurant. From behind a copse of trees, they heard raucous laughter, growing louder.

"Sounds like a bunch of drunks. Could be some homeless people," said Flood. "How many do you think there are?"

"Only a few," said Yablonsky.

"We'd better steer them away from Tavern. New York liberals love the homeless—as long as they're far away."

As they moved along a well-lit trail, the noise receded. Yablonsky glanced to his right. A great pyramid of ice and snow had formed over the Wollman Rink. But under the street lamps, Yablonsky glimpsed a smear of red.

From outside on the terrace, the three cops heard glasses being smashed in toasts. Near the pyramid's bottom, it looked like someone had rubbed a red crayon.

The men shot past the topiaries, through the trees, puddles of water, and melting snow. The rain had made the snow and ice slippery. Branches scraped by them.

They stared at the body inside the giant bank of snow, made soft by the rain.

Shouts of joy and wishes for a good new year spilled from the translucent, insulated restaurant. Flood ran his hand over his bald head. "My God, we've got a crime scene here."

Yablonsky forced himself to act. Putting on his gloves, he started scooping the soft snow from the victim's fingers, face, and body.

"Won't you destroy clues?" Flood asked.

Yablonsky looked around. Any footprints had long since been washed away by the rain. No fibers, no signs of struggle. Clues? There weren't any.

"We won't be able to lift any fingerprints off the snow, Captain." He handed Flood his car keys. Flood left to bring back the equipment they'd need.

Withers had recovered his composure. Despite his arthritis, he eagerly scraped the snow away. "I can't wait to see who this guy is. Murdered and frozen inside a pyramid like a pharaoh."

Flood returned with rolls of plastic tape and Yablonsky's lucite malachite kit. "Christ, look who it is. Skinny McPherson."

"If we work quickly and quietly," Flood said, "maybe we can keep them out of it. Control the crime scene."

Skinny had been investigating Yablonsky's precinct, seeking to write an exposé on police corruption there. Cops and detectives in the precinct were tied into a bordello on the East Side. They owned a piece of it, and were shaking down street peddlers, confiscating their goods and later selling it as swag.

McPherson had spoken to Internal Affairs, which was always on the lookout for crooked cops. Police rumor had it that once he handed in the article and it was published, several cops in the precinct would get burned. But whatever Skinny's exposé would do to other cops, it would exonerate Yablonsky.

"One of Skinny's stories dealt with corruption in our precinct," Yablonsky told Flood.

"Yeah, but we don't know how many goddamn cops he planned to burn when it got published," said Withers.

"Bullshit," Flood said. He looked down at the body encased in ice. "No cop could have done this. Cops wouldn't have had the resources. They wouldn't have had the connections to pull this off, or the money to come up with airtight alibis."

"Let me catch this case," said Yablonsky.

"This one's going to be high pressure. A red ball all the way."

"I was the first on the scene. I want the case."

"If Skinny had any notes from the story about my precinct, I'd be real interested in you finding them." Flood paused. "We've got to get them before I.A. does. Did McPherson burn you?"

"No," said Yablonsky. "His story clears me."

"Good," said Flood. "My precinct's still busy trying to prevent terrorism. Now the murder rate's up. Too many detectives are being devoted to Homeland Security. In New York these days, murder is legal."

TWO

Three a.m.

Flood and Yablonsky faced each other at Hanagan's bar, an East Village hang-out for the journalists at Skinny's paper, the *Guardian*.

"Skinny's murder hasn't become public knowledge yet," said Flood.

Patrolmen Henderson and Saunders came in. Familiar faces from the precinct. "Here's the rest of your team," said Flood. "I know this is a major murder, but we can only give you two people."

The tall black cop moved easily through the crowd. Saunders, much shorter, even shapely in her uniform, followed in his wake.

"Both of them are ambitious," said Flood. "They're willing to work double shifts to help solve Skinny's murder."

"I know them," said Yablonsky. They were a decade and a half younger than him. "I can work with them."

"Good to see you, Alvin," said Henderson. Turning, he studied the party-goers. "Skinny used to frequent this bar, right?"

"One of many," Yablonsky said.

"Anyone from his paper here?"

"I don't know yet," Yablonsky said.

Saunders scooped peanuts onto a napkin. "What's been done so far?"

"We've canvased the area surrounding Central Park. Interrogated people in the homeless encampment."

"Any results?"

"No one saw anything."

Yablonsky looked around at the photos of journalists that lined the walls. Since the *Guardian* was a left-wing paper, none of the photos were of booze-friendly writers, made mellow by literary chatter and gossip. Instead, the faces that stared back at him were solemn, weighed down by acting as the city's conscience. Photos of Skinny took up one corner of the bar, him sitting next to a manual typewriter, then an electric, followed by a word processor, a large computer screen, and finally a tiny laptop. Photos of other columnists, the newspaper's owner, Raymond Staples, and even photos of Sully Barnes, Abbie Hoffman and Jerry Rubin, leading violent antiwar demonstrations from the sixties, lined the opposite corner. Barnes had a look of fury on his face, a bottle to throw at cops in his hand. Decades later, Hoffman committed suicide. Rubin had been killed while crossing a street in California. Only Sully was still alive—rehabilitated, a male version of Mother Teresa, the newspapers said, running worldwide charities and homeless shelters for the U.N. He'd turned his life around, and had the citations to prove it.

"None of the photos match any of the people in this room," Yablonsky said.

"Pressure from Skinny's political friends come down yet?" asked Saunders.

"Not yet," said Flood.

Henderson crossed his long legs, frowning as he looked at the glasses of water on their table. "It's New Year's, do we drink to our future success?"

"Let's be the only cops who don't get drunk this New Year's," said Yablonsky.

"If I'm gonna be running interrogations at the *Guardian* tomorrow I'll have to check into the blue motel."

"It'll be the day after New Year's, the staff'll be skeletal," said Flood.

"I might pick up a few things," Henderson said.

The blue motel was a room in the precinct, usually filled with farting, snoring cops, who, just finished with or about to begin their shifts, tried to catch up on sleep.

"No blue motel for me," said Saunders. "My old man won't be home again tonight. I never should have married a fireman. When we both work shifts, we hardly get to see each other."

"Light some fires," Yablonsky said.

THREE

At his apartment, Yablonsky flicked on his VCR, wanting to see the tape he'd made of people actually celebrating the holiday. The tape rolled. The screen filled with the familiar visage of Dick Clark, a giant face that blocked out the revelers behind him. Like the rest of the country, Yablonsky had been watching Dick Clark not age for years now. But as a kid, he usually found himself turning the channel to Clark's competitor, Alan Freed, enjoying the authenticity and talent of the mostly black entertainers who performed on *The Big Beat.*

There was one more phone message. He thought that nothing else tonight would be able to surprise him, but he was wrong. His ex-wife, Arlene. Why was she calling?

After their marriage had ended, she had "married up," to the head of security for Harrah's in Atlantic City. She had caught Yablonsky on TV, on the evening news two nights ago. Then a sudden drop in her voice. She used this urgent, plaintive wail whenever, despite all his shortcomings, she decided that she needed him. "Merry Christmas, Alvin. Happy New Year. You must call us immediately. We're in trouble."

We're in trouble. Though he had wanted children, she had wanted none. Not with him. Not with anyone. So she had to mean her and her husband.

He was tired. He would call, but not this morning. Out of all the not-too-many women he had known, only his ex-wife would have the gonads to suggest that he rush to help the last man with whom she had cuckolded him.

He'd met Arlene after a handball game at Manhattan Beach Park. As he was handing over twenty dollars to Leroy White, she said, "Such a shame. You could have used that money to take me out."

The first visit to the Dolcis' had been memorable. Her father filled the door frame, holding garden shears and snapping the blades together, raising them over his head as Yablonsky fled with her to the door, swearing that he got the message. "Have a good time with my daughter. Don't forget. I'm also an electrician, so I do wiring."

As soon as he opened the car door for her, she placed her hand between his legs, cupped his testicles, and told him, "Let's have a good time." She slept with him on their first date.

He remembered their two-year marriage. After a couple of good weeks, it had started to founder, because unlike most other cops' wives, she wanted him to be home *less*.

"I grew up poor, and like Scarlett O'Hara, I never wanted to be hungry again. You're a cop, for God's sake. Get out there. Hustle. Make a buck."

In fact, she had been raised in Bath Beach, the doted-on daughter of a prosperous electrician who did all the wiring for the Profaci family. As a kid, Yablonsky had made the mistake of growing up with middle-class values in a lower-class neighborhood, East New York. He spoke patiently to her, beginning to agree with her months-old argument that she had married the wrong kind of man. "Arlene, I won't change. What do you want me to do?"

"I want you to be ambitious. Everywhere you look cops are getting rich. Don't be a grass cutter, Alvin. This city's made for the taking. Half of my father's uncles are cops. They all have homes on Todt Hill in Staten Island, Lake Wallenpaupak in the Poconos, and at The Landings in Fort Lauderdale. Go out there and be a man, for Christ's sake. Be a meat eater."

Lady Macbeth had probably scolded Mr. Macbeth in much the same way, he thought. And like Lady Macbeth, she seemed to be washing her hands of him.

"You don't understand, Arlene. As a cop, I really can't break the law too much."

"What the hell are you so afraid of anyway? As a cop, you never break the law—because you *make* the law."

"I'm afraid of getting caught."

She shook her head with disbelief, and it was obvious that she was far more reckless than he. "All my exhortations, all the patience I've shown, it goes right over your head. You refuse to be educated. The great miracle here is that no matter how many people they arrest, there's always so much more to steal."

Months later, when she had finally written him off, she made the admission that rocked him and ended their marriage.

As the weeks passed, he realized that she no longer seemed to expect skillful corruption from him. Yet she continued to urge him to leave their apartment and do his job. All the clues seem to be there, he thought. She's having an affair.

He lay back in bed, watching her as she brusquely entered the room, returning from a night out with her girlfriends. She slipped out of her clothes, quickly deposited them in the bathroom hamper. She returned wearing his bathrobe.

"Who did you see?"

A pause. The hesitation made him feel sick. "I was out with Connie and Marie. What's it to you?"

His clumsy interrogation continued. "Where'd you go?"

"You know. Out. The movies."

"What'd you see?"

"It was a movie. I forget."

He hoped he didn't show how sick he felt. "You forgot the name of a movie you saw tonight?"

"I didn't really go to the movies." Another pause. "What the fuck does it matter? And I'm not one of your motherfucking murderers, so enough with the questions."

"You've been unfaithful, haven't you? I've been faithful to you."

There was no answer. "Have you been monogamous?"

"Mostly."

She had hesitated before answering. In that millisecond, he died. He'd never given infidelity a passing thought. Though obviously she'd been doing enough thinking about it lately for the both of them.

She stood leisurely before him, unconscious that her bathrobe had opened and he could see all of her beautiful, curvy body. "I'm glad everything's finally out in the open. I know I'm supposed to feel guilty, but I won't play that game. I'm too honest for that."

"I see. You call what you've been doing being honest?"

"I do. You look so hurt, Alvin. In half the marriages today, one of the spouses commits infidelity. I didn't really cheat on you, because it's all just statistics."

"I see. Tell me, Arlene. How many times did you answer this statistical need?"

"More times than you'd like to know—and you'll never know how many times."

"I'd like to at least know where. Tell me."

"Of course. The Golden Gate Motel."

It hit him in the pit of his stomach. She'd cuckolded him in the most notorious temple to infidelity in Brooklyn.

"I guess I'll have to end our marriage, Arlene."

"Who's talking about ending our marriage? We'll end this marriage when I'm good and ready. I mean, if you sued for divorce, there we'd be in court, you making all these wild accusations as if we were in some soap opera. And I'd probably lose the apartment. And it's a great apartment, Alvin. We've got the best view of the Verrazano in the city. Anyway, when you come down to it, I didn't really cheat on you. If I'd been cheating on you without thinking you'd been cheating on me, then I'd have been cheating on you. But since I assumed you were cheating on me too, no cheating's really been going on."

He understood exactly what she was saying. She smiled at him, suddenly looking very pretty and winning. "I mean this is the twenty-first century. We're not Fred Astaire and Gracie Allen."

"Fred Astaire and Gracie Allen lived in the *twentieth* century. And it's not Gracie Allen. It's Ginger Rogers."

"Who?"

"Ginger Rogers. That's who he danced with."

"Okay, no big deal. Ginger Rogers. What the fuck are you so angry about?"

Unsuccessful in shaking or shaming her, he was determined to press on and win this argument. "Fred Astaire and Ginger Rogers. They were the most romantic couple in the movies."

She rolled her eyes in exasperation. "Okay, so I made a mistake. You always do that. Making a big thing out of every little mistake I make. That's not charitable. But back to the main point. My apartment. Please don't divorce me, Alvin. I've been so happy here."

Except for their arguments over his lack of ambition, he thought he'd been happy here too. Suddenly he hated their apartment. "I like the view of the Verrazano, too. I swear to you, Arlene, you'll never get custody of this apartment."

"Please don't do this to me, Alvin. You're a nice guy, but you're acting like a baby. If I knew you were going to react like this, I never would have cheated on you. Lots of partners go on after infidelity."

"I can't be married to you anymore, Arlene."

"Such a kid. So unambitious. So unsophisticated. Alvin, you force me to go to a lawyer, and I swear I'll tell him to stomp in your head in court."

"Arlene . . ."

"No. You're the one who wants to end our marriage, not me. That means I'm not responsible for anything I did in the past or anything I do to you in the future. I'll tell all the world how you've treated me."

She had seen too many talk shows. Everything was all wrong. The adulterous wife unrepentant and indignant. The cuckolded husband ashamed.

"Arlene . . ."

"No. You're not a nice man. I need help and understanding. I need probation. As long as I'm in this apartment, I'm willing to remain faithful. And I want you to know, I've always been faithful to you in my mind."

An image of all the men she'd made love to at the Golden Gate with her mind came to him. He knew that to her, he must look sick, a weakling.

He saw her shudder, then stare at him as if he were Hannibal Lecter. "I swear, whenever you look at me like that, you scare me to death. Think about it. I've been battered, Alvin. Assaulted. My children have been abused."

"We don't have any children, Arlene."

"And whose fault was that? Yours, not mine. I always wanted kids, Alvin. I would have been a great mother."

"Arlene, let me bring you back from Fantasy Island. Whenever I brought up having kids, you always told me, 'Not me. No brats. Not ever.' "

"Because I was afraid of having children with a father like you."

But she now seemed willing to forgive him his sins as a would-be father. Slipping out of his robe, she faced him, proud of her sloping breasts and blond pubic hair. "You're gonna have some proof of what a good wife I'm gonna be for you from now on." He had always liked the fact that she was confident about her beauty, but how many other guys had liked that, too?

He wanted no part of her. As she headed south, she smiled in what she believed was a sexy way. "Let me slip onto something more comfortable."

Afterwards she snuggled against him, certain she had won a great victory. "You see what a great wife I'm gonna be from now on. For you, I'll be more than monogamous. From now on there's nobody but you for me in this apartment. Why did I ever stray? I wish that the entire year could be a 'do-over.' "

"No more trips to the Golden Gate Motel?"

"No more trips." She smiled up at him. "That kind of thing's for Marie and Connie now. Not me."

"No more nagging me about making more money?"

That one made her hesitate. "As a valued civil servant you make a good living. I should be content to live on a detective's salary. I should be satisfied in knowing that at the end of your career there'll only be your pension for us to live on." She smiled at him sweetly, a demure and devoted wife. "I have a great idea, honey. Next week we'll start redecorating this place. *Our place,* Alvin. Together. To reflect your new confidence in me."

He drew her face next to his, gave her a hug, and smiled as if he were overcome with love. "I'm still going to divorce you, Arlene."

There was a pause. "Fuck you," she said. "You choose to kick me after I went down, but I will strike back, motherfucker."

She spoke to him triumphantly, as if his ruin had already been accomplished. "There's just one more thing I want you to know before I never talk to you again. You're nothing but a child, and you make love like a child. Just now was no different from any other time. Once again you managed to reach all my erroneous zones."

But in the battle that was their divorce, her lawyer continually outmaneuvered his. As promised, she meted out vengeance with a gusto that even impressed and astonished her own attorney. The baubles, zircons, and fugazis in their safe deposit box disappeared. The $2,800 in their joint savings account somehow suffered the same fate. And he would have to pay out alimony for five years. But the apartment with the view of the Verrazano went to him.

As the moving men packed away the last of her things she finally broke her silence. Her eyes set with determination. "I will return, Alvin," she vowed.

Full of confidence, he smiled back. "I don't see how."

He learned from other cops' wives that she could barely contain her fury when, two weeks after the divorce decree became final, he handed over the lease to another cop and moved out.

Now, from his apartment in Sheepshead Bay, he savored the memory of his one small victory. Even though no corpses were present, he lit a cigarette and bitterly remembered how it had turned out. The cop he had so cheerfully signed over the lease to was a bachelor. It was all very romantic and unplanned. A chance meeting between his cop buddy and his ex-wife at a Fifth Avenue bar that was frequented by the Bay Ridge Precinct. For a month there was a laser-like focus on doing anything and everything to please him. The trips to the Knick games. The devoted smiles as she sat demurely, watching him and his buddies bowl and drink beer. The many moments of sharing and caring. Yablonsky watched in helpless admiration as the whirlwind romance continued. Five weeks after meeting this hardened, streetwise cop, Arlene returned in triumph to the apartment. One week later she proudly etched her name alongside her fiancé's on the lease, where she lived happily with Yablonsky's ex-buddy until she met the man who would become her new husband, and fled the often dark and dingy place with a tacky view of a rusty bridge for a three-bedroom penthouse suite next to many of the high rollers he would oversee for Harrah's in Atlantic City.

Yablonsky replayed the message, again hearing the plaintive voice asking him for immediate help. Forget about that, he thought. He'd wait a while before calling.

Before he went to sleep he heard the familiar wail of a car alarm. Alarms were always going off at night. The urban melody helped him sleep.

Four a.m.

He heard a ringing and stumbled to the door. He lived on the ground floor of a house on a tree-lined block that was steps away from the beach. His apartment, half of a two-family house, was enormous and he paid reasonable rent. Lately his Russian landlord had been harassing him, trying to get him to vacate allegedly so he could give the apartment to relatives. It was probably him.

"I'm not vacating," he said. "Go away."

The ringing persisted. "Who is it?"

"The police."

He opened the door. Deputy Mayor Robert "Hey" Abbott, flanked by two uniforms. A couple of months ago, pulling a late shift on a pair of double murders, he'd seen Deputy Mayor Abbott clandestinely enter the after-hours bondage club Tops 'N Bottoms. Why the hell wasn't he there now, being spanked?

"What do you want?"

"Detective, get dressed and follow us."

"What the hell's going on?" Yablonsky asked.

"Just follow us."

The cars drove through the Brooklyn Battery Tunnel into Manhattan. As they got out and walked, three guys surrounded Yablonsky.

"Where are you taking me?"

"Just come along, Detective," Abbott said.

At the southernmost tip of Manhattan, there was a wide open space that served as a heliport.

The three men delivered Yablonsky to a waiting, silent helicopter. As he climbed the steps, then bent to enter, the mayor of the City of New York opened the door.

"Have a seat, Detective. Care for any coffee?"

Yablonsky declined. The mayor took the container of Starbucks out of the holder and sipped. "I have them delivered all the time. I'm on my way to Washington to attend a conference on young people and crime. I'm against it. You vote for me, by the way?"

"I did." Yablonsky answered truthfully. This mayor's predecessor had delivered on his anti-crime platform and the murder rate had plummeted. The new mayor was definitely under pressure.

"It's ironic. Skinny, writing for that left-wing newspaper of his, did nothing but accuse me of buying the election."

The mayor, one of the richest businessmen in the city's history, had spent millions of dollars to earn his mayoralty. That had come out to about a hundred dollars for each vote he'd received. Skinny had written that he should have paid the money directly to each voter.

"I've only been mayor of this city for a few months. Morale is low. Crime is up. Now a reporter's been murdered. One of their own. I guarantee you this story will knock funerals for firemen off the front page. This is my first crisis. Make sure you solve this case, Detective."

"I'll solve it."

"Good," said the mayor. "I'll be at this goddamned conference for three days. What can you give me concerning his murder?"

"Skinny was shot with a nine. The murderer had accomplices. Central Park was just the dump site, not the scene of the crime."

"That's little comfort. Central Park is the most famous park in the world. I don't like to be called at two in the morning and get told that one of the top investigative reporters in my city's been killed and

dumped in the park like some holiday joke. Especially since he was a political enemy of mine. Do you have a time of death? I'm assuming he was
killed before Christmas."

"Not yet."

"Do you have a suspect?"

"Not yet."

"I understand that he was working on a piece investigating corruption at the two-one, your precinct, when he was murdered."

"That wasn't the only story he was working on," Yablonsky said
quickly.

"No mayor wants to be more pro-cop than me. But if your investigation uncovers cops, you'd better fucking follow it. For your own sake."

"He wasn't killed by a cop."

"Enlighten me."

"Cops are street guys, sir. They wouldn't have the resources or ability
to murder in such a premeditated way. The most a cop can do is kill a
perp in an alley and plant a drop-gun or knife."

"Perp?"

"Perpetrators. Cops aren't able to plan a killing, set up an alibi, or
pay off politicians to get them off, if they get caught for conspiracy to
murder. And Skinny's murder was a conspiracy. I assume that he was
working on other stories. One of the other exposés he worked on, or was
about to work on, resulted in his murder."

"Maybe. But will you still want to solve this murder, Detective, if
the doors you open lead to cops?"

"Yes."

"Good. Tell me why."

"Because the story McPherson was working on about precinct corruption exonerated me."

"That's a good, selfish reason. But when a journalist gets murdered,
it's major headlines. How do you react to pressure, Detective?"

"I'm used to it."

"Good," said the mayor, sipping his Starbucks. "If this case gets shit-canned or derailed in any way, there's gonna be consequences. Do you still want this case?"

Yablonsky nodded.

"Good," said the mayor, finishing his coffee.

"They'll drive you back." The detective disembarked, staring at the whirling silver guillotine-like blades.

While Yablonsky was being driven back to Brooklyn, three of the men who killed Skinny McPherson met on Front Street, half a mile from where the mayor's helicopter had taken off. They climbed up a fire escape, cut the bottom pane of the apartment's bedroom window with a glass cutter, and pried the window open.

After entering the bedroom, they gently placed a plastic bag around the head of a sleeping man.

Two of the men watched as he expired. The third replaced the broken window with an old pane, identical to the others, then swept up the shards. As they climbed down the fire escape, one man said, "I heard that guy had AIDS."

"Yeah, looks like a suicide to me."

FOUR

Sully Barnes, winner of the Nobel Peace Prize a couple of years ago for his tireless work with the homeless for the U.N. and now the city, looked down at the celebrity-filled audience.

"The greatest thing about Skinny was that, though he knew he made enemies with his stories, he kept on writing. He knew he wasn't invulnerable. Sometimes he'd tell me he was frightened of the risks—but he'd never back off a story. Never. The proof of that is his murder."

Julie Benfield slowly mounted the podium. She was almost as tall as Sully, Yablonsky noted. Though formerly a model, Benfield didn't believe in makeup. Her eyes were swollen with tears and grief.

"Even though I'm on the editorial board of the *Guardian,* McPherson wouldn't show me his copy—wouldn't discuss his work with me. Usually I had no idea what he was working on. But then the story would break, and all hell would break loose. Sometimes the bad guys would be arrested, but a lot more often, though he exposed them, they got away with their crimes. He hated that. McPherson drank too much, ate too much, smoked too much. Sometimes," she said, "he'd even brag too much." She paused as people laughed. "But maybe all of that was because he cared too much. He was beautiful."

The service was over. The crowd spilled out of Campbell's, some to accompany the hearse to the cemetery, others to return to City Hall, their newspapers, or their network TV stations.

Guardian staffers moved toward the line of waiting limos. Sully Barnes approached the lead limo. He moved through the crowd, which parted out of respect, to embrace Julie. He hugged her for a moment; then her grief made her turn away.

She left Sully, walked through the streams of mourners.

"Alvin?"

He waited for her to reach him. She took his hand.

"Alvin. Please walk with me."

Moving away from the crowd, she said, "Too long."

"Too long?"

"The funeral service. My eulogy. Not good enough. There were too many eulogies." Of course, "If Skinny were alive, he would've loved it. He liked praise."

"He had a lot of friends."

"Obviously, though, someone didn't like him. You'll be here for me, won't you?" Looking up at him, she shivered. "Looks like I'm in a jam again."

"Jam?"

"I hate being alone."

"You're not alone. You're a celebrity."

"I *was* a celebrity." She squeezed his hands. "I hate being alone, Alvin. Since Skinny died, I feel like paying someone just to stalk me. At least it'd be company. If I was still famous I'd have an entourage. Now I only have you. I can count on you, can't I?"

"Of course."

"Good. I'm going to get through this. I've been through tons of divorces. This is my first murder, though."

"I'm going to be spending a lot of time with you, Julie. There will be a lot of questions. I'm sorry about that."

"No. No, I want his murderers found. There had to be more than one. Accomplices, to drive near where they wanted to dump him. Then drag him near the skating rink." She looked at him, her eyes narrowing, a reporter once again. "You check with forensics?"

"Last night."

"What'd you learn?"

"He was killed with a nine. He'd eaten shortly before he'd been killed. Egg rolls. Tacos. Chinese food."

"That was my Skinny. The guy had no discipline."

"If I can find out where he last ate, I'll be able to come up with a day and time of death."

"The last time I saw him was a couple of weeks ago. I told you that night at Tavern on the Green. I assumed he was in his country house in Stockbridge. He liked to go up there to write. Usually he kept the phone off the hook. Are they pressuring you yet?"

"No one's pressuring me."

"They should be. Alvin, you'll go with me to the cemetery, won't you? I need a guy I can lean on."

The procession was ready to take off. He followed her into the funeral car.

FIVE

Under the salesman's gaze, Yablonsky felt anorexic. "I'm a detective, remember? I have to speak to Walter."

"Walter's over at the buffet, organizing things. That's the *Obese Release,* to the uninitiated."

"How do you know I've never been here before?" asked Yablonsky.

The salesman laughed. "With that stomach, it's obvious. Here in Sales for Whales you're as skinny and svelte as Kate Moss."

"Maybe I'll come back here then." Yablonsky smiled. "How do I get to the buffet?"

"Take 'Gleason Glen' for half a click. Then make a left at 'Brando Boulevard,' which widens out into 'Orson Welles Way,' and you're there." He hesitated. "Watch yourself, though," he warned. "You're heading into dangerous territory. Once you grab a plate, you're on your own. Beware of claim jumpers."

"Claim jumpers?" Yablonsky asked.

"People who hijack or kidnap your food. It's not uncommon here." For a moment he looked uncertain, then continued. "May I give you some advice?"

"Of course."

"If someone has designs on your food-filled plate, it's best to surrender your portion. A pile of food's not worth your life, is it?"

"Of course not," Yablonsky said.

"Some here would disagree. Remember, you're on your own. Good luck."

Making a left, Yablonsky found himself on "Brando Boulevard." To his right and left, mythic, gargantuan figures, a few who did not want to expend the calories necessary to trudge fifty feet to the dressing rooms. They stayed in the aisles, struggling in and out of suit jackets. As soon as the detective reached "Orson Welles Way" he heard a low rumbling that grew louder as he neared the end of the trail.

There was a final dogleg to the right, then a sharp intake of breath as the detective entered a scene that was right out of the Serengeti.

People were gathered around enormous trough-like chafing dishes. Some made quick sallies toward a table, scooped up a portion of food, and speedily darted away. To his right, a group from a tour bus had staked out a territory near a series of benches and refused to let anyone else through; the males gathered around the territory to protect the entire pride as they ate. Waiters rushed past Yablonsky, carrying trays of roasted chicken, duck, and turkey. Often the tray would be nearly empty by the time they made it through the throng. The sole purpose of other waiters was to continually fill and refill the enormous plates with fresh delicacies. Signs on the buffet table read: *No Fingers, No Dunking.*

Scavengers, Yablonsky thought. What impressed him was the enjoyment they took in the act of eating. All of these people came from different walks of life, had different jobs and experiences. But they had this in common: they were all people who had crossed a tacit human boundary. As they chomped down on the food brought before them, they seemed to acknowledge that unlike most people, the world they lived in had no limits.

Walter Lumiere stood on a raised platform in the middle of the buffet he had christened the *Obese Release,* with a microphone in his hand, yelling instructions to the waiters.

Yablonsky stuck out his hand, but Lumiere was too preoccupied to shake it. "Section five needs roast beef, Arthur. And chafing dishes." He turned back to Yablonsky. "We did have a robbery last night. Still, I'm surprised they would send a detective over a few thousand dollars in cash. I'm impressed. We got it all on videotape." He paused. "When they made off with the cash *and* two chafing dishes, I almost lost it."

"I'm not here to talk about the robbery." A team of waiters carried in a series of two-pound lobsters and rib steaks.

"Hors d'oeuvres," said Lumiere. He called a waiter over and handed him the microphone. "I have to talk to this gentleman, Michael. Make sure everything keeps coming, but I don't want our supply lines overextended."

Yablonsky followed Lumiere as he marched away from the noisy buffet, back to "Brando Boulevard."

"When I spoke to you on the phone I told you that the coroner's report described what was in Skinny's stomach at the time of death, just before he was murdered. And three of his friends told me he headed up here. What time did he come in?"

"He was here, Lieutenant. December twenty-third at around five p.m. I remember because I refused to let another salesperson wait on him." He dabbed at the droplets in his eyes. "I always wanted that honor for myself. Like most celebrities he liked the four-star treatment. I'd escort him personally to the Obese Release." The proprietor turned away. "When I think about his murder, I get carried away. What kind of man steals another person's meal, Detective?"

"A hungry one," Yablonsky said. "How long did Skinny stay?"

"He was here about an hour. Left at around six. Said he had an appointment to keep."

Yablonsky was careful not to show his excitement. Unless people saw him after the twenty-third, that was the day of the murder. "Did he say where he was going?"

"No."

"Was he with anyone when he came in?"

"Not this time. Some days he'd arrive with that girlfriend of his. You know, I'd always ask myself what it was he saw in her, Detective. She was too thin. How can a man get excited by proportions like that?"

Yablonsky, who was himself well aware of Julie Benfield's proportions, said, "It takes all kinds to make a world."

"While we don't get that many skinny people in here as customers, this country grows bigger by the minute." He stretched out his arms like Charlie Chaplin playing with the world. "Our movement is expanding, Lieutenant. With each pound gained, we gain another victory. Sooner or later, everyone's going to shop here. I've seen the future of the next millennium in America, Lieutenant. It's not God. It's food."

"Maybe," said Yablonsky. "None of McPherson's clothing was found in Central Park. By now, we assume that his murderers have probably disposed of everything he'd worn. But the crime itself was so unorthodox that they could've done something equally unexpected with the garments as well. Often, items are removed from the victim for the murderers to keep as souvenirs. Do you remember what McPherson was wearing?"

The clothier to the fat didn't hesitate. "Top overcoat by Calvin Klein. Dark gray. No suit, just casual. Relaxed-fit slacks and a white banlon shirt he bought weeks before in our 'Tents for Rent' section. And now he's dead, Lieutenant, and aside from losing a fine reporter and dear friend, we've lost yards of material."

"It definitely wasn't in the holiday spirit. Did he purchase anything while he was here last?"

"No clothes this time. He was just here to eat. I'm good about that kind of thing, Lieutenant. A customer doesn't have to buy anything to enjoy the Obese Release. For me, it's always been, 'Give us your hungry, your poor.' Even the Statue of Liberty beckons the famished."

"You were Skinny's friend. Did he mention who he was going to meet?"

Lumiere shook his head. "Like all great reporters, he was usually pretty closemouthed."

Two men rumbled into Lumiere's store. Yablonsky saw the proprietor's face light with a glow of excitement as he stared at two six-hundred-pound identical twins. "My God," he said, "the Thomas twins. As I live, eat, and breathe. The great ones. In my store." He turned back to Yablonsky. "Are we finished? There are the Thomas twins. You must've heard of them. Of their accomplishments."

"I'm afraid I haven't," said Yablonsky. "Who are they?"

Lumiere laughed. "Each twin is capable of clearing half of my buffet in minutes. With those of us in the Back to Fat movement, their deeds have become folklore. Unlike Skinny, they never call ahead to warn us they're coming. I've got to get ready."

"I thought you were concerned about Skinny," Yablonsky said. "I thought he was like a son to you."

"My function in life is to serve the living, Lieutenant."

As the Thomas twins rolled into aisle four, taking "Arbuckle Alley" to the "Tents for Rent" section, Lumiere hurried in their wake. "Would you like to join us, Detective?"

One hour later, Yablonsky was on the curb, feeling bloated but satisfied, knowing he'd just participated in one of the great banquets of his life.

The rotund doorman stepped outside the shop and waved. "You did well," he said. "Come again."

SIX

Shelly Townes, ex-borough president of Brooklyn, rolled out of bed, stretched his skinny arms, and brushed his teeth. Then he assiduously reviewed his schedule. At 9:45, he was expected in the kitchen, to be handed first a broom, then a mop, just like the other prisoners. Then, after an hour of rigorous sports, free time and contemplation. In the afternoon, group therapy and another lecture on rehabilitation—which he didn't need.

As he shaved, he cut himself, one of the few men to do so while using an electric shaver. He grimaced. He'd already served six months, but was determined to get through the rest of his sentence.

Fuck it, he told himself. He could skip steering a broom and mop around for today; he'd accept the demerits. But the sports and therapy sessions were a must.

He slipped into a pair of designer jeans, then raised his thin arms and wiggled into a sweatshirt with the "Catskills Minimum Security Facility" logo. It resembled the kind of impulse buy that tourists spring for on vacations to New York.

He noticed that his bungalow-mates were not around. Thank God; they'd be at the indoor volleyball court, where he was expected in half an hour. Then his ordeal would begin.

Sighing, he walked outside, passing by a small series of signs with arrows pointing to the different facilities: Golf Driving Range. Restaurant. Boating. Health Club. Spa. Not Open to the Public, Guests or Wives of the Inmates.

He passed by prisoners lugging bags of new seed to the sheds, to be used on the fairways and greens when spring came. He was in the state minimum security facility, but behind it sat the annexes and facilities for a federal minimum security prison. As there were no barriers to enter and leave the place, he and the other state white-collar criminals had lucked out.

He walked by the lot leading to a series of trailers that were used for conjugal visits by the prisoners' wives, then past the indoor resort-sized swimming pool. The prison in fact had once been a resort for Orthodox Jews, before it went out of business and had been taken over by the state. As Orthodox Jewish men and women didn't swim together, the prisoners had two of almost everything: two volleyball courts, two spas, two pools.

Seeing no one was around, Townes jimmied open one of the vending machines and had his breakfast. Of the dozen vending machines serving candy and soda on the prison grounds, he'd managed to have two machines of his own slipped in. The delivery guy and franchise owner, from Brooklyn, were part of his constituency.

Outside again, he forced himself to walk to the volleyball courts. With no twenty-foot barbed-wire-tipped walls, or guards with rifles impeding the view, the panorama he had of the bare fields, the rolling hills, was terrific.

Approaching the volleyball court, he saw that the guys were already choosing up sides.

His nemesis, Sid Wolfe, held the ball. Wolfe was a former inspector of traffic lights who'd used his job as an opportunity to strip metal from the lights and sell it.

Glancing at Townes, he said to the opposing captain. "Chose you for him. Odds or evens? Loser gets him."

"You lose. He's yours."

Reaching the tennis courts Yablonsky noticed two teams of men playing volleyball. He recognized the man about to serve as Shelly Townes. Before his imprisonment he'd been the borough president of Brooklyn.

As Townes struck the ball, Yablonsky thought that he looked like the flabby, skinny kid who sat at the beach and let everyone bigger and broader kick sand at him.

The ball went into the net. A man Yablonsky had known on the outside, Sid Wolfe, groaned.

"Not again!"

"Spastic," another man grumbled.

"Sorry," said Townes. After serving, he rotated to a position on the front line. Yablonsky watched as a man from the other team served. A feverish volley ensued. Jumps. Passes. Spikes. Yablonsky realized that the health club situated behind these men had obviously kept most of them fit. The ball was hit to Townes. He had a great opportunity to spike, leapt up in the air, swiped halfheartedly at the ball, and missed. Yablonsky saw the men on the front line of the other team smile.

"Our secret weapon," one of them said.

"Shelly, do us a favor," the inspector of traffic lights barked. "You wanna see us win?"

"Sure."

"Then pull your hapless ass out of the lineup. Leave the game. You're banished."

Yablonsky noticed that Townes did not seem to be humiliated or embarrassed by the barbs. Smiling at his teammates, he walked off the court.

He'd acted the same way during his trial, Yablonsky recalled. Agreeable, friendly, contrite.

The feeble efforts he'd made before to serve and then spike the ball had caused him to sweat profusely. As Townes bent down to pick up a towel, Yablonsky approached him.

Townes looked up, and the towel slipped from his hands. "Oops," he said.

Yablonsky picked up the towel and handed it to him. He noted that despite the harsh conditions of Townes's incarceration, he was bearing up.

"Thank you," Townes said, fumbling for the towel. "I'm really clumsy today."

"You'd never know it," said Yablonsky. "I'm the detective who called earlier."

"Right," Townes said. "Let's go inside."

"How they treating you?" asked Yablonsky.

Townes shrugged his thin shoulders. "I can't complain." He was shorter than the detective and looked like a stiff winter breeze would knock him over.

Yablonsky followed the former borough president across a stretch of greenbelt to his bungalow. Despite the winter, a group of inmates were practicing their putts next to a series of bungalows. Others were stringing out netting that would go on the tennis courts.

"I thought you all had jobs here," Yablonsky said.

"We do. I work in the prison print shop. On the sly, I print up literature for the party, possibly for my future campaign."

Yablonsky supposed that breaking or bending the law in a minimum-security prison wouldn't be too difficult at all, just like on the outside. He walked with Townes up the steps, across a porch, and through an unlocked door into his prison cell.

The bungalow had been divided into six cubicles of equal size. The room had been pleasantly painted in blue and beige. Though there were

TV and music rooms in the visiting center, a few prisoners listened to personal disc players or watched satellite TV, keeping the volume low or using earphones out of consideration for the other inmates. The guy who lived in the cubicle just before Townes's was watching a movie video.

"We have a video library. We get all the latest releases. Great, right?" said Townes.

Yablonsky did not disagree. Townes led the detective to his own private nook, throwing his towel in a laundry hamper in the corner of his room.

"You should see the laundry facility," he said. "Right out of *My Beautiful Launderette.*"

"Appropriate," Yablonsky said. "Considering most of the men are here for trying to wash their cash."

Townes chuckled. "That's funny. You know, you have a good sense of humor for a detective."

Yablonsky looked around at the pleasant bungalow that seemed right out of the Chateau Marmont in Hollywood. "I'm beginning to believe that this time the joke's on me."

Shelly Townes reached for a hand weight resting on a shelf near a stack of books. He lazily pumped his arm up and down, dropped the weight, but managed to move his foot away in time. He left the weight where it'd fallen on the floor.

"Sorry about that," Townes said. "Personally I think all the effort that a guy puts into sports is silly and unproductive, unless you're a professional athlete and getting paid for it. But my cardiologist told me I gotta get in shape, you see. I'm too frail. That's why you saw me playing ball outside. I gotta be like Rambo."

Townes flung himself on his bed, then crept to its edge and sat with his skinny feet hanging over the rail. "You wanna ask me some questions, right?"

Yablonsky pushed a chair to the side of the bed and took a seat. "The article Skinny wrote resulted in your imprisonment. You also lost one of the most prestigious jobs in the city. I know you couldn't have murdered him yourself because you were in here when he was killed. But did someone else whack him for you?"

"A million times, no," Townes said. "I'd never do anything like that, Detective. I was the borough president of Brooklyn, for God's sake. That's one of the whitest white-collar jobs a guy can get. Besides, blaming other people for your problems is not what prison's all about. I want you to believe me, Alvin. I'm the guy who fucked up. I'm the guy who let everyone who trusted me down. Even the book that's gonna be written about me's gonna emphasize my sense of guilt. And when you're mea culpa in a book, you create a permanent record. The whole world's gonna know how sorry I am for all the things I tried to get away with."

"Come on. Don't bullshit me, Shelly," said Yablonsky. "A borough president has all kinds of connections. Some nosy writer causes your imprisonment and you're not sore? *Tauchis offen tisch,* as the Jews say. Put your cards on the table."

"Okay," said Townes, "I was a little sore. But I never got angry enough to do anything about it. On the lives of my wife and children. Besides, how could I blame Skinny? Everything that happened was my fault."

Townes slipped out of his shirt and tried to twist it into a tight knot so he could toss it like a basketball. He aimed for the hamper and missed. He made no effort to pick up the shirt. He looked at the detective and smiled. "Where was I, Detective?"

"You were talking about your rehabilitation," Yablonsky said with a smile.

"Right. But what I just told you isn't true. Being in this prison hasn't made me a new man. Even before I was sentenced, I had rehabilitated myself. If they freed me tomorrow, I'd have the inner strength to reject the cons and scams that would have tempted me before. Ask the prison psychiatrist. He'll tell you that nobody in our group accepts responsibility and guilt better than I do. If Skinny hadn't written that article, I'd never have had the opportunity to transform myself. I really am a new man."

Yablonsky unconsciously reached for a cigarette and lit it. "Enlighten me," he said.

From outside the cubicle, both men suddenly heard a voice roar. "Where's my fucking soda, Shelly?" There was a pause in which both men heard a refrigerator door slam. "I had a six-pack here. Three cans are gone. Stolen. Where are they, Shelly?"

Yablonsky looked to the borough president, who waved a skinny hand dismissively. "It's nothing," he said. "Where was I?"

They heard a series of loud, fast footsteps. A big, jock-like guy stood in Townes's doorway, filling it. He was red-faced. "Three cans of my six-pack are gone. Where are they, Shelly?"

The accusation didn't seem to bother Townes. He smiled slightly at the detective. "For chrissakes, Mel. Don't get your fucking balls in an uproar. It's only soda, not the crown jewels."

Yablonsky recognized the angry guy who filled the doorway. His name was Melvin Harris, and he had once been the comptroller for a chain of New York banks. So many accounts in Geneva were so flagrantly laundered that even the morally neutral Swiss finally washed their hands of him and dropped a dime. He was currently serving two years for misappropriation of funds.

Harris turned to the detective. "If it was the crown jewels, somehow this cocksucker'd find a way to boost them even in prison." He turned to Townes. His voice was flat. "This is the second time this week. I warned you."

"Where were we, Detective?" Townes said, but his thin arms shook slightly. "I was telling you about my downfall, right?"

Harris stepped into the room, his hands knotted into fists. "You motherfuckin' slimy worm, I told you before. This is not like life on the outside. Here we're supposed to be good to each other."

The former borough president looked at Harris, smiled, and shrugged. "Inside, outside, what's the difference?" He turned back to Yablonsky. "Watch, Detective. This guy's gonna give himself a heart attack over a can of soda."

The man crouched, thrust his hands forward. "I told you I'd beat your slimy brains in if it happened again."

Yablonsky heard laughter from men in the other cubicles. Townes looked at his accuser blankly, not reacting to the insults.

"We are talking, right, Detective?"

Yablonsky nodded. The former bank comptroller moved forward swiftly, grasping Townes by the neck and shaking him. "Thief," he hissed. "Worm."

Yablonsky stood, but Townes waved him away. "It's okay," he gasped. "Let the maniac vent."

Harris pulled back his hand into a fist, changed his mind, and slapped the unresisting Townes as if he were a girl. Townes fell back on the bed, remaining motionless.

"You finished, Harris?" he said. "I wanna know."

The man was still red-faced. "Steal my soda again, wise guy, and you'll know. If there's a next time, they're gonna put me in a real jail over what I'm gonna do to you." The physical exertion had made his chest heave. He turned to Yablonsky. "Sorry for the interruption, Detective. Watch your wallet." Wheeling, he left.

Townes lay motionless on the bed. Yablonsky saw his pipe-like arms slide around his chest and he rocked back and forth. "Will my punishment ever end?" he said loudly enough for the other men in the bungalow to hear.

"Are you okay?" Yablonsky asked.

"I'm not okay," said Townes. "You want me to help you, you have to help me up."

"Sure," Yablonsky said. Grabbing the detective's arm, Townes pulled himself to the end of the bed and dangled his feet over the railing. "Sorry you had to witness that," Townes said. "We fight among ourselves constantly. It was only a can of soda. I guess that trivial people fight over trivial things."

"As a cop, I wouldn't call what I just witnessed a fight," said Yablonsky. "It was more like an assault." He thought about the many street fights he'd had and lost as a kid sentenced to life in East New York. "Next time, try fighting back," he said. "They'll respect you more."

Townes displayed his thin arms and smiled ruefully. "Do I look like a fighter?" he asked. "Besides, fighting in prison's against the rules."

There was derisive laughter from his cellmates. "No one respects me, Lieutenant. Not even my constituents. If they did, they never would've sent me here." He pointed to the resort-like bungalow as if it were Devil's Island. "Detective, I'm okay now. I tell you I'm gonna rehabilitate myself, even if the entire city's against me. And when I get out at last, I'm gonna forgive Harris. I'll forgive McPherson. Even the big donors and voters in my campaign who spoke to Skinny and questioned all my financials. The men who investigated me were more crooked than I ever was."

That was probably true, Yablonsky thought. He noticed that Townes spoke about his constituents as if they had robbed him blind, and not the other way around. Yablonsky lived in Brooklyn. He remembered the building projects, the additional traffic lights put in at intersections in his neighborhood that had cut fatalities. As venal as Townes had been, he'd also been an effective borough president.

The former borough president and accused soda thief leaned closer to the detective. Townes smiled. "Confidentially, Detective, I never expected to win. I never wanted to win. I ran more times for office in Brooklyn than Vito Battista. I always had my eye on the campaign contributions. You remember those junkets to Europe I'd always make after each campaign? As long as I lost, my financials were seldom scrutinized. I had everything a man could want. A beautiful wife, summer and winter homes. With each loss my lifestyle always managed to improve a little. I tell you, Alvin, I lived much better than that Democratic hack who ran against me and always won."

Townes stopped talking. Yablonsky watched him reach inside his pillowcase, take out a can of Pepsi, and sip it. "But then, close to a decade ago, a new candidate for mayor comes along," he said contemptuously. "A Republican who guarantees that he'll lower crime. That there'll be no more riots or racial boycotts like in Crown Heights or Flatbush. And because of his record as a prosecutor, the voters believe him. He's elected, and the mook's got long coattails, because I'm swept into office right along with him."

Townes wiped his lips and thrust the Pepsi towards Yablonsky, but the detective declined the offer to split the liquid swag. "You know, we may be in minimum security here, but it's still a prison. If you don't care enough about your possessions to safeguard them, then it's your fault when they disappear." He took another sip. "Where was I, Alvin?"

Yablonsky remembered the quiet, inauspicious way Townes made his junkets to Europe, taking his wife and two teenage children along with him as his assistant and recording secretaries. He glanced at Townes with new respect, despite the weaknesses he'd witnessed before. "You were telling me how your problems began once you won. And no lies, Shelly."

"That's right," Townes said. "And I don't lie, Detective. Not anymore." He smiled, making a lip-smacking sound as if he wanted Harris to hear him. "All my problems began once I'd won. Winning was my Watergate. After I took office for a second term, a reporter made the trip from Manhattan over the Brooklyn Bridge to visit my borough. I was eating lunch in Queen, that Italian restaurant across from Borough Hall, when he approached me. I already knew all about him. He wrote exposés for the red rag in the Village, the *Guardian.* I immediately threw a double sawbuck on the table and left.

"The next day I was in Queen again, eating prosciutto, and he came back, promising that the article would be laudatory, a tribute to the tenacity that led to my success. The theme of the piece would be how I was able to ignore my four prior defeats and at last win office."

"So you agreed?" Yablonsky asked.

"Hell no. I declined again. But he wrote the article anyway. It was unauthorized, but I knew that even while he was asking my associates and friends all these alleged innocent and complimentary questions he was mixing the mortar for my tomb."

"He destroyed you, under the guise of complimenting you," said Yablonsky. "You must've been furious. Brooklyn politicians are notorious for being vengeful."

Townes sipped his soda, nodding reflexively. "There was no reason to be vengeful. He buried me with praise. To this day I remember the seemingly harmless questions and statements that turned so deadly. 'There's another side to this great man besides his tenacity. How he was able to accumulate three vacation homes and a stock portfolio managed by *Sanford Bernstein* I'll never know. He must be a financial genius.' Then there was, 'What one has to admire most about Townes is his frugality upon assuming office. No more European trips for him. As long as the ever-vigilant Townes is borough president, Brooklyn voters can rest easy.' " Townes's fingers gripped the can of Pepsi as if he were strangling it, tossing it weakly toward a wastepaper basket near the laundry hamper. It bounced off the rim. He made no effort to pick it up. "You know, Alvin, to the day Skinny died, I don't think he was even aware he'd written such a deadly exposé." He nodded thoughtfully, reaching into his pillow case and bringing out another can of soda.

"You didn't have Skinny whacked? Despite the fact that, even though you've already been here for six months, you still have to serve another two years?"

Townes smiled. "Don't let what you saw before give you those kinds of ideas, Detective. I was depressed and angry because Harris has beaten me up before."

"Over what?"

"Small things. There are five other guys living in this bungalow, yet whenever something is stolen they come to me."

"If I were serving my time here, you'd be the logical place I'd look." Yablonsky nodded toward the can of soda. "You told me before you were completely rehabilitated."

"If going from being accused of stealing a million and a half dollars to being blamed for boosting three cans of soda's not complete rehabilitation, I don't know what is."

Yablonsky admired the way Townes avoided admitting guilt by maintaining he was only "accused." "You've gone from stealing millions of dollars to swiping cans of Pepsi, but you're still stealing. Stop bullshitting me, Shelly."

"I'm modifying my behavior, Detective. Slowly winding down. As far as being sore at Skinny for being stuck in prison, believe me, I know I got off easy. There were people who really wanted me to pay for my shenanigans. Here, as long as I give them thirty hours of work a week, I have complete freedom. You saw those trailers when you first came in, right?"

Yablonsky nodded.

"My wife and I meet there twice a month for conjugal visits. I see and sleep with her more in here than I ever did on the outside. Before, my entire life was campaigning. Now I got satellite TV, I eat cuisine that's so good the prison chef oughta be rated by Zagat. You saw me playing volleyball. Arnold Schwarzenegger I'll never be, but my health's improved since they put me in here. I'm enjoying my life much more in 'Club Fed' than on the outside. My life's changed, all right, Detective, it's gotten better."

Yablonsky digested this. He looked at Townes, studying him without seeming to. He saw a lot of things in the man's face, but not murder.

"Prison's freed me, Lieutenant. When I was living on the outside I was really in jail. That's the God's honest truth."

Yablonsky reached for another cigarette. He'd heard that kind of speech before from many inmates, usually when they were before a prison board seeking parole.

"Since the article was unauthorized," Yablonsky asked, "did you ever talk with him again?"

"Never," said Townes. "He was there during my trial, watching the proceedings, but I still wouldn't speak with him."

Yablonsky pulled out a pen, and began to take notes on his pad.

"How often did Skinny show up?"

"He was there for the duration, but not every day. Most days."

"How long did it last?"

"Just three weeks. I had a kangaroo court."

"That's a good one, Shelly." Yablonsky paused. "Was Skinny ever with anyone else?"

"Not to my knowledge." Townes smiled ruefully. "Believe me, Detective, I wasn't paying close attention to him. I had other things on my mind."

"Did you ever see him interview anyone in court for his article?"

"Sorry, but no. During sidebars with the attorneys, he was allowed to listen in. The party chose my lawyer, not me. If I would've had decent counsel and a fair-minded judge, I'd still be on the outside."

"But then you wouldn't have been rehabilitated," Yablonsky said.

"That's true."

"Who was the presiding judge?"

"The Honorable Robert Dillon. In nearly every ruling, he favored the prosecution. I think he was scared of being reversed on appeal, and that's why the sentence was comparatively light."

"Did Skinny ever confer with him?"

"He might have. I didn't notice him interviewing Dillon during my trial, but he might've met with him after, you know, to sharpen his ax for the job he did on me. And I'm not lying about that judge, Alvin. Five weeks after my trial, they transferred him to divorce court so he could keep company with the rest of the fuck-ups."

Another question occurred to Yablonsky. "Did you notice anybody in court watching Skinny while he was watching you?"

Townes shrugged. "There are always spectators in court."

They were interrupted by a low chirping sound. Townes rolled lazily off the bed. "Sorry," he said. "Gotta get my cell."

"They're having a lockdown?" Yablonsky asked sarcastically.

Townes laughed and picked up a cellular phone. "No, Lieutenant. This is what I'm referring to. Who thiz? Murray?" Townes looked up. "I've got Murray Kornblum on the line."

Yablonsky listened to Shelly's end of the conversation, noting that, for a guy in prison, Townes still had access to the people in power. Kornblum had been the Republican party leader of Brooklyn for the past decade. Townes took a sip of soda and spat into the phone. "No, Murray. No. No. A trillion times, no. That name is to be removed from the appointments list immediately." For a moment he listened, then barked, "I don't care diddly squat if he's the compromise choice. I didn't choose him. I'm not gonna let Valdez push this cocksucker through." Ernesto Valdez was Townes's successor as borough president of Brooklyn. "He's Valdez's man, not mine. You tell Ernesto that I may be stuck in a mousetrap, but I ain't nobody's piece of Velveeta."

Yablonsky rose to leave.

"Why don't you sit back down?" Townes asked. "Split a pizza with me. I'll call the Domino's in Liberty and in twenty minutes we'll share a pie. It's ironic, Detective. There are parts of Brooklyn where the delivery people won't go because it's considered too unsafe."

"Watch yourself, cop," Yablonsky heard Harris shout. "Don't share anything with him. You'll see him split the pie right down the middle, but somehow your share'll only be a piece of crust."

"That's right," another voice yelled. "Townes'll swipe your tube of toothpaste right out from under you even if you're brushing your teeth."

Townes made the call and ordered the pie. "I hope you ignore my fan club, Detective." His voice grew louder as he spoke to his tormentors. "I guess I'm not gonna get your votes after all."

"Not unless you steal it!" shouted Harris.

"Mine neither, and I'm a Republican. Hey," the other voice yelled, "my toothpaste *is* gone."

Yablonsky didn't want to split anything with this thief. "Sorry, I have to leave," he said. He paused. "I've been offered much better bribes, Shelly. I turned those down, too."

Townes threw his cell phone on the bed and got up. "So have I. That's why I'm really being rehabilitated, you know. From the things they didn't catch me for."

"Where's my fucking toothpaste?" one of his bungalow mates roared.

Yablonsky, about to leave the cubicle, instinctively glanced back at Townes, who, rummaging through a drawer, had taken out a new tube of toothpaste and was in front of a small mirror by a sink, brushing his teeth with a Pepsodent smile.

SEVEN

Clerk Jimmy Johnstone, entering his presiding judge's chambers in front of the shapely novice attorney, dunked the money-filled envelope into the open desk drawer with the practiced skill of Michael Jordan.

"Two points, Jimmy," said the judge. The bailiff nervously pivoted, for he had gone against every survival instinct by depositing the envelope in front of a third party, but Judge Dollars Dillon had ordered him to do so. However, Johnstone ignored the judge's casual wave of dismissal to linger in the room a moment longer. Both men looked at the curvaceous beauty sitting across the desk, to gauge her reaction.

The attorney was petite but stacked. Both men inwardly sighed as she thrust her shoulders upwards, and they could see the ripples of her power suit, the faint impressions of her pointed nipples struggling for liberation against her brassiere.

"You need anything, Judge?"

Dollars Dillon cast wary eyes at his competitor. "Everything's just fine, Jimmy. See you later."

The judge stared at this luscious piece of ass solemnly, pondering the weighty judicial matter at hand: whether to immediately pocket the envelope, or, just this once, to decline the proffered payoff.

The attorney was Shoshanna Tuvia. She passed the New York bar exam five months ago and had taken the first steps to establish a career by becoming a divorce lawyer and setting up an office with three other attorneys on lower Broadway, not far from the family court building on Centre Street. Two weeks ago, she had tentatively joined the pack of lawyers who hung out by the rear bench in Dollars Dillon's courtroom, hoping the judge would steer litigants who had arrived in his courtroom without an attorney to her. Even with his thick glasses, he had noticed her sitting in the back row and had promptly assigned to her one of the petitioners in the Forster case. In choosing her to represent one of the litigants, he had in effect granted her what was called "grazing rights" in his courtroom. According to the dictates of justice, she was expected to kick back part of her fees to him.

The judge took his eyes away from her as he heard a knock, and Vincent Cook, one of the courtroom's deputies, entered.

"The casebook's already been assigned, Your Honor."

Judge Dollars Dillon grunted, "Everyone happy out there?"

"Smooth as a goose giving head, Your Honor."

"Glad to hear it."

The twenty-six-year-old attorney's eyebrows furrowed. "What was that all about, Judge?"

He made a dismissive gesture. "Nothing, my dear. Just taking inventory. Something you'll learn all about in the future, once you understand the inner dynamics of a courtroom." She would not yet be aware of the great judicial battles between his courthouse deputies and clerks, who repeatedly clashed over who would pass on the files of prospective clients to the waiting attorneys and therefore pocket the bribes. In the battle over the money, the deputies had all the advantages because, unlike the clerks, they had mobility and weren't restricted to their desks. They could waylay the litigant as soon as he or she appeared in court, before reaching a clerk. The atmosphere lately had become poisonous between the two competing groups, and Judge Dillon had utilized his courtroom savvy to come up with a scheme in which both groups pooled part of the bribe money and therefore shared in the profits.

Once again it seemed that the wheels of justice were running smoothly. He turned back to Shoshanna Tuvia. The problem with her was that she was too damned good-looking to be a lawyer in matrimonial court and may well have been sent over by his enemies, those pimps in the judicial investigation department, to entrap him by proffering a bribe. If she was what was called in the world of politics a "honey trap," then he knew that his conduct would have to be faultless, at least until he determined whose side she was on.

He moved to the coffeemaker on top of a small refrigerator located in the rear of his room, dipping his hand into the drawer so she could see him pocket the envelope. The desk drawer was used so frequently for financial aggrandizement that the denizens in his courtroom referred to it as "the tollbooth."

She stirred slightly with surprise, but there was no other reaction at his brazen display of greed. His pencil-thin, graying eyebrows furrowed in a friendly way as his eyes traced the line of her pale thigh to where her black pantyhose began.

As he headed back to her, carrying a cup of coffee with one hand, his other hand patted the envelope in his pocket. He wanted to begin her education. "Justice functions best when everyone has a share in it." He placed the coffee on the table and executed a mock bow. "Your espresso, my dear. All part of the service." Staring at her chest, he asked, "One lump or two?"

"I usually take two lumps with mine."

"I can see that," he said, lost in admiration. "When I saw you enter my courtroom two weeks ago, so new and idealistic, I swore to myself that I was going to show you the ropes. Are you willing to place yourself in my hands? There's so much about the law that I can teach you."

She leveled her gaze at him, displaying a tiny gold ring on her left hand. "I'm married, Your Honor."

"So am I, my dear." He saw that this was no time for crude looks and suggestive language. If she was what she claimed to be, an honest attorney who could be bribed and trusted, then she still might have made a deal with some clerks to cut or gyp him out of his rightful share. It was a common practice for a clerk, pretending he was the judge's representative, to waylay an attorney who had just entered the courtroom, hand the lawyer files of the cases the judge had assigned him, demand a gratuity, and keep all or part of it for himself.

He put down his cup of java. "Did any of the clerks approach you on your way in here?"

"Yeah, but I waved him off."

"Who approached you, Ms. Tuvia?"

She did not react. From his perspective, her refusal to roll on a colleague was a good sign. "I'm glad to see that you're no rat, my dear. I'm also happy that you waved him off. Even though the clerk hands you the file of your new client, you're supposed to come to me directly to show your gratitude. Always bring the envelope to me."

She reached in her pocketbook to hand him the thick envelope, but he drew back in real horror. "No. No. No. How would it look, you handing money to a judge?" He yanked his chin toward his open desk drawer. "It goes in there." He pointed to an overcoat draped over a wooden hanger. "Or in there. Do you understand? I don't even have to be in the room when you make the deposit. You leave it, I promise you I'll find it."

She said nothing, so he continued. "Lawyers like you pay referral fees all the time," he said. "So when I refer a client to you, you show your gratitude and split part of your fees with me. That's how it's done."

"I understand."

"One more thing, my dear Ms. Tuvia. In this courtroom the bailiffs have a tradition of talking directly to the client and intimating they can deliver a judgment in his favor. If I give them a favorable ruling, then the client assumes it's because of the golden handshake and everything's okay. I expect you to be a regular gal and look after my interests when you split the gratuity with the bailiff. If I didn't rule in the client's favor, the rule of thumb here is that the bailiff returns the money only if the client makes a pest of himself. If your client drops a dime to you about what the bailiff did, it's permissible for you to ask for a kickback to help him get back the rest of his dough. Whatever your client kicks back to you, you keep all of it. The bailiff's not supposed to ask you for even a penny of it. And don't let him hand you that shit about courtroom custom. What I'm telling you is the right tradition. He won't resent you for not sharing. He gambled and he lost. What I'm trying to teach you is the due process of how our laws function."

Without a word she passed by his desk, flipped the envelope into the drawer. He repressed the desire to mutter "swish" in consideration of any uneasy feelings she might have had.

She was no longer a cherry, he thought, feeling elation tinged with caution. After all, she might still have been sent over by the Investigatory Division to string him along. Was he being Naga'd? Was there a third, metallic nipple in between those two delicious breasts? But the apprehension lasted for only a moment. A person didn't get far in this world without trust. "I hope I've managed to teach you something about the law, Ms. Tuvia," he said, modestly.

"I learned a lot, Your Honor. Thank you."

She was about to leave. He knew he only had time to get in one final hint of sexual complicity. Did the situation call for Judge Wapner or Judge Wachtler? That is, should he be avuncular or somewhat more aggressive? Wapner won out.

"My chamber will always be open to you, my dear." As she left, he congratulated himself for having executed a subtle, graceful pass that showed him off to her as a man of the world who seemed interested only in pursuing a friendship. He saw her shut the door, but could not see her shake her head to his secretary and say, "I gotta tell you, that is the dirtiest-minded magistrate I've ever seen."

The secretary smiled knowingly. "You haven't met too many judges, have you, Ms. Tuvia."

The skinny, bespectacled judge glanced at his Rolex. Eleven forty-five. He was already over two hours late. Time to bag it.

Pressing his buzzer, he notified his secretary to usher in two attorneys to converse with him about their case.

He greeted the men with a broad grin, already anticipating conflict. "How the fuck are you guys?"

The two competing attorneys shook hands with each other, and then with him, in a friendly way, not at all as if they were soon-to-be bloody pugilists in the ring. They pulled their chairs close to his desk and sat down.

The three men ignored the No Smoking sign and lit up, dipping their cigarettes in the already overflowing ashtrays. The judge gave one of the men, Fred Thoroughbrow, a significant look. "I can use a couple of new ashtrays there, Fred. For your comfort, guys, not mine."

Thoroughbrow crossed his lanky legs. "It's taken care of, Your Honor." Catching a glimpse of white in the desk drawer, he said, "I see that business has been good lately, Judge."

"I got no reason to complain," he said modestly, cursing himself for not immediately removing the envelopes. Then, "Turn around, guys."

Both men understood that he wanted to insulate himself from his own venality in front of them, and swiveled their chairs so they wouldn't actually see him scoop the envelopes from the desk drawer and place them in the inside pocket of his suit under his robe. The awkward moment ended and they turned around to face him.

"Actually, all that's in one of them is a couple of tickets to a Knicks game," he said, believing the non-monetary gift lessened his culpability.

He felt exonerated, cleansed. Although he'd been splitting fees with one man for years, and the other for months, he'd continued his practice of never actually allowing an attorney to see him pocket any money. Over his three-decade career in the judiciary, he'd always been known for taking this precaution. He never directly received any of the bribes he so diligently pressured and labored for. Of course, he continued this custom upon finding himself in Matrimonial Court. Although he'd been here for only a short time, he made it a point to learn the habits and lifestyles of the attorneys he permitted to be in his stable. Konigsberg, the other lawyer here to see him, had toiled on Court Street in Brooklyn Heights for years before recently emigrating across the bridge to set up shop in Manhattan, where he hoped to get his share of the much more bitterly fought and asset-laden divorces of that borough. As soon as Dollar Dillon's clerk, Johnstone, had informed him that Konigsberg had just purchased a three-bedroom loft in TriBeCa with outlandish monthly carrying charges and a balloon mortgage, the judge, always on the lookout to nurture new talent, knew that the financial pressures would make the attorney eager to do business and so had started assigning him cases. The move had paid off nicely for both of them.

Thoroughbrow was a different story. He and the judge had known each other and conducted business together for twenty-five years. From the beginning of his career, Thoroughbrow had fastened onto the judge as if he were his own personal talisman and had followed him from branch to branch, switching his field of practice to conform to whatever division of justice the magistrate found himself in at the moment, as easily as a driver changes lanes. They'd met and befriended each other in Taxi Court, happily splitting fees until the judge was transferred. When Dillon was moved to Legacies, Thoroughbrow studied the field so he could join him. When the magistrate was moved yet again, to Criminal, the indomitable attorney mastered that field, too. Six weeks after, the judge was transferred to Matrimonial. Within eight weeks, the resourceful attorney had joined the rest of the team on the rear bench. In this relationship, the judge was the shark, and Thoroughbrow the complacent pilot fish, content to follow in the wake of the leader and grow corpulent off his leavings.

Because he was favored above all other attorneys in the courtroom, Thoroughbrow was expected to attend to many of the judge's temporal needs. He bought him his suits, paid for his meals, and furnished his apartments. And since the judge's wife was in real estate, the couple expected the attorney to change addresses fairly frequently, and Thoroughbrow complied with this, always using the judge's wife as his real estate broker.

The three men knew that the case they were conferring over now was a piece of typical matrimonial shit, but it had humorous aspects. This was a battle over the custody of children. The judge who'd originally been assigned the case had churned it along skillfully for many years. The kids, high school students when their parents' divorce proceedings started, had now evolved into adults with divorces and custody battles of their own. So time had taken care of that problem. The case had been lateraled off to Dillon eight months ago.

By continually delaying rulings and churning out motions, the three men, working in concert, had forced the battling couple to sell off their jewelry and to liquidate two of their homes to raise cash, so at least their assets had been disposed of. Finally the proceedings were drawing to an end. However the last asset to be disposed of was definitely not liquid. During happier times, the housewife had requested that her husband bestow on her the gift of breast implants, a request which the architect, anticipating many years of happy usage, happily granted. The cost was to be $18,000. Because this procedure was considered cosmetic surgery and was not covered under their medical insurance plan, the husband had agreed to put down $3,000 and pay off the rest in installments. Now that their marriage had soured, however, and since she had initiated the divorce, the architect balked at making the remaining payments, claiming that the construction of her two edifices implied usage. Now that they were to be divorced, her boyfriend was reaping the benefits. Therefore he should be required to make the rest of the payments. The architect's wife steadfastly maintained that since her breasts were not a building, the laws of usage and possession did not apply. The battle over these fleshly mounds had become fierce. Konigsberg represented the architect. Thoroughbrow was the attorney for the wife.

Dollars Dillon's skinny fingers lit a cigarette. "Guys, this piece-of-shit case has jerked us around long enough. It's time we wrap up. Normally, I would tell you to work it out among yourselves, but it's been weeks and you guys can't seem to reach an accommodation. So it's up to me to do a little prodding. One of you has got to be a mensch and give in a little on this breast business."

Both men remained silent. "I want this finished some time today, gentlemen, before gravity takes over."

Konigsberg ducked his head. "My client feels he's been screwed, Your Honor. He's laid a foundation, overseen construction, and now the building's being occupied by some stranger. He feels betrayed. It's Fred's turn to be reasonable."

"I understand the poor guy's point," said Dillon. "I feel for him. Like any great creator, he has a vision. He imagines that wife of his slipping into a new pair of breasts. Now after the task's been completed, he discovers some backdoor man's taking his place and he's been cut out of the picture completely."

Konigsberg nodded. "Not only that, Judge. He didn't initiate divorce proceedings, she did. Now he's deprived of one of the estate's most valuable assets. Is that fair?"

"It don't have to be fair, Your Honor, it only has to be the law," said Thoroughbrow. "A contract is a contract. My client wants the full fifteen thousand."

"Yeah," said the judge. "But seventy-five hundred a tit, that's highway robbery."

Thoroughbrow shook his head stubbornly. "She's entitled to the full fifteen grand. It's not her fault the marriage tanked right after completion of the job. Sometimes things just happen that way. Let's dispose of it, close the case, go out to eat, and have a good laugh. Dinner's on me."

Dillon gave Konigsberg a sympathetic look. "We're not in a courtroom, but I'm leaning in Freddie's direction. There's no room for compromise. I think your client's gonna have to honor the contract."

Konigsberg said, "I see this as a custody battle, Your Honor. This is a court that rules over custody. If my client is being asked to fund the cost of a breast job, shouldn't he retain custody over that which he's nourished and paid for?"

"Maybe we should arrange for visitation rights with them on weekends," Thoroughbrow said. He turned to Dillon. "This is ridiculous, Your Honor. Those breasts are my client's. They're part of her. She goes to sleep with them, and she wakes up with them. It is impossible for her to surrender them in custody. This is a question of keeping what is hers after a divorce, not a division of assets."

The resourceful Konigsberg immediately countered. "My colleague may be the one who raised the issue, but I'm glad it's now out in the open. This is an asset of their marriage like any other and should be divided equally between them."

Dillon appeared to be undecided. Thoroughbrow shook his head. "This is too much, Judge. These breasts belong solely to my client. This is not lend-lease."

Dillon looked thoughtful. "You've raised interesting legal issues, Mel, but I gotta tell you, I'm still leaning toward Freddie on this matter."

But Konigsberg refused to acknowledge defeat. "Judge, I can back up my argument with science. Don't think of what my client contracted for as breasts. They are mere mounds of silicone, compounds of chemicals the architect added on to her as if he were building the wings of a house. They're ornaments that my client contracted for, so his wife would look and feel better about herself. They should not be considered real flesh at all. They are essentially jewelry and should be seen as community property. When a marriage dissolves, the assets of the estate are split between the parties. The cost of the breast job should be split here, too."

"I'm afraid I'm going to see things Freddie's way, Mel."

"Thank you, Your Honor," said Thoroughbrow. He gave his colleague a smile. "I guess in this matter, the law won out after all."

Konigsberg swatted the table like he had just eliminated a pesky fly. "You don't have to rub it in so fucking much, Freddie. Even before I entered the judge's chambers I knew how things would turn out."

Thoroughbrow and Dillon exchanged a smile. "What are you saying, Mel?" the magistrate asked.

Konigsberg said, "It's just that since both of us are gonna hand over envelopes, I expect justice from both of you. I feel betrayed. I feel ganged up on. How could my side prevail when you let Freddie over here buy all your suits for you? I guess I was stupid to expect a compromise. I know I was a fool to think we'd be going by Marquess of Queensberry rules."

"I don't like conflict in my court," said Dillon. "Since we each hand over and share in the profits of the justice system, each of us has a stake in keeping things running smoothly. Our system was invented and subscribed to by us. It is not imposed on us by an outside force like the Mafia through fear. So, gentlemen, we've all got to get along. I can't have one attorney leave chambers pissed off at my decision. The system can't function if one of us holds a grudge."

It took both men a moment to realize that the system the judge was referring to was their fee-splitting system and not the system of justice.

The conciliator patted the weary combatants on the shoulders. "Freddie, this time around the dice went your way. Be gracious about it. Mel, while it's true that this time you crapped out, next time you might be the winner. I know you feel like you've lost a war here, but you've got to put that aside. Pull yourself together. Be a mensch, not a mook. We don't need one hothead running off and colliding with one of those rats from the Investigatory Department."

"It's my client's birthday today, Judge. A day he should be celebrating. What kind of present is this gonna be?"

"I intend to give your client a special gift, Mr. Konigsberg. I'll serenade him, even though he has only himself to blame for my ruling."

"But how can any of this be his fault? He's not responsible for you two ganging up on me."

"He was careless. He should've prenupped those nipples."

Dillon heard the clerk say, "All rise," and as he moved swiftly toward the courtroom, he raised his hands slightly over his head, a champion about to enter the ring. Since divorce was something that affected all people, he loved seeing the fear in people's eyes once he told them he was a matrimonial judge.

The tiny, mustachioed man nimbly mounted the steps to his great seat and stared down at the inhabitants of his arena. The lawyers were standing next to their now-seated clients. Thoroughbrow, a contented look on his face. Konigsberg, glum but resigned.

The courtroom was silent, but was disturbed by a sudden buzz of activity and noise from outside. Dillon frowned, knowing the reasons behind the sudden clamor.

While the inside of the courtroom belonged to Dillon and his favored group of lawyers, hallway hustlers were anarchists, attorneys who set up shop outside his courtroom. Any client who appeared to be unrepresented was waylaid by these claim jumpers who lined the hallways, as they took a last stab at trying to convince a client to let one of them represent him before he entered the courtroom and became Dillon and his crew's property.

This practice cut into the courtroom habitués' profits, so its practitioners were naturally resented.

The judge crooked a finger at Stephen Gomes to approach the bench. "I know what's going on out there," he told his bailiff. "Clear those hallway hustlers out of this courtroom at once."

"They're allowed to congregate out there, Your Honor."

"Then tell them to shut the fuck up," Dillon whispered. "If I hear one more word from out there, I'll remove them from this chamber."

"But, Your Honor, they're outside your courtroom," Gomes said softly. "They're already removed from your chamber."

"Then I'll find the bastards in contempt."

"They can be found in contempt once they enter your courtroom, Your Honor. As long as they remain outside, they cannot be found in contempt."

"Please, Stevie. Instruct them to find some other courtroom to place under siege. Tell them to migrate to another branch."

The burly bailiff nodded and left. For a moment, there were loud sounds of protest, then murmurs, then silence. Gomes returned.

The judge called the bailiff over to him. "Have you succeeded in at last quieting those jackals out there?"

"One of the litigants about to enter the court is deaf. They're all busy signing or pretending to sign to him to choose one of them for his attorney."

"That figures," the judge said. "Justice is no longer blind. Now it's deaf and dumb as well." He motioned to the two attorneys. "Step forward, gentlemen. As the three of us know, the disputants have managed to agree to the division of their liquid and non-liquid assets. Only in the matter of the breast job is there a dispute. We're about to solve that now." He turned to his clerk. "Call the case and have the litigants approach the bench."

He beamed at Thoroughbrow's client, who was a dish and a half. "Don't let the ordeal you've been through alienate you from our justice system, my dear." Turning to the architect, his smile became a beam. "Your attorney tells me it's your birthday. Is this true?"

Suddenly Konigsberg's client's dejected eyes filled with the belief that because of this happy coincidence, he was about to save a few thousand dollars. "It is, Your Honor."

"Then I'm gonna serenade you," Dillon said. "Listen and learn, Mr. Brown." To the tune of "Happy Birthday," he sang, "You must surrender the dough. With your counselor in tow. Appeal this deal, and it's off to jail you'll go."

Glancing at his watch, he noticed that it was one-thirty. So far today he'd managed to dispose of one case. Justice was really rolling along. He motioned to his bailiff. "Tell everyone we're adjourned until three p.m."

Before the detective had reached his chair inside chambers, Dillon stood casually by his desk and checked that the drawer was closed. He returned to his seat and smiled. "I've heard good things about you, Al. That Mexican case. I heard you really had Internal Affairs over a barrel."

Yablonsky ducked his head at the compliment. "I was dealing with delegates from the U.N.," he said. "By the way, I've heard about you, too."

"Then you know me. During my stint in Criminal Court, before they transferred me out, no judge was more pro-cop than I."

Yablonsky's impassive face softened slightly. Dillon gave him a shrewd look. "I know all about what you did to stay afloat during their investigation of you, and I approve." He smiled at the detective encouragingly, for though the cop had called ahead to arrange a meeting, Dillon didn't really know why he was here. "Now why'd you come to see me? Do you want me to buy two tickets to the policeman's ball?"

Yablonsky smiled. Dillon offered him a cigarette, which he declined. "I only smoke at a murder scene, Your Honor. Calms the nerves." He paused. "You must remember the headlines a week ago, Judge. Someone decided to celebrate Christmas by having Skinny McPherson killed and his body dumped in Central Park."

A thin wisp of smoke settled on the judge's mustache. "You the primary?" So this was only about McPherson; the judge's relief showed on his face. "If I remember correctly, McPherson was a big man. The guy was unmistakable, like a precious New York landmark. It's hard to recall. The case was over a year ago. Since then, they've transferred me to yet another branch."

"His paper treated you roughly from time to time. I've heard you're a man who knows how to nurture a grudge, but I only want to find out a few things about Skinny during Shelly Townes's trial."

Was the detective coming up with a motive for him? This was ridiculous. He'd never have anyone killed. Somehow, if he ever could, he'd make the detective pay for this. Dillon didn't betray a flicker of anger. "McPherson never wrote about me, only his paper did. And what you heard about me isn't true. I don't hold grudges."

Not against Skinny, Dillon thought. Journalists were just like anyone else almost. They married and they divorced. Some of those muckrakers would inevitably find themselves in his courtroom; and when that happened, nothing, not even the thickest envelope in the world, would discourage him from taking the sledgehammer of justice to their assets.

"I'd like to be able to help you, Alvie. I remember now that McPherson was in my courtroom."

"Good," said Yablonsky. "How long did Townes's trial last?"

"It was a while back, before they discovered they needed me back in Civil Court. I believe it lasted for two weeks. Not at all an unusual length of time for a corruption case. My sentence naturally shocked him.

I think he thought he'd hardly have to serve any time at all, but my sentence was appropriate. The usual in corruption cases."

"How many times did McPherson show up in your courtroom?"

There was a silence as the judge thought. "He was a diligent reporter. He was here most days during Townes's trial."

"Did McPherson and Townes ever speak to each other during the trial?"

"I'd assume so. But if they had, it would've been in the rear of my courtroom. I wouldn't have been privy to what they said to each other."

"Did either of them ever appear to be angry? Rack your brains, Judge."

"That I don't recall. I seldom see anger in my courtroom."

"Yeah, right," said Yablonsky. "No one gets angry in Matrimonial Court. Did anyone else besides Townes ever speak to McPherson during the trial?"

"Despite his size, I didn't notice McPherson that much. I mean, I was running a trial, Detective, not a Weight Watchers session. He may have spoken casually with some of the other people in court during the trial. But there was nothing unusual about Townes's trial at all. Only the fact that it was a borough president defending himself against corruption charges. A shameful thing. I was sorry I had to give him such a harsh sentence, but it was in line with what was being handed out for similar crimes."

"Don't worry too much about Shelly," said Yablonsky. "I recently visited him in the Catskills. He didn't appear to be suffering."

"That makes me feel better," said Dillon. "It's justice I believe in, not vengeance."

That was a wrap, Yablonsky thought. "How many cases did you dispose of today?"

"We managed to dispose of one."

"If I ever find myself going through another divorce, and you're the judge who's presiding, I hope you'll remember our talk and be merciful."

"Sorry, Lieutenant, but personal relationships never influence me. Next time show better judgment in choosing a spouse. Take me, when I divorced and remarried, it was to a much younger woman who looks up to me. I know I'm a lucky man, Lieutenant, and I cherish her. She cherishes me. We'll never get divorced."

"I hope I have your luck in the future, Judge."

"It's not luck," said Dillon. "It's character."

After the detective left, the judge glanced at his watch and knew it was time to get ready. On cue, the side door of his chambers slid open and into his room stepped a tall, thin, red-haired younger guy, Judge Earl "Recused" Richards. Dillon stood and began slipping out of his robe.

"Recused" Richards raised his arms, removed his jacket, and placed it over one of the folding chairs. "It's good to see you, Your Honor," he said, deliberately formal, kidding around.

Judge Dillon handed his black robe to Richards, then went over to his closet to put on a top coat. Richards shrugged into the black robe. "I feel like I'm at a costume party."

One judge smiled at the other. "It's good of you to accommodate me this way, Earl. I'm bushed. I need a pinch hitter. It's your turn to step up to the plate."

"No offense there, Dollars, but it always seems to be my turn to come to the plate. In case you forgot, I'm a jurist too. Not your designated hitter."

Dillon moved to the mirror in the bathroom to adjust his tie. "What do you mean?"

"This is the second time in a row I've mounted the bench for you. We're supposed to reciprocate. You owe me."

The judge looped his tie and spoke from the bathroom. "You're absolutely right. How stupid of me." He came out of the bathroom and inspected his slightly taller substitute. "The metamorphosis is complete, Earl. You make a good-looking me."

He handed Richards a folder. "The cases to be calendered today." Both men heard the angry voices from outside. "You better get out there fast, Earl." He smiled at the judge. "Be suave. Be sophisticated. That's the least you can do when you're pretending to be me."

"Okay," said Richards, adjusting the robe slightly to compensate for the height difference. "But you owe me, Dollars. I expect you to be at my branch tomorrow afternoon. Last time when you didn't show, I had to use one of the clerks from the courtroom next door."

"How'd he do?"

"Actually, he did well. He calendered two more cases than I would have."

"No," said Dollars Dillon. "I mean how did he *do?*"

"Oh. I hear he made out okay. He got two lawyers from two of my newer cases." He paused. "Sometimes I think we shouldn't let them take from our table. Since we're the law it should all go to us."

Dillon shook his head. "That's impractical, Earl, and unfair. If a guy's willing to do you a favor, he should be able to keep what he can earn."

"I guess you're right. I only hope I can live up to the standard that he set. Where are you going, by the way?"

"I'm gonna spend some time with my wife."

"I've seen your wife. You're lucky."

"Not really, Earl. Eventually you get tired of being served the same flavor ice cream every day."

Richards laughed. "You mean she's a consolation prize. You're not gonna tell me that you're running out of people in New York to commit adultery with. No one can."

"As impossible as it is to believe, I temporarily have." He watched as his substitute exited, reached his bench, and whacked his gavel on the desk, saying, "Silence. God has spoken." The waiting, feuding families went back to their separate sides of the room. Dillon smiled approvingly and left, knowing that his courtroom was in good hands and that he had played a part in the preservation of a valuable tradition.

EIGHT

In a precinct cubicle, Henderson and Saunders were carefully sifting through piles of garbage. They wore green outfits and had on thick surgical gloves.

Yablonsky stood in the doorway and peered in. Henderson was going through a pile of soiled napkins from the McDonald's on West 71st Street, searching for evidence that the perpetrator might have discarded. He was only in his late twenties, tall and matchstick skinny, with a pencil-thin mustache. He planned on taking courses at John Jay to help him become a detective. Yablonsky liked the fact that he was ambitious. "Stench de la Manhattan," Henderson said. "My favorite *parfum*."

Saunders stood over another pile. Her weight, currently at 130, fluctuated with the city's murder rate. She said, "The mayor's thinking of bottling and marketing it to Jersey. It's amazing. For years Skinny did nothing but rag on him. Now we're working twenty-four-seven to find Skinny's murderers." She paused. "Do you think the mayor did it?"

"No motive," Yablonsky said. "He doesn't need more money."

"Did Androtti find anything out during his canvass?" Henderson asked.

"Only that most people don't go out on their terraces during winter."

Captain Flood tipped his lounge chair at an angle and leaned back. "You're fifteen minutes late. How come?"

"Going over the reports. Look, Captain, some mook stole my squad car last night. I'm the lead detective on a major murder case. I need another car—and quick."

"I sympathize, Alvin. But with the budget cuts, we're not repairing vehicles or replacing anything that goes out of service. Take a taxi. Submit an expense chit. They'll be approved. What you got for me?"

"Okay, but I do want that car. The forensics report. Interrogations conducted within the neighborhood. Read 'em and weep."

Flood leafed through the documents. "No DNA. Any possible clues melted in the snow and rain. No recovery of any weapons. Prints impossible to lift because of the weather. Canvasses as to potential witnesses, so far unsuccessful. Christ, how are we supposed to prove that no cops did this?" He paused. "Patrolman Billings is out as a suspect, right?"

"He's going to be transferred. Then retire within a year. No motive. I've already met face-to-face with the mayor at his heliport and told him no cops were involved."

"You met with him? Face-to-face? What'd you say?"

"I told him the truth. That street cops are too blue-collar to plan and execute a complicated murder like this. I think Skinny was murdered by some prominent guy, or guys, who wanted to conceal a major crime."

"That's good," said Flood. "If the media ever learns that Skinny was investigating corruption in my precinct, that's what I'll tell them. Did Skinny ever speak to you? Which cops was he going to burn?"

"Mainly Patrolman Billings. But there were others. Skinny told me he estimated that, at one time or another, 75 percent of uniforms had made dirty money off hookers, parking tickets, and swag. But in the world of corruption, that's pretty minor-league stuff."

"I know," said Flood. "Why can't the media concentrate on the honest 25 percent of the cops in my precinct?"

"He was a good man."

"In about half an hour, I'm going out there to be Q-and-A'd by the newspapers and the networks. Can you give me anything to tell them?"

"There're witnesses."

"Who?"

"His accomplices. Skinny weighed three hundred pounds. Whoever killed him had to have help in disposing the body."

"The only other witnesses to the crime are the guys who helped murder him?" said Flood. "I really feel encouraged now. By the way, after you interrogate Ortiz, and hopefully break him, I'm gonna have to ask you to put all the other murders you've been trying to solve on hold. Once you do that, our solve rate's gonna be even lower."

"Stet them and forget them?" Yablonsky asked. "But two of my cases concern the murder of children. I think that, with all the help from Discovery and the rest of the department on this one, I can at least keep the investigations on the kids going." Except for the murder of a cop, nothing was higher on a detective's priority list than child killings. They were considered "real victims" because they were defenseless and innocent.

Flood shook his head no.

"Shit. Double shit," said Yablonsky. The cliché picked up from detective novels and TV shows was that there was no such thing as a perfect murder, when what Yablonsky and every other detective knew was that hundreds of perfect murders were achieved every day.

If the detective could tell from the crime scene that this was a sloppy murder, with a thousand clues, but due to constraints of time, he had to stet and forget the case, then the killer had gotten away with murder. Men who assassinated strangers and left their bodies on the side of a highway or in the woods, with dozens of brutal wounds and tons of fingerprints, committed a perfect murder as long as they eluded capture. A felon could carry out the sloppiest, dumbest, and most easily solvable killing in the world, but if he remained free, then he'd executed a perfect murder. The murderers of these children joined the list of perps who'd committed perfect crimes.

"Ask yourself, Alvin, even if you nabbed these men, how much time would they actually serve?"

The criminal seldom went to prison for what he did, but what he and his attorney would agree to be charged with and sentenced for. Therefore the criminal was now in the position to determine how much time he should receive. The justice system would be forced to function this way as long as sufficient amounts of crimes existed to tie it up. In effect, each criminal became the other's ally, because the more crimes they committed, the less time each of them served. So their very criminality insured them against having to serve heavy time.

Flood unrolled the chart that contained yet another image of the park and the neighborhoods that surrounded it. A clearance rate of less than 60 percent was considered by the community politicians to be disastrous, and during the past eight months, the precinct's solve rate was considerably lower than that.

Yablonsky studied the chart Flood had unrolled. Each black mark meant that the detective had solved or cleared a murder. The red on the chart stood for the murders that were not solved or cleared. The crimson tide overwhelmed and threatened to drown the scant amounts of ebony.

"Once I show the media this, I already know what they'll be printing tomorrow. So both days are ruined for me."

"Statistics are tricky, Captain," the detective said. "Half the cops are still involved in antiterrorist efforts. We've got a manpower shortage."

"The media doesn't care about that anymore. They only care about the rising murder rate."

"If we were to switch colors, make red stand for our cleared cases and black for the uncleared, things would look much better."

"You may have something there," Flood said slowly. He shook his head, plainly in awe. "Goddamn, Alvin, you've managed to solve the crime problem."

Yablonsky opened the metal door. Fernando Ortiz was short and muscular. Despite the fact that it was winter, he wore a muscle T-shirt. As the detective took a seat opposite him, he grinned confidently and flexed his mighty but small arms. They were full of tattooed daggers and striking cobras.

Mr. Macho, Yablonsky thought, already knowing how he'd play him.

" 'Nando, you declined Patrolman Cumming's offer of a cigarette like the down guy you are. Mind if I smoke?"

Ortiz gave him a wary smile. "You can stick that cigarette up your ass for all I care. I want my attorney."

Yablonsky smiled pleasantly at Lattrell Cummings, the cop who made the arrest. He turned to Ortiz and laughed. "You've outsmarted yourself, Fernando. You're such a tough guy, being a member of the Latino Nation, that every shyster I know's too petrified to rep you."

In all the years Yablonsky had fooled suspects into confessing he'd yet to understand why anybody would blurt out the truth to a detective before his attorney showed up. Yet somehow a detective was able to con a skell into believing that he indeed was helping himself when he admitted his crime. "You Carmen Miranda'd Fernando, didn't you?"

Lattrell Cummings instantly understood the script that the two men were to play out. "It's all on the tape. He's been Miranda'd."

The young man scratched at his arms. "Where's my attorney?"

"Don't worry, Fernando. Cochran, Shapiro, and Bailey are on the way over to arrange bail even as we speak. So there's only a little time, I'm afraid, for me and you to get to know each other." In fact, no one at the precinct had yet sent for Ortiz's attorney. But the courts had ruled that the police could make use of treachery and lies in their struggle to wrest a confession from a suspect.

"In the meantime, 'Nando, I'd just like to ask you one thing."

"Ask away, dickhead. I won't answer. Where's my attorney?"

The young man's clever verbal sallies seemed to upset the detective. What he was really thinking was how amateurish a hoodlum Ortiz was. Real original gangstas were usually polite, too familiar with the rules of interrogation to trip themselves up by showing anger. "Tell me, Fernando. You and twelve other members of the Latino Nation courageously beat up a boy merely because you suspected he was gay. You've just insulted me by telling me to stick my cigarette up my ass. How come you're so fascinated with assholes, asshole?"

"Qué?"

Yablonsky reached for a stack of papers, held them up to his nose and pretended to read the blank sheets. "This is the most recent study in *El Diario* of people who are assumed to be gay. It says that up to 80 percent of you ultra-macho gang members are believed to have pronounced homosexual tendencies, that you disguise this with extreme displays of what you believe to be heterosexual behavior."

Ortiz recoiled as if he'd been shot. "Stick those goddamn papers up your ass!"

Yablonsky smiled. "There you go again. You can't seem to tear yourself away from assholes."

"I ain't no fuckin' faggot. I'm a pussy pounder!"

"You're a faggot," Yablonsky said. He waved the papers in the air. "It says so right here. Reported by your own newspaper. Written in your own language."

As the young man stood, for the first time Yablonsky noticed the shiny ring on the index finger of his left hand.

The young man flexed his muscles. "Let me get this straight. You calling me a maricón, right?"

Yablonsky's casual grin was maddening. "Your friend and fellow gang-banger, Tito, just confessed an hour ago that you, more than any of them, enjoyed kicking in your victim's head. I'm saying that makes you the gayest gangsta in the bunch."

Ortiz sat down and smirked at Yablonsky. "Tito'd never roll on me. You almost had me. You ain't never gonna get us to confess."

"I don't want your confession, Fernando," Yablonsky said. "You should be punished for what you did. Sending you to prison, where you'd be raped every day, would be no punishment for a man like you. Anyway, why should I give a fuck about your confession when Tito's already confessed for you?"

Ortiz did not look so certain now. "I still ain't saying nothin' until my attorney gets here. What did Tito say?"

"He told us he saw you cop that ring from the kid you beat up."

Ortiz laughed. "That's a lie. I couldn't boost no ring because I wasn't there. Anyway, it was Tito who copped from the Herb, not me. He took the faggot's sweater. I know, because after it was over I ran into him," he added hurriedly. "He told me all about it."

"Where'd you run into him?"

Ortiz smiled confidently. "The corner of 175th and Broadway."

"What time?"

The young man hesitated. "Five-thirty."

"Morning or evening?"

"In the morning, man. In the p.m., I was back in my crib, sleeping."

"You sure about the time?"

"Oh, yeah."

"How can you be so sure when you're not wearing a watch?"

"Tito was wearing a watch," Ortiz said triumphantly.

Yablonsky read the section from Cummings's report that said Tito Martinez had surrendered a Rolex and a bright yellow sweater along with the rest of his property. Yablonsky shook his head decisively. "That watch was too new and expensive to belong to a mutt like Tito. He must've boosted it, along with the sweater you told us about when you rolled on your friend."

"I never rolled."

"You just admitted you did. It's on the tape. Anyway, only a man who has such strong homosexual tendencies that he can't control them rolls on his best friend. That's in the article in *El Diario* too. Right, Lattrell?"

"I read it there this morning."

Ortiz looked as if he'd been hit by two successive right hooks. "That's a lie."

Yablonsky waved the stack of papers. "You can read it here yourself. Unless you're illiterate."

The young man looked indignant. "Don't you call me illiterate. I had a mother and a father."

"And they'd be proud of you now," continued Yablonsky. "The instigator of an incident that probably paralyzed a boy who did you no harm. Tito said you were responsible for this mighty act of manliness."

"I want my attorney."

Yablonsky waved him off. "He's on his way. In the meantime, tell us, Fernando, were you on the left side or the right side of that poor young man? Your freedom's on the line."

Ortiz paused as if in thought. "I was on his right side."

He smiled slightly at seeing how upset his response made the detective.

"You were on the right side," Yablonsky said slowly. "But most of the injuries were on the left."

"The right side," Fernando Ortiz said happily. The detective looked shaken, and there seemed to be no doubt that the gang member's statement had thrown off the cop's deductions.

"Please, Fernando. Think about this. You're claiming you were on his right side?"

Ortiz smiled. "The right side. You can ask me all night and I won't change my story."

"The right side?" Yablonsky repeated.

Fernando Ortiz looked bored. "Yeah, cop," he said patiently. "I was on his right."

"Then you *were* present in the schoolyard when that young man was stomped," Yablonsky said softly.

For a moment Ortiz stared, not comprehending the detective. Both he and Cummings were wearing wide grins. "Hey," he shouted. "You tricked me, man!"

"You tricked yourself, original gangsta." The detective turned to Cummings. "He's yours."

In the street cop's eyes was the excitement of a hunter who had just pursued and captured a wild animal. "I owe you one."

"I'll get it back when we catch Skinny's murderer."

On the detective's desk were more reports from the task force: Discovery, the Interrogation Unit, the Coroner, and the Trace Evidence Lab. All of them, by their very brevity, emphasized the difficulty of catching Skinny McPherson's murderers.

Playing his messages, Yablonsky smiled as Julie's voice thanked him for accompanying her to the cemetery. It was the most kindness and consideration she'd been shown since Skinny's death, she said. He was definitely a guy she could depend on in a jam.

He put the "follow-ups" down and stood before a scale model of the section of Central Park that contained Tavern on the Green, the park's entrances and exits, and a tiny statue of Fred Lebow, just outside the children's playground, his hand pointing dramatically in the direction of the Wollman Rink, and the rink itself.

Talcum powder, representing snow, covered the twigs, and a plastic building stood for the restaurant. Shiny mirrors suggested the lakes and the reservoir. The entire tableau resembled one of those picturesque scenes inside a snow globe, and for a moment Yablonsky believed that if he gave the replica a shake, snow would fall.

He stood over the model, measuring the distance between the 65th Street entrance and the dumpsite.

Why not dump the body in the reservoir? Yablonsky wondered. Idiot, he thought. It was too far from the park road. If the driver was coming from the East Side and seeking a place to dispose of the body, why travel all the way through to the other side of the park? Whoever got rid of the deceased would be looking for a spot where the body could be speedily disposed of. Therefore they had to come from the West Side.

Skinny's newspaper's printing plant and some of its offices were located on Eleventh Avenue and West 65th Street. The murder must've taken place in or around the building.

On his way downstairs, he passed a group of cops peering out a window, watching attorney Sterling Roth, about to hold a press conference on the precinct steps. He'd forgotten about Roth. Best to slip out the back. The cop-hating, headline-loving lawyer was just crazy enough to spark a confrontation with him.

NINE

Cops who arrived or left the station house stepped pointedly around attorney Sterling Roth and the surrounding media in frigid silence. Roth grinned at the cops who ignored him, knowing that his friendly facade would antagonize them. Although he admitted to loving publicity and living for it, he motioned to the reporters: mikes down.

The reporters, temporarily deprived of the performance they sought, drifted down the steps and began steering the satellite vans over to the plaza in front of the precinct house, readying cameras for Roth's future client's arrival. Since cops were now forbidden to subject a suspect to a perp walk, it'd probably been Roth who notified the media.

Patrolmen Donovan Beatty and Mark Bridges stopped to confront the defense attorney. "Free any more cop killers lately, Sterling?"

"No," Roth said. "But I'm about to."

"What I'd like to do, Roth, is get you into an interrogation room and ask you why you're so eager to represent any skell who kills a cop," said Bridges.

"Willing to rep any black skell who murders a cop, that is," added Beatty.

"It's the juries who free them, my friend, not me. The juries I pick know that most cops on the stand testa*lie*. And with this country's racism, I believe it's impossible for blacks to be responsible for what they do and to really be criminals."

As Roth talked, his ponytail was break-dancing back and forth. He spoke softly, not wanting the reporters who'd headed off to set up for Darius Moody's arrival to hear him. "Besides, to tell you the truth, every time one of you mothafuckas are shot while trying to arrest a brother, I feel like doing a little dance. I feel sorry for your widows and kids, but never for you. Not when mayors are elected by white votes to put bullets in the backs of black people. Every cop who's contributed to lowering the crime rate does so by hassling black kids and beating black suspects. You're shooting brothers all the time for the sole crime of being B.A.D., Black After Dark. Of course, you cops have other ways of destroying people." He paused. "Just ask Alvin Yablonsky."

"You grew up in Brookline. You went to Harvard," said Patrolman Bridges. "Why do you have to come off like some 'down' guy who's a man of the street?"

"Well. I have to maintain street credibility with the brothers. Besides, at least one of my offices is uptown, not downtown with the other rich shysters. You'd be surprised, guys, at the people I deal with in my office. Crooks. Politicians. Even detectives."

A police car pulled up and four doors opened. The accused murderer Roth wanted to represent got out, and the four cops who guarded him moved around the car to flank him. Reinforcements marched out of the station house to surround them as cameramen and reporters surged forward, ready to tape and talk.

"The guest of honor has arrived," Roth said. "Gotta go, guys. I smell chum."

Darius Moody was only about five-feet-nine but he had biceps that dwarfed Arnold Schwarzenegger's. Though the handcuffs succeeded in immobilizing those mighty arms, it still took the pressure of the six cops behind him to keep him moving up the steps.

The twenty-year-old felon had been a member of the most dreaded drug posse in Harlem, the Jherri Curl Boys. He'd been walking along the northern end of Central Park with his girlfriend when they'd come upon another member of the Jherri Curls, Delray De La Mumba, grappling on the ground with a cop over a gun.

De La Mumba, who would later give a statement against Moody, stated that the fellow Jherri Curl had pulled out his weapon and "threw down," that is, shot and killed the patrolwoman, Maria Tomas. Moody's girlfriend also supplied the police with a statement. Once in the station house, the gang leader confessed and swore vengeance against his former friends.

One week after his confession, during his arraignment, where he was adamant about wanting to represent himself, he claimed that the confession had been coerced by beatings, and it was in fact De La Mumba who had killed the cop. The high-profile case caught the attention of many celebrities in the theater and literary worlds, who circulated petitions and did TV spots claiming that Moody's confession had been coerced.

Responding to the surrounding cameras, Darius Moody brought the entire procession to a halt by refusing to move any further.

Pressure was applied to Moody's back, but he was an unmovable force now. "Get your mothafuckin' hands offa me!"

"Moody," one of the cops by his side said, "let's go. Now."

Moody turned, spat in the cop's face, and laughed. "No, mothafucka. I'm tired. All fired up. Can't take no more."

The cop who'd been spat upon wiped his face and dried his hand on Moody's cheek.

"Shut up and move it, Moody. Now."

"Why should I? You think I don't know what's gonna happen to me once I'm locked in my crib? I'm gonna be one dead nigga."

The squadron of cops grabbed his powerful arms and tried to drag him up the steps. Moody shook some of them off. The stalemate continued.

"Chill, brother, chill. Maintain." Roth trotted down the steps, his hands raised to Moody in a soothing gesture. "Right now, I need calm from you, not confrontation. In court, I promise you, we'll have plenty of time to deal with these racists. But now's the time for chillin,' my brother, not killin'."

"Who the fuck axed you? You another cop here to arrest me?"

Roth laughed. "Just someone who's here to help." Roth stuck out his hand as if Moody would be able to shake it.

Moody recoiled from the seven-foot giant. "Fuck you, Jew. Get your hymie ass outta my face."

The virulent anti-Semitism made both the cops and the media react with shock. Roth remained unbothered.

"I'm not Jewish," he said.

"You shuckin' me—you a long-nosed mothafucka and that means you Jewish."

"I don't consider myself Jewish."

Moody spread out his hands as far as the handcuffs would let him. "What you want from me? You my landlord and the rent's due?"

"I wish you'd chill. I want to represent you in court. Together, we'll take on these racists."

Moody edged up closer to Roth. Instinctively he dropped his voice, though the cops and reporters could still hear him. "How you gonna help me? They got my confession. On tape."

"Only a crazy man would confess to a crime he wasn't responsible for committing."

The admitted cop killer moved closer, easily dragging the half-dozen men who held him. "You callin' me crazy now. Take these chains offa me, we see who be crazy."

"I won't discuss my strategies of justice with you on the steps of a police precinct, my friend. That's oxymoronic."

"First you callin' me crazy. Now a moron. What up? You frontin' on me?" But there was no heat in Moody's voice. The tricks and turns of the lawyer's mind were beginning to intrigue him. "Why you say that? Why you want to rep me anyway?"

Roth grinned. "The reason you're crazy is because you won't let me be your lawyer. The reason I want to rep you is because I love cases like this: a black man minding his business, gets harassed by some cop and has to defend himself. The death of the cop doesn't really bother me. But I am bothered when they use that as an excuse to put yet another black man in prison. You are a political prisoner. In the face of this racist society, a black man can never be held responsible for what he does."

"You can be my lawyer," Moody said.

"Good," said Roth. He turned to the cluster of newspaper and TV people. "Our defense is this: Darius is the victim of a mental condition common to black men in America. The blatant racism my client's encountered in his life has driven him to madness. There's a name for the disorder Darius Moody suffers from: black rage. The cop hassled him when she shouldn't have and my client snapped." He turned back to Moody. "Now you can do something for me."

"What?"

"Strip off your clothes once we're inside so they can photograph you." He looked meaningfully at the cops. "This is one brother you won't be able to touch. If there are any additional bruises or scars on my client after he's been photographed, we'll know where they came from. Now, Darius, it's pointless to give yourself and these cops such a rough time. Follow me and my reporter friends here into the police station. My firm'll mount a real defense for you. Interviews with celebrities. Protest letters. Lots of media attention!" Roth clapped his hands. "I love a case like this. Just follow us inside, my friend. The only way we'll get a chance to free you is if you let them put you in jail."

"If I'm so mental and crazy, like you say, then why'd I be able to listen and cooperate when they say I gotta move on up and go in there?"

"Like most unbalanced people, your condition comes and goes. Right now you're lucid, but the strain can make you crack anytime. Don't worry, my friend. We'll get you off." He turned to face the reporters. "In reality, my friends, this man is the victim."

"I'm the victim here," Moody repeated. He managed a smile. Since Roth was not offended by his client's anti-Semitism, the reporters weren't, either. They approached Moody, whispering excitedly, like future members of his fan club.

TEN

Most parking garages in the city were in constant use. Yablonsky glanced at his watch. He'd been here for almost twenty minutes, and had not seen a worker enter or leave. The garage, with two floors and basement, was almost completely enclosed. No parking attendants. The only security camera was in front. No one else came in—the garage was closed to the public, used only by workers at the plant. The detective stared at the walls of thick concrete. Thick enough to muffle any sounds of conflict.

He walked around the half-dozen cars scattered throughout the top floor and peered along the uneven, sloping garage floor. He looked for drops of blood, torn clothing, anything that would seem out of place. He picked up a cigarette butt and placed it in his evidence bag. As he stepped around dried oil slicks dotting the vacant parking spaces, he noticed window slits had been set into the concrete walls. From inside the garage he could see West End Avenue. But there were no parallel buildings across the street, nowhere for someone to see anything that might have happened there.

Following a trail of cigarette butts, he descended to the next level, first picking up each smudged butt and placing it inside his evidence bag. The traces of lipstick on the tips meant a woman smoker.

He found two crushed cans of Stroh's beer on his left and placed them in his evidence bag. Many of the ceiling lights no longer worked. He took a flashlight out of the bag, shone it on the rough-bottomed surface. No flecks of red. The ground was littered with Snickers and Mars Bars wrappers. He walked the entire level again, but spotted nothing. No jarring signs of struggle that meant murder.

When Yablonsky reached the basement of the garage, he cast the flashlight against the ceiling, but there were only spiderwebs and whorls of graffiti from street crews. Despite the broken windows and rows of lights, the place was dark.

He walked to one of the exits and forced open the rusty iron door, shining his light on the landing. Bits and pieces of gum. A dirt-stained handkerchief. They'd never get any prints off it, but slipping on a pair of surgical gloves, he plucked it off the ground anyway. Then he opened the bottom door and was back at the lowest level. His coat stained with sweat and dirt, he methodically paced off and searched one section of the basement level after another. Dust from the stagnant air caked the insides of his nose. He'd grown used to the solitude and liked it. Again, he worked diligently across the entire level, eyes moving systematically from the walls to the floor to the ceiling. He didn't know what he was looking for. If McPherson had been murdered here, the killers could have come back to remove any evidence.

A mound of concrete led to a glimmer of light that meant he was approaching the rear exit. Yablonsky felt like he was walking up a hill. Following the beam of his flashlight, he spotted two faint oil smudges next to one of the building's columns. During his first canvass, he'd missed them. They were just over the front yellow line that denoted a parking space. He crouched and studied the dirt-encrusted smears. He could discern the faint outline of a man's knees, and cloth fibers as minuscule as specks of dust were mixed in with the oil.

He stood, beaming the flashlight over the parking spot. A man or woman bending down to fix a flat could have made the imprints. But few could repair a tire from the front of a car. The slits that held the jack were usually on the car's sides. He bent down, spread his knees, and measured the distance between the oil blots. Someone much bigger than himself had made them. An image came to him of McPherson being shot, sinking to the basement floor, and leaving these fading prints. He grimaced, suspecting that his instincts were correct. This was the murder spot.

Half an hour later, a five-person team of men and women from the trace lab came down, and he told them they were taking samples that might help him solve the murder of Skinny McPherson.

He turned to a five-feet-ten, good-looking black guy named Bobby Cale, the lead tech of the team. "Don't leak any of this to the press."

"Tight-lipped," said Cale.

"Don't even tell the other cops."

Cale nodded, understanding that it was important for the primary detective on a high-priority red ball case to be protected and close-mouthed about anything he uncovered. "No leaking of any information to other cops."

Yablonsky directed the two teams to the area he wanted covered. As one group began lifting oil samples and placing the smears into the glassine bags, Yablonsky recorded the procedure on a steno pad. Two uniforms followed him as he pointed to areas where he wanted powder spread; the column next to where he'd found the imprints, the floor area surrounding the oil blots.

As he watched Cale crouch down next to one of the oil smears with a tiny scraping knife, he knew it was best to start the bargaining now.

"When can I have my report?"

Cale smiled. "Ain't gonna bargain with you. Six weeks."

Yablonsky shook his head. "You know the case I'm working on. Two weeks at the most."

"Ain't gonna bargain. Four and a half weeks."

"This victim meant something to a lot of people. If I solve the case, I'll make sure you lab guys get most of the credit."

"*If* you solve the case," Cale said. "Ain't gonna bargain. Three weeks."

"Two and a half weeks."

Cale sighed. "Two and a half weeks."

Yablonsky's smile showed his appreciation. "Thanks for not bargaining."

Cale casually pointed to two barely discernible blood spatters on the ground. "Bingo," he said.

"Jesus, Bobby. Lucite malachite it." The test would determine if it was human blood.

Cale was crawling on his knees, taking a scraping and applying a solution. "Did you spot this before?"

"No," said Yablonsky. "I missed it."

The mixture failed to turn brown. "It's just a preliminary test, but I don't think it's human blood at all," Cale said. "Probably a rodent's. The spatters appear to come from two separate animals. It chills me to say this, Alvin, but what we have here is the work of a squirrel who may be a serial killer."

"Don't squirrels hibernate in winter?" Yablonsky asked without a smile.

"Nope." Cale appeared just as solemn.

"That means he's on the wing."

Cale nodded and looked thoughtful. "This is no psycho rodent murdering out of passion or thwarted ambitions. Notice, Alvin, that there are no corpses or any other signs of victims. The killer must have dragged them off. Maybe the first victim was killed during an argument over food. Maybe the second was about to roll and claim his reward of nuts. That means premeditation. Should I spread the crime tape and have the tech guys look for latents?"

"Unfortunately, my hands are tied," said Yablonsky. "I have no jurisdiction over the animals in my precinct."

"So the squirrel walks?"

"I'm afraid so. Somewhere in this city there's a squirrel who got away with double homicide."

"He killed them, then disposed of the bodies. I tell you, this is one motherfucking squirrel I wouldn't want to tangle with. Back to Skinny. No bullet shells. No cartridges. We still have a crime scene here?"

"We still do, Bobby. The blood spatters may be the result of some terrorist of the squirrel kingdom, but he didn't leave those knee prints. They were caused by a man who was shot, sinking to the ground."

ELEVEN

Raymond Staples sat at his desk in one of the fifteen buildings he owned in the city. Scratching his hairpiece with one hand, he leafed through the weekly newspaper he owned. On the front cover of the *Village Guardian,* his employees had juxtaposed a photo of Raymond next to a night crawler. The caption underneath read: *Who is the bigger worm?*

Looking up at one of his office walls, filled with photos of him accompanied by celebrities, he wondered why they said such things about him.

"When are we giving the go-ahead on Tompkins Park Plaza?" he asked his assistant, Kathy Burke.

"Next week, Mr. Staples."

He looked at the figures, then once again at the newspaper's headline. The latest canard was that he was displacing fifteen families on East Tenth Street and Avenue A.

"I'm displacing no one."

Pressing a button, he switched the overhead TV to CNN.

"I believe there's something on about me," he said. "Care to watch?"

"There is. But I wouldn't watch that now, sir."

"Why not, Kathy?"

"I read the TV page this morning. The news spot they're running on you? It features that remark you made last summer."

"Alleged remark," said Staples. "Let's watch it anyway. I've always had an open mind."

Last August, he'd been returning from a business meeting in Westchester. Encountering a traffic tie-up on the FDR, he ordered his limousine driver to use side streets to take him to one of his buildings. While driving down a block in Harlem, they stopped for a red light. Staples noticed a group of inner-city kids running in and out of water spraying from a fire hydrant. Upset that his car would get wet, he asked his driver, "What the hell do these kids think they're doing?"

Now the CNN reporter turned on the security tape Raymond's ex-chauffeur had handed her during her investigation. "When it gets hot like this they use a wrench on the hydrant to jimmy it open so they can cool off," the driver said.

"Why don't they just use air-conditioning?" he heard himself ask.

Staples and his secretary watched attentively as the reporter recounted the facts. Staples, shaking his head, said, "Kathy, I never said it."

Statistics and incidents filled the screen. He'd been one of the few restaurant owners who refused to donate leftovers to Sully Barnes's homeless shelters. Not true. No one cared more about the homeless than he.

A call from Martin Burrows, a senior executive at the ad agency BBD & O, was put through. "Raymond, we want you and Larry Miller in a pizza commercial for Luigi's. Both of you tycoons are splitting up the pizza between you as if it were the city." He added, "If you two can work things out between you, that is."

"I wasn't aware that Killer Miller and I were quarreling," said Staples.

"I'll remind you, Raymond. When *New York* magazine decided to use him on their cover instead of you, you declined to be interviewed."

Staples's hand brushed through the widow's peak of his toupee. "That'd be narcissistic and self-absorbed behavior. I never said such a thing."

"They have it on tape, Raymond."

"Tapes lie," he said, smiling.

"You did a preliminary interview with them. They videotaped it."

"Videos distort."

Looking at his watch, he decided: lunchtime.

Outside on the street, he brushed by a couple of newspaper reporters who always hung around his building in hope of a story.

Of course they'd missed the big story of the day. That stocky detective who'd interrogated him this morning about Skinny being found in one of his buildings.

Seeing a detective in his office, the thought that a man he'd liked had been killed in one of his own buildings had shaken him. He'd immediately offered to help, giving an alibi for the twenty-third, the night Skinny'd been killed.

The heavyset detective smiled, told him he was only there to ask routine questions about when he'd last seen Skinny or talked to him. Just because Skinny'd been murdered in one of his buildings didn't mean that he was a suspect. There'd been no need for Raymond to supply him with an alibi.

Of course, since the alibi he'd supplied wasn't really true, it didn't matter anyway.

The detective recited a series of names. As Skinny's employer and occasional social companion, had McPherson ever mentioned any of them?

"I don't know these people," he answered.

He stopped walking in front of Ma Maison. He tried to push through the revolving door leading to his restaurant, furious that the maitre d' stood behind it, preventing him from getting in. But at last he forced himself inside.

"What's going on here, Harold?"

"You were insistent, Mr. Staples. You told me not to let you in here. You said you were trying to lose weight."

"I never said that."

TWELVE

Yablonsky and Julie Benfield carried the crates of Skinny's notes into McPherson's now vacant office.

The door open, he could see the entire press floor of the *Village Guardian.* In this pressroom, there were no rows gleaming with modern Macs and IBMs. The four computers for this news organization were clustered in a section of the cavernous room, just under a draped sign reading *Free Mumia.*

The *Guardian's* walls were scarred with slogans. "Che Lives." "McCarthy in '68." Half the wall was covered by a trio of yellow posters that said, "War Is Not Healthy for Children and Other Living Things." Right under this was a blown-up photo of Jerry Rubin, Abbie Hoffman, and Sully Barnes tossing bags of urine and shit at army recruits during the protest march they'd led down to Washington to levitate the Pentagon. Beneath the photos someone had pasted a record album cover of Arlo Guthrie's antiwar song, "Alice's Restaurant."

Earlier he'd been ushered into a staff meeting by a secretary. The revolutionaries were arguing.

Bob Stone introduced him. Yablonsky asked his questions. How come no one had wondered where Skinny had been the past two weeks? No reason to wonder, they said, Julie Benfield told them Skinny was heading to his country home for the holidays.

Julie Benfield stood as Yablonsky entered her cubicle. Like most men, when he was younger he'd been drawn into a sexual frenzy every time he encountered tall, blond, successful-looking women whose blank faces and perfectly formed features emphasized their unattainability.

She'd been married three times before she'd reached thirty, but the brevity of her marriages, rather than the number, made her infamous. She'd gone into each marriage as casually as an ice cream addict in a Häagen-Dazs store chooses another flavor. One of her marriages, this one to a record producer, had lasted for five months. She decided to put the second one to rest two days after the nuptials. The third didn't even make it through the honeymoon. Before that marriage she called one of her brothers, the one who later committed suicide, to ask him to attend, and he'd answered, "Not this time. But I'll be sure to make it to the next one." The detective wondered if she'd had to pay a psychological price for her past celebrity. Surprisingly, many famous people didn't. They didn't have complex interior lives. But it was obvious that she did.

She'd been famous for about twenty years. She had a royal name, one that had been prominent in New England for many decades. The Pilgrims started their passage to this country on ships the Benfields had built. Benfields had founded Groton, and they considered Harvard, to which they donated money and buildings, to be a private club. Their family tree went far back, its roots deep yet delicate. Some Benfields never made it through childhood, falling prey to typhus or influenza, while others, as they got older, could usually be counted on to attend the best universities and finest sanitariums.

He'd read about how she grew up. In the 1950s, Julie's branch of the family had emigrated to California from New England because of the milder climate. She'd grown up on a 7,000-acre ranch outside of Santa Barbara which had its own zip code and village. When the children reached school age, their parents built their own school and staffed it with tutors. Until they attended college, the children were seldom allowed to leave the ranch.

After graduating from Radcliffe, she drifted down to New York. Although she received invitations and attended parties for a group of people who still believed that debutantes should be balled upon coming out, she gravitated to the drug- and amphetamine-soaked world of Warhol's Factory, where she modeled clothes, sang along with Nico and Lou Reed for a while as one of the co-lead singers of The Velvet Underground, and appeared in a few underground movies directed by either Warhol or Gerard Malanga. In her most famous movie, *Undercover in Chelsea,* she lay motionless in bed alongside an actor for two hours, sleeping. The climax in the film came when she turned over and the audience realized she'd been naked all along.

In this poster-filled newsroom, although she'd been a legitimate celebrity, her cubicle was bare.

Benfield placed her coffee mug on her desk. "Tell me, Alvin." She motioned toward the conference room. "Were you just in there?"

"Yeah. I had to ask the staff a few questions about Skinny."

"What'd they say about me? Around here, I'm the house conservative."

"Nothing."

"Alvin, I know they talked about me." She gave him a smile. "My protector."

He looked away from the wall, still lined with Skinny's articles. "You've told me. I'm a good man to have around in case of a jam."

"Yeah." She casually squeezed his hand. "Now let's get to work."

They went through the piles, dividing the paper into two categories: Skinny's published articles and his notes. She looked through the articles. He, the notes.

"You seem to be right about the notes he left to himself," he said. "He kept nothing on the computer. And whatever he wrote to himself, mostly on cocktail napkins from bars, are like hieroglyphics. They're indecipherable. Julie, Skinny was just starting to investigate corruption in my precinct when he was killed. His interviews have got to be around somewhere." Yablonsky moved over to the wall, started reading one of Skinny's investigatory articles, a piece he'd done exposing kickback practices between Brooklyn politicians and attorneys in commercial real estate. "How long did it take him to write this one?" he asked.

"That was before my time with him. I used to tell him to be more organized. I told him to drink less, to eat less, to be more careful about himself. But he was a guy with large appetites." She paused. "I told him a lot of things."

Yablonsky moved back to the desk, leafing through a pile of indecipherable notes in frustration. "I really liked Skinny, so I can imagine what it's like for you."

She'd begun organizing McPherson's articles by the month and the year. "So many columns," she said. Looking through an article he'd written about doctors in the Bronx taking cocaine, she said, "Yeah, I miss him. If only he'd taken the bribe."

"Bribe?"

"Well, it's just that I assume since the guys he was going to expose were powerful and prominent, they would have tried to bribe him first."

"You should be a detective."

"I'd be a better detective than a reporter," she said. "Working on this paper, seeing the feuds and cliques and pettiness, doesn't exactly make a person an advocate for speedy social change. No one, except for the people who write for it, take the paper seriously at all. And most of the people we give it to read it only for the movie and music reviews."

"Then why would a conservative guy like Staples own this paper?"

"It's just a business to him, I guess. He's got a lot of businesses, Alvin." She paused. "Now that Skinny's dead, I'm the only one who still speaks her mind against their silly policies, regardless of the consequences. Skinny had integrity and it killed him. One thing about me," she said, her voice dropping, "I never cave into pressure. Never. Not me. Now I'm the only one left with any integrity."

"You forgot Sully Barnes," he said. "Skinny was killed on December twenty-third, Julie. When you didn't hear from him over Christmas, didn't you try to call him?"

"I lived with the man for two years, Alvin. I knew his habits. I had no way of knowing that he never made it to Stockbridge. He always kept the phone off the hook up there. When he went up there, it was to drink and write."

"How come you didn't go with him?"

Her eyes narrowed. "I have family in Lenox—that's nearby. I don't like to go up there during the holidays."

"I see."

Marsdon Phelps and Mike Kakowsky, two men whom Yablonsky recognized from the staff meeting, walked by.

"I tell you, we ought to be more like PEN," said Kakowsky, referring to a famous New York City–based writers group. "They censor any writer who disagrees with their policy. A writer's group that censors their writers. Good politics."

They laughed.

Since there was no door by Julie's cubicle, Marsdon Phelps stood in the entrance and knocked on the wall. He walked in with a smile and handed her a sheaf of paper. "Sorry to interrupt you and your cop. Your obit on Paul Rogers needs to be rewritten. You make him out to be some kind of John Reed. Too laudatory."

"I don't see how," she said, an edge to her voice. "All the salient points are there. The man was incredibly wealthy, but gave away most of his money for left-wing causes."

"But not to us, so fuck him. The guy had lots of dough, but to us he was a regular Cyrus Warner. Whenever Roland and Sully tried to put the arm on him to subsidize the paper, he'd turn us down flat."

"But he gave so generously to so many other causes." She hesitated. "How should I change it?"

Phelps stood over her shoulder, looking down at her copy. "The phrase 'giving generously' should read 'giving impulsively.' In your sentence 'gave away much of his fortune to a myriad of liberal causes,' change the words 'a myriad' to 'a few.' In the sentence 'he enjoyed politics,' change the word 'enjoyed' to 'dabbled in.' Instead of 'his largess evolved out of his altruism,' say 'his largesse evolved out of his guilt.' Any questions?"

"When do I change the name *Village Guardian* to *Pravda*?"

Phelps seemed amused as he glanced at Yablonsky. "Very funny. Why this sudden crisis of conscience? You've always done it before."

Benfield smiled bitterly. "The *Village Guardian*. We write all the news that fits to print," she said.

"That's not us," said Phelps. "We make no pretense here of objective reporting. Our credo's always been 'All the news that supports our views.' We may be a weekly, Julie, but you're already an hour over deadline."

"But I'm already working on the muggings from the Mitchell-Lama Housing Project."

"Fuck that," said Phelps. "Listen, Julie. I know Skinny's dead, but believe me, you've got to start focusing more on your work. Mourn in your apartment, not the office. I suggest you press that button on your keyboard and file both stories within an hour."

He left. "Fry in hell," she muttered. Turning to Alvin, she said, "This is one jam I wish you could help me get out of. Working here. I don't know why I write for this rag. I guess I still hope that I'll accomplish something someday."

"But you're famous."

She smiled at him, and Yablonsky once again felt that he was naive. "No," she said. "I became famous because I always remembered to stand to the right of the person being photographed so that the next day my name appeared first in the newspaper caption under the picture."

"To most people, becoming a celebrity's accomplishment enough."

"The only thing I've accomplished is stretching what should've been fifteen minutes of fame into twenty years. The older I get, the less proud I become of all my crazy antics from the past. I'm in my late thirties, Detective. It's time I accomplished something because of my talent."

"I'm sure you will." He handed her a sheaf of napkins. "Here, maybe you can do better with this than I did."

"I never could read Skinny's handwriting. What'd you learn about his case so far? By the way, Alvin, I'm going to bring you a present. Some of his sixties rock albums. He was a man who still listened to LPs, like you. Me, I'm strictly a CD gal."

"My task force's made a lot of progress. Skinny was killed on December twenty-third, after six P.M. I think he was killed while meeting one of his sources in your boss' building."

"Good," she said. "No matter how intense the pressure gets, you won't back off, will you?"

"I'm going to solve it." He paused. "That's what you want, isn't it?"

"Of course," she said. "It's just that I've already lost one guy I cared for. I don't want to lose you." She paused. "I loved that guy—but he was a man whose life was filled battling against his problems. I've always needed and been looking for a guy who cares enough about me to help me with mine. With a guy like you, I'd be more stable."

She squeezed his hand. He stood. Beautiful, brilliant, but moody and complicated. What did she look like naked? "We've accomplished nothing today—concerning my investigation, that is. Concerning my feelings for you, we've accomplished a lot."

"I'd like to see you again, Alvin. And not only because of Skinny."

He smiled at her. She was thin, but seeing that space between her legs would be heavenly.

Seeing the look in his eyes made her laugh. "I won't let you fuck me in my office, Alvin. For one thing, there's no door." At last she dropped his hand. "But we're going to see each other soon."

"When?"

"Give me a call."

He turned to leave. On the street, whenever he'd pass by an attractive woman he'd feel compelled to turn around and watch her walk away. He swung around. Julie was still in the alcove, watching him.

"I'll call you, Julie."

"Alvin, you were the one fucking guy in this world who tried to help me and didn't expect the usual thing in return."

I expect it now, though, he thought.

THIRTEEN

The homeless camp on the East River was divided into two parts, just like the East and West Sides of Manhattan. The section closest to him consisted of jumbled, haphazard masses of large packing crates strewn together with planks of wood and pieces of metal to form small, square-like squats. Shards of forty-ounce bottles lay scattered in pools of water, oil slicks from the FDR overhead, and puddles of dirty, melting snow, led to the camp. Many of the squats had bent chimney pipes from which smoke drifted. Electrical wiring and cables twisted through the encampment like boa constrictors, tapping into Con Ed's power lines. Yablonsky smelled rotting food and human waste.

The other part of the encampment was across the FDR, built on the jogging promenade bordering the East River. Broad wooden planks separated the squats into rows of streets, intersections, and avenues. Dozens of people streamed into and out of the camp. Yablonsky spotted garbage cans overflowing with refuse. The Sutton Place apartment buildings and balconies of the rich and middle class just two blocks away looked down on the encampment. Graffiti that had been scrawled on the side of one of the squats read, "Homeless Hills, Phase One, Sold Out."

At the camp's other end, scavengers had surrounded an unwary jogger and were bringing him down. "Hey!" he yelled, but no one paid him any attention. The detective quickly turned away.

Debris, pieces of furniture from an earlier homeless encampment recently destroyed by a thunderstorm, were flung throughout this village of shacks.

Yablonsky walked past a group of quarreling men that were lined up for food.

"Motherfucker!"

"That ravioli's mine."

"Don't be so fly with me. This ain't even ravioli. What this is, motherfucker, is Spaghetti-O's."

Two young white men dressed in baggy gray coats tore off from one of the food lines and shuffled towards the footbridge.

"I got the untreatable strain of T.B., but that fucking Sully came right up to my face with some food and fed me anyway."

His friend shook his head. "Amazing."

"I mean, he came right up to me, with that forgiving and understanding look. He treats you the way you want the world to treat you."

Four vans had been lined up side by side at the edge of the pedestrian walk. The backs of the vans were open as men and women moved sluggishly forward, in spite of the cold, to be served chili, orange juice, and coffee. Yablonsky inhaled the burnt-coffee aroma, wishing it were strong enough to wipe out the smell of feces, garbage, unwashed bodies, and urine.

The wind knocked over a stack of Styrofoam cups teetering on the lip of the rear of one of the vans.

Next to Barnes, near the tailpipes of the other vans, four men and a women with buttons reading "Homeless Coalition" handed out coffee, vegetable soup, and orange juice. Inside the vans were stacks of glassine plastic bags filled with magazines, clothing, and disposable needles. Yablonsky realized with a shock that he recognized the fourth man, a tall, clean-shaven guy in his thirties who, trying to blend in, wore the same shapeless non-designer dirt-smeared clothing of these grifters. It was the actor Charlie Kudos, who'd flown to New York from Hollywood two weeks ago to study Barnes for a cable movie being produced about the Nobel Prize–winner's life.

Kudos made it a point to stay involved in liberal left-wing causes, from PETA to the rights of illegal immigrants. Unlike most of West Coast Hollywood, he wanted to be perceived as a serious-minded East Coast man. He'd just finished up a big action picture for the money, had recently divorced his third or fourth wife, moved into his second or third home, and had recently fathered his fifth or sixth out-of-wedlock child. He was known for flying left-wing, liberal politicians and heads of social advocacy groups out to his East Hampton house and throwing them together with the beneficiaries of their causes. Yablonsky had read about a fund-raiser for the Powhattan Indians during which the town cops had to be sent for to throw the recipients of the actor's largesse, the Indians, off the premises. Kudos decided to hold his summer charity function in a series of cavernous lawn tents resembling tepees. The evening had started out with friendly celebrities prepared to hand over blank checks and ended with an angry shaman doing a war dance.

Right now, however, Charlie Kudos stood with the other coalition workers, far away from his troubles, handing out cup after cup of chili to shivering men and women. Like Sully Barnes, the actor wore the famous turned-around Brooklyn Dodger baseball cap, along with the by-now familiar Barnes uniform of a gray shapeless overcoat with mud-spattered Nikes. A silver earring dangled from his right ear.

Barnes, half a foot shorter than the six-feet-two actor, ladled out a cup of soup to an old woman wrapped in a blanket. "It's motherfucking cold out here, even for winter," he said. "You can use a coat, Hannah. You can use a scarf, too." He smiled at her. "Now you look like a Fifth Avenue model."

Barnes patted the old woman on the shoulder, then turned to a short, chubby guy in a white coat with the Beth Israel hospital logo sewn on the front. The short guy, out of breath and coughing, stuck a cigarette in his mouth.

"You been through the encampment?"

"Me and Dr. Goldkin, just like you asked."

"Were you able to see everybody? Or did they all hide from you?"

The doctor's eyes narrowed. "I'm not you. I saw only those who didn't ask for money and who didn't threaten me with mayhem. I figure I was able to give a quick, non-obtrusive physical to ten men and women."

"There are over a hundred people living here."

"I know. None of them too healthy. They should be in shelters. Sleeping out here in winter destroys the throat and lungs."

Barnes nodded. "Who's in the worst shape?"

"Three of them have T.B. Probably untreatable. The rest, various degrees of pneumonia and bronchitis."

"Can you take them to one of our hospices?" Barnes paused. "At our facility on East Eleventh Street and Avenue B, there's room."

"Look, Sully. I'm not Marcus Welby. Some of these people aren't even lucid. I'll have Brisco take me over in one of the vans, and if they're willing to come, great. But I'm not gonna force them."

"Of course you'll force them. Take along Brisco, plus Stevie Winslow over there. Wear the gloves, wear the masks, but get those crazy people's asses into the van."

Yablonsky, having entered the camp, headed toward the cluster of advocates. Charlie Kudos approached him. Clasping his hands before him, he gave him a Buddhist bow. "You'll have to wait in line there, buddy, along with everyone else."

"I'm not homeless," said Yablonsky. "I'm here to see Sully."

"You and the rest of New York. You sure you don't need some coffee and chili? You look like you could use a good meal."

Yablonsky smiled. "I have a home. I'm the detective who spoke to Sully earlier about McPherson's murder."

The actor made a horrified face. "Let me guess, you're trying to put together a deal based on your experiences in cracking a case, right? What's your above line? Ten-five? Play or pay, right? Well, you've got to sell off the international rights first and then have a distribution deal. Then maybe, if its legs seem long enough, and I'm guaranteed first dollar gross, we could climb into bed together."

"It's nothing as complicated as that. I'm only trying to solve a murder."

"Really," the actor said enthusiastically. "Whose? Did I know him?"

"Skinny McPherson's. So far I haven't been able to detect whether you know him or not."

"I didn't know him," said Kudos. "But I thought his murder had been solved already."

"Sully was McPherson's best friend on the paper. He may have information that would help my case."

The actor slipped his arm around the detective's shoulder. "So you're a detective? I feel like such a putz. But every cop who introduces himself to me usually has an agent trying to sell me his story. How long you been working on this case, anyway?"

Yablonsky didn't answer.

"I been here two weeks, and already Barnes is kind of letting me run interference for him," Kudos said. "Before I let you speak to Sully, you ought to watch what he says and does with these people for a while. It's good for the soul."

"Miguel says he needs a scarf over here, Sully," said one of the women activists.

"Shit," said Barnes. "We're out of 'em. First thing we do after we finish up here is call Bendheim Clothiers. You speak to them, Doris. Tell their manager, that cheap cocksucker Morty Gunther, that if he doesn't contribute ten dozen scarves pronto, I'll have a dozen dangerous derelicts in front of his store tomorrow. There'll be hunger strikes, nasty signs, the works. How many customers does he think will be brave enough to go through that gauntlet?" Doris and he exchanged smiles, and Yablonsky got the feeling that this was not an unusual tactic for them. "On the other hand, if he comes up with the clothing, my people will set up an exclusive five-minute spot with one of the networks on how his store symbolizes the post-Christmas spirit."

Yablonsky recalled how, during the Reagan era of tax cuts and trickle-down economics, this skinny, frail-looking man had been the first to take on the administration by breaking into a just-closed shelter in Washington, D.C., and refusing to leave until Congress came up with the money to reopen it and keep it going. That time he'd fasted for two and a half weeks, just a few days shy of the three weeks of starvation that meant automatic death. Congress caved in—and came up with the money. His then girlfriend whispered to him that he'd won, then had to step into the ambulance that was taking him to the hospital where he'd be fed intravenously to save his life. Since then, he'd participated in over a dozen hunger strikes. Hollywood celebrities who respected his guts and confrontational style rallied around him with free publicity and do-nations. Since his first victorious fast, he'd burned money at the New York Stock Exchange, chained himself to the White House gates, and with his coalition, created Hooverville-like homeless encampments in Washington, D.C., Chicago, Los Angeles, and New York to dramatize the tragedy of the homeless. The threat of one of his hunger strikes sent waves of anxiety through some of the most powerful and successful people in the city.

"I'll do that, Sully, but you're not gonna fast because of a few dozen scarves, are you?"

As Barnes talked, he continued to ladle out cups of soup. "Of course not. A hunger strike is for something really big. Do it too often, people become used to it and it loses its power to shock. But Gunther doesn't know that."

"Motherfucker!" a homeless guy screamed at a tall, powerful-looking man. "What right you got to cut into line? I was here before you."

The other people on the line cursed and laughed. The taller man started toward the shorter one, shoving people out of the way. "Gonna cap your ass, nigger!"

A couple of activists started to run to the soon-to-be-fighting men. Barnes, stepping out of line, said, "That's enough, Rollo. Calm down there, buddy."

"It's cold, Sully. I been waitin' fifteen minutes and I am one cold motherfucker."

"Sorry about that, Rollo. You got to wait on line like everyone else. Can you use another coat?"

"Shit, yeah."

Kudos whispered to Yablonsky, "He's out here every fucking day in the cold like this, dealing with violent, crazy people like that. I don't know how he can stand it."

Yablonsky said, "From a distance, on the footbridge, I saw some men from this camp attack and mug a jogger. I want to tell Sully. He's got to send some people over to help him. I radioed for a squad car. They'll be here soon."

Kudos's voice was flat. "We don't like it when cops come here. And you'll see Sully when I say so."

Yablonsky looked at him. "Charlie, fuck you."

He approached Barnes. Barnes looked him over, his eyes hard. "I'm busy here, buddy," he said. "Please state your fucking business."

"I'm Yablonsky."

"The detective who spoke to Myrna? You're here to speak to me about Skinny, right?"

"I am," said Yablonsky. The tall actor, following in the detective's wake, came up to them. "I told this cop you're busy, Sully. He shook me off. He claims that some of our people jumped a jogger. A squad car's on the way."

Barnes sighed. "All you cops do is hassle us. When do they get here?"

"Soon, I hope. There's an APB out on one of the guys you helped before. Rollo 'Street' Williams. He's suspected of robbing several convenience stores in Queens. He's here at your camp."

"I don't make any judgments about how these people live. If you want to pinch Rollo over there, you cops will have to do it by yourselves."

"They will." Yablonsky recalled that many years ago when Barnes was younger, after leaving college without graduating, he'd been out on the streets, too. His relationship with the police had always been adversarial. Barnes had been arrested half a dozen times for committing petty crimes like burglarizing cars, breaking into subway turnstiles, and smashing parking meters and telephones to jimmy out the money. Then in prison he'd met the Corrigan Brothers, two radical Jesuit priests who'd been put in jail for vandalizing army recruitment centers to protest U.S. policy in South America. Under their tutelage he slowly began to undergo a spiritual transformation, and upon his release into parole, Barnes became involved in social causes. Once again he was jailed, but this time for protesting the conditions of men and women who lived on the streets and in the shelters. Two years ago, the Nobel Prize committee had cited him for voluntarily setting up homeless shelters for the U.N., caring for AIDS patients and drug addicts, devoting his time to the weak and defenseless populations of society. Yablonsky had read somewhere that some time ago, when he was a street guy, Barnes had married and fathered a kid, then deserted them both, but to the media and the city politicians he supported and campaigned for, the possible unhappiness of a wife and kid counted little compared to the thousands of people and lives he had saved.

"Take my place over here and continue feeding these people, Charlie," said Barnes. "It'll be good practice for when you have to play me once you start shooting that movie about me."

Turning to Yablonsky, he said, "Let's go in the van, sip some coffee, and you can ask me your questions, Detective. It's as cold as a witch's tit out here."

The two men sat in a van that smelled of unwashed bodies. Sully's breath smelled of coffee and cigarettes.

"Sixties rock," said Barnes. "It's amazing how listening to Simon and Garfunkel's 'Fifty-Ninth Street Bridge Song' relaxes me, really soothes the savage beast."

"I'm the same way," Yablonsky said. "I have to ask you, though. What's it like, winning the Nobel Peace Prize?"

"Surprising," said Barnes. "Like me, you're a guy who grew up in Brooklyn, right?"

"Yeah," said Yablonsky.

"I could tell," Barnes said, nodding. "Over sixty years ago, there was this small gang of Italians and Jews living in Brownsville. Their job was to go all over the country and hit anyone the mob wanted out of the way. For years they got away with it. One of these shooters was a guy named Abe Reles."

"Right," said Yablonsky. "My father knew him. Kid Twist."

"Yeah. Anyway, the Brooklyn D.A. brought him in on a pinch, and some guy trying to save his ass over another charge rolled over on him. The truth about Murder Incorporated came out. After questioning Reles, who likewise turns out to be a rat, Burton Turkis, the D.A., looks at him and asks, "What was it like, killing all those people?' And Reles, who used to favor an ice pick, answers, 'I bet it was probably a lot like you when you tried your first case. At first you were nervous, right? Then you got used to it. Same with me.' Unlike a lot of these political types, I didn't lobby at all for it, so when I learned I won, I felt stunned and nervous, but then I got used to it. I won a couple of years ago, right? All the money went for beds and blankets. For repairs and renovations for the shelters and new vans. Believe me, the money didn't go very far, help too many people, or last too long. I've been out on these streets for over ten years, and the problem gets worse and worse. The numbers of homeless continue to grow. Sometimes I feel like returning that citation and telling the committee to crumple it up and shove it up their asses. But other times, I gotta confess, I love the attention, socializing and schmoozing with celebrities." He smiled. "Even when I'm pretending not to. That kind of attention, all the acclaim you get can become addictive. It can turn you, if you let it, into just as much of a junkie as"—he gestured toward the window—"those poor slammin' smackheads and cokehounds out there."

Barnes turned up the radio volume slightly. The song, "Down On Me," with Janis Joplin singing lead vocals, was from Big Brother and the Holding Company's first album.

Yablonsky said, "I was touched when you donated the entire amount of the prize to keep all the shelters you'd set up, going. I don't think I'd ever be capable of giving up two million dollars."

Barnes shrugged, "It was because of these people that I was awarded the money. Why shouldn't it go back to them?" He smiled at Yablonsky. "But yeah, it was hard giving it up."

Tommy and Rocco returned with the van, Rocco pulling alongside Sully. Rolling down the window, he said, "Didn't see that jogger. Wasn't able to find him. Guess the cops will have to find him."

Yablonsky turned and studied the two men. "Where'd you find these two guys?" he whispered to Barnes. "They look like the kind of head slammers who used to fight in clubs and smokers. Are they teamsters?"

Sully swiveled around, pouring himself a cup of coffee from one of the tureens. Yablonsky declined Sully's proffered cup. "You're right. That's the cop in you. They are teamsters. They deliver the newspapers to news-stands each morning and sometimes moonlight for me doing security work. Since each of them has their own private fiddle going with the newsstand owners, I estimate twenty percent of what goes out in circulation ends up in their pockets, not in Staples'. I've been doing this kind of work now for over ten years, and the one thing I've learned is that everyone in this city has their hands in someone else's pocket." He paused and pointed to the no-longer-organized line of derelicts. "Except them. Look at them, Detective. Even having to wait patiently on a line to be fed's too much for whatever emotional resources they possess."

"Looks like you do a lot of ordering people around yourself," Yablonsky said.

"The only time I succeed in helping them is when I act like a cop," Barnes replied. "There's got to be order and organization, even among us leftover-from-the-sixties anarchists. Look how quickly Charlie's let everything disintegrate out there." He rubbed his silver earring as if to ward off an evil spell. "I've got to go back and straighten things out before that Hollywood hustling parvenu, with access to all those liberal deep pockets, fucks things up so badly it'll be the homeless who're serving my staff and not the other way around."

"In the days right before Skinny was murdered, how often did you meet with him? Did he ever discuss his future writing projects with you?"

Barnes sipped his coffee. "Obviously I don't work with the *Guardian* full-time, but I recall that I met with him at least once. They hired me right after I won the Nobel." He smiled. "Which was, I'm sure, just a coincidence."

Yablonsky smiled back. "How did you manage to live before they employed you?"

"I wasn't on salary, but I kept part of the donations for living expenses. The I.R.S.'s been through our accounts a dozen times, like with all charities. Everything computes. The three-room apartment I keep up, on Bleecker Street in the East Village, now basically's evolved into a drop-in center. I have one room, people who really need a place to flop share the other. Some nights I even find bodies sprawled all over my kitchen, but it's not that bad."

"I'll bet it's not," said Yablonsky. "Why'd you decide to take the job with the *Guardian?*"

"Because it's an advocacy paper," said Barnes. "My position on the editorial board's just ceremonial. The real reason I let the *Guardian* put my name on the masthead was because they promised me my own column, which I use as a platform to promote my views. Even though Staples is a compulsive liar, he's kept his word to me. He's never interfered with what I write. Do you read my column? Do you agree with what I've been saying?"

"There's a difference between helping a guy or woman who's out there busting his or her hump trying to make the weekly bills and assisting heroin addicts, crack addicts, and other disturbed and violent people move into a neighborhood and make it worse. But I admire the passion that fuels your views. Someone's got to help these people and most of us don't want to do it."

"That's progressive thinking for a cop." Barnes paused. "Can I put the arm on you for a contribution?"

"When I'm out on the street, I give. But if you invite me to one of your famous fund-raisers, I'll reach into my wallet for you."

"It's a deal. Are you finished with me yet? Look at that pompous insecure asshole out there, fucking things up."

"Unfortunately, I have to ask you a few more questions. You were Skinny's best friend on the paper. Did he ever consult with you about what he planned to write?"

"Never. Since I had my own column, he was always afraid I'd steal his work." Barnes sipped his coffee and flicked the radio volume down. "How are you doing on this case, anyway?"

"I've got the date of the murder, the time and place. All I need is a suspect."

"You know when he was murdered? And where?"

"December twenty-third. In the garage of the newspaper's printing plant."

The wind came in through a crack in the van's window. "You're not gonna shitcan this case, are you, Detective?"

"I miss Skinny too fucking much to shitcan it. Since you're on the editorial board and help run things, how about letting me go through the *Guardian*'s back issues? I need to find past exposés written by Skinny that I might have missed, or go over articles written by your other reporters. I'm looking for connections between people."

"Come anytime you want," said Barnes. "I'll tell Myrna to let you have complete access to our files."

"I'll also have to speak to Benfield again. I like Julie. Is she a reporter now? What hours is she in your office?"

"She basically does all our obits. Recently, she's been allowed to do some actual journalism for the paper. So she's out there on the street sometimes, and that can be dangerous. She's really something, all right. One fucking beautiful woman. A lot of brains. A lot of ambition."

"Good for her," said Yablonsky. "What's she working on?"

"She plans on doing a series about a mostly welfare housing development in East Flatbush and its effect on the surrounding neighborhood. Of course she's got to stick to the party line and not write about the increase in crime. She understands that."

"When she goes to these projects, will your newspaper send a security escort with her? Will she have a photographer?"

"We ain't *The New York Times*," said Barnes. "There'll be a photographer, but we don't have the staff to send along security people. You don't have to worry about her, Detective. She'll be fine. The project association expects her. They already know what kind of article she intends to write. You promised me a check, remember?"

"I forgot," said Yablonsky. He reached into his coat pocket, pulled a check out of his wallet, and began scribbling.

"Make it out to the Homeless Coalition," said Barnes. Yablonsky handed him the check.

"Thirty dollars?" said Barnes. "For thirty dollars I promised to let you attend our next party? You got a good deal." He smiled. "But remember, our next social function's a fund-raiser." He shook Yablonsky's hand. "Be happy to see you there. That is, as long as you bring your checkbook."

Yablonsky stepped around the patches of weeds that were still growing, even in winter. Under the footbridge, shards of whiskey bottles and discarded needles gleamed in the disappearing light. Climbing, he thanked the god of People-Who-Had-Homes that he was leaving the encampment unmugged and only thirty dollars poorer. The squad car still hadn't arrived. He called the nearest precinct, once again gave dispatch the location of the incident with the jogger.

From a distance on the tiny bridge, he saw a skinny white man running toward the encampment. Yablonsky could not make out what the guy was yelling, but he seemed to be heading toward Barnes.

Tensing, the detective leaned forward, wondering if he could get there in time to help Barnes. The man began screaming. Charlie Kudos, seeing a crazy person rushing toward him, wheeled. Yablonsky, moving forward, saw the actor run toward the van. The lines of homeless people broke up and the men and women scattered. The guy, shouting obscenities, headed for Barnes.

Rocco, Tommy and Kudos ran toward the derelict. Yablonsky watched the teamsters toss him on the ground as if he were weightless. But the sheer physical power of Rocco and Tommy was not enough. The street guy scrambled up, lowered his head and rushed Barnes. Before he could reach him, Kudos stopped him with a diving tackle. Tommy and Rocco approached warily from behind, obviously afraid of having close physical contact with a guy who might have AIDS.

Standing on the footbridge, Yablonsky saw Barnes walk over to the guy who was self-destructive enough to try to attack him in front of so many witnesses. The homeless advocate seemed to be saying comforting words, then gently patted him on the shoulder. The guy turned his face away from Barnes.

The teamsters gripped the still angry man's shoulders and escorted him out of the camp, but he turned back to Barnes, still cursing. Yablonsky couldn't hear what he said, but despite the violence he'd tried to commit, the detective felt sorry for him. The guy looked pathetic, wearing a full-button coat that he was too mentally disturbed to close. He wore dirt-encrusted sneakers with untied laces like an inner-city kid. Yablonsky wondered why this guy would be crazy enough to attack Barnes, and to do so in front of so many witnesses. He let out a long, slow breath as he watched Barnes and Kudos return to feeding the homeless.

FOURTEEN

The wind banged against the boarded-up buildings. Across the street next to the roller coaster was a white-faced brick building that displayed giant paintings of Nathan's frankfurters and French fries. Seagulls flew over row after row of deserted amusement stands. Down the street from Nathan's stood the burnt-out frame of an abandoned bathhouse. Traffic lights blinked as the occasional car drove down the street.

The detective headed down narrow alleyways, away from the jumble of vendor stalls. Used furniture and clothes spilled out of the labyrinth of alleys that was the Russian-run souk in Coney Island.

Some stalls in the souk had contained boxes of gray market batteries, counterfeit jeans, and knockoff car parts. Some stalls sold nothing but wind-up watches and transistor radios. One of his street sources, Nicholas, a Georgian in his twenties, nicknamed Midas, had been given permission by one of the Russian *mafiya* families to set up the market. Every product that the rest of America disposed of or junked could be sold here. Anything that was manufactured, no matter what the condition, would eventually find a buyer. If you were a New Yorker with a home and a family that had been here for more than a generation, you didn't know this place existed. But if you were homeless or an immigrant who lived in Brighton Beach, Coney Island, or Sheepshead Bay who disposed of roomfuls of furniture as deftly as you disposed of your past country, then this thieves' market was your own personal shopping mall.

The detective knew his way around this marketplace. Years ago, Yablonsky, a man who often guessed wrong on the technologies of the future, had collected scores of eight-tracks while confidently disdaining cassettes. Whenever he had needed another eight-track player, he came here to search for a replacement. Whenever he needed needles or cartridges for his record players or to look for LPs, this was where he came. If the manual typewriter he still used needed a ribbon, he walked from his basement apartment in Sheepshead Bay to this marketplace. All these objects from the end of the twentieth century, before joining the horse and buggy, blacksmiths, and community ice houses—the detritus from the end of another century—were recycled one last time here. This time Yablonsky had come because the market was a good place to hear things.

"The Pulitzer Prize–winning writer who was murdered," he'd asked Midas. "Skinny McPherson. You hear anything about it?"

"I can't help you with that one, Detective. But, like in Russia, find out who offered the bribe. Whoever offered the bribe is your murderer."

"The reporter was killed because he turned down the bribe."

Midas looked at him incredulously. "Then you'll never find the killers."

A car seemed to be following him about half a block away. Leaving Surf Avenue he walked under the overpass leading to the Brooklyn Aquarium. Since he was just a mile or two away from Sheepshead Bay, he decided to walk near the beach to get home.

To his left, he saw the silhouette of the Cyclone, then the Wonder Wheel, then three thousand miles of Atlantic Ocean.

Only the seagulls were out today, searching, then dive-bombing for food. Today no one was sitting on the benches of the boardwalk. No joggers. No women walking baby strollers.

He remembered coming to the Steeplechase as a kid, riding the speedy metallic horses, then after the ride ended, being smacked by obese clowns with sticks that gave off slight electrical charges. His gang of friends, a tough bunch from East New York, climbed the steps to be the only kids to wreak vengeance on the clowns by spitting on them from overhead.

Underneath the boardwalk, he heard muffled sounds, the sounds of struggle. Shoving his hand in his pocket he ran down the steps.

Now on the sand, he saw shadowy figures under the planks. As he turned to close with a figure on his right, a kick to his back sent him staggering. He smashed his fist against one of the guy's jaws. Figures behind began to pummel him. Slowly he sank to the sand. He felt hands gripping his shoulders. He heard the roar of the ocean as if it was inches away.

He tried to reach for his gun amid the bodies, but the fall had knocked his gun away in the sand.

"Son of a bitch," he said.

He heard feet above him on the boardwalk, scurrying away from the sounds of conflict

Smart, he thought. As a detective, he'd run toward the sound of struggling.

He took punches in the face—kicks to the legs, stomach and chest.

"You can have whatever money I have on me," he gasped.

A long, pale face loomed in front of him. He tried to grasp the guy's neck, choke him, but he found his arms pinioned.

"You still haven't got a fucking clue, do you?" The accent: white male from the Bronx. "Shitcan your investigation."

Yablonsky tried to brace himself to rise but couldn't.

The men backed off, fled.

He lay there breathing heavily for what seemed like hours. At least they hadn't taken his gun, he thought. That would have been the ultimate humiliation.

Once he'd retrieved his gun, he pulled himself to his feet. Staggering drunk-like on the boardwalk, he leaned against the railing. "Bastards."

He sat on a bench, his hands going over his body, assessing damage. Bruises, a cut mouth, aching kidneys and lungs. No broken bones. He knew from his old street-fighting days in Brooklyn that he'd need three weeks to heal.

From a distance he saw apartment buildings. Farther away, the Verrazano. To the right, the Brooklyn curves and shoreline that led to the rest of Long Island, then the country's end.

He needed help.

A radio cab pulled into view. The car that had seemed to be following him.

He tensed, gripped the gun inside his pocket, then let his hand slip away from the gun.

It was Milo. Milo, originally a Russian immigrant, had been in this country for decades.

Over the years, they'd known each other casually. Milo drove a radio car for a cab service while maintaining a minuscule fleet of yellow cabs, which he leased to other drivers. Uniforms throughout the city's precincts, including Yablonsky's, would give him a call if their wives or girlfriends were using the car and they needed a ride into the city or back home.

Milo approached. He was an average-sized, weather-beaten guy with heavy, muscular arms. The cabdriver brushed the two columns of hair that created a bald aisle on his skull. "What the hell happened to you? Were you mugged?"

"I was threatened. I saw you before, driving down Surf Avenue. Why'd you hang around here for hours?"

"Hours? You were gone from my sight for less than two minutes. Then I see you stagger up the boardwalk. It's lucky for you I like being a cop groupie. Let me take you home."

Inside the cab, despite the detective's injuries, the cabdriver tapped a drumbeat with a pencil on the dashboard, zapping the rigged meter.

As Milo drove him home, the detective peered out at the streets, looking for any white males who seemed out of place, but he saw only shabby Russian babushkas, heading with their strollers to the playground. Men, despite the cold, played handball at the courts.

Milo drove along Surf Avenue, then under the train tracks of Brighton Beach Avenue.

The rigged meter continued to lunge forward. Yablonsky was too exhausted to care. Milo was merely engaged in the usual small-time corruption. The men he was after were engaged in big-time crimes.

The car moved along Brighton Beach Avenue, passing Coney Island Avenue, Mrs. Stahl's Knishes, and Golden Appetizers.

"Why were you walking home, Alvin? What were you doing in Coney Island?"

"What were you doing down here, Milo?"

"I've got a real franchise, driving Pakis from the farm, Kennedy Airport to Brooklyn. Sometimes I get these short, jerk fares to Surf Avenue. What the hell is a detective with a gold shield doing taking the D train down to talk to one of his street sources?"

"How the fuck did you know that?"

"What else would you be doing? If you didn't taxi down, how else would you get here?"

Yablonsky gave him a bitter look. "My squad car was stolen. I demanded another one. Those Rear Echelon MotherFuckers in my precinct still haven't replaced it. I need a car. It's hard to get a taxi that's willing to leave Manhattan."

"I'll drive you."

"What do you mean?"

Berry continued zapping the meter. "You know how I like hanging around cops. Let me be your chariot."

"How?"

He made a left onto West End Avenue, then another left onto Oriental Boulevard, the main thoroughfare in the Manhattan Beach section of Sheepshead Bay. "If you need to be taken to a crime scene or do a little investigating, call ahead."

"You'll drive me?"

"If I don't have anything else breaking—yeah. Before I'm through zapping the meter on you, your department'll wish they bought you your own fleet."

A checker cab made a right off Oriental. Milo leaned forward. "Look at that. They're not supposed to even be on the streets anymore. I got a collection."

"Of what?"

"Checker cabs. Someday I got to show them to you. Five beauties. I keep them in a lot on Cozine Avenue in Brooklyn. I ain't never gonna put them on the street working for me, though. They got shocks like a tank and a transmission like an airplane. You gonna use me, Alvin? I'll steal less from you than other cabdrivers."

Ahead he could see party ships lined up along the bay. In the evening they'd journey miles out into the ocean to act as floating casinos for people who liked to gamble. Rubbing his bruised jaw, he said, "Sure."

At two in the morning, New York City police brass swam in the pool at the New York Athletic League Club, ran on the treadmills, and relaxed in the sauna.

Yablonsky stood before Police Commissioner Hodges and Michael Lascari, one of his deputies. They lounged inside the weight room, watching two precinct commanders work out with twenty-pound weights on Cybex machines.

"What happened to you?" Hodges asked.

"I took a walk along the beach. The tide was rough."

"I see. You know we've placed a task force at your disposal. You still want to lead it?"

"More than ever."

"Good. Solve this case, and in a couple of years, we'll put you behind a desk instead of on the street and you can start enjoying perks like this," said Lascari.

"The manager of this club and me are good friends," the police commissioner said, smoking a cigarette across from a sign that said No Smoking. "When it's late at night, the facilities are opened up for our use."

"No dues," said one of the deputy commanders. "Always for free."

"Care for a smoke?" the police commissioner asked.

"I brought my own," Yablonsky said, the only man there who didn't light up.

"We hear," said Police Commissioner Hodges, "that you've already met with the mayor about the McPherson murder. Is this true?"

"I did," said Yablonsky, "at his heliport pad."

"We also hear that he already believes cops were responsible for murdering McPherson to quash the exposé he was working on about corruption in the two-one. Your precinct."

Diagonally across from them, two fat precinct commanders were playing paddleball. The detective heard splashes and shouts from the pool area. "He never said that. What he did say was that if it *was* the motive for the murder, I should pursue it regardless of who it leads to."

"What do you believe?" asked Lascari. "Is it cops?"

"A cop wouldn't have the resources to pull off this kind of murder. It had to be individuals with much greater power—enough to cover up crimes greater than money ties to a bordello and selling confiscated goods from street peddlers."

"You mean one of McPherson's other stories that got him killed—and not the exposé on police corruption. If you're so certain cops didn't do it, why'd you find it necessary to question Patrolman Billings?"

For a moment, Yablonsky wondered whether it was only patrolmen who had ties to that bordello. But only for a moment. "My investigation into Billings's activities the night Skinny was killed cleared him."

"Good," said Hodges. "If word ever leaked that the reporter was in the process of uncovering corruption in the two-one, half the people and politicians in the city would assume cops killed him, no matter who you bring in for the crime. I'd like very much to see that article he was writing. I want any speculation about dirty cops in the two-one stopped before it becomes public knowledge. If you uncover the article, turn it over to us. If our political friends get ahold of it, God knows what they'll do to us next."

"I want to find Skinny's article, too. It exonerates me."

The police commissioner paused. "Do you want it published? We don't."

"Only if word leaks out and I.A. undertakes their own investigation."

"Great," said Hodges, finishing his cigarette and lighting another, all in the same motion. "We're on the same wavelength."

After Yablonsky left, Police Commissioner Hodges flicked on the giant-screen TV at the end of the gym. The men watched a large image of Sterling Roth.

"CNN's replaying the press conference Roth held earlier today," said Hodges. "That means he's already kicked off his campaign to try to free that cop-killer Moody. No matter how it turns out, he's going to make the department look bad." He cased the sparse crowd listening to Roth, zoomed in on the screen when he spotted something. "What the hell are Patrolmen Bridges and Beatty doing outside the main defense perimeter? Can't we even do this right?"

"Do you think cops like protecting Roth?" said Lascari. "Half the uniforms there, especially those who lost partners and had Roth defend the skells who murdered them, would probably like to pop him themselves."

"More than half," said Hodges and laughed. "My wife's sister's cousin was murdered by one of Roth's clients a couple of years ago."

Lascari sighed, watching the attorney spew anti-cop rhetoric and prime the crowd. "I'm glad I don't have to deal with him. I pity the poor street cop who does."

The detective was driven by Milo to Munson's Diner on the West Side, the place where he'd meet his most important informant.

Sliding into the booth he faced the man who'd been furnishing him with enough information to solve four murder cases in the past two years.

"You're fifteen minutes late, my friend," said Roth, glancing at his Rolex.

"Sorry."

"Next time I won't wait. It's bad enough you turned me into a snitch," said Roth. "But to keep me fucking waiting for you like I'm the lowest C.I. on your list, this, my friend, is real chutzpah, even for a cop."

At 3:30 a.m., Munson's diner, except for the detective and his stoolie, was deserted.

"Dinner or breakfast?" asked the waiter.

"I'll have a tuna salad on rye," said Yablonsky.

"The usual for me," said Roth. "You see that? I can say 'the usual' because you and I are meeting so regularly that even the waiters recognize me. How much longer are you gonna insist on your fucking pound of flesh?"

"A very long time, my friend," Yablonsky said, munching on a dinner roll.

Two years ago, while working with the Feds on a money laundering case, Yablonsky learned that Roth uncovered information on one of the government's biggest prizes in the Witness Protection Program, a deposed right-wing dictator of a Latin American country. He'd informed on his drug cohorts in exchange for being allowed to live in America. Roth had promptly furnished his left-wing contacts with enough information for them to kill him, even though he was in the Witness Protection Program. Yablonsky had used the information he had on Roth to turn him into his most valuable C.I., confidential informant.

"What kind of detective blackmails an attorney into stooling for him? What kind of cop will use information he has on a man to destroy him and everything he believes in? I could never live with myself if I did that."

Yablonsky buttered a dinner roll and ate it. Roth pushed his away.

"A detective who wants to solve more murders," Yablonsky offered. "What do you got for me?"

"Since Skinny's murder I've had my ears to the street. I've heard nothing."

"You better get a hearing aid, then," Yablonsky said.

"I heard it was cops."

"It wasn't cops. You knew and liked Skinny, so did I."

"I don't like any reporter enough to jeopardize my life so you can get the credit and can continue to own me like this. If I find anything out, I tell you and you solve your case. Then I'm off the hook with you, my friend. I've dropped my last dime."

"Deal," said Yablonsky.

FIFTEEN

Gripping both ski poles, edging away from one of the many precipices of the exclusive ski resort in upstate New York, Raymond Staples said, "I don't understand why you're here. No one cooperated with you more than me."

It'd been years since Yablonsky'd skied. Looking down at the resort's panorama, he felt dizzy.

"How long did it take you to come up here from the city, Detective?"

"Two hours."

"What with getting out to the heliport, you almost beat me and my private copter. I'm envious."

"Don't be. As soon as I got in the cab, my driver claimed the hundred-dollar fee we'd negotiated was only for one way, so he doubled the price."

"You've never skied before, have you?"

"Not for years. Certainly not extreme skiing."

"Don't be frightened. All you got to do is focus. Don't look down, adjust your right ski so it's not pointing up the cliff, like it presently is, and you'll be fine." Staples took in another deep breath. "For me, it's exhilarating. Whenever I'm up here, I feel triumphant, like I just climbed Everest."

"I read a book about Everest a couple of years ago. It was written by a Russian guide who managed to climb, then descend Everest during a storm in which eight climbers died. A month after his book was published about his experiences up there, he was killed in an avalanche while climbing another mountain in Nepal. Give you any ideas, Mr. Staples?"

"Yeah. Let's work our way up higher so we can descend faster. A tip, Detective. Whenever you do something risky, ignore all premonitions of death."

Wind blew through the trees and sheets of snow and ice rumbled down. "Why ignore them? The first time I questioned you in your office, Raymond, you made sure to tell me you were vacationing in the Caribbean on the night that Skinny was killed."

"On December twenty-third?"

Pulling off one of his gloves, Yablonsky reached into his pocket. "Patrolman Henderson found these in the *Guardian*'s research room." He showed Staples a series of photos. Most were of him, Shelly Townes, and Dollars Dillon, taken at various times by photographers in front of Dillon's condo in Fort Lauderdale, at The Landings. The caption under one of the Reuters photos said: Will New York City Survive? Judge Robert Dillon, Boro President Shelly Townes, and Zillionaire Restaurateur and Developer Raymond Staples have fun in the Florida sun.

One of the pull quotes from an article read: "Judge Robert Dillon proclaims, 'Anyone who returns to the Big Apple with a better suntan than me's gonna get sentenced to a year of community service!' "

Staples stared at the most recent photo, taken at the condo fuckpad, of just himself and Dillon. Shelly wasn't in this photo; he was in jail. The date on top of the photo was December 23. The day Skinny was murdered.

Staples stared at the photo of the judge and himself. "That's not me," he said.

"The article says you were with Judge Dillon. You vacationed with him. He's a buddy of yours."

"I don't know him. That's not me in the photos."

"It is you."

"It's me, but the photo's been doctored."

"Friendships with men like Shelly and Dollars are often just excuses to do business together. Was that why you told me you were in the Caribbean, instead of in Florida with Dillon?"

"If I was with the judge that night, then I couldn't have been in New York with Skinny, right?"

"Maybe you were with him for only part of the weekend."

"You have my word, Detective. I was with him for the entire weekend."

"Your word?"

"I never lie."

"Who'd you do more business with, Judge Dollars Dillon or Shelly?"

"I barely know them. May I continue skiing now?"

"I spoke to your assistant. I know you're currently taking one of your famous mini-vacations in which you get flown to a resort, have some R and R for a couple of hours, then return to the city. How'd you like to give me a lift back on your copter? When are you going back?"

"I won't be back until late tonight. You probably have to return right away."

"I don't feel like being charged double by my driver, Raymond. Let me fly back with you."

"It's only a two-man copter."

"What do you have planned once you return to New York?"

"We go to a gala at the Met tonight."

"Once you return, how'd you like a police escort? Make sure you get to where you want to go."

Smiling, Staples said, "I hope they like the opera."

Yablonsky pointed to the picture. "Dollars?"

"I was with him for the entire weekend. You have my word."

"Your own newspaper called Dollars Dillon one of the worst judges in the city last year. He's not the best character witness."

"He's still a judge. And a man of impeccable character."

"You won't be meeting with the judge? Going over your alibi?"

"I won't be contacting Dillon, Detective. You have my word on that."

SIXTEEN

The two attorneys who entered Judge Dillon's chambers were agitated. He noted to himself that this pair of litigants had never made an effort to ingratiate themselves by attempting to join his bull pen. Nevertheless he greeted both men effusively. He always made it a point to prowl his courtroom halls for fresh talent. Somewhere within this disaster of a case he knew he'd be able to pry out a victory.

The taller of the two men, Mark Fob, said, "This case has dragged on for over two years. No complaint about that, Judge. I enveloped you just as you wanted—and I still haven't gotten a favorable decision."

The other attorney, Mike "the Mutt" Ludlow, said, "Bullshit. You know very well, Your Honor, that the preponderance of the evidence is on our side. I was promised that if I gave you an envelope, I'd get a favorable ruling concerning child support, in addition to a more generous settlement. I kept my word, but so far there's been no ruling. So the case drags on and on, and my client and I wait and wait for justice. Mark's given you money. I've given you money. Which way on this case you gonna go?"

"He's right, Your Honor," said Fob. "We've both enveloped you. How you gonna go?"

The judge looked thoughtful as he pondered a way around this impasse. At last he clasped his hands. "Gentlemen, the solution's been staring us in the face. Each of you hand me five grand, and I'll decide the case on its merits."

Standing to usher out the two resigned attorneys, he poured compliments on each man, praising each's courtroom abilities as he walked them to the door. It was always good strategy to end a sidebar like that on a good note.

Luigi came into his chambers to cut and style his hair. The judge turned his palms down. "I want a real good nail job, Luigi. Go easy on the file, but heavy on the polish. I want these nails looking as buffed and as shiny as a new pair of shoes. I got a matinee with my wife today."

"Like a car wash, Your Honor. No scratches."

Snip and cut. The judge relaxed, enjoying as always the spectacle of someone engaging in trivial and repetitive work on his behalf. As he heard the hypnotic melody of the razor and clippers, he allowed his mind to wander, and his fantasies led him inexorably to the great dream. The newspapers were full of flattering stories and ass-kissing articles about him . . . the newest appointee to the state supreme court. Other jurists' dreams were far more spectacular, but he knew that if he kept his dreams more modest, the state supreme court, instead of the real big-time, the federal, then God would reward him for not dreaming too grandiosely.

There he'd be, ascending the podium, a figure almost regal in his dignity, the cruel articles and ten-worst lists forgotten as he prepared to assume his new, sober responsibilities, live a different, more elevated kind of life, and at last cleanse himself by serving the public, dazzling jurists, lawyers, and litigants with a series of briefs and rulings that would make New York law and shape jurisprudence for half a century.

* * *

Now standing next to the vendor's table, touched by the awakening of his long-slumbering honesty genes, he knew that for as long as he lived, he'd always remember the stunned looks on the barristers' faces. He knew that gossip about his forbearance would spread. He was on his way to becoming a Swinging Supreme.

Putting back the cheap trinkets, he reached across and fingered a fake silk scarf and gloves. He decided to reward himself for the virtue he'd shown by purchasing a gift for himself instead of his wife. Where love already existed, weren't presents and tokens of affection superfluous?

"How much for the scarf and gloves, Muhammad?"

"Five for the scarf. Six for the mittens. Don't look so upset, Judge. My prices, like the cost of justice, have gone up."

"I'm not upset, Muhammad, only surprised, that's all. I mean, you know who I am. I didn't think I'd have to pay retail."

The vendor shrugged. "I don't get no discount, why should you?"

"I should get a magistrate's discount. You know me."

"If you can't afford a pair of gloves for six dollars, then buy one glove for three. And yeah, Your Honor, I know all about you."

The judge handed him eleven dollars. He wrapped the scarf around his neck and put the gloves in his overcoat pocket. "What do you know about me, Muhammad?"

"I know that as long as you're sitting on the bench, I should love my wife and never get a divorce." He turned to face the next customer.

Making a left on Church Street, Dollars Dillon continued his walk to Battery Park City. The streets were full of traffic, and he twisted around to see if Billy was still following him. The diligent chauffeur was. Streams of people rushed back and forth around him. Pushcart vendors sold fruit, knockoff CDs, American flags and place mats with pictures of the World Trade Center on them, and cheap watches whose batteries would run out as soon as you purchased them. He bought half a pound of cashews at the corner of East Broadway, then signaled Billy to pull up for him. He enjoyed sinking into the plush leather. He'd purchased the car a couple of months earlier, in anticipation of spending his new found wealth, and he loved the fact that the new-car smell inside had not yet faded. There was no smell as sweet as the scent of a just-purchased limousine. His wife thought so too. It was an aphrodisiac.

He thrust the bag toward the window separating him from his driver. "Care to partake, Billy?"

The chauffeur scooped a handful of cashews out of the brown bag and munched noisily. Billy handed him a sheaf of traffic summonses, but Dillon ripped them up and threw them in the garbage bin, along with all the others.

"I'm late for a very important date with my wife, Billy. Please step on it and get me home. By the way, how's your wife and kid?"

The chauffeur wove his way through the busy streets. He didn't respond to the question. He'd seen the judge in action before, and never knew whether Dillon's probes about his family were innocuous social pleasantries or inquiries about future business.

Billy drove onto Chambers Street, then from there made another left, entering Battery Park City, where the judge and his wife lived.

Dillon patted down his remaining strands of hair and sprang out of the car without waiting for the door to be opened.

His chauffeur walked him to the entranceway of his luxury apartment building. In the expanse of ground between the coastline and the expensive condos was a park for children. For a moment the two men watched mothers wheel baby strollers into and out of the park.

Billy pointed with his chin to the parade of strollers. "There go your future clients, Judge. What time you gonna need me for?"

The judge's eyes lingered lovingly on the younger generation, anticipating the future. More than half of those kids being chauffeured around by their mothers would be in court one day. "Tell you what, Billy. When I need you I'll beep you. But before you pick me up, drive over to Twenty-Third Street and take out half a dozen glazed mini-donuts from Krispy Kreme. Then you can drive me uptown for dinner."

"Hi there, Hugo," Dillon said, smiling as the doorman let him in.

"Beautiful day, Your Honor, isn't it?"

"Seems like," said the judge. He took the speedy elevator up to the thirtieth floor. The apartments in Battery Park were small, but there were compensations. He entered and called out his wife's name. There was no answer. She must be busy, he thought. Arranging herself for him in one of the bathrooms. He fixed himself a few finger sandwiches to eat, then strolled over to the bay window. Across from the harbor, tiny joggers ran laps on the Brooklyn Heights Promenade. To his left was the watchtower sign of the Jehovah's Witnesses. His eyes drifted toward the Statue of Liberty. Patting the thick envelope in his inner suit pocket, he grinned and waved at the statue. He'd always wondered what the green girl was concealing in the folds of her tunic.

He glanced at the area where the World Trade Center used to be. Three thousand people unable to get divorces, a tragedy.

There was a soft knock on the door. Turning, he waited for his wife to get it for him, but she didn't seem to be around. Maybe she'd gone to visit another neighbor on their floor. The knock on the door meant nothing, he reassured himself. Probably his wife had had something delivered, or else it was the newspaper franchise once again trolling for a tip. The judge's normally benevolent expression vanished. He didn't like having his domestic harmony disturbed.

Opening the door, he stepped back. Three men entered. He recognized the shortest one. The others were stocky. Instinctively he stepped back again. Trying out a smile, he said to the one he recognized, "Can't you leave a guy in peace? I had a rough day in court and I had to re-calendar everything. So in the end nothing was accomplished." He hurriedly added. "If you wanted to meet with me, I'm open for discussion. I mean goddamn it, you didn't have to bring along Laurel and Hardy."

One of the men started to laugh. The other snickered. The guy Dillon knew wagged his finger at him and said, "Objection overruled, Dollars."

Dillon took another step back. To his horror, the men followed. The tiny judge smiled tentatively up at the trio. "Is there a lesson for me to learn in all of this? You bet there is." He paused, not understanding why he felt a jolt of fear. He was a judge. Time for him to take command. Assert himself. "We had a dispute. I have my point of view. You have yours. Let's discuss."

The guy he knew returned his smile. "That's just what we want to do, Dollars. Come with us downstairs for a walk-and-talk. We'll discuss. We'll reach an accommodation."

The judge stepped back yet again. One of the men left the group to shut the door. Once again Dillon's eyes searched the apartment. Where was his wife? She should be dialing for help. What he said was "I'm relieved to hear that." He spread out his hands and swaggered a little to establish that it was he who was in charge. "We had a falling out, that's all. It wasn't your fault, but it wasn't my fault either. So what's the problem?"

The guy he knew nodded sagely. "I've talked and talked to you, but all you do is re-calendar my conversation. So now you've got to come with us."

Again he stepped back. "I say we ought to talk about our concerns up here. Over coffee and danish, like gentlemen."

"Okay, we'll talk. What do you say to a motherfucking welsher? What do you tell a guy who's too greedy to hear?"

He strained to hear the footsteps of cops or security in front of the door. He admitted to himself that the sudden presence of these men shocked him, despite their prior threats. He knew why they had come, but hope surged through his valiant little body. He was certain that somehow aid would come. It always had before. He'd always gotten away with everything he'd tried. There had never been any real repercussions, except frequent branch-to-branch transfers, and that had only enriched him. He ardently wished that his wife was in the apartment, but she was gone, and no one else had come along to render help. He turned away from the men, suddenly saying, "I think we should talk here. I don't wanna go."

The guy nodded to the other two, who approached the tiny magistrate.

As each of them grasped a shoulder, aside from digging his heels into the plush carpet, he offered little resistance. "You guys know who I am, so take it easy. I don't wanna go with you." Somehow he felt that if he apologized sincerely, he could make things better. "I'm sorry," he said to the man he knew. "I'm so sorry. But I don't wanna accompany you downstairs." He turned to the two big guys, hoping his heartrending pleas would get them to change sides. "He's gonna have me killed. Don't let him kill me."

At last the guy nodded to his two compatriots. One of them shoved him roughly toward the door. "Hey!" the judge yelled.

The guy he knew approached him. He said softly, "Come on, Judge. Relax. What do you think I am, *upatz,* to kill a judge? You think I'd have a guy with a sterling reputation like yours murdered? Do you think I'd take the chance of having a man of your standing killed? We gotta take you to a place where we can have a conversation without that sexy wife of yours walking in on us. We just want to take you to someplace quiet, where everything between us can be cleaned up, sorted, and straightened out."

He was probably in for a beating, the judge told himself. In the flood of emotion and relief that came from the realization that they weren't going to kill him, he said, "Can I leave my wife a note? She worries about me."

"Unnecessary," said the guy he knew. "We'll only be gone for a short time."

The judge searched his face. "You're not gonna kill me?"

"Of course not."

Dillon closed his eyes for a moment, tried to relax. He opened his eyes at last, but the men were still there. His knees felt weak. One of the men put an arm around his shoulder as if they were friends. The pressure was gentle but insistent. The judge moved along with the three toward the door. Before he left he swiveled to look again at his apartment. There was his wife, hiding behind the living room curtain that led to the bathroom. He signaled her frantically with his eyes. Their gazes locked. His beseechingly, hers terrified, but strangely enough also filled with an icy composure. He knew why these men wanted to meet with him, and it had nothing to do with her. Why wasn't his loving wife dialing the police? His eyes pleaded with her for help, but she just watched him. He started to cry out to her, but a hand was placed around his mouth. He saw his wife, staring at him in silence from behind the curtain; then he was out the door.

They ushered him onto the hallway landing. Very few words were exchanged during the thirty-flight walk downstairs.

"Jesus, you guys are scaring the hell out of me. I'm gonna hand over everything I owe, so there'll be plenty for everybody. I can be trusted."

The walk downstairs seemed unending. The judge saw muted lights and even occasional graffiti. In all the years he'd lived in this building, he'd never had occasion to use the stairs. The leader of the three wasn't in good shape either, and there were frequent pauses to let him catch his breath. Always after a few moments' rest, Dillon would be pushed and would walk compliantly. He resigned himself to being worked over by the two powerful men hovering behind him. All he could do was hope that the beating wouldn't cripple or accidentally kill him. He and their leader were panting hard. The other two were like Schwarzenegger and Stallone, barely out of breath. "All I can say is, you guys succeeded in frightening me. When do we talk?"

One of the guys behind him said, "You fuck. I ought to kill you just for making us walk up and down thirty flights of stairs."

When they reached the ground floor, he lurched toward the door but was held back. His crotch and armpits were sticky with perspiration. "Where are you taking me?" he cried out.

They descended one more flight. One of them went ahead and came back seconds later. "It's okay," he said. "No one's doing laundry."

"Except us," said one of the men.

The leader leaned against the wall between the elevators. His breath shot out in gasps, then finally became regular. "You better lay chickee," he said to one of the men. "Keep watch."

They reached the laundry room. It was deserted. The judge looked around. A line of perhaps two dozen washers and dryers stood against the wall opposite them. Posters with instructions for using the machines were at either end. A box of Tide rested on top of one of the dryers.

The guy behind Judge Dillon said, "I wonder if he takes starch."

Dillon's scream was cut off by a hand. The leader smiled at him, then patted the thick envelopes inside his suit pocket. He wagged a finger at Dillon. "We're gonna launder your money for you, Judge."

The judge tried to twist away. He bit at the huge hand looming in front of his mouth. The guy stared at the pinprick of blood. "The little motherfucker bit me."

"There's no reason to kill me," the judge sobbed. His eyes closed and he swayed. "I'll hand it over to you. I swear it."

The leader shook his head. "It's too late to be sworn in, Judge. Besides, a lot of premeditation went into this. We took the service entrance in, we'll take the service entrance out. We already 'tossed' this room. No video surveillance." He paused, and gestured toward the washing machine. "This time I ain't gonna walk away with nothing."

The judge trembled. "Kill me and you'll never get anything. Kill me and not a penny goes into your pockets."

The guy he knew came back from locking the door. "That's okay. We'll keep a close watch on your wife."

The judge wrestled with the hands holding him. "She doesn't know anything. I'm the only one who can get you what you want."

The guy in front wagged his finger at him. "I don't believe you. Take it easy, Judge. Go quietly. Go like a man." He walked over to one of the washing machines and put in three quarters. "Think he'll make it through the spin cycle?"

The tall guy chuckled. "I think he will. He could use some good 'spin' around now."

"Judge," the other said, "we're gonna dump you in one of the big double loaders over there."

He felt their hands grasping him harder and shook his head violently back and forth, but could not resist. He was paralyzed. "Please, guys," he sobbed.

As he was pushed closer to the washer, he yanked his chest and arms away from the machine, but he was securely pinioned. "No matter how small they are, they always struggle," the taller guy said. "It's instinct."

The other guy nodded his head. "Scientific," he said. Lifting the judge effortlessly, he slammed him into the washing machine. The judge screamed, then moaned. His legs dangled out of the double loader. Despite the shock, he tried to crawl out of the machine legs first. The two men stuffed his recalcitrant limbs into the double loader as though Dillon were a package they were cramming into a small piece of luggage. The taller guy closed the door, and leaned his weight against it. There was the sound of water rushing in through the hoses. The frantic kicking against the door at last grew more feeble, then stopped.

The two burly men gazed through the window as the judge started to revolve around in the machine. "Shit and double shit," said one. "We didn't separate the colors from the solids. I bet the fabrics run." He added, "A dime says he don't last two minutes."

"You're on." They watched the judge spin around, his eyes wide open and his mouth firmly closed. Whenever they saw him, his eyes were dilated with terror but his mouth was still tightly shut.

Long moments seemed to go by. The struggle continued, but at last, inevitably, the distinguished arbiter and great innovator of so much urban corruption exhaled and expired.

The taller guy turned away from the lifeless body revolving before them and glanced at his watch. "Ah, shit," he said.

"You must owe me a dime," said the leader.

"It's not that. He didn't last the two minutes, so I won."

"So what's wrong then?"

"In all the excitement, I forgot to put in the detergent."

SEVENTEEN

The grieving widow Dillon sat demurely on a low divan in the living room, slyly managing to cross and uncross her shapely legs as she fielded the questions.

"Who discovered your husband's body?" asked Officer Wendell Henderson.

Her eyes closed and she rocked back and forth on the divan a few times. "A woman on the twelfth floor was doing her laundry. Robert's machine had long since turned off and it looked like just clothes were inside there. After her stuff dried, she came back to the laundry room, and wondered why no one had emptied that machine. She opened the door and Robert's legs spilled out. So she sent for security, and they pried poor Robert out of there. He was so white, so wrinkled, and wet and pale." She shifted back on the cushions, surrendering to a fresh onslaught of tears. "If only I'd been here, I could have tried to stop it. He didn't deserve to be murdered like that."

Officer Denise Saunders turned away from the tray of rainbow bakery cookies on the table. She was a binge eater and murder always made her hungry. "No one deserves to be murdered in any way," she said. "So you weren't at home when your husband came in. Where were you?"

"Probably walking in the hall or the stairwell. During winter I exercise a lot indoors. I race-walk the halls and use the stairwell as a Stairmaster. It's good for you."

"I can see that," said Henderson. "Exercising in the halls could be a real piece of luck for the investigation. Detective Yablonsky's theory is that the judge wasn't taken down to the basement by the elevator. He was forced to walk down the thirty flights of stairs to avoid residents and doormen. Did you run into anyone in the stairwell? Spot anybody who didn't look like they lived here? Remembering anything at all could really help us solve this case."

She looked at the two officers and her features broke with grief. She buried her face in her hands. "I lied. When my husband came home, I was in the bathroom."

"What time was that, Mrs. Dillon?" asked Saunders, picking up a rainbow cookie and eating it.

"I believe it was around one."

"We've already spoken to his chauffeur and court clerk, Mrs. Dillon. We know that he planned to see you. Didn't he call out?" Saunders paused. "Didn't you hear a struggle?"

"I wish I had. Then I would have called for help. But I heard no sounds of any struggle. He came home. Then I didn't hear anything for a while. When I came out of the bathroom, he was gone. I assumed he'd come up to take care of a few things and then left."

"But why would he leave when he came expressly to visit you, Mrs. Dillon?"

"Because he wasn't up here to see me, Detective. If he ever came back here in the afternoon it was only to pick up something he'd forgotten to take with him when he saw his other women." She gave them a smile. "I always understood his need to cheat. I didn't consider our marriage the worse for it. Robert was a man. Men cheat. But we were the love of each other's lives. He always came back to me."

"Then why did he tell everyone else that he planned on seeing you?"

"Out of concern for me, Officer Saunders. Naturally, when he planned to be with one of his whores, he'd tell everyone he was spending time with me. It was his way of shielding me from any embarrassment before his colleagues. I told him, 'Who you fuck is your own business, Robert, but do it in my backyard and it's your balls. I'll grind your gonads into the ground, guy.' So he listened."

"Do you know who your husband kept company with?"

She straightened slightly. "I just told you, I didn't know or care who or how many women Robert fucked." She paused, adding wearily, "I always did my best not to know who they were. I learned to forgive. And to cherish the time we spent together. Look at these headlines," she said, gesturing to the newspapers displayed on the coffee table. "My husband was older, but he was full of life and knew how to make me happy. You won't find any stories of his kindness in any of those articles," she said, sighing. Henderson and Saunders shifted their eyes to the city newspapers, each of which related yesterday's murder in its own unique style. The wood of the *New York Post* said, "Dirty Judge Murdered in the Cleanest Way." The headline of the *Daily News* was "Crooked Judge Comes Out in the Wash."

The *Village Guardian* was also a tabloid, though it was a weekly. Its front-page article was written by Sully Barnes himself and read, "Judge Who Topped Ten-Worst List Killed—Part of the Problem, Not the Solution."

"Right now our task force is interrogating the single and married women in the apartment buildings your husband's chauffeur drove him to. He maintains he can't help us. That he never saw the women the judge met in these buildings."

"Billy was on salary, and I suppose he was paid for his discretion as well as his driving skills. Do you think those women will really tell you anything? I knew and loved my husband, and I didn't know half the things he was involved in. If a wife doesn't know, how do you think a whore will?"

"Did you know about his condo in Florida?" Henderson asked.

"I knew all about my husband's weaknesses and his occasional romps down south."

"I'll need his address book and Rolodex, receipts, records of credit card payments and any bank statements."

"My husband's murder took place downtown, out of your jurisdiction. How come they assigned you the case?"

"Your husband knew Skinny McPherson, the reporter who was murdered a couple of weeks ago. The chief detective feels the two murders might be connected, so he put in a special request to the one-nine, the precinct near City Hall, that I be assigned to this one as well."

She stood. "I'll have his personal items ready by next week. May I assume you're finished?"

"Just a few more things."

"But I'm so tired. Look, yesterday I hear my husband enter the apartment. Ten minutes later I come out of the bathroom, and all I see are a few of these fucking finger sandwiches he used to make. So I'm thinking, great, he's gone. Who is that husband of mine fucking now? Then a couple of hours later a security guy comes up here to tell me they've just fished my husband out of the wash. I wish I could help you nail the bastards who murdered my husband, but I can't."

Henderson and Saunders believed her. If she hadn't been in the bathroom when these men dragged her husband down to the laundry room, she'd be dead.

There were no signs of struggle. A prominent public figure lured away from his apartment or his office by someone he knew, same as Skinny. Either they followed him or they were already aware of when he'd be in the building, same as Skinny. And the victims were either forced or tricked into descending into the building's basement, where in a secluded spot they were killed.

"When your husband was fished out of that double loader, a waterlogged roll of twelve thousand dollars also came out in the wash," said Detective Saunders, pulling at a strand of loose hair. "Was that money he carried with him? Or money that was given to him inside the courtroom about half an hour earlier? We found a bag with a scarf and gloves he bought from a vendor outside the Civil Court Building. Even with the lower crime rate, I think twelve thousand is a little too much money to carry around for spending cash. Since you run a successful real estate business from your apartment, Mrs. Dillon, and since most of your clients are attorneys who argue cases before your husband, you two had to have exchanged confidences, and both of you knew what was going on concerning your business. Did this twelve thousand have anything to do with the real estate business your husband helped you run? If not, do you have any idea where the money came from?"

"I wish I could say that money was mine. But I have no idea where it came from."

"Okay," Saunders said. "We believe that some time yesterday your husband received the money in court. Since there were two envelopes, that means there were probably two payments."

"Are you implying that my husband was carrying the money around because he'd just received a couple of kickbacks?"

"That would seem to be the case. Unless he was about to hand off to someone else," said Henderson.

"Officer, if he was about to hand off to someone and didn't, then the money should be returned to me."

"Why? Was it you who handed the money off to him, Mrs. Dillon? To make a payment to someone for you?"

"I have no idea who my husband was about to hand off to. I told you, he was always very secretive about his judicial responsibilities."

"From what we can surmise, the route this kind of money traveled was usually from some other guy's pocket into his. Not the other way around."

"Okay. Assuming you're right and a couple of attorneys kicked back to Robert, why investigate it? Obviously, whoever paid my husband did so for services rendered. Robert must have been killed because of some deal that went wrong. But I can't imagine Robert finding a new, untapped area of corruption. He wasn't that resourceful."

"Maybe he was," said Henderson. "How often did the judge fly down to his condo in The Landings, Mrs. Dillon?"

"Every couple of months, I guess."

"Did you accompany him?"

"It was strictly boys only. Wives were never invited. In fact, the only reason he bought it was so that he'd have a place to exclude me from."

"The last time he vacationed there, the weekend right before Christmas, did he tell you who'd be going with him? What we're investigating is whether a man who accompanied him to his condo needed your husband to furnish him with an alibi. We're looking into business dealings of anyone the judge took down to The Landings with him."

"Robert was a journeyman judge who rendered junk justice. He was transferred from branch to branch and borough to borough. How powerful could he be?"

Saunders sipped her cappuccino. "The fact that he spent time in so many branches could also mean he had the opportunity to accumulate a lot of favors and become involved in a lot of deals. Had he mentioned any recent threats?"

"No threats."

"Did he discuss any business deals he was involved in?"

"No business deals."

"So your husband's murder is a complete mystery?"

"A complete mystery."

Mrs. Dillon leaned back into the sofa, thumbing through one of the tabloids. Sensing their eyes on her, she peered up. "I'm reading these articles, but my mind's not on them. I was simply remembering the kind of man my husband was and the way he always made me feel. Especially the last time I saw him."

EIGHTEEN

lobe after globe of light hung from the ceiling to usher the
party guests into the main room on the fourteenth floor. Lac-
quered in gold, it was shaped like a duomo, with rows of
windowpanes for the revelers to look out upon Central Park.

Part of the room had been set up to resemble a soup kitchen. Giant
tureens of rice and beans rested on tables, and celebrities stood behind
them, cheerfully ladling the soupy meals into plastic bowls for other
celebrities.

Yablonsky could see lines forming by two metal grates, under which
fans had been placed under slits in the floor blowing smoke through the
bars in order to resemble steam. Next to these was a row of cots under
spring frames, with signs reading, "No Drinking. No Urinating. No
Drugs." A guest at this party could lie down on a cot, or doze in one of
the background fugazy storefronts, complete with iron security mesh
gates. "Tonight, We Are All Homeless."

A tall, handsome guy wearing sunglasses emerged from the crowd.
He was clean-shaven, and a pirate's long, gold earring hung from his left
ear. The button he wore said, "I'm White but Feel Guilty About It."

This was Charlie Kudos. Stopping in front of the detective, he said, "Sully told me he invited you to our fund-raiser."

"Yeah, he did," said Yablonsky. "Where's Julie?"

"Benfield?"

Yablonsky nodded.

"How do you know her?"

"The case."

"She hasn't arrived yet."

Yablonsky put his hand forward, but the actor made no attempt to shake it.

Kudos removed his sunglasses, winced at the artistically placed muted lighting, and slipped them back over his eyes again. "Sully told me I gotta apologize for the way I insulted you at the homeless encampment. So I'm apologizing. It was all a misunderstanding. Do you care for food?"

As he spoke, the actor was methodically spooning food out of a plastic bowl and into his mouth. "Is it any good?" Yablonsky shouted above the noise.

"It's crap," said the actor. "But Sully suggested I eat this way while my movie's being shot so I'll be more authentic when I play him. You know I'm filming a movie for HBO based on his life, right? When Sully visits the encampments he always makes a point to eat the same food as the homeless. So what can I do?"

Yablonsky noticed Henri Batiste, the famous French designer, in a conversational cluster to his right. The designer must have seen him and recognized that the detective was wearing one of his suits. He broke away from the group and headed toward the detective. As he drew closer, Yablonsky, anticipating a compliment, was already stretching out his hand to greet the great clothier. Instead of grasping his hand, however, Batiste snapped open his lapels, placed a hand on Yablonsky's shoulder and quickly unbuttoned his suit, ripping off the label that bore his name.

Pulling back, he said, "I'm a designer, not an upholsterer." Yablonsky, stunned, turned to Kudos. "Did you just see that?"

Kudos smiled. "You shouldn't let it upset you. Or cause you to want to leave early."

Before them, several people were ladling rice onto paper plates. "In Afghanistan, this would be a feast."

"They shouldn't have fucked with us. If they ever get a bomb . . ."

Kudos sighed, "I always thought the best defense against war is peace. The best antidote to hate is love."

"I'd like to think that in the next terrorist or chemical attack you'll be spared," Yablonsky said. "You're too moral to die."

Kudos gave him a look, but said nothing. As they approached the cluster around Barnes, Kudos murmured in a low tone, "Look, I know you're only gonna be here for a short time, but please don't monopolize Sully. Don't waste his time by asking him a lot of questions. He got sick last night while we were in the van making rounds. Maybe he caught bronchitis from one of the encampments. We don't know, but he's been on antibiotics since this morning. And don't let on that you're overwhelmed at being here. Drinking and snorting lines are okay, but only in moderation and only outside on one of the terraces. When you're inside, stick to Merlot or the white Rothschild. There are no six-packs or bowling balls here."

Yablonsky started to say something, but thought better of it.

Barnes was dressed like Yablonsky had seen him at the homeless encampment, a loose-fitting, unpressed cloth winter coat covered a black sports jacket and a T-shirt with a button on his collar that said, "Just for Tonight, I'm Homeless." On top of his head, with the brim reversed, was an old Brooklyn Dodger's cap from the '50s.

The Nobel Prize winner took out a handkerchief and blew his nose. He turned away from the half-dozen people staring in rapt attention. "Hi, Alvin. Good to see you. Eat as much as you want. Stay as long as you like."

"That won't be long, unfortunately," Yablonsky said.

Kudos jerked a finger at him and smiled. "He's embarrassed. A minute ago Henri Batiste noticed he was wearing one of his suits and pulled his name off the lapel."

"I would've found it fucking suspicious if that greasy little frog hadn't ripped his name off your jacket," said Barnes. He took a step back, whispering to a guy holding a tiny cassette recorder, "Strike that."

For the first time, Yablonsky noticed that long tables had been set up at the rear of the party room. On the tables sat rows of white linen, gleaming silverware, china, and a seemingly endless arc of chafing dishes. Waiters and waitresses dressed in beige uniforms with chef hats served spoonfuls of food to long lines of people. The lines were much longer than at the ersatz soup kitchen in front. For a moment he wondered how he'd missed it. I must be slipping, he thought.

"Now that's some fucking buffet," Barnes said. "It took the catering service hours to set up."

"And this place," said Kudos. "Isn't it fantastic? We've already collected over twenty thousand dollars, and that's just at the door."

Yablonsky smiled, seeming to agree, but thinking: Only celebrities in East Coast Hollywood would throw a party designed to sensitize people toward homelessness by having it at one of the most exclusive and wealthiest co-op buildings in Manhattan.

"Don't feel self-conscious about being the only guest here who's not rich and famous," said Kudos.

"I don't feel self-conscious," Yablonsky said. "I'm the only one who can arrest anyone I want."

The half-dozen people in the group looked at the detective as if seeing him for the first time. The guy with the microrecorder, who Yablonsky now noticed was wearing a Press logo, stepped away from Barnes.

"I don't care what your editor says, my friend," Barnes said. "I work for a newspaper too, and I know how it's done. You don't put a Nobel

Prize winner on the inside page, you put him on the cover. You also give him final quote approval. Or you get shit. Suppose I say no to your fucking profile?"

"You wouldn't do that to me, Sully."

"I may. If we have to debate over whether or not I get quote approval. Why should I deal with a news group that makes me have to defend my rep? I shouldn't have to defend it, not in this town."

The reporter thrust the microrecorder toward Barnes. "Anything you want, Sully. You hold the recorder. You send me the tape of the week we spend together for my article. I know who you are. I respect the rep of a man like you. What more can I do?"

"You can leave," said Barnes.

Barnes watched a new group form around him that seemed to be hanging on his every word. "Anyone in the market for a thrown-away citation from the Nobel Prize committee?" Barnes asked. "Just let me know and it's yours, my friends, along with all the fucking scrutiny that comes with it." He stepped back, Kudos and Yablonsky following.

"Bullshit," said Kudos, looking at Barnes with great affection. "I've studied you for three weeks, Sully, and don't try to pretend that you're some selfless, egoless Gandhi. You're more like Martin Luther King. You know, not an ascetic, but a guy with balls, and a ton of energy to go with it."

"Okay," said Barnes, edging toward the buffet, the two men following. "So it flattered the shit out of me to win it. All the time people expect me to be so blasé and matter-of-fact about it, and all the time I'm thinking, Holy shit, but this is so motherfucking great. I won the Nobel Peace Prize. I was a petty criminal, and here I am talking to presidents and lecturing prime ministers. The most powerful men in the world kissing my ass. What an accomplishment for a guy who started out on the street. That's why I've got to be a pit bull when I guard my rep. Any dirt gets dug up on me, and my entire organization suffers."

"There's no dirt currently available on you," said the detective. "By the way, where's Julie?"

"Currently available," said Barnes. "Julie's supposed to arrive later."

A waiter ambled by, handing drinks to Barnes and the actor, and leaving before giving one to the detective.

"Excuse me . . ." said Yablonsky.

"Alvin!" Kudos was mortified, staring as if he'd just committed the faux pas of the millennium. "Remember what I told you," the actor said a bit too loudly. "No bowling, and no beer."

"I don't bowl, and I drink beer only to get through your movies," said Yablonsky. "The waiter didn't give me a drink."

"Leave him the fuck alone, Charlie," Barnes said. "I've seen you at an encampment with a roll of toilet paper trailing out of your ass like a tail. Not exactly Martha fucking Stewart yourself, are you?"

Kudos flushed, glared at Yablonsky, but said nothing. "This isn't some party filled with ball-breaking billionaires like Alvin'll find when he goes over to Staples's yacht later," Sully continued. "He doesn't need to hear that patronizing shit here, so loosen the fuck up."

The handsome actor stroked his cheek, then his earring. He whispered, "Sorry, Sully."

Two guys and a woman dressed in the beige uniforms of the catering staff rolled a speaking dais into the center of the room. Sully walked over to the podium but ignored it, standing in front of it to speak, declining to be on a higher level than his audience.

Silverware tinkling against champagne glasses quieted the party-goers.

"It's make-a-donation time," whispered Kudos. Yablonsky nodded, pleased that he'd already given his check.

Barnes faced the hundreds of people in this room, his hands casually in his sports jacket pockets, emphasizing how at home he felt with them. He said, "I won't give a long speech tonight because I believe in short sentences."

Barnes reached into one of his pockets, pulling out a rolled-up newspaper article from *The Times* and showed it to the crowd. "The operators of the dog shelters in San Francisco have suggested that homeless men and women be allowed to live there with the dogs." He paused. "What's next? Putting them to sleep?"

The article fell from Barnes's hand to the floor. "Fuck that," he said. "In *Wall Street,* Michael Douglas tells Charlie Sheen and a bunch of wealthy stockholders, 'Greed is good.' I'm gonna substitute the word *guilt* for *greed.* Today guilt's unfashionable, but it's good. When you walk or drive by a homeless man or woman, shivering or sleeping in front of a storefront, if you don't toss them a little gelt, then you should feel guilty. When you step out onto your Central Park terraces and see people shivering below you in cardboard boxes, you should feel guilty. Guilt is important. We can use it as a lever to change and improve lives. Tomorrow my newspaper's gonna go to press and talk about two big society events that were held tonight. There's ours, held to collect money for the homeless. And there's Raymond Staples's, collecting guests on a two-hundred-foot yacht, anchored off the Seventy-ninth Street boat basin, so that the wealthy can dine on any endangered species, oblivious to the dozens of homeless who are shivering, trying to sleep or stay alive next to his yacht in Riverside Park. Staples and his buddies may feel safe on his tumbrel-like yacht, but what I'd really like to do," he said, his voice rising emotionally, "is make Raymond and everyone else who thinks like him an endangered species. There are some people in the world who never feel guilt about anything. But here," he continued with a smile that embraced everyone in the room, "and for tonight, at least, successful people in the city are breaking bread with street people. For tonight we don't need and won't accept any cash from you that is denominationally deprived. Just for tonight, I'm demanding credit card charity and checks with at least three or four zeros in them. Tonight I know that I'd rather be in this room with you good people than on Staples's boat with his coldhearted and desensitized billionaires. My people are beginning to make the rounds. Please don't disappoint them. Don't disappoint yourselves."

Barnes stepped back into the crowd. For a long moment there was respectful silence. Then the party buzz began again. Young men and women wearing the "For Tonight I'm Homeless" buttons made their way among the guests, carrying big black garbage bags similar to those in which the homeless lugged around their possessions. Everyone in the room had reached into their suit pockets and were either writing out checks or dropping non–denominationally deprived bills into the bags.

Yablonsky started to walk from the buffet to the terrace. Then he spotted Sterling Roth, standing with Barnes in the center of a crowd. The detective waved to his chief source, but Roth turned away.

Yablonsky saw Kudos drop his money-filled Hefty bag on the floor and head over to the buffet.

The actor asked, "Where's the calamari?"

"Sorry. Everything in the Italian section's gone."

"Shit!"

Yablonsky watched as Charlie, the guy who'd lectured him on social manners, wended his way along the length of the buffet. Whenever he spotted fried squid on a discarded plate, the arbiter of social graces industriously shoveled the leftovers onto his. People were still arriving, but no Julie.

Yablonsky slid the glass door open, stepping onto the terrace.

Ahead, across the park, shining like a necklace, were the lights of Fifth Avenue. Imagine a world where views and condos like this were taken for granted, he thought.

Years ago, when he'd just started his career as a cop, he guarded famous politicians and celebrities who arrived in New York.

Below him, on Central Park West, he detected movement.

Two men roughed up a woman, preparing to drag her into the park.

"Hey!" he yelled.

They hadn't heard him.

Taking out his cell phone, he called for backup.

In the gallery he waited for the elevator, but it wouldn't come.

Scrambling down the fourteen flights of stairs, he paused in front of the building to catch his breath.

He looked into the park. Where'd they take her?

"Come with me!" he shouted to the doorman, pulling out his badge.

They raced across the street, his eyes scanning the trees and terrain.

The squad cars he'd sent for would be here in minutes. He stopped running, tried to listen.

Up ahead—a woman's muffled screams.

Racing along a wooded path, he saw them. Copses of trees lined either side of a footbridge. They were about to drag the woman under the bridge.

Crouching, his hands steady, he pulled out his Glock. "Police. Don't move!"

But they moved. Yablonsky glimpsed shiny objects that could be guns or knives. No time to think. Aiming at the bulky bodies, he tried to fire away from their victim.

He watched one of the men stagger away, the other, grasping his fellow assailant by the arm, led him into the woods.

Where were the squad cars?

Reaching Julie, he saw she was limp and unconscious, lying on a bank of dirty snow.

NINETEEN

The SoHo Branch of the Bank of Manhattan was between Mott and Mulberry. In front of the bank were Chinese-style lanterns that management had placed there to acknowledge an ever-expanding Chinatown. An Italian flag and an image of Garibaldi covered the customers from Little Italy. This area was also inundated with artists and galleries, so the logo in front looked scrawled, a piece of street graffiti.

Inside, the bank was L-shaped, like many Manhattan apartments. Irene Nuñez was in front. Short and shapely, her face framed by brown waves of hair, she looked delicate despite her security guard's uniform. She was nodding her head at a large, fat, bald man.

Stopping a few feet before them, Yablonsky heard loud, angry whispers. "Ease off, honey. This bank hasn't been robbed since Jesse James. Our customers don't need to see you twirling your nightstick like it's a dick. You don't have one, Irene. You never will. You want to be fired today, or what?"

"Of course not, Mr. Thompson."

"You fucked up big-time, baby." A pudgy hand pointed overhead to rows of video cameras on the ceiling. "Let them do all the security work.

You're only here because we want to give the illusion that our customers are completely safe. What do you have in store for us next? Gunplay, like in *The Rifleman?*"

Smiling at the fat guy, she said, "Of course not, Mr. Thompson."

"I know this is your first week on the job. Just relax, babe. No more patrolling up and down like you're guarding fucking Fort Knox. You're no longer a cop. It only makes the customers nervous. They assume there's some reason you're being so vigilant. Got that, Ms. Nuñez?"

Nuñez wearily closed her eyes. "Of course, Mr. Thompson."

"One more thing."

She gazed at him expectantly, hoping for some kind of parting compliment, probably thinking that since he'd just decapitated her verbally, at least he'd be perceptive enough to offer some encouragement. "Yes, Mr. Thompson?"

"Your boyfriend may be a big-shot middleweight in the ring and all that shit, but I don't want to see that animal in my bank anymore. If we decide to let you go, no confrontations. I don't want him in here, shadowboxing on our carpets, throwing punches at the columns. This is a bank, Ms. Nuñez. Not a training camp. Entiende?"

"I'm Italian, Mr. Thompson. Tito's a super-lightweight, and he's my husband, not my boyfriend."

"I'm happy for you, Ms. Nuñez."

"Thank you, sir. *Stu gazu.*"

"What's that, Ms. Nuñez?"

"Who gets the next watch?"

Thompson rolled his eyes plaintively, asking God why he'd been burdened with such help. There was no response. Nuñez left.

She smiled at Yablonsky. "I hope that was as painful for you as it was for me." Dropping her voice, she said, "You weren't specific on the phone. What's up?"

"We have to go downstairs—to the computer room. I need some skinny on a guy."

"That, I figured. I don't really feel like eating. It's my lunch break, but I'm not hungry. I want to be out on the street. I need to chill."

Yablonsky reached into a pocket, came out with a small brown bag. "I know. I brought you some Brooklyn haute cuisine."

Without opening the bag, she said, "Don't tell me what it is, Alvin. A bagel, right? I told you I'm not hungry."

"Why not? The cream cheese is an inch thick."

Jerking her head in Thompson's direction, she said, "Why in the hell should I be hungry? You just saw that *cazzu* over there make me eat a truckload of shit."

"So then, Irene. You can help me now."

"Okay," she said. "I guess I owe you that much. You pulled the strings to replace your buddy Dwyer at this great job. But if you need skinny from me, you better act fast before he fires me and it's good night, Irene."

"How come you and him don't get along?"

"I don't know," she said and sighed. "Like you and the pseudo Art Deco in here, I guess we clash." Her voice dropped. "You want the usual?"

"Yeah," said Yablonsky.

"Okay," she said. "Fill out a form requesting to visit a safe deposit box. I'll escort you."

Downstairs, the video cameras faced iron bars enclosing rows of safe deposit boxes. Yablonsky pointed with his chin to the glassed-in computer room, empty now. "How come they have no surveillance here?"

"These days, who's going to break into a bank and rob computer records, when all you have to do is hire a hacker to break codes for you? No eye in the sky, no rolling tape. We're free to say anything we want." She pointed to page three of a week-old copy of the *Daily News,* lying on a chair. The article detailed the assault on Julie Benfield and the detective's brief gun battle with the assailants. "How the hell are you?"

"I'm fine."

"How is she?"

"Shaken up, badly bruised. But she's back at work already."

"Is what the newspapers say about you true? Are you two involved?"

"I've helped her in the past. I worry about her."

"Someone ought to worry about you, Alvin."

She sat down at the PC and clicked the mouse. The sheen of light from the interior windows made her squint. "Who do you want me to bring up on the screen?"

"My task force is currently interviewing anyone who Skinny McPherson's exposés put in prison."

"Just give me the name, Alvin."

"Raymond Staples."

"What's his favorite quote, 'Fuck with me and I'll triple-fuck you back'? Alvin, it's been years since I've been fucked three times by a guy. Now I'm worried about you for sure."

Bending her head to the task, she brought his name up on the screen, as well as a long list of banks in which he held accounts. "Holding companies. Corporations. I'll have to make calls to trace the Cayman stuff."

"Whatever he's covering up that's been semi-legally or illegally gained, you've got to help me find it, Irene."

He met Nuñez when he was a detective third grade and she was an earnest rookie patrolwoman at the Central Park Precinct. Yablonsky had just drawn a pair of threes, during one of the parties in the precinct's basement. He began asking Irene about boxing. According to *Ring Magazine,* her husband, Tito "El Niño" Nuñez was the number one contender for the super-lightweight title. Wanting to get to know her, hoping to promote a few free tickets to the Garden for him and his friends, he'd asked, "What's it like being married to a sports hero? Great, right?"

Ignoring the clichéd question, and the corresponding pat answer, she'd said, "Not as great as you think, Alvin. I wish El Niño'd spend as much time putting me on the canvas as he does his opponents."

But Tito must have spent at least some time with her on the canvas, because a couple of months later she told Flood that she was pregnant and planned to quit the force for good at the start of her last trimester. After the kid was born she was looking for part-time work, and being a cop was 24-7. Yablonsky, knowing that his buddy Dwyer planned to retire and move to Florida to manage a motel, asked him to recommend Nuñez to be his replacement at the SoHo branch he'd been transferred to. So she now did security work part-time, and when Tito was training or on the road, which was a frequent occurrence, she raised their kid by herself.

"Suppose I find stuff on him that points to other crimes. Illegal stuff that can't possibly be connected to Skinny's murder? I know how you work, Alvin. Usually you never let the various illegalities you uncover distract you from your primary investigation."

"Anything dirty you uncover about Staples I can use. Want some coffee, Irene?"

She stared at the screen. "Maybe later." Normally, computer information was privileged. In practice, though, the information was too valuable to be kept secret. A vast underground had evolved, both on the Internet and off of it, which traded in gray-market computer skinny, for money or for favors.

Irene held the printout in her hands. "This is just the first installment. Holding companies. Cross-ownerships and dummy corporations. Raymond Staples really knows how to cover his assets. Give me a week and I'll have more for you. If I'm still working here, that is."

"Heavy," Yablonsky said, hefting the paper, then sliding it into a manila envelope. "Thanks for the help. If these people are dumb enough to can you, I'll get you another job."

She shrugged. "Maybe I shouldn't have been so quick to retire from the force. Where are you going now?"

"I'm meeting Julie Benfield. There's a cop guarding her now twenty-four hours a day. This is my shift."

"I saw photos of you and her in the papers. Even beaten up, she looked beautiful."

As he stood to leave, he sensed her sadness. He hesitated. Taking her hand in his, he asked, "What's wrong, Irene?"

"I'm fine."

He stayed put. "You sure?"

Avoiding his eyes, she said, "Quit Q-and-A'ing me, cop." She dropped his hand. "I could give you all the dope on my husband. But what's the point? No one can force Tito into behaving like a character on a bubble gum card. Anyway, it's my own fault. I knew it'd be rough before I married him."

"Is he beating you, Irene? We have guys at the precinct who—"

"Who can what? Keep Tito's dick away from him so he won't use it on half the women in the United States?" She paused. "There's nothing no one can do, Alvin. Not as long as I continue to be married to such a shooter."

"Then divorce him."

"Not so easy." Glancing at the *New York Post* photo of him leading Julie to an ambulance, which was titled, "The Detective and the Debutante," she said, "I wish I could be like her. Look how elegant she is. She'd never screw up her life this bad."

"The reality of her life's nothing like that. It's never like that."

Her brown eyes smiled. "Guess I have a bad case of celebrity envy," said Nuñez. "But I'll snap out of it, like always. Say good-bye and leave, Alvin."

TWENTY

Picket signs saying "Homeless In, Murders Up," and "Give Addicts the Needle Someplace Else," waved in the air. Approximately one dozen people, all wearing sweatshirts that read "Community Coalition Against Addicts," paraded back and forth before a storefront with "East Village Shelter" in the window, and four video cameras. A couple of satellite vans were parked nearby on the sidewalk.

The shelter was sandwiched between a Puerto Rican church and a Lithuanian social club, across the street from a newly built Starbucks. Twin lines of homeless and addicts meandered out of the storefront and snaked around the corner, to East Fourth Street. Condoms, broken forties, disposable needle packs, and glassine bags littered the street. Three months ago, before the shelter and soup kitchen had decided to hand out disposable needles, a twenty-nine-year-old former dancer for the Rockettes had been murdered by one of the men who'd shown up an hour early to wait for a meal. Most of the picket signs referred to the newest urban tragedy, a nine-year-old girl stabbed by a hypodermic and her family not sure if she'd been given AIDS. But a couple of signs carried the name of the young woman who'd been murdered, Marisol Rogers.

A couple of people screamed, "Out of our community!"

Benfield edged closer to one of the protesters, an elderly Hispanic woman who hefted a sign with a drawing of a needle resembling a gun pointed at some school-aged children.

"I'm from the *Village Guardian*," said Benfield. "How long have you been out here? Why are you demonstrating?"

"We've had enough. This neighborhood has many social services, but when a young girl is stabbed, it's time for this damned shelter to get out. Pronto."

Benfield slipped away, back to Yablonsky. "You watch, Al. My last column will be slugged something like 'Hard-Hearted Inhospitable Community Shuts Door to the Needy.' But that's why I'm not coming back."

Turning away from him, Benfield pointed to a tiny recorder. "Shouldn't your community be open to everyone?" she asked a short, bald guy who wore a gray-spattered painter's cap, a faded lumber jacket, and trousers with smears of blue around the knees.

"Why?" answered the man. "As long as these fucking animals are allowed to eat and shoot up here, our community's closed to us."

Benfield shook her head, and for the first time since Yablonsky'd known her, looked regretful. "A great line," she whispered to him. "But too incendiary to use. My 'Press Clips' column, referring to Sully, will say, 'A prophet in his own backyard, scorned.' " She paused. "One day, though, I'm going to be able to write what I want. You'll see. For another newspaper."

Yablonsky said nothing. The demonstrators waved their signs in the air and yelled, "Leave fast or leave slow. Junkie hookers have to go!"

Microphones were stuck in Sully and Roth's faces as they crossed the street, approaching the demonstration. Roth wore jeans and a peacoat. Sully wore his usual outfit, including the backwards Dodgers baseball cap.

"What do you think of this demonstration?" asked Bob Anders of the *News*.

"It's disgraceful, Bob. I'm shocked that these people would manipulate the media, exploiting some poor girl's tragedy in this way," said Roth.

Barnes said, "I suppose they have the right to protest. Otherwise, I have no fucking comment."

Sully left the group, walking over to the derelicts who stood on line waiting to be fed. Yablonsky saw him gently lift a middle-aged homeless man who was leaning against a supermarket shopping cart that held two plastic bags of clothes. First he ushered him into the storefront; then he came back to wheel his cart and his possessions into the building. When he returned to Yablonsky and Roth, he was speaking on his cell phone. "I spoke to Staples just the other day. He's the one restaurateur who's too fucking cheap to make a donation to feed the hungry. Christ, we're not even asking for money, just food."

There was silence as Barnes listened. Turning to Roth, he said, "Raymond's been warned. The only thing to do is mount one of my patented hunger strikes. Sterling, you and I are so close, we practically share the same Rolodex. How many cams and glams can you get to mount a demo in front of one of his restaurants? We'll go to La Parisienne, his flagship." Barnes was stone-faced as he gave out orders. "We have Charlie Kudos. He'll be a big help in rounding up some celebs." He spoke to Roth so that Myrna, the person on the other end of the cell phone, could also hear his conversation. "It doesn't matter who he gets, as long as the people are famous. They're all interfuckingchangeable." There was a pause. Then Barnes's voice, flat. "Raymond deserves the whole treatment. This is the scenario as I see it. The first day, I'm down there by myself, I want the news cams making wide-angle shots of the restaurant, making it look huge, to emphasize the David and Goliath aspect of the demo. The second day, bring along a few of our people, make sure they're competent and won't get crazy or violent and embarrass us once the TV cameras go on. Rotate the people who are being shot, but always have some of them there, because after all, they're what my fucking fast's really all about. On the sixth day, cameras cover me around the clock with hourly bulletins as to my health. Put an ambulance in the foreground, not background, along with two concerned doctors hovering nearby. I'll wear loose-fitting street clothes so I'll look more frail. Make sure there's a stretcher. Remember, we're going for spontaneous empathy, and that always has to be planned out." He looked at Roth and grinned, already savoring his triumph. "That's how I see it."

Roth's ponytail bounced madly in the breeze. Turning away from Yablonsky, he said, "I don't know about this, Sully. Raymond's not your ordinary guilt-saddled leftie or lib. He likes bad publicity. Take it from me. I know. This fast can win only if the guy or government you go up against has a conscience. I think we're gonna lose."

"No way," said Barnes. "His ass is ours." Slapping Yablonsky on the back and winking at Benfield, gestures that made the detective think they were two of his most intimate friends, he said, "Now we gotta go."

"Where to?" asked Roth.

"First we migrate back to the *Guardian,* where you can check out my Rolodex and combine the names on it with yours."

"Then?"

"Where the fuck do you think, Sterling? You've been through this before. We hit the McDonald's on Broadway, so I can load up on Big Macs."

"Hey, Sully," said Julie.

"What?"

"Your ex-wife and kid are already up there, waiting for you."

"Shit," said Barnes in exasperation. Then he gazed around guiltily, but no other reporters or media people besides Julie had heard that remark.

Roth and Barnes walked away, skirting both the protesters and the reporters. The father of the nine-year-old girl, seeing where all the news mikes had been pointed, edged up close to Barnes and thrust his sign up and down in the air, his daughter by his side. Yablonsky was surprised. Roth, the moral mouthpiece of the world for just about every cause, was silent. Sully, so compassionate with his own people, had no words of comfort, breezing by the man without a word.

"I guess that poor guy and his daughter just aren't part of Sully's constituency," Julie said.

"He's like most social advocates I've met," said Yablonsky. "You mount a demonstration against him, and he feels threatened. So what?"

"Yeah," said Benfield, adding, "They're a real threat, all right. Let's go to my apartment. I've had just about enough of award winners. I've seen enough rotten, lousy parenting for today."

Crossing the street with Julie, Yablonsky ran into Patrolmen Beatty and Bridges, badges off and in plainclothes.

"What the hell are you doing here?" from Bridges.

"You're always turning up where you aren't supposed to be," said Beatty. He paused. "Sorry, Alvin. I'm just surprised to see you."

"I'm surprised to see you," said the detective "without your badges and out of uniform. What's going on?"

Moving closer to Yablonsky, Bridges, the tall, stocky cop, whispered, "Roth's our chief source on the street."

"We're protecting him."

"From who?"

"We can't tell you."

Julie opened one of the windows, causing a slight breeze to blow the lingering scent of her in the apartment toward him. He breathed it, and thus part of her, in.

My first trip to her apartment, he told himself. Although she said she detested Warhol as a person, the living room was filled with photos of her modeling for him and his magazines, posters of her posed to shock, promoting his underground plotless movies. Glossy pictures of the designer clothes and fragrances that had been marketed with her name on them had been hung on most of the walls throughout the room.

"You shared an apartment with Skinny for two years. Change anything since he died?"

"I haven't had the time."

"Whose apartment was it originally, Julie. His?"

"Mine. He moved in."

"Well, that eliminates you as a suspect."

She laughed. "In New York, murdering someone to take over their lease is a legitimate motive for murder."

Yablonsky looked around, feeling like he was in a shrine to her famous past. Two walls filled with her triumphs. A tiny part of one wall reserved for Skinny's. There was his framed citation for winning the Pulitzer Prize. A few investigative articles of his hung like paintings on his section of the wall.

Benfield said, "Warhol may have been attracted to me only because of my looks and family name, but all this is still the closest I've come to fame. I'll get a job on another newspaper."

"I thought you were only taking a few days off."

"I'm taking a leave of absence, Alvin."

"Why?"

"Because I like the atmosphere at the *Guardian* even less now than when I first started working there. The assault made me see things."

"But you're no longer in any danger. There's always a cop protecting you now."

"I don't trust cops, except for you." She took his hand. "You're always there for me. The one guy I can count on. I'm going to have them both. Fame and accomplishment. I'm coming back."

"Sure," he said. "How come Skinny merited so little space?"

Staring at him, Benfield said, "Because he was a lot more secure than me."

"At the party, I spoke to Charlie Kudos. Did you go out with him?"

"Alvin, I've fucked lots of men." She smiled and began taking off her clothes. She was thin and had beautiful legs. The nipples on her small breasts were erect, the patch of hair between her legs very blond.

* * *

Afterwards, leaning against his chest and staring at his penis, she reached down and fondled it, as if adjusting it. "That tasted better than Häagen-Dazs."

"I'm glad you enjoyed it."

"You up for another licking?"

Yablonsky laughed. "I'm a middle-aged guy. I need some more time."

The detective looked around. There were more photos of Julie side by side with famous people she'd either known or fucked, Yablonsky thought. Lavender walls with tiny whorls of flowers. Purple comforters and throw pillows.

"Skinny must have loved living in this apartment."

"Yeah," she said, and laughed. "Remember when I promised you those records?"

"Yeah. How are you going to get them?"

"I've already been to two flea markets. I managed to find you the *Mike Bloomfield/Al Kooper Supersession* recording. I love that we like the same music, Alvin. I've dated lots of celebrities. A big mistake. At last I found a guy that'll care about me more than his fucking movie career or getting his name in a publicity column. You really love me, don't you?"

"Oh yeah." Now he was up for another licking. "Want me to prove it?"

On her lilac-colored dresser was a row of photos. Family shots. Smiling kids playing croquet or horseback riding before a huge house. She had a good-looking family. Yablonsky thought of the Kennedys, cavorting in their compound in Hyannisport. The photos on the surface showed a happy, functioning clan.

"Who are the two good-looking guys in the front?"

He felt her stiffen. "Jimmy and Tommy, my brothers. See that guy behind him? The real handsome one? Amazing how such a comely fellow could be such a lousy father. He's two for two."

"What?" said Yablonsky. "Baseball?"

"No," she said. "Two sons. Two suicides."

"I read about one a few years back," he said carefully.

"That was Tommy. Shot himself after flunking out of Harvard. Not because he was afraid to go back home, but as a way of avoiding the fact that he had no place else he could go. He spoke to me on the phone, right before he did it. I pleaded with him not to. 'Stay with me,' I begged him. 'I'm no good,' he said, 'and I'm tired. Tired of always failing. Even before I went to Harvard he told me it was lucky I was handsome. That all I was good for was marrying some rich girl. I'm tired of having the shit kicked out of me. Besides, he's right.' I heard the shot, then the phone went silent."

"Your parents must've been upset at the funeral."

She laughed. "My parents don't go to their children's funerals. What they do is ship the bodies back to Lenox, to join the other eager Benfields in our family plot. I'll never forget it, Alvin. Not for as long as I live. You read the papers, right? Two days before Jim hung himself, the cops found him running around with his clothes off in Gramercy Park. 'Please come east,' I said. 'I know that seeing you would help him. He needs you.' My father got on the phone. All he said was 'You've upset your mother enough.' 'Please come,' I begged. 'After my golf tournament,' he said."

Wiggling away from him, she picked up a photo, held it in her hands. "See how handsome Jim was? He was an angel. Now look. The last photo of him before he killed himself." The picture in the frame showed a tall, fat, middle-aged man trying to smile. His face, puffy and unfocused. The face of a drug addict.

"It took tremendous effort for me to break away from my parents. It consumed nearly all the spiritual resources I had. Thank God I did. My brothers never really could. We moved to California and that twenty-thousand-acre ranch. Last week, when my mother called me and told me my father wanted to apologize before he died, I felt like saying, 'I bet he's still healthy enough to lay the nurses on the floor.' Growing up, because of my father's health, we had to move from Massachusetts to that ranch in Southern California. We had our own zip code. Our own post office. Owned our own town. Flew our own family flag. When it was time for us to be educated, my father, like all middle-class parents, built a schoolhouse and hired a staff to live near the compound and teach us. To his way of thinking, public schools were full of blacks, Asians, and Jews. Even private schooling wasn't exclusive enough . . . What was your father like, Alvin?"

"Strong," Yablonsky said. "Being my father's son was like being Hercules' kid. People were always coming up to me, telling me about his feats of strength."

"Like what?"

"One time one of my cousins told me he'd seen my father as a young guy lift up a car's front end past his knees. 'Did you really do that, Dad?' I asked.

" 'My son, it was a small car,' he answered. Another time in East New York, I saw a teenager named Guiseppe smash into an eighty-year-old woman, my neighbor who lived across the street. I told her family who did it, the kid was a member of a street gang, and within minutes I had thirty guys looking for me. My father used jujitsu on their leader, threw him on the concrete so he'd land on his head. Then faced down the rest of the street gang. He had a temper, but you felt protected."

She held his hand. "I never felt protected by my father. I don't really want to tell you the kinds of feelings he had for me."

"I miss my dad," Yablonsky said.

"I don't miss mine. When I became a teenager, like every other girl I'd invite girlfriends to stay over. My father, martini in hand, would hit on each of them." She paused. "Some of my girlfriends he succeeded with. Last week when my mother called and said my father wanted to apologize, remembering Jim, I said, 'Please don't talk about my dad. You've upset me enough.' 'Will you come?' she asked. 'Please?' I answered, 'Maybe after my horseback-riding lesson.' My father deserves to die alone. Thank God I've broken away from him."

* * *

Yablonsky took a quick shower and dressed. He scribbled a note to Julie, telling her how special she was to him, how much he loved her. Placing it on the bed alongside her, he kissed her lightly on the cheek and smiled. She purred softly, her arms wrapped around a pillow.

Shrugging into his winter coat, he gently closed the door, walked down the three flights of stairs, exited the tenement and came out onto the street. Crossing Barrow, he walked along Hudson, which was wide. There were patisserie stores on the corner, reminding him of Paris. Reaching the Cubby Hole, a lesbian bar, he stopped. Women lingered inside or came out into a waiting taxi. Yablonsky waited his turn.

Earlier in the day, Sterling Roth had held a press conference at the steps of the Criminal Court Building at One Centre Street. The purpose of the conference was to raise questions about Darius Moody's imprisonment. Instead, the reporters asked whether a former client of his, Lewis Markham Robb, a terrorist from the 1970s who'd built bombs for the F.A.L.N. and the Weather People before losing two fingers and part of his face when one exploded, was back in town. Robb, whose bombs had killed both cops and civilians, had eluded capture for over two decades.

After Roth denied he knew Robb's whereabouts and the press conference ended, he called Detective Yablonsky. "Through contact with one of my street informants, I believe I may know the identity of one of the men who murdered Skinny McPherson."

"Tell me."

"Not over the phone. You could be taping me for even further blackmail. Later tonight. Three in the morning. I'll be checking you for a wire."

"The usual place?"

"Never," said Roth. "It's got to be a place I choose. Near where I live. A grungy after-hours club called the Mars Bar. I liked McPherson. Like me, he stood for something. I find it hard enough to live with myself and what you make me do. Remember, Detective, if something comes of this, I'm never going to inform for you again."

"That was our deal."

The taxi driver drove down Bleecker. Even though it was two-fifteen in the morning, the jazz and rock clubs on Bleecker were filled with people. Yablonsky looked left as they passed Lafayette Place, glancing at the *Guardian* building. He saw newspaper vans crossing the city, dumping stacks of dailies in front of stands. The blinking lights of a truck denoted a newspaper delivery guy squeezing a ream of paper into a vending box on the other corner of the Bowery. The further the taxi drove into the East Village, the emptier and dirtier the streets became. Yablonsky thought that tonight the East Side looked like a feudal village whose inhabitants dumped refuse out of their windows and onto the streets. At last the driver stopped to let Yablonsky off in the middle of the block.

The detective stood on the corner of East Fifth and Second Avenue, across from the new tenements that used to be the old Fillmore East. Lighting a cigarette to keep him warm on this chilly night, he crossed the street. After seeing Roth, he told himself he'd head for an after-hours cop bar only three short blocks away.

He rounded the corner and stopped in shock when he saw Bridges and Beatty, crouching behind a ten-year-old dirty yellow Saab, guns drawn and staring tensely at him.

Bridges, motioning him down, hissed, "What the fuck are you doing here?"

Beatty, knowing that the detective frequently did not carry his service revolver, reached down to his ankle holster, handing him his drop gun.

Yablonsky didn't answer. He stared at the whitewashed tenement on East Second Street, standing by itself, surrounded by a demolished block of vacant lots filled with discarded, rusting appliances and bricks. "What's going on?"

Beatty, ducking lower behind the car's shell, his Glock pointed steadily at the shadowy, unlit building, spoke quickly. "We were off-duty, on our way to Billy's Blue Lounge," he said. "I spot Lewis Markham Robb shopping for motherfucking Macintosh apples and seedless grapes, in front of a Korean fruit stand on Second Avenue. We follow the scumbag until he makes us and ducks into this building. He's somewhere in there now. Five minutes ago he told us anyone who rushes the building will be one dead motherfucker."

"No hostages, right?" asked Yablonsky.

"Thank God, no," said Beatty.

Bridges, gun also drawn, said without looking at Yablonsky, "One of us will have to draw fire so we can shoot him. Until we pinpoint him, it's a stalemate."

Beatty, bracing himself on the ground, rose slightly, edging an inch or so over the car, hoping to draw fire without taking too much risk. Nothing. No gunfire.

Bridges crawled to another parked car, peering out from the side carefully, so he'd be able to bring down Robb if he was dumb enough to try and escape through the rear of the building.

"When are the blue-and-whites going to be here?" asked Yablonsky.

"We're off-duty," whispered Beatty. "No radios." Many cops chose not to carry beepers, so what Beatty said made sense. But why hadn't one of them crawled to a pay phone for assistance? Any rookie patrolman knew that in this situation you talked reassuringly to the would-be doer, got him to talk back. Talked and stalled. Bridges and Beatty were veterans. What the hell was going on here? Then, looking at the grim-faced men, he knew.

"You can't execute this guy," Yablonsky said. Bridges, without bothering to look at him, said, "Sure we can." Beatty raised himself another half-inch over the car. "Do you have a fix on this fuck yet?"

"No."

Yablonsky's beeper was back at Julie's. "I'm crawling away for help," he said. "I'm calling for assistance."

Bridges, with two hands steady on his Glock, said, "See anything, Beatty?"

"I can have a negotiating team down here in ten minutes," Yablonsky said, trying to begin a negotiating process of his own with the cops. Talk and stall.

"Don't go anywhere." Bridges took a deep breath, turning slightly to look at him. "Shut the fuck up, Alvin."

"You can't execute this guy. You can't murder him."

"Robb's back in New York either to blow up more buildings and kill a few more cops, or because he decided he'd like to come in from the cold and hire an attorney to deal down the decades-old murders to jay-walking offenses. Then he can be out on the street in a couple of years and become a famous media darling." Bridges, shaking his head, said, "That's not gonna happen. Not tonight."

"We're not murderers," said Yablonsky.

"It's not murder if a murderer who threatens to kill you gets popped. As soon as I can figure out how to get a fix on this guy without one of us getting shot, this motherfucker will go."

Bridges stopped talking. From half a block away, a tall man, easily recognizable because of his size and swinging ponytail, stepped around the corner and into the streetlight.

A quick look of unparalleled cunning crossed Bridges's face as Roth drew closer. "Here comes the solution to our problem." The cop paused, he and Beatty exchanged glances. "Okay?"

"Okay," echoed Beatty. "Two pricks blown with one motherfuckin' stone."

As Yablonsky's most important source came closer, he peered into the deserted tenement. No noise. No boasts or threats. Robb was a real pro; quiet and lethal. "Let's try to talk to him," he said hurriedly. "Try to get a response out of him and keep him talking."

"Fuck you, Alvin," said Bridges. "This is out of your hands. For once, let one of *them* get killed and not us. Alvin, afterwards we got to be D and D on this all the way."

Beatty nodded. "Test*alie* or fry."

"I'm going for help," said Yablonsky, staying where he was, too scared to get shot by some cornered, cop-hating terrorist whom he was trying to save.

Roth was here. Seeing three cops in the late-night darkness with guns drawn and hiding behind cars, he quickly read the situation. Crouching alongside them, he said, "Who's trapped?"

"Lewis Markham Robb."

Roth breathed in deeply. "When did it happen?"

Bridges glared at the attorney in anger, as if his presence here was the last thing he wanted.

"This situation developed only moments ago," Bridges said. "What the fuck are you doing out here at this time of night? On the way to a meeting with him? Having knowledge of a fugitive's whereabouts and not telling the police is a serious offense."

Roth didn't answer. There was the struggle in him to appraise the situation coolly, but his skepticism concerning cops won out. "You want to kill this man. I won't let that happen."

"Calm down, Roth," said Bridges. "Robb's just across the street. Any noise he hears coming from us might spook him, and that's the last thing we want to do. The negotiating team hasn't arrived yet. Meanwhile, this dirtbag says he's gonna blow away the next dumb motherfucker he sees walking down the street. We can't let that happen."

"Roth, don't go. It's a trap," said Yablonsky.

"Why the fuck should I believe you?"

"If I even see that motherfucker blink, I'm gonna shoot him," said Bridges. "We've asked him to give up. But you know your client. He won't negotiate with us."

"Is this true, Alvin?"

"Don't go in," said Yablonsky.

"I'm tired of you telling me what to do."

"Why risk your life?" the detective said, glancing at Beatty and Bridges.

Raising himself on his haunches slightly, Roth said, "I'll talk to him." He stood, edging around the car, taking a tentative step closer to the shadowy building. Nothing. No response.

"Stay put, Roth," said Yablonsky.

Roth took another few steps. When he was close to the building, Bridges double-checked both sides to see that there were no witnesses. Bending over the car hood, he fired sudden bursts into the front of the tenement, to the left, wide of Roth. Beatty joined in. There was a quick flash of returning gunfire from the tenement. Roth went down. Bridges and Beatty fired at the flashes coming from the second-floor landing. The three cops glimpsed a shadowy figure, staggering backwards, then lurching out the window and onto the fire escape. Rhythmic, quiet popping sounds came from Bridges's automatic. Dropped for good, Robb's arms hung from the fire escape.

The two cops stood, moving along with Yablonsky to check on Roth. Roth's hands rested on his cheek. His head lolled to one side like it had been snapped and broken, almost torn off by a bullet shot through his left ear. There was very little blood. His best and most reliable source was dead, thought Yablonsky.

The three men stared down at him, breathing deeply, struggling to control the adrenaline rush. Bridges's voice, very calm. "What do you think, Demi? Head or body shot? How could Robb, in this darkness, catch him in the head? Me, I think this was supposed to be a hit to the body that went bad."

"Makes sense," said Beatty. "I don't think Robb ever intended it to be a mushroom shot."

"Who cares if some left-wing lawyer gets popped by his own client?" asked Bridges.

Beatty, peering down at the inert attorney, smiled. "Now that he's gone, fuck him."

Yablonsky looked away from the dead attorney. "For God's sake . . ."

Beatty approached him, asked for his drop-gun back. "We'll have a day to meet with our union reps before they begin the Inquisition. This gun wasn't fired, so obviously I don't have to surrender it. Back it goes." He slipped it into his ankle holster.

"The techies will analyze the building's spray patterns. Forensic will run tests. So they'll know that only two guns were fired. Our two guns," Bridges said, staring at Yablonsky.

The three men heard the faint sounds of sirens. "Here's our story," Bridges said. "We got to emphasize this to Infernal Despair. They're gonna find Robb's gun, know he was armed and dangerous. Roth was killed with his bullets, not ours. Why was Roth passing by at this time of night? Paying a social call on a friend at four in the morning after an exhausting arraignment with Darius Moody? No. Roth must've been heading for a meeting with Robb, his future client, whose jacket is fat with the murders of cops and civilians. Once Roth saw what was going on, he told us he'd defuse the situation and get his client to come out."

What were these two cops really doing on the street at two in the morning? wondered Yablonsky. They were on the day shift.

"Goddamn you," said Yablonsky. "You've destroyed me. I won't testalie for you."

"Bullshit," said Bridges. "Look at this hood. No surrounding houses, so no videotapes. The press will buy what we tell them. So will Infernal Despair, as long as you keep your fucking mouth shut."

The sirens grew louder.

"What about spray patterns?" asked Beatty.

"At first we thought he was shooting at us from the first-floor window. Then seeing him, we directed our fire toward the second landing and nailed him."

"Demi," said Bridges, "why didn't we phone for help?"

"You should know," said Beatty. "We're off-duty when we make a known fugitive and tail him to a building. We have no idea if anyone else's in the tenement. Maybe his confederates were waiting for him. They could also be armed. Beepers are only required for cops on special assignment and commanders, so it's just too risky for any of us to leave and call for help. We had to stay here to keep an eye on the building and shoo any innocent civilians away."

"This is one fucking time there won't be any cops marching in any funerals," said Bridges. "Still gonna file a report, Alvin?"

Yablonsky glanced at their drop-guns. "I never said I'd file a report."

"You gonna roll?"

During the inquiry, thought Yablonsky. "No," he said.

Sirens roared. Lead police cars raced onto the street, pulling up midway on the block as other squad cars blocked off the ends of the intersections, cutting off access to pedestrians and drivers as they mounted a level one mobilization. Cops with guns drawn tumbled out and took shelter behind their cars. A sergeant and three cops, beginning to set up a phone command, went to land lines, phones that could not be listened to by reporters.

From behind the barriers and flashing lights, reporters read live feeds into satellite vans. The sergeant recognized one of the plainclothes cops who appeared to be standing next to a tenement house. He saw that their guns were put away and yelled, "You're blue and you're okay, right?"

"Fucking right," said Bridges. "We're okay."

The sergeant stood; the squad of police put their guns away and moved closer. "Anyone down?" asked the sergeant.

"Two down," said Beatty. "The perp and a civilian."

"The building clear?"

"We ain't been inside," said Bridges. "We're off-duty so no flashlights, but my intuition tells me that the one on the landing's the only one in there. We were tailing him. He ducked into the tenement. To meet with him." Bridges jerked his chin down, pointing at Roth.

Turning to a uniform, the sergeant said, "You, Martino and Gale, get flashlights. Check the tenement out." Then, back to Bridges. "You know who they are?"

"Yeah," said Bridges. "We managed to nail Lewis Markham Robb. This guy, his attorney, is Sterling Roth. They set up a meet. His own client shot Roth while he was trying to get into the building to defuse the situation. We ordered him to stay put."

The sergeant's eyes quickly swept the crime scene. "Jesus Christ," he said. "Two big names."

Dropping his voice, Bridges asked, "Any brass here?"

The sergeant laughed. "Those Rear Echelon MotherFuckers only come after they're sure the bullets have stopped flying, never during the exchange of fire. They'll be here later, along with their publicists and press kits. I've got to speak to the negotiating team. Tell them they're not needed." Staring at the dead attorney, a tech kneeling over him with chalk, he said, "What a shame. He might've hated cops, but if you were literate and read newspapers, you liked him."

"Me too," said Bridges.

TWENTY-ONE

Inside the conference room, brass and R.E.M.F.s were not only lined up from one end of the table to the other, but along the sides of the table as well, so it would appear to the cops, once they sat down, that they were surrounded. The sheer weight of the number of men arrayed against them would surely choke the truth out of the outnumbered, outflanked cops.

As a veteran detective, Yablonsky knew or had casual dealings with most of the men seated around the huge table. Two deputy commissioners. Flood, blank-faced and therefore appearing to be neutral. He also knew August "Sparrow" Smith, and Elmo "Rollover" Robbins, from I.A.

Deputy Mayor Robert "Hey" Abbott, whom Yablonsky had seen clandestinely entering an after-hours bondage sex club a couple of months ago, apologized for arriving five minutes late and sat down.

"What we have here," began Arnold Feeny, a deputy police commissioner, "are two cops who tried to put a murder scheme over on the department and our city. They are the lowest of the low, dirty beyond belief." His gaze swept over the three men and their union reps. "We have forensic reports. We have the slugs. We have the guns. We have the spray patterns. We already know what happened. We already know who's guilty here. Your famous blue wall of silence will be pierced."

Bridges and Beatty stuck to their story. Roth's death had been a tragedy, an accident. They had tried to restrain him. The spray patterns showed that they'd steered their fire clear of Roth. The attorney'd been killed with Robb's gun, not theirs. When Yablonsky was questioned, he was evasive.

Deputy Commissioner Feeny stood, turned off the recorder and video. "I swear to you three fucking musketeers, one of you is gonna, roll." Wheeling toward Sparrow Smith and Rollover Robbins, he said, "Okay. Let's begin the march of dimes."

Beatty and Bridges were taken away to be further questioned. Their union reps went with them. Yablonsky stayed behind. It'd be easier for him to roll if he was away from the presence of the other cops.

Rollover Robins said, "You were the real ringleader here. You set up Roth, using those two dummies to murder him."

"You need proof, gentlemen," said Phillip Young, his union rep.

"McPherson's article would have exposed corruption in your precinct. We know he talked to you, Detective. You only want to solve his murder so you can get your hands on his notes and destroy them."

"Those notes proved my innocence," said Yablonsky.

"We saw you meeting with Roth at Munson's. We know he was one of your sources."

He was a detective, yet he had no idea he'd been under surveillance. Instead of rolling on the other two, he was fighting for his life. "Why would I have one of my best sources killed?"

"He was an unwilling source. He learned you were dirty and planned to come to us with that news."

"That's bull. Insinuations aren't proof," said Phillip Young.

"We have Roth's body. That's proof enough. If you admit that you recruited the other two to set Roth up, we'll shift the blame to them and go easier on you."

"You'll what?"

"Admit your part and we promise you, the other two will take the fall."

The tape recorder and video, which had been running when the inquiry started, had been turned off. He recalled watching tapes of Roth's press conference with the brass at the health club, then at the precinct, spotting Beatty and Bridges just beyond the defensive perimeter. He remembered seeing the two cops in plainclothes moments after Roth and Sully had left the demonstration against the homeless shelters. Had the two cops been stalking Roth, waiting for an opportunity? He realized that by implicating them in Roth's murder to I.A., he'd only be further implicating himself. Staring at the blown-up photos of Roth, remembering how he'd looked lying so still on the cold, dark pavement, he said, "I feel sick."

"It's your conscience," said Abbott.

Yablonsky turned the video and recorder back on. "You think I planned Roth's murder?"

"We know you did."

"Suspect, you mean," said Phillip Young. He took off his glasses, ran his hand through his crewcut Afro.

"Suspicions are often enough."

"Not this time," said Young. The other two patrolmen were brought back into the room. "They're still sticking to their bullshit story," said Rollover Robbins.

"It's not a story," said Bridges.

"The reason they're sticking to the story is because it's true," said Young. "There's no reason to call a grand jury. Roth brought on his own death, and that was tragic, but he did so because he ignored Patrolman Bridges's orders not to expose himself to the possibility of gunfire. He was an attorney. This was his client who the police had cornered. He knew the risks."

"Patrolman Beatty should have restrained him better," said Deputy Mayor Abbott.

"And risk getting shot by Robb if a struggle broke out? Then we'd be participating in another all-too-familiar ritual: more police funerals. Please remember that a dangerous felon was killed, a man whose bombs might've one day reached your offices. Or blown up some of you or your relatives' children who decide to become cops."

Deputy Commissioner Feeny stood, flicking off the tape recorder, signaling an assistant to turn off the video. Facing Beatty and Bridges, he said, "We will not forget how you men colluded to avoid prosecution. You now have another motive to solve McPherson's murder, Detective. If you even jaywalk in the future, Yablonsky, we'll bring you down."

"Maybe he should be off the case," said Deputy Mayor Abbott.

"You don't really have any proof against him," said Flood. "Just suspicions."

"No," said Feeny. "I want the murder solved, and he's just proved he's resourceful enough to solve it. Don't ever forget, Detective. It's your head that's in the vise, now."

Outside on the street, the two cops and the detective vigorously shook hands with the union reps, who then left.

The three men crossed the street and turned the corner. "I knew in the end you'd tell the truth," said Bridges.

"So Roth was a source of yours all along," said Beatty. "Who'd have guessed?"

"Want to come with us to Farrell's and celebrate?" asked Bridges with a smirk.

Yablonsky winced. Accident or premeditation? On his way to meet with the detective, Roth had been killed. Had he been set up? Who had the connections? I.A. was stunned that Roth had been killed and thought that Yablonsky was as dirty as the other two. He knew there'd be attempts to entrap the three of them. What the hell had he gotten into? "I want no part of you," he said. "You set Roth up. You're killers."

"You shouldn't forget that," said Beatty. "If you're thinking of rolling on us."

In his office at the precinct, Yablonsky sat staring at the scale model of Tavern on the Green, Wollman Rink, and the surrounding area of Central Park. The reams of paper that awaited him on his desk were uninviting. Maybe if he avoided looking at them, they'd get up and flee the scene.

"Entrancing, isn't it?" Flood said. "Just like a postcard. But Currier and Ives' paintings of Central Park never had any murders committed in them."

Flood sat down. "Sorry I couldn't be of greater help to you, but you survived. Internal Affairs and the mayor may be perfectly willing to lay McPherson's murder off on us. If his murder isn't solved, the only story that will resonate with the public is that he was killed because he was investigating corruption in my precinct. Roth's death is big news—and he was killed by cops."

"I was there," said Yablonsky.

"It was lucky for us that your gun wasn't fired."

"Lucky? I'm a detective. I don't believe in murder."

"Some cops do. Roth was your chief informant, killed on his way to meet you. Why?"

"He said he had information about the McPherson murder."

"I don't believe in murder either. Especially by cops. Did Beatty and Bridges execute him?"

Yablonsky hesitated, then said, "I.A. did a thorough investigation. They might not have wanted to clear us, but they did."

"I.A. accused you of setting up the entire thing. Why would they say a detective would eliminate the snitch who's going to help him solve an important case? I.A.'s always the ally of whatever politicians are in power. Do these politicians really want this case solved now? I hate the idea of Bridges and Beatty out on the street."

Yablonsky reached for his coffee. "There's nothing you can do. They were cleared."

"Right. But why would I.A. scapegoat you and minimize their part in this? We've got to give them a murderer quickly. We can't have cops implicated in the murder of an investigative reporter. Have you been able to do anything since that goddamned inquiry?"

"On the twenty-third, when Skinny was murdered, Raymond Staples took a private plane to Teterboro Airport in New Jersey and was driven to New York."

"How'd you learn this? Why is this important?"

"A week ago, I asked a taxi driver friend of mine to put the word out on the street about McPherson's murder. This morning I met with the driver of a car service in Washington Heights. Raymond Staples used a phony name, but the driver recognized him anyway. I have his logbook with his record of the trip. The driver also remembered that Staples came off the plane with no luggage."

"Why's that important?"

"No luggage meant he was planning on returning to Florida. If he'd stayed in Manhattan, the doormen and anyone else would've seen him."

"I've been looking through Beatty and Bridges's files. Did you know that six months ago for a three-month stint, they moonlighted as security guards for one of Raymond Staples's buildings?"

"Was it the building where McPherson died?"

"No, but that's unimportant. They have a relationship."

"I asked to see Discovery's latest surveillance reports. A couple of months ago, the Department of Traffic set up secret surveillance cameras at intersections to entrap speeders. While taxi drivers make it their business to learn the locations, and avoid them, the average citizen's unaware they're there. Look at this photo. It shows Raymond Staples's car. We checked the license plate going through an intersection on West Sixty-fifth and West End Avenue. I've already spoken to Raymond's limo driver. He's got an alibi for that night, a good one."

"So he took the car out by himself. God, I hope he's the doer."

"I was thinking of using Henderson and Saunders. Setting up surveillance teams . . ."

"No teams," said Flood. "Do it yourself."

In his office, Yablonsky stared at surveillance tapes sent over by the Department of Traffic. Patrolmen Henderson and Saunders had coordinated the photos of drivers and names for the evening of December 23. Yablonsky smiled slightly as he looked at the underlined last name on the list.

TWENTY-TWO

I thought I was dealing with a professional." Raymond Staples squared his ample shoulders and looked away from the TV cameras shooting the commercial. His costar, a nine-year-old boy, pulled back, saying, "Mister, I'm a pro. But you keep stepping on my mark."

"I never stepped on your mark," said Staples. "I don't have to take this shit. This is my commercial. This is for my restaurant. Any more lip from you and you'll be on your own."

"Raymond, please," said one of the agents standing offstage.

His coactor, turning to his agent, said, "Mr. Williams, he steps on my marks."

Staples reached into his pocket, drawing out one of his strongest Cuban cigars. Taking a long, leisurely puff, he blew smoke over his costar's head. The boy, stepping back between coughs, said, "You also moved into my key light."

Staples threw the cigar down, nodded to his entourage, and left the building. Yablonsky and Milo watched Staples's limo pull out. Milo turned his cab into the traffic. "How many cars you want I should keep between us?"

"At least one other car."

"Okay," said Milo. "This guy's so full of himself, he's oblivious to the street. We could climb in the limo with him, and he still wouldn't know he's being tailed."

The two men watched the limo make a left onto the West Side Highway. There wasn't much traffic. Staples's driver made another left at West Thirty-ninth Street, then drove several blocks before stopping in front of the Jacob Javits Convention Center.

Ten minutes later, three men came out and entered the limo, hidden behind the opaque windows. They could see nothing. The detective, with his knowledge of the city, recognized them, noticed they sat in the back with Staples and huddled up. Damion Carnes, booker of special events. Darion Gatt, chief of security, who'd been given this job by the head of one of the construction companies who'd built the center. And the last guy, Billy Davis, a teamster union official.

The detective hadn't reached the point in his case yet where he could go before a judge with a writ that would result in cops placing bugs in Staples's limos. He guessed they were meeting about the notorious pilferage that came out of the convention center. Anyone showing off their wares at the center always had to bring more of whatever they were exhibiting to allow for theft. From Kosher food exhibitors to booksellers, a good part of the product always ended up falling off the trucks.

In the cab, Milo turned to him. "The new auto show's not like the old ones. That's because they no longer exhibit checker cabs. Someday I'm gonna drive you over to the lot on Cozine Avenue in Brooklyn, and you'll have a chance to really view those beauties of mine up close. I've got six checkers there. They go up in value every day. All mine. My legacy."

At the corner of Staples's flagship restaurant, La Parisienne, on West Fifty-second Street, they watched as the doorman ushered Shelly Townes out and over to Staples's car. As the doorman craned an umbrella over his head, Shelly, carrying a vinyl gym bag, reached for the door. Milo's eyes rolled up as Shelly fumbled with the bag while trying to unzip it. Typical. The bag landed in a rain puddle and upended. Yablonsky expected money to fall out. Instead what rolled into the street were cans of Pepsi. Townes couldn't even open the car door, the handle was too wet. Finally, the driver scrambled out, picked up the soda, and guided the hapless ex-borough president into the car.

"What the fuck is Shelly Townes doing in a limo?" asked Milo.

"I don't know yet."

"You going to call Catskills Correctional? Tell them they got a prisoner on the loose?"

"No. If I call them, Staples and Townes will know they were tailed. Maybe he's on a work-release program. I want to find out where they're going."

"Why am I busting my hump so hard to make a living when these guys in minimum state security have it made in the shade? It never pays to be honest."

"You're not honest."

"So slip the bracelets on me, Alvin. Let my vacation begin. I bet he's at the halfway house on Borden Street, in Long Island City. I can just picture Shelly during the day with a mop in his baby-white hands."

"You know this guy?"

"I drove him a few times. I know he used to be borough president. The idea of him swabbing the decks of some factory during work-release is outlandish."

There was another stop in front of a bakery on Ninth Avenue that sold Veniero's, the best Italian pastry in the city. The driver returned lugging a box filled with cannoli.

Milo's voice filled with admiration. "You've got to hand it to Shelly. He lives better in prison than most of us on the outside."

As the limo pulled away, Shelly opened the window, tossing the bags filled with leftovers onto the street. The car drove past Lincoln Center on

Broadway, then made a left. The car ahead drove by Staples's building headquarters on West End Avenue without stopping.

Staples's driver turned up West Seventy-second, past the Pier Seventy-Two restaurant, then made a quick right onto Riverside Drive, heading for Riverside Park, which, unlike neighboring Central Park, was a long, narrow sliver of green that was bordered by Riverside Drive on the east and the Hudson River on the west.

The detective watched as up ahead, Staples's car made a left into the grassy tree-covered underground amphitheater that served as the parking garage for the small marina's boat owners. The limo stopped near the rear of the garage. Staples and Townes got out of the car; Shelly dropped his umbrella and picked it up. The two men walked toward one of the metal gates leading to the promenade and boat basin.

Yablonsky signaled for Milo to park outside the garage at its edge. He slipped his shoes off, waited for Staples and Townes to exit to the marina, then followed, seeing the footprints the men had made on the oily garage floor's surface. Even though he might cut his feet on glass, he didn't want them to hear the echo of his footsteps.

He could see the two leaning against the chain-link fence that led to the docks and moored-up boats. Seagulls hovered over the marina, diving with exultant screams whenever they spotted a fish in the dark waters of the Hudson. The lazier but smarter gulls scavenged through the overflowing garbage cans from the boat basin.

Yablonsky expected Staples to head for the yacht he owned, but the two lingered by the chain-link fence, talking softly and gesturing. Yablonsky remained where he was by the door. He wasn't able to hear what they were saying, but didn't want to risk being spotted coming closer. Straight ahead were moored boats, including Staples's huge yacht. To the right of the marina was chain-link fencing, topped with rows of barbed wire. Behind the fencing were huge construction machines: derricks, cranes, and bulldozers. The trailers for the construction crews had been boarded up to safeguard them from homeless climbing in, cutting the wire, and living there. The Portosans were locked. The site had been idle for months.

For five more minutes, the men talked in low tones, then walked back to the garage and Staples's limo. Yablonsky stepped back, crouching behind a parked car. An image of him kneeling behind a parked car the night Roth was killed came to him, but he repressed it. Yablonsky stared at the bare, dim overhead bulbs that illuminated the garage so poorly. Rainwater seeped through the amphitheater's roof, vines grew through the soft cracks. Like a spelunker in a cave staring at ancient Cro-Magnon paintings, he noticed layers of graffiti and scratchitti on the walls, as indecipherable as cuneiform. It seemed to Yablonsky that the entire marina had been left by the Manhattan politicians to slowly atrophy.

Yablonsky watched the two men walk to the limousine. After the car U-turned, he ran to Milo's taxi. All day long, he'd seen Staples pull up to a building or construction site and wait. Politicians or businessmen and women would come to him. His talks were always conducted in his limo, his associates would leave, and then it was on to the next meeting.

Milo braked his car while they were still on Riverside Drive. Just before the approach to Seventy-second Street, Staples's driver parked next to a hydrant. Milo zapped the meter like a junkie frantically tapping a vein. Yablonsky wished they'd roll down the opaque windows so he'd have a better idea what the two men were discussing, but the windows remained up. Ten minutes later the limo pulled away without dropping Townes off.

Once again the limo entered traffic, turning onto West End Avenue. Opposite Munson's Diner on Eleventh Avenue, a redemption center had been set up. The street was crowded with derelicts wheeling shopping carts filled with soda and beer cans. They'd feed a can into the redemption machine and out would come a nickel. Sheets of plastic had been placed over the tops of the carts to prevent the cans from slipping away in the rain.

Milo had to stop for a red light, one traffic light behind Raymond. One derelict muttering gibberish inched closer to the redemption center. Cars slowed to avoid hitting the scores of homeless who made their rounds between cars, diligently hitting up the drivers for money. A guy would stand in front of a car and refuse to move until coins were tossed on the pavement.

Up ahead Yablonsky noticed that the window was rolled down on Shelly's side. Out went a few coins. The light changed. Once again Staples's great white limo was moving through traffic, easy to tail. Yablonsky anticipated finding out additional skinny on Staples and Townes: where they were heading, who they were meeting.

Milo's foot moved from the brake to the gas, about to follow. From out of the corner of his eye, Yablonsky saw a tall white man approach their car from the driver's side.

"Give me a dollar," he growled.

The guy was about six-foot-five, had a huge bushy reddish-white beard, and seemed crazy enough not to respond obediently to authority if Yablonsky showed his shield.

"That sounds fair," the detective said.

"Fuck off," said Milo. As Yablonsky began to roll down his window to toss some money, the derelict, nodding to himself, loomed over their car window. Lifting both windshield wipers in the air, he snapped them off.

"Cocksucker!" yelled Milo. The derelict moved across the street, hoisting the wipers overhead triumphantly. Yablonsky watched the rain inundate the windshield, making it impossible to see.

Milo's car remained where it was, unable to move any further. Other drivers inched around, then past, the disabled automobile. Milo, refusing to apologize, used his cell phone to call for a tow truck. From the rolled-down passenger window, Yablonsky watched helplessly as Staples pulled further away into traffic. At last he lost sight of the vehicle. Leaving the car, flashing his shield, he tried to commandeer the first few cars he saw. In the rain, drivers ignored the shield, although some threw a few coins out on the street.

TWENTY-THREE

Yablonsky crossed the street, away from the *Guardian*'s office, having responded to Julie's call to meet her and Sully concerning Roth's death.

Barnes, after dodging another attempt by his kid to see him, had called Raymond Staples, trying to pressure him into donating the leftover food from his restaurants to Barnes's shelters. Sully threatened a hunger strike and press coverage if Staples declined, but Raymond was adamant: no donations. Barnes hung up the phone, puzzled at dealing with one of the few people he'd been unable to bend to his will.

"I've heard some scuttlebutt, Alvin. Was Roth one of your C.I.s?"

"Not at all," Yablonsky answered.

"I have a newsman's curiosity. Was Roth coming to you with information as to who murdered McPherson on the night he himself was murdered?"

"He was not," Yablonsky said.

Yablonsky walked along the East Village streets, making a right at the Starbucks across from Tompkins Square Park. Stopping for a traffic light, he walked by the Starbucks on Eighth Street. When he reached the Starbucks on the corner, he crossed.

On Third Street, Yablonsky rounded the corner, coming upon the breakup of the lonely, unattended-by-the-media demonstration that protested Sully's coming into the community with yet another homeless shelter. They'd been demonstrating a couple of hours each day for a week. The father of the girl who'd been stabbed with the needle and possibly had AIDS hoisted a picket sign into the van. They'd run ads, taken out radio time. They needed money. Yablonsky walked past a bearded Hispanic man carrying a protest sign and dropped a dollar onto the blanket on the street that'd been laid out for donations.

"Traitor."

Yablonsky glanced up. Charlie Kudos. The actor, tall, handsome, and despite the winter, tan, smiled down at the shorter, stockier detective. Rubbing his earring, he asked, "Where you heading?"

"I'm on the job," said Yablonsky. "I just left the *Guardian.*"

"What a coincidence. That's where I'm going." Yablonsky noticed that Kudos was lugging along one of the tabloids, open to a page with some gossip about him and Benfield. "To see Sully, of course," he added hurriedly. "Not Julie." There was a pause. "How come you're helping out the opposition? They want our shelter out of here."

"I thought Sully always makes a point to donate charity to any bona fide group that has difficulty collecting it. The more despised a group is, the more Barnes gives."

"Yeah, but this bunch is despised by us. They're fighting our presence here every inch of the way. These aren't progressive people."

Yablonsky, who was still in the process of learning the vocabulary of diversity and multiculturalism, said, "I'm a detective. The only progressive thing I do is catch murderers."

"As long as they're poor, as long as the people they kill aren't left-wing attorneys." Towering over him, Kudos gave him a tight, superior smile, tapping the newspaper he held by his side. "I can't understand it," he said. "You and her. By the way, how's Sully?'

Yablonsky wanted to say: paying attention to everyone in the world except his own family. What he said was "He's fine."

A tiny path in Central Park led to a hidden basement door in the rear precinct. No media cameras. No reporters, Yablonsky noted with pleasure. He took the elevator, getting off at the second floor where the detective bureau was located. Inside his small office, he studied the scale model of Tavern on the Green, Wollman Rink, and the West Side section of Central Park that Discovery had constructed for him. It seemed exhaustive in its detail, faultless, with scale-model taxis pulling into the parking lot, along with tiny horses and carriages and longer tourist buses. Inch-high doormen stood outside with brooms, sweeping the entranceway and the approaches clear of snow.

The detective plugged the extension cord into an outlet. What was he looking for? he wondered. The blue lights that had been strung from tiny trees glowed. He stood over the top of the eight-inch restaurant and Wollman's ice skating rink. The icy pyramid in which Skinny'd been found near Wollman's was two inches high. Even scale-size models of the topiaries had been put in. Everything was there, except the answer.

He stared at the narrow, curving streets that led into and out of the park on Central Park West and Fifth Avenue. You can't stop a car, get out, dump a body not far from a restaurant filled with curious tourists in the early evening. If there'd been premeditation, and there had to be premeditation, the murderers had to meet with Skinny early in the evening and murder him. Then store the body in the back of a car in the seldom visited garage, below Staples's office in the West Sixties. They'd dumped the body at three or four in the morning, when the restaurant and rink'd be closed.

What the fuck was he missing? He studied the approaches closest to the restaurant and rink. He looked at the spot where Skinny's body had been discovered. If you went into the park on the West Side, you took West 65th Street through the park. If you drove in from the East Side, you took East 66th Street and exited at West 66th. The west side of the park had separate entrances and exits. The car or van that carried Skinny's body approached from the West Side. The road curved, separated by a triangle of sidewalk from the emerging East Side traffic; when inside the park, though, the roads ran parallel to each other. There was an entranceway in the wall, separating the park from the road. If the car or van pulled up on the sidewalk near to the entranceway, as though disabled, several men could get out, carry McPherson's body to the dump site, then bury him during the snowstorm. But Skinny's sheer size and weight worked against this solution. Special agencies had to be sent for to carry McPherson's body out of the park. They'd needed a gurney, Yablonsky remembered. Three or four men would never have been able to carry a 300-pound dead guy such a distance.

Dead end.

Was Skinny alive when they brought him into the park? Remembering East New York, he knew that Mafia people were often conned into accompanying their buddies to the designated murder site, where their best friends would then kill them. But what would McPherson be doing in a park at three or four in the morning with these men? Led here, killed here? Not even Jimmy Breslin would be in Central Park at that time of night during a snowstorm.

Dead end.

But if they removed the wooden barriers, they could drive into the restaurant's parking lot, wheel across the bridle path to the rink, leave the car, and carry the body the few yards over to the dump site. Burying McPherson would take all of fifteen to twenty minutes. The snow storm would quickly fill the tire tracks, and all traces of them being there. No evidence. The parking lot at that time of night'd be deserted. No witnesses.

Sitting back in his chair, he again raked his eyes over the hub of Manhattan. He studied approaches, small hills, miniature copses that had shielded the murderers burying a grossly overweight man in a sepulcher of snow that would soon turn to ice. He removed tiny horses and carriages, workers, and cars until it was empty of people. Then he realized what it was he'd missed.

Twilight. He stood at the crest of a deserted path in Central Park, near Rat Rock, a hill located near the ball fields on West Sixty-fourth Street. In the distance, he could see blue and red chalk marks on the tiny cliff's surface, made by rock climbers to denote toe and finger holds. City alpinists had transformed the miniature mountain range into their own Mount Everest. In the non-winter months they'd scale its summit.

Taking the path to the right, Yablonsky walked a short way through the woods. He descended a few steps, then stopped when he reached the clearing.

The area was serene and still had patches of snow, but they were drying up and evaporating in the warmer winter weather.

Up until the time of Skinny's murder, there'd been a nearby homeless encampment, even during the winter months. Now, no scattered bottles. No junkie's needles. He'd been here before during one of his canvases of the area. The precinct was a twenty-minute walk from this area of the park. Why hadn't he noticed this before? The area's tranquillity should have tipped him off immediately.

Traces of the homeless were still here. A rusted shopping cart without wheels. A cardboard condo was still standing, along with scattered pieces of carpet and plywood framing.

He sat on an ancient La-Z-Boy easy chair. All over the city, the mayor's task forces were attempting to chase the vagrants to the city's edges. But no one had moved these people, they'd moved themselves.

Even the people who lived in the bigger encampments by the esplanade and band shell were gone. They'd left shortly after Skinny's murder. Why? Had one or more of them witnessed something that night? Why would they be so upset at witnessing a murder that they'd leave an area they'd lived in unmolested for years? Desert an encampment in such close proximity to tourists, joggers, money, and food? Cops were too frightened to enter the park at night to roust or chase them. Young punks from street gangs were too scared to come into the park at night to pour kerosene over them while they slept and set them on fire, a habitual way for some of these kids to enjoy themselves.

Many of these vagrants were not the cleaned-up, antiseptic, endearing, free-spirited street naïfs that people were shown in movies or on their TV screens, but hard-core violent criminals. Last year, seven people had been murdered in the park, four of them by homeless people committing robberies for drug money.

Yablonsky thought: If one or more of them did witness this murder, maybe who'd been murdered was not as important as who committed the murder.

Skinny considered himself a guy of the streets, in touch with everybody he thought played an important role in the city's operations, but Yablonsky doubted that these derelicts would know or care who he was. Possibly one or more of them had recognized not the victim, but his killer; and that was what had frightened them enough to make them leave.

Why shouldn't they run? The doer had accomplices. Aside from organized crime, how many killers were powerful enough to order other people's help in committing murder? Because the guy had cronies who'd also murder them in the blink of an eye, the killer would be a guy who was too powerful to blackmail. Report what they'd witnessed to the cops? The cops had always been, and would always be, their enemy. The thing for them to do was flee. He'd have to find them.

*   *   *

Back at the precinct, Yablonsky conferred with a team of detectives, second grade, from Robbery who'd been sending decoys into the park for the past year. He went through dozens of past surveillance photos, matching faces. In the months preceding Skinny's murder, several vagrants had lived in the smaller encampment near Tavern on The Green. Most of them came and went. But some remained constant, regardless of the month or season. The detective slipped the photos into the inside pocket of his sports jacket, along with Raymond's bank statements, and left. Staples had offered a phony alibi because he'd committed something that was bad enough to be covered up. So far Staples was his only suspect. It was time to have a team of detectives really squeeze him to see what he offered up.

TWENTY-FOUR

Raymond Staples's West Side garage. Poorly lit. Seldom used. Three people sat in the tiny booth where people had waited, before Staples closed the garage to the public, for their cars to be returned to them.

"What we want to know from you is why you murdered Skinny," asked Patrolman Wendell Henderson. "What story was he working on about you that forced you to murder him, Raymond?"

"I wasn't here when he was killed."

"Arranging a meeting with Skinny was easy," said Henderson. "You were his boss. But at the meeting, I suspect you didn't really want to murder him, hoped you wouldn't have to. But he refused to accept your bribe, so you had him murdered in this garage."

"There was no bribe. I was in Fort Lauderdale."

Patrolwoman Saunders said, "This is where your employee was murdered. Doesn't it distress you?"

"Doesn't it bother you taking me here? Why'd you take me here?"

"We both felt we needed to reacquaint you with the murder site. Maybe some memories would be reopened." Henderson paused. "We didn't mean to upset you."

"I'm not upset, I'm just impatient. You couldn't upset me, Wendell."

"Bullshit," answered Saunders. She was only five-feet-two. Her feet didn't even reach the floor under the bench. "Homicide detectives upset everyone. If you're innocent, the detective reminds you of whatever else it is you have reasons to feel guilty about."

"Do you know who detectives deal with most of the time, Raymond? Amateurs. When a gold shield shows up at a crime scene, he looks for inconsistencies. If he's really good, every inconsistency he finds at a crime scene or draws from a suspect's statement becomes a clue. You've left clues."

"I've had enough. I'm calling my lawyer."

Detective Henderson reached into a manila envelope. "Detective Yablonsky gave us this."

"I thought that since Roth's death he was off the case."

"He's still running things. That night you said you weren't in New York? The Department of Traffic set up surveillance cameras at certain intersections to catch speeders. We have photos of you here on December twenty-third."

Raymond stared at a dated photo of one of his cars. "It's not me."

"It is you."

"When Skinny was murdered, I was in Florida, and I have a witness to prove it."

"Who, Judge Dillon?"

"He's dead," said Saunders.

"The photo shows me with him."

"The detective says you were with him for only part of the weekend."

"That's a lie. Someone else must've driven my car."

"So it is your car?"

There was a long silence. "Maybe I was mistaken about my whereabouts on that night. But just because you can prove I was here doesn't mean I killed anyone. If I came back to New York it was to meet someone, but not McPherson."

"Who'd you meet with, Raymond?"

"My accountant."

"You flew into a private, out-of-the-way airport late at night so you could meet with your accountant? No, you murdered the reporter, flew back by private plane to Fort Lauderdale, and continued working on your suntan."

"Why would I sneak back into New York, then jeopardize everything by using my own limo to murder someone?"

"You probably didn't realize you'd end up being photographed by the Department of Traffic," said Henderson. "Few people even know about the surveillance cameras. Still fewer know their locations, only taxi drivers."

"Your chauffeur wasn't in the limo. Only you and your accomplices."

"Maybe somebody borrowed my car to frame me."

"Bullshit. You used your own car because you needed to take Skinny to the dump site in Central Park. I know a lot of cabbies. Even they wouldn't be stupid enough to give a ride to someone who's been murdered. Who would pay them?"

Henderson handed him a sheaf of his financial statements, taken from offshore banks. "These are copies of your business transactions."

"These are not my transactions."

Henderson gave Saunders a look. "Isn't this your name on these statements, Raymond?" Saunders asked.

"It's my name, but you forged it."

"You're an easy guy to do a tail-job on. Detective Yablonsky watched you meet with Shelly Townes at the Seventy-ninth Street boat basin earlier today. Shelly was supposed to have been at a halfway house in Long Island City. I guess if a minimum security prison can't control Shelly's acquisitive instincts when he's supposed to be in jail, they certainly can't control him once he's on the outside. So he's involved in this, too."

"I don't even know Shelly."

"The detective saw you schmoozing with him last night at the boat basin."

"That doesn't mean I know him."

"But your meeting with him at the boat basin wasn't about his rehabilitation. You killed the reporter so whatever under-the-table deal you two are involved in could proceed."

"I'm never even gonna see the guy again. If you don't believe me, you're welcome to stalk me some more."

"What are you and Townes covering up?"

"Didn't the detective hear what we said to each other? There was never a cover-up."

"You were consorting with a known felon. You'd do anything to keep from ending up in prison like Townes."

"Proceeding with something we covered up was the furthest thing from our minds. You can't believe that we were involved in something so crooked that, in order to keep it from becoming public, we had to murder some reporter. That I had him killed to stay out of prison."

"You killed McPherson."

"Shelly's too honest to be involved in a cover-up. I'm probably the most successful businessman in the city. Do I look like the kind of guy who'd commit murder?"

They didn't answer.

"If I was involved in something, it goes without saying it'd be white-collar stuff. These days, committing a white-collar crime is so common, it's practically legal."

"It's still against the law, Raymond."

"If you only knew how few under-the-table deals I accept out of the hundreds I'm offered, you'd nominate me for a Nobel Prize."

"This is instructional," said Henderson. "I wish Yablonsky could hear this. A real lesson in modern penology. Go on."

"You got to admit that a guy like Shelly spends more time on the city streets than in jail. Even if Skinny was dumb enough to turn down an offer that would have made him a rich man, I wouldn't be dumb enough to murder him just to stay out of such a place."

Staples stood. "I severed my ties to Townes, that's what our last meeting was about. If you don't believe me, you're welcome to keep stalking me. I got the tail end of a ballet to catch at Lincoln Center. Are we through wrestling, officers?"

Some interrogation, Henderson thought. The cops were exhausted, drained. The suspect full of adrenaline, triumphant. "For now."

TWENTY-FIVE

Only one café was open on Henry Street, in the mostly Italian neighborhood of Carroll Gardens. Though it was late, groups of teenagers and men stood at each intersection, hanging out. Yablonsky had cannoli and sfingi at Nino's, then returned to the cab.

"Where to now?" Milo asked him.

"Mr. Chang's."

"Jesus, Detective. Not another restaurant. We just ate. I guess the scuttlebutt I heard about you is true."

"What's that?" Yablonsky asked, perking up.

"That you're ruled by your stomach."

"Isn't everyone?" Yablonsky asked. "Chang's isn't a restaurant, Milo. It's a factory. Chang owns it, runs it like a 1920s sweatshop. I want to see if he's still using child labor in his factory."

Before Milo signaled left, he looked repeatedly in the rearview mirror, watching for traffic. He parked the car on Hamilton, rolled his windows up, and said, "I'll wait here."

Yablonsky walked around the corner to Court Street, watched a dark beige van slow for the light, then make a right onto the Gowanus Parkway. Heading for Manhattan, Yablonsky thought.

He stepped into the after-hours sweatshop. Bare lightbulbs hanging from fixtures in the ceiling lit the room. A panorama of women and men hunched over small tables, with garments piled high. There seemed to be no children hiding in the one bathroom that serviced both floors. He climbed to the second floor, but spotted no children. Six months ago, acting on a tip, he had visited this sweatshop. In the early morning he'd found large numbers of kids working the sewing machines. He couldn't stand to see kids being used this way. He'd warned Chang, the owner. "If I see any more of this activity going on, I swear I'll ship your current mistress back to China. She'll look real good walking down Tienanmen Square."

"I promise, no more kids."

"Be moral, Mr. Chang. Exploit adults, not children."

Now a moral glow seemed to suffuse Chang and he bowed his head. "You came like you said. You come back whenever you like. You not find kids."

"I'll still be back, Mr. Chang."

On the street, Yablonsky stood for a moment, clearing his head from the reeking smell and noise. He took deep breaths. After being in the sweatshop, the air from the polluted Gowanus Canal nearby seemed sweet.

From behind, he heard the metal door of the factory close. As he walked toward the taxi, three men came out of a doorway, pointed guns at him, motioning for him to climb into a dark beige van.

"No," he said.

One of them hit him on the head with his gun butt. Suddenly the van was up on the sidewalk. The door slid open. He was dazed. Lowering his head like a battering ram, he charged one of them, knocking him backwards. His arms were grabbed. The men scrambled into the van with Yablonsky and slammed the door shut, pointing their guns at his head and his groin.

One of them opened his collar, took his gun out of his vest holster. "He's a cop," the driver said. "Check for a drop gun."

The guy to his left bent to look for an ankle holster. It made him vulnerable, but there were still two guns pointed at him.

"What do you know," he said. "Not a thing."

"You don't carry much deterrence power," the guy with the gun pointed at his groin said.

They drove down a dark street, no lights. Another one. Yablonsky knew where they were. An industrial area, deserted at night. The car approached the tiny Union Street Bridge. A block over was Third Avenue, at night the beginning of a hooker's stroll. He looked up. Through the windshield he could see the nearby curve of an elevated train. The car stopped. He was made to get out and walk. His entire life flashed before him: buffet by buffet, banquet by banquet, meal by meal.

He almost slipped on the cobblestones as he walked up the tiny bridge. No cars. Only a few scattered tenements in the distance. In the night, the construction cranes in the distance resembled huge giraffes.

His knees felt weak. He looked down into the Gowanus Canal, saw the shimmering yellow-green toxins from its polluted waters. The semi-solid chemicals swayed and shimmered like giant rattlers. Thousands of needles, tossed away by junkies, rode the crest of the stagnant water like foam. The water was so filled with rusted cars, ancient machinery, and concrete kimonos you could almost walk across it.

They stopped him at a break in the rail. From far away he saw the F train, progressing caterpillar-like to the next station, Ninth Street. The screech of brakes as it pulled into the station, then the sound of gun butts and kicks.

The water revived him, but still he went under. He was dazed, but he instinctively started to tread water. He shook his head, but couldn't clear it. A shadow loomed just before him and fear gripped his stomach. It was one of the old wooden piers, but he was too tired to swim to it. His fear increased. It was foolish going on. He was exhausted.

"Yo!"

Hands reached in for him at the break in the rail, pulled him up. He was wet, cold, covered with phosphorescence but alive. It took him ten minutes to compose himself. He'd been saved by three hookers near Third Avenue, who, hearing the noise, waited until they saw the car leave, then ran to Union Street.

Yablonsky, propping himself up against the bridge, looked up.

The tallest woman was dressed in a tight red dress which ended about six inches under her navel. "You connected, mister? Was this a mob hit?"

Yablonsky decided not to tell them he was a detective. They might throw him back.

"Yes," he lied.

Still breathing hard, he muttered words of thanks to them for saving him, started to reach into his pocket to give them what was left of his water-soaked wallet.

Each of them accepted a hundred dollars but no more. "We ain't accepting the money for helping you"—the tall one smiled—"but because our macks expect it."

The two other women nodded. Yablonsky showed them what was left in his wallet, but they still wouldn't take it.

"You gonna need it to get home. Come with us, we'll flag down a taxi for you. Don't be afraid, we ain't gonna yang-yang you."

"You didn't save my life to rob me," Yablonsky said.

One of them said, "We entertain these mob guys all the time. At after-hour joints. Or they come here. When they want to cheat on their mistresses. Mister, if it was one of them that jumped you, I suggest you pack and leave town."

"Or join the Witness Protection Program," the tall one said. Her eyes filled with concern. "Otherwise, you gonna end up compacted in an auto salvage lot or part of a cement column at a construction site. Now get behind us. You look too disreputable to be picked up on your own juice. A cabdriver sees us, he thinks he's gonna get a double-decker sandwich before he finishes his shift. Which family you in, anyway?"

"Flood's," Yablonsky said.

As the cabbie pulled up next to his apartment, the driver looked back at him with disgust. Then he turned on the lights and stared in horror.

Yablonsky silently got out of the cab, throwing some wet bills on the seat as a tip. The driver paid no attention to the bills and showed no interest in Yablonsky's state of being. He was focused on the backseat. "Look at my seat. Look at the stains. How am I supposed to clean them? You couldn't at least be bleeding? Blood's a hell of a lot easier to clean than this."

Turning the key to his lock, he entered his apartment. Someone sat on the sofa, waiting for him. An enemy. "What are you doing here, Arlene?" he asked his ex-wife. "How'd you get in?"

"I spoke to your landlord. He let me in. He doesn't like you, you know."

"They're forming a club for all of the people who don't like me," Yablonsky said. He noticed that she was looking at him. At last she'd noticed the shape he was in. At last there'd be a little compassion. After all, she was his ex-wife.

"I've been waiting here for over an hour," she said. "You're covered with chemicals. There's mud. You're dirty. What the fuck have you been doing, bathing in New Jersey?"

"I was beaten up. Some guys threw me in the Gowanus."

"Detectives don't get beaten up. Knowing you, it's more likely that you slipped."

"Okay, I slipped," he sighed. "Arlene, I'm tired. I need to take a bath, to get all the toxins off me, and to go to sleep. Please tell me why you're here. What's wrong?"

"The focus of everything is always you. I'm here because you don't answer my calls. I'm your ex-wife, but you show no concern."

"I've been busy trying to catch a murderer."

"That's you. Always busy trying to catch murderers. I could fall off the fishing pier in Atlantic City and you wouldn't blink an eye."

"Atlantic City's out of my jurisdiction. Aren't we divorced? Aren't you your husband's responsibility now, you know, the guy you dumped me for?"

She moved toward him. "I've got problems, Alvin. I've got troubles."

He stood before her, dripping yellow ooze on the floor. "You mind if I at least towel off while you complain?"

"You know my husband's been running security for Harrah's now for over two years. Three weeks ago one of the replacement dealers came into the counting room, caught him skimming the skim. Now he wants money. What do we do?"

"Don't go skimming the skim," Yablonsky said.

"Of course he shouldn't have done it," she said, her head twisting slightly with impatience. "That's not the point. What are we supposed to do now?"

"Pay him."

"What the fuck kind of detective are you? If we pay him, he'll only want more."

"Then don't pay him. Your husband'll find other work."

"But not in the casinos. Not after they blacklist him. If they don't dump us both in the ocean first. What should we do?"

"Leave town," he said. "Go on the wing."

She stepped toward him, her face flushing unpleasantly. "What is wrong with you, Alvin? If we pack up and leave town, what kind of life are we gonna have? No more schmoozing with celebrities at all the free shows. No more leased Cadillacs every year. No more parties for high rollers. No more comps at all."

"You shouldn't have jeopardized your lifestyle by skimming money from the casinos."

"That's ancient history. The fucking point is, what do we do now?"

Yablonsky leaned against a stool in his kitchen nook. He tried to think how he could help her. He wasn't angry. He'd seen this kind of childish thinking many times, mostly from criminals. When confronted with their crimes, they tried to weasel out, either holding others responsible for their actions or ignoring the fallout entirely, expecting that the results would all go away simply because they wanted them to. "I need some time to think."

"You're no help at all."

Yablonsky tried to rub away the aches in his elbows from where they'd thrown him in. "You do something, you have to live with the consequences. That's called being an adult, Arlene."

"I am an adult and I don't need lectures, Alvin. Please don't tell me again how we shouldn't have stolen money from the casinos. We weren't stealing. We skimmed from the people who were skimming. And don't fucking remind me about consequences. We know there are consequences. What the fuck do you think we're trying to avoid?"

He stood and sighed. Thank God he had Julie. "Please go, Arlene. I need some time before I can try to help you."

"But we don't have time." She stood, holding her pocketbook before her. "I don't feel guilty about what we did, either. In this country, any dream worth having is worth stealing for. Don't you know that?"

Yablonsky walked ahead of her, leading her to the door. "I guess not. I'm a cop."

She moved toward the door. "I'm gone," she said. "Thanks for the help. You know, I'm glad I used you as my trampoline to get out of Brooklyn. I'm glad I never came back to you. I followed my instincts. Look how you live. By yourself in a basement apartment. According to your landlord, pretty soon you won't even be living here."

"That's probably true."

Two steps closer to the door. "I've read about your affair with that washed-up Warhol whore. You know she's probably gonna dump you."

Never, thought Yablonsky. Just a few more steps and she'd be out.

"You never learned how to dream big. You'll never be a meat-eater like my new husband. I know something about your case. Heard you have contacts with a real mover, Shelly Townes. We know Shelly. He often comes to Atlantic City."

"Before or after they sentenced him to prison?" Yablonsky asked.

"After," she said. "There's so much you can learn from Shelly. He's one in a million."

"What can you tell me about Shelly?"

Near the door now, she turned to look at him incredulously. "You tell me you're not able to help me, yet you expect reciprocity?" She paused. "If you'd been able to get us out of this, I'd have been so grateful. Your loss."

She was out of the door. Was there a suggestion of sex in the air? Sex, but no reconciliation. He remembered. Even at the beginning of their marriage, when things were better between them because of her ambitions for him, he'd felt that being inside her was like being inside a cash box.

He showered and toweled off. Naked, he went back to his living room to go over his mail.

From Irene, there was a letter thanking him for urging her to leave Tito. She was giving him another chance, but wanted to show her gratitude with a gift.

Yablonsky fingered a large gold crucifix. Smiling slightly, he slipped it over his neck. After all, he wasn't ashamed to be a Christian.

He turned on the TV, but lowered the sound. Before he went to sleep he ran the message on his machine. There were a few guttural Brooklynese phrases. "Word on the street is that your reporter was whacked, but not by the guy who owns all them restaurants." The video he saw was a real oldie from the eighties, *I'm in Love with a Working Girl.* He watched as a beautiful smiling working girl tossed her boyfriend into a swimming pool.

The light flashing from the TV disturbed him and he turned it off. Yablonsky, his body bruised, acted and moved like a man in his nineties. Before he blacked out, he remembered that he'd always loved the ocean.

TWENTY-SIX

Yablonsky stood in a field full of weeds in Far Rockaway. The wind that blew in from the beach was cold. The gates that had been padlocked to prevent people from entering Fort Tilden kept no one out. Taking out the photos with one hand and holding dollar bills in another, he moved further into the decaying complex. He wasn't worried about being robbed, because his hand was outstretched in the classic philanthropist's pose: giving out money. Nuclear-tipped missiles had once been kept here. Above a rise, batteries of guns still pointed toward the Atlantic.

Crouching, he slipped through a concrete bunker, saw embers of glowing fires, rolled-up mattresses, and the usual beer bottles. In the flickering light, the detective scanned layer after layer of indecipherable graffiti, all names of people that no one else would ever care about. He gave out dollar bills to the vagrants, shining a flashlight in front of the surveillance photos, but no one knew these people.

Outside, a homeless guy, followed by a German shepherd, wended his way through the tall grass with a shopping cart. He chattered to himself, then to his dog. Yablonsky, stopping the cart, handed him a dollar bill, showed him the photos.

"You ever see any of these people before?"

The guy gave him a lingering look, as if he were the one who was crazy, then negotiated his way through a crevice between the twin gun batteries. The detective left. The trip back to the city took forty-five minutes.

"Come in. Come in."

He stepped through a torn chain-link fence on Fifty-first Street and Eleventh Avenue in Manhattan.

"Have a seat," Eddie Johnson smiled. "Take a load off."

Only one person lived in this lot. Johnson actually had enough furniture to set up a living room and bedroom. Electrical outlets snaked into the Con Ed power lines, so there was even a DeLonghi heater and refrigerator. The place actually looked like a cozy model home. You could walk from one room to another, but the only things missing were walls and a roof.

Eddie Johnson pointed to his patched-up La-Z-Boy. A gracious host, he offered Yablonsky coffee, went to his hot plate to put it on, then brought it back to him. "This'll warm you up."

Sitting on a vinyl rocker, Eddie Johnson spread out his arms expansively. "You like my setup?"

"State of the art, Eddie. Real *Town & Country*."

The derelict pointed to his wall-less, roofless home. "I've been here now for five months. I'm a regular homebody now."

Yablonsky handed him a twenty-dollar bill. "For a rainy day."

"The rain don't bother me," Eddie Johnson said. "I'm putting down roots. People like you drop in here all the time."

"Well, you've always been a hospitable guy, Eddie." He showed him the photo and watched him stare at it for a long time. He handed it back to the detective.

"I know him. Billy. We used to meet in the park. Cup together, then look for deposit cans. Billy's okay."

"Billy who?"

Eddie Johnson was silent. Foolish question, Yablonsky thought. No one had last names on the street. "Does he have a street name?"

"It's just Billy. You're not the only one who came here looking for him."

"Who else is trying to find him?"

"A tall guy with a ponytail."

Roth.

"When did you see Billy last?"

Eddie Johnson looked thoughtful. "I saw him about a month ago, at the recycling center. He said he was scared to live in the park now."

"You're sure about this?"

"I remember because he was acting strange. He had clothes piled up in his shopping cart. Not too many cans. I'm sure the clothes weren't his."

"How do you know they weren't his?"

"Too big. They looked like a big man's clothes. Why you after Billy? What he do?"

"It's not what he did, but what he saw. Can you tell me where he said he was heading, Eddie?"

"Can you hit me with another Jackson?"

Yablonsky handed him a twenty-dollar bill.

"Billy say he gonna try his luck in Brooklyn. But I don't know where he's at."

It felt like everything was pulling together. He scribbled his name and a few complimentary phrases on the back of his business card and handed it to Eddie Johnson. "Next time a cop rousts you, show him this."

Back at the station house, Yablonsky did twenty minutes of paperwork, then studied the model of Central Park again. If the men in the van drove up here, parked here, and Billy was nearby, around this spot, he might have seen the murder. If Billy had somehow stolen Skinny's clothes, that meant the murderers were probably looking for him too. Should he ask Barnes, Yablonsky wondered, with all his homeless contacts, for help? Barnes was still a journalist, and the detective didn't quite trust him to keep the story to himself. It was nearly eight in the morning. He pictured Julie waking up, flinging her bedcovers off her shapely, pale legs. He needed to hear her voice, wanted to remind her that he was having dinner with her at her apartment later tonight.

The phone was picked up on the sixth ring.

"Julie?"

"It's me," said Charlie Kudos. "This the detective?"

"That's right. Charles, what the hell are you doing in her apartment?"

"It's all perfectly innocent. Sully sent me. We're trying to convince her to return to work. What's that tall black cop doing outside her door?"

"Taking a civil rights poll." Yablonsky paused. "He's her bodyguard."

Kudos laughed. "She was only mugged, Detective."

This from an actor who six months ago, along with PETA, had trashed the office of a prominent furrier, and then had repeatedly refused to accept punishment for his vandalism, saying he would choose the type of community service he'd perform. Yablonsky bit his tongue.

"Just let me speak to Julie."

"She can't come to the phone now, Detective, but I'll tell her you called." The actor hung up the phone.

Flood was downstairs in the basement, playing both hands of a two-handed poker game. "I never lose when I'm playing against myself," he said. "What you got for me?"

"I tailed Staples last night, saw him meet with Shelly Townes. The meeting looked interesting, especially since Townes was supposed to be at a halfway house in Long Island City."

Flood shrugged. "Did you overhear anything incriminating during the meeting?"

Yablonsky shook his head. "While I was able to work a tail on Raymond to his meeting place, the Seventy-ninth Street boat basin, I couldn't get close enough to overhear them."

"Who's tailing him now?"

"Patrolwoman Saunders. I spoke with her half an hour ago." Yablonsky smiled. "Since our chief suspect expected it'd be me doing the tail, we had someone else do the surveillance." He paused. "When I take over tonight, I'll be doing a front tail."

"Watch yourself, Alvin. Yesterday I got calls about you from the mayor's office. They want me to put another detective on the investigation. You're handling a high-profile murder investigation and a high-profile girlfriend. I read about you and her in the papers a couple of times a week now. You're a celebrity now," he said, "Soon you'll have lots of people besides I.A. stalking you."

"No one's stalking me." Except for the people who threw him into the Gowanus, he thought.

At six in the evening, he rang the bell of Julie's brownstone apartment on Barrow Street in the West Village, then let himself in.

She was waiting for him on top of the landing. When she'd been friends with Warhol and had posed for magazine covers and posters, she modeled the most sensational and avant-garde clothes in the country. Now she wore simple tight-fitting black stretch pants and a white blouse, her small breasts swelling underneath. To him, she was one of the most elegant, desirable women he'd ever seen.

She tried to kiss him, but he pulled away.

"Alvin. You look terrible. Haven't been going for any midnight swims, have you?"

"How the hell did you know about that?" *Was she fucking Kudos or not?*

"After Skinny's murder, I inherited most of his sources. One of them called me a couple of hours after it happened." There was a pause. Then she sprang gracefully to her feet. "What else is wrong? I tried phoning you last night. Several times. But you were always busy."

After listening to his phone messages, he'd taken the phone off the hook. He followed her into the dining room, which was still full of Skinny's award-winning articles and exposés. Now some of her articles appeared on the walls too. Sitting across from her he said, "Luckily for me I know how to swim. When I called here this morning, Charlie Kudos answered the phone."

"He was trying to convince me to go back to the newspaper. That's all."

"Kudos is famous. I'm not. He goes through other people's lives like a wrecking ball. I don't. The same time you've been sleeping with me, you've been fucking him. You're a whore, Julie."

She gripped his arm. "I told you I loved you. Don't you break up with me."

He looked at her, laughed bitterly. "You used to sleep with two guys at the same time. Plenty of times."

"Not any more."

"Not any more."

She started to cry. He hesitated, then reached for her. She led him to her bedroom. He watched her undress and they made love.

Sprawled on the bed naked, she reached for the remote and flicked on the TV. "It's better than having a cigarette," she said.

Yablonsky smoked, even though this habit was usually reserved for corpse viewing. He may have fucked her, but he was still steamed.

The phone rang. She reached for it absentmindedly, then looked alert and alarmed, motioning for him to stay.

"Yes, Mom," she said. "I know who this is." She paused. "Why should I see him now? Of course I care that he's sinking. But I really can't come now, Mom. I can't face it. I'm sure I'll get a pre-death apology from him for being such a shitty father. I understand that it will be help-ful, at least for him, so he can die in peace. But I still have to go on. Did he go to Tommy's funeral? When I called about Jimmy, begging him to come east, to help Jimmy when they found him wandering around naked in Central Park, I'll never forget what he said. 'Calm down,' he said. 'We're not coming. It'll upset your mother.' Well, now it's his turn."

She paced back and forth slowly, holding the phone. "Well, that's you, Mom, not me. I could never be loyal to a man who treated me with so much contempt. I know he's in the hospital. Every other time he was in Cedars, he made sure to sleep with practically every nurse he could get his hands on." She paused, listening, her voice lowered with resignation. "Yes, I know he's my father. I also knew he was my father at the ranch when my girlfriends told me he was coming on to them. And I knew he was my father when he ridiculed my 'forever girlish' figure. He always seemed pissed that I was his daughter and not a potential girlfriend." Her voice lowered as she forced calm. "Maybe he's *not* the reason I'm so fucked up, Mom, but he's the reason I think I'm so fucked up. I don't need closure. I don't need to forgive him for Jimmy and Tommy. He doesn't deserve it." Click. She hung up.

She turned to him, looking frightened. "Where the fuck do you think you're going?"

"I have to take over the surveillance of my chief suspect in Skinny's murder."

Her face flushed with anger. "First you start a fight with me. Then we ball. Now you're gonna leave me. No, motherfucker. You're going to stay with me. All through the fucking night."

With this woman, emotion was being drained from him like a Duracell. "I'm going on the job, Julie. I can't stay."

Fear crept into her voice. "Please don't leave, Alvin. I'm afraid of what I'll do to myself if I'm alone."

"I have to go, Julie."

"You're running out on me, Alvin? You too?" She sank on the couch. "Go ahead. Make tracks. Do the usual male thing. Leave and take everything with you when you do it, including your fingerprints."

He was already late to relieve Saunders. "I'll stay with you for a while, but then I've got to go."

She stood, marched over to the dining room, poured herself a drink, then watched the decanter crash to the floor. He looked at her, barefoot and surrounded by shards of glass.

"And that's just the beginning of what I'll do to myself if you don't stay. You're staying for as long as I need you. *Don't you go.*"

He took a deep breath. "I won't."

At two a.m., he pulled away from her. She was sleeping. It was safe to leave. Writing a note reassuring her that he loved her, he said he'd be back some time earlier this morning. He'd certainly try.

He slipped into his pants and shoes, then out the door. Henderson sat in a chair outside her apartment. "You're a rock, Wendell."

Henderson put down his wallet, opened to photos of his kids. "Where you going now, Detective?"

"Surveillance. I'm meeting Saunders. When does your shift end?"

"In two hours. Double A's relieving me. Then it's home to the wife and kids. Of course my kids'll be in school. Alice and me'll be able to have a late breakfast together."

Yablonsky'd seen photos of Henderson's kids before. "You have a nice family to go home to, Wendell. Good night."

Yablonsky sipped his cup of coffee and watched Staples leave the Flatbush Diner, a restaurant in the West Fifties in Manhattan that he'd just bought and was refurbishing. The lights inside and outside the diner went off. Raymond dismissed the foreman and the non-union construction crew.

Staples was alone. He walked over to his limo. Yablonsky observed him getting into the driver's side of the car. So far the incidents Clements had witnessed had been nonincriminatory. Yablonsky wondered where Staples would go.

Staples drove his car for a block along Eleventh Avenue before the detective started to follow. Now that it was dark, there was no need to do a front tail. Raymond stopped the car next to an all-night Cuban bodega on Fifty-Sixth Street, came out of the store carrying two humidors of cigars.

Raymond got back into his car. The light changed. Yablonsky followed, now two blocks behind. To his left stood foreign auto repair shops. To his right were the hidden rumbling bridges and culverts of the no-longer-used railroad cargo stations.

Raymond continued to drive along the city's edge. Although it was late at night there was still lots of traffic. The limo drove by Staples's printing plant on Eleventh Avenue, the same place where Skinny had been killed, then past the giant multi-apartment complexes of Lincoln Towers. Yablonsky glimpsed thousands of lit windows and terraces. The limo drove on.

Up ahead, Staples turned left onto Seventy-second Street, then right at the next fork, heading toward Riverside Park. The limo slowed, braked, then turned into the underground parking lot of the boat basin, just as Yablonsky knew it would.

The detective parked by a hydrant, then got out of the car.

Staples walked through the underground parking lot, down the steps, across the path, and to the barbed-wire fence separating the boat basin from the park. Rivulets of stored-up rainwater splashed down from the roof of the parking lot, running across the amphitheater's steps, resembling an urban waterfall.

A man came down the steps. His footsteps and the rhythm of his walking weren't regular. Whoever was meeting Raymond was struggling to keep his balance on the slippery, smooth surface of the concrete steps. At night, an aisle of streetlights lit the promenade, but the rest of Riverside Park was in fog.

Staples's voice, low and cautious. Shelly Townes's voice, friendly and relaxed.

They moved to the promenade, elbows leaning over the wooden seawall that separated the park and city from the Hudson River, New Jersey, and the rest of America.

Yablonsky decided to remain where he was, out of sight, ten yards away from the two men. The tones were distinct, the words less so.

This was not a meeting between antagonists. The voices were earnest, but mostly in agreement. Shelly's hands were everywhere, pointing to the park, the empty construction site, across to New Jersey, then expansively to the rest of Manhattan. Staples's voice, still too low for the detective to make out, spoke cajolingly, almost pleadingly. The voices rose and fell, almost in synch with the rhythm of the cracking river ice.

They conferred for another ten minutes. Staples pulled away.

"So you're with me on this, Shell?"

"All the way."

Raymond left. Yablonsky waited, watching him briskly climb the steps, a hell of a lot more surefooted than the fumbling ex-borough president.

Yablonsky heard Staples's limo start up, but remained where he was, continuing his surveillance, but with Townes now as the target. There was no need to follow Raymond anymore tonight, he thought. Everything was going his way. At last he'd made some right decisions. He was not surprised at their clandestine meeting; he'd expected it. His chief suspect was ready to be taken in.

He continued using the trees for cover, waiting for Shelly to leave. Why the hell wasn't he?

Inside the underground parking lot, a car pulled up. He shifted as quietly as he could and moved behind another grove of trees. The car door opened. Another set of footsteps moved down the path.

"Looking motherfucking good, Shelly."

"You too."

TWENTY-SEVEN

Inside Sully Barnes's East Village apartment, workers conducted a small clinic, handing disposable needle packs to addicts, urging them to throw away the needles once they'd shot up so they wouldn't get AIDS, then leading them to two card tables, cajoling them to eat steaming bowls of chicken stew.

In the living room were piles of winter coats, gloves, and blankets. People rushed through the hall on their way to carry out errands. A couple of homeless people emerged from one of the rooms, adjusting new pairs of gloves. An addict cursed softly as he waited to be handed his needle pack so he could go outside on the steps and have his fix.

"I'm listening to you people, man," he chanted. "Ain't sharing no spike, but I'm hungry and it's hard."

Piles of unwashed dishes lay scattered on an old wooden dining table in the kitchen. There were no carpets, hardly any furniture. People slept in rolled-up blankets on the floor. The walls were decorated with Basquiat-like graffiti slogans and posters urging middle-class people to donate clothes and money. Half a dozen homeless men lay sprawled on cots in a small bedroom. The smell of unwashed people permeated the apartment.

Sully, sitting behind one of the card tables, smiled when he spotted Yablonsky, stood, and came over to him. Behind him was Charlie Kudos. Adjusting his Brooklyn Dodger baseball cap so the brim was backwards, Barnes said, "It's good to seee you again, Kojak. You said you wanted to see me. Let's get the fuck out of here."

"But you told me to meet you at your apartment," Yablonsky said.

"You actually think I'd live in this fucking place? Let's drive uptown to where I really live."

Kudos, edging closer to Barnes, said, "You sure you don't want me to come with you?"

"Don't worry, I can handle it," said Barnes, then guided him back through the makeshift needle-dispensing center and food shelter. Kudos followed, a concerned look on his face.

"Sully . . ."

"Can it."

In the car, Sully said, "I've got to explain about the apartment. The lease is in my name, but about a year ago, it became impossible to live there. You've seen the filth and the chaos. I'd go nuts if I stayed there."

"Hey, I understand," said Yablonsky. "You live where you can afford to."

"You'll keep this quiet, won't you? I don't need any more bad publicity."

Yablonsky was surprised, because as far as he knew the media worshiped Barnes. Already most networks and news organizations had promised prime coverage of his upcoming hunger strike. The talking heads all seemed glad he was taking on Raymond. The few articles that criticized Barnes's social policy of coming into a neighborhood, opening food shelters, and dispensing needles were either spiked or received scant coverage. If there were ever casualties because of Barnes's social activities, they didn't usually make the papers.

Yablonsky, leaning forward in his seat, asked, "Where are we going?"

"Just take the West Side Highway. Drive uptown."

At last the precinct had come through for him and had given him a car.

Yablonsky continued uptown. On their left was the Hudson River and the Palisades. Across from them was the small neighborhood of Spuyten Duyvil, the devil's spit.

Driving over the bridge, Yablonsky looked at the ball fields and the cliffs, the last things you saw when leaving Manhattan. Making a left and crossing the parkway, they entered a world of rolling hills, country clubs, and Tudor houses. Mist drifted up from the river. Yablonsky passed a one-pump gas station.

Barnes lived in a narrow pseudo-French chateau just off the road. "The top half is mine," he said. "The landlord hasn't raised me yet, probably because I'm such an important person." He added quickly, "I'm kidding, of course. Maybe he's waiting to be invited to one of my testimonial dinners."

"Or maybe he's hoping to put in a plaque saying that you lived here."

Barnes laughed. Yablonsky pulled his car off the road in front of the cottage. Further down, at the end of the road, were tracks and a train station. "When I take it, I'm in the city in half an hour."

"Convenient," Yablonsky said.

Barnes's apartment was decorated with Sixties leftovers from the *Guardian.* Posters from Fillmore East and every rock concert of the era except Woodstock hung on his living room walls.

Barnes motioned for him to sit on the couch. He remained standing. "You're probably wondering why I didn't hang anything up from the Woodstock festival. Because when I was there, I hated Woodstock. Woodstock was about money, not music."

Yablonsky was silent. Barnes threw his baseball cap on a chair and said, "All the rumors of Peter Townshend of the Who smacking me on the head with his guitar are untrue. It never happened."

Yablonsky, who was sitting a hundred feet away from the stage and had seen it happen, said, "I'm sure the stories are baseless. But I've got to ask you some questions, Sully."

"Okay, Detective, ask away."

"Why'd you meet with Shelly Townes last night?"

The smile vanished. "How'd you know? I wasn't meeting with Townes. Were you tailing me?"

"I was tailing Raymond. First Raymond met with Shelly. Then Shelly met with you. Why?"

"Let me get this fucking straight," said Barnes. "You're asking me to account for my actions? You expect me to come clean about why I met with a known felon?"

"You got it," said Yablonsky.

"Isn't this taking you away from your murder investigation, Detective? It shouldn't matter, you know, that Townes was a felon. At one time, Alvin, I was a fucking felon."

"I agree. It shouldn't matter. So why'd you meet with him?"

"Okay. I realize you're a motherfucking cop first."

"Don't ever forget that, Sully."

"Shelly and I met to make a deal. When he comes out of prison, he wants to get back into politics. But because of the conviction, it'll have to be from behind the scenes. He's already handpicked the guy he wants to succeed him. Bobby Clavern, a guy who's not even backed by the borough party machine. What does he get from me? A promise to canvass and raise money for him."

"What do you get from him?"

"What I get from Shelly and his friend are additional shelters and clinics in Brooklyn. Most communities oppose us when we come in. They'd have to be nuts not to. When we come into a neighborhood, the violence increases. The people who live there get to see lots of new urban landmarks, like winos staggering in the street and urine puddles. Their kids have to be careful not to stick their hands in garbage cans or they'll pull them out stuck with needles."

"Why help these people at all, then?"

"Because no one else will. Now tell me, Detective, are you fucking finished with me?"

"Almost," said Yablonsky. Peeking at Sully's partially open desk drawer next to him, he asked, "Why do you keep a gun in your apartment?"

"Every goddamned celebrity in this country has at least one stalker, Alvin. And I don't wear blinders. I know that some of the people we help are violent and it scares me. Some of them know where I live. I'm a street guy, right? Any of these crazy motherfuckers breaks into my apartment, I'll blow them to kingdom come."

That's exactly how most communities feel about Barnes and his derelicts, Yablonsky thought, but he was silent.

"Also," Sully said, "this is a wealthy neighborhood. There are always burglaries."

"I thought you didn't believe in capital punishment, Sully," the detective said. "I thought you believed in rehabilitation."

"I believe in self-defense. Just the fact that you're questioning me is embarrassing. Why don't you take my gun over to your ballistics people? Have them check it out. Then you can dismiss me as a suspect."

"You're not a suspect," Yablonsky said quickly, not wanting Barnes to line up his powerful political and media allies against him. "I only had to clear up a few questions. Now you know why I sometimes hate my job."

"Now you know why I sometimes don't like cops."

"I know that in this city there's always an interconnecting web of relationships between people. Sometimes street derelicts bump up against tycoons. Nobel Peace Prize winners meet with convicted felons. But you've got to be more careful who you're seen with, Sully."

"From now on, I will be, Detective."

TWENTY-EIGHT

T he *Guardian*'s records room consisted of long rows of metal shelving, the middle shelf containing the label of the month and year of back issues.

Ignoring the boxes of microfiche reels, Yablonsky and Henderson focused on issues from the past decade. Starting with the oldest issues first, Yablonsky methodically went through each weekly, skimming over "Press Clips," photos of club kids who'd died from overdosing, first on speed, then ecstasy, then cocaine. There was a full-color spread in the usually black-and-white newspaper of the annual Village Halloween march which started at Washington Square Park and ended up at Christopher and Gay Street. He saw a reveler dressed as a four-cornered table. Other participants were costumed as court jesters, clowns, and gigantic garden tools.

Earlier he'd parked his car in the precinct parking lot, and when he'd come out, some other cop had commandeered the vehicle and it was gone. He was no longer surprised at having his car stolen, least of all by a cop.

Sipping cups of coffee, they went from one shelf to another, returning to the table with stacks of back issues, then looking through them all.

"This is drudgery," said Henderson.

"It's better than being on the street."

"Was that what your career as a cop was like?"

"My career as a cop consisted mostly of showing up late at crime scenes."

Henderson laughed. In the March issue of an old *Guardian,* he saw an article about the proper techniques of sadomasochistic sex. "You've got to see these photos, Alvin."

Yablonsky stared at some of the more inventive positions, shook his head. "My ex-wife said I had no imagination."

"That's probably why she's your ex-wife."

Yablonsky leafed through more issues. There were articles about the dangers posed to Greenwich Village by encroaching developers, an article by Skinny detailing the mob links of the midtown convention center. Yablonsky stared at the byline, wondering what other corruption Skinny would have exposed had he lived. Occasionally he read Julie's obituaries. No matter what the subject's accomplishments, she wrote about them in the same flat, unimpressed tone, as if maybe she expected they would actually die again.

Wendell Henderson put down a three-year-old July issue. "Alvin. Bingo."

Every issue of the paper had been complete, but in this issue, someone had scissored away a column from the "Press Clips" section.

Yablonsky went to a projector, looking up the date on microfiche. Again, this was the only page of information missing.

"Let's log the date and year of the column," Yablonsky said. "We'll visit the other newspapers. Maybe we'll be lucky and find out what's been deleted. Once we know what, maybe we'll know why."

Yablonsky had already talked about the missing microfiche. He put the article he'd found in the "Metro" section of *The New York Times* away. It detailed how Shelly Townes, Dollars Dillon, and Sully Barnes had purchased one of the most expensive tables together at a fund-raiser for the former head of the Taxi and Limousine Commission, who was now running for Congress. The story stated that the trio had become friends several years back when Judge Dillon was at the beginning of his career, trying cases at taxi court.

Across the East River, the scattered factories of Long Island City beamed their lights. The two men leaned against the promenade. "There's Shelly's halfway house, Sully," Yablonsky said. "You think he's safely tucked into bed at last?"

"Knowing Shelly, he's probably renting a suite at the Waldorf, partying the night away with his security guards."

"Exactly," said Yablonsky. "Knowing Shelly." Beyond the promenade stood the last great land edge between the East River and the Atlantic Ocean. All of Long Island stretched before them in shadows, scattered lights, and fog. Barnes returned the photo of Dollars, Townes, and himself, taken at the fund-raiser.

How well did he know Dollars Dillon?

"Not well at all." The three men were relaxed. Their eyes were unguarded. They'd socialized or done business with each other before.

What was he doing the night McPherson was murdered?

"What night was Skinny murdered?"

"December twenty-third." He'd been at home, by himself. Hadn't he been concerned when Skinny failed to call or report in afterward? Barnes had assumed the reporter had been working on a story and had left town to interview sources.

"I can't believe you're still questioning me," said Barnes. "Do you believe I'm involved in these murders?"

"I'll stop questioning you when I get some answers."

Later, at Barnes's hunger strike in front of Raymond Staples's La Parisienne restaurant, Yablonsky saw Barnes leave and come back with another cup of coffee.

Good idea, Yablonsky thought. He got out of the cab and walked past York and First Avenue, away from the TV cameras.

On Second Avenue, a car slowed down next to him.

The door opened. From inside he glimpsed Deputy Mayor "Hey" Abbott, accompanied by his friend from Internal Affairs, Sparrow Smith. The detective instinctively backed away.

"Get in."

Yablonsky sat between the two men. The limo moved south down Second Avenue, away from the demonstration.

"Have a cigarette?" said Deputy Mayor Abbott. "We already know you smoke."

"Take the pack," said Smith.

"No thanks," said Yablonsky. "A pack is something offered to a guy who's about to be executed."

"Nobody's going to execute you," said Deputy Commissioner Abbott.

"If you play ball," said Sparrow Smith.

"Where are you taking me?"

"On a cruise to nowhere," said Sparrow Smith.

Yablonsky stared at the driver's mirror, studying the two burly men. Smith looked like a teamster. Deputy Commissioner Abbott, though strictly white collar, resembled an ex-college football player who'd been drinking six-packs for a couple of decades.

"We're not gonna keep you long," said Sparrow Smith. "Ever since we met after Roth's murder, I've felt you're a pretty bright guy. But being too bright sometimes benefits no one, least of all yourself. There are ways for you to help yourself that a guy like you, a street cop, is not even aware of yet. We already know the major part you played in Roth's death, which we're willing to overlook."

"If anything, I tried to stop it," said Yablonsky. "What's the quid pro quo?"

"There's no quid pro quo at all, strictly speaking," Deputy Major Abbott said. "This investigation you're on, pursuing it helps no one."

"Sometimes there's no point in finding out who murdered who," said Sparrow Smith. "Sometimes it's better to stet it, forget it, and go on. We're both taking the time to advise you. Rein yourself in."

"I understand," said Yablonsky. "Why not take me off this case? Tell everyone I was removed because of my deficient skills."

"This case has been a stinker from the start," said Deputy Mayor Abbott. "We get rid of you, we look like fools. Eventually the media will forget about the murder, but right now they're still giving it column space."

"Which is unfair if you ask me," said Sparrow Smith. "They wouldn't give a rat's fuck if an ordinary citizen was murdered in Central Park." He paused. "They're elitists. Not street guys, like you and me. A street guy always knows when it's in his best interest to bend a little. To compromise."

Should he use what he had on "Hey" Abbott—his afternoon bondage breaks? Not yet. "The mayor said to solve the murder regardless of which doors are opened," said Yablonsky.

"Unlock any doors you want," said Deputy Mayor Abbott. "Just don't open them."

"Assign an additional team," suggested Yablonsky. "Gradually let them take the case away from me."

"We thought about that. But we want this to fade away and die, not get reinvigorated by another team. The fewer detectives who know about this, the better it will be for all of us. Of course we want you to solve it, as long as you keep away from the people you're interrogating." He paused. "That's one fucking dead end."

"In other words," said Sparrow Smith, "pursue as many leads as you can find, Detective, as long as they're different from the ones you're pursuing now."

"I like Sully," Yablonsky said. "I was as protective of him as anyone else was until I began to interrogate him."

"No need to show off by mentioning names," said Smith. "Sometimes the most skilled and appreciated detective is the one who knows when not to probe, who not to ask. Sometimes that's the best way to clear a case."

"How can a case be cleared if I refuse to solve it?"

"It's solved when the people above you are satisfied with the results," said the deputy mayor. "It's solved by a refusal to dog an icon when he insists he's innocent. We trust him. Our assurances should be enough. Your case is solved because you survived."

"I want to survive."

"We want you to survive too," said "Hey" Abbott. "But you can't be expected to if your investigation makes some people nervous. What we're going for is a simple change in your methodology. Most murder cases are solved within twenty-four hours or they're never cleared anyway."

"I was making progress," said Yablonsky.

"You don't make progress by shutting down the top social activist in the city. When a detective becomes a threat to the best people in the city, it's time for him to retire."

"You mean Sully?"

"Hey" Abbott nodded. "And he's not the only one. There are big bucks at stake here. One of the two main political parties in New York can't have a loose cannon shooting off his mouth and harassing one of their biggest earners, a guy who's definitely innocent. And that's the thing. He's definitely innocent."

"How do I know unless I investigate?"

"Investigate all you want, just not him. Look at it from his point of view. For reasons known only to yourself, you've decided to zone in on him. Once word of this gets out, his reputation's ruined. His reputation supersedes any evidence that you might believe you have. His reputation should be enough to eliminate him as a suspect."

"What do I do about the media?" Yablonsky asked. "One of McPherson's exposés uncovered police corruption in my precinct."

"The media doesn't enter into it. If you sidetrack this case, you safeguard your precinct."

The car slowed at the corner of Second and Eighth. "You followed me during my meeting with Sully, didn't you?" Yablonsky asked. What was worse? Being tailed or not even knowing it?

"If you're a smart guy, you won't have to see us ever again," said "Hey" Abbott. "Not about this case. Not about Roth. Retire with honors in a couple of years, open your own restaurant, step in as chief of se-curity for Raymond Staples. All with our blessing."

The driver pulled further down the street and stopped for Yablonsky to get out.

"Of course we're gonna keep watching you for a while," said Sparrow Smith. "Until we're sure you can be trusted to run your investigation the way it should be run. Get the message?"

Yablonsky closed the limo door. "Like a telegram."

Across the street from Sully's demonstration, Yablonsky, still inside the taxi and aware he was probably being tailed, waited.

The dead of night. No glamorous cameras, no glitzy media or admir-ing crowds. The middle-aged woman Barnes had offered a blanket and cigarette to began to cough, then sob. Sully knelt. Yablonsky heard him say, "Don't go pussy on me, Sheila. Hang in there."

The woman coughed again, rolled herself up in the woolen blanket. Barnes and his assistants went back and forth to the van, lugging used coats and pairs of boots. The people sleeping between the damp carpets were awakened, handed woolen blankets and boots.

Sully and his assistants made rounds, stealing over the Manhattan Bridge to Brooklyn, pulling up next to an approach ramp near Henry Street. Before the detective signaled his driver to dim the headlights, he glimpsed people sleeping under the ramp. The van made a few more stops before Yablonsky followed it back to the site of Sully's hunger strike. Before he and Kudos joined the derelicts once again, Barnes turned the lone TV camera still out on the street around so it was once again focused on him.

On the corner of Mulberry and Crosby, off Houston, stood a church.

Yablonsky turned onto the street and walked through the iron gate. He knew that the parish priests kept the church open twenty-four hours a day for their congregation, who were mostly street people. Yablonsky walked past two reproductions of Michelangelo's *Pietà*. The church was a different denomination from his own, but he didn't think God would mind.

He entered a pew in the back, sat next to Deputy Police Commissioner Michael Lascari and Precinct Commander Larry Flood.

"Why this place?" asked Flood.

"We'd know immediately if I.A. came in, so they have to stay outside. It's like our sanctuary."

"Give us the latest," said Lascari.

"On the McPherson murder?"

"On I.A.'s investigation of us."

"They said if I kept away from Barnes they wouldn't lay Skinny's murder off on us. Essentially, I'm supposed to shelve my investigation."

"Do you think he's guilty?"

"As soon as I start investigating Barnes, I get pressure to stop."

"Don't shelve it," said Deputy Police Commissioner Lascari. "I don't trust them."

"Once we give them what they want, cops are going to fall like clay pigeons," said Flood.

"We still want you as the primary detective. We know you won't bend under their pressure. Just remember you're one of us. No matter what they promise, don't fuck this up. We're going uptown. Need a ride?"

"I'm staying," said Yablonsky.

"What for?" said Flood.

After they left, Yablonsky sank to his knees, clasping his hands before him. Looking up, he saw giant sheets of stained-glass windows depicting famous biblical scenes. He bowed his head, thinking, What should I do?

"Help me," he whispered. "Guide me."

TWENTY-NINE

In daylight, Yankee Stadium looked golden. Milo drove Yablonsky by the bodegas on River Avenue. There was a homeless encampment near Orchard Beach that the detective wanted to search.

"See, Detective? No phony meters today. No zapping. I've turned over a new leaf."

Yablonsky smiled. Milo slipped through the red light on 175th, slowed, and pulled a gun. "Hand over your Glock, Alvin. Slow and careful."

Yablonsky opened his coat and let Milo take his gun away from him.

"From what I've heard, you don't even carry a drop gun."

"What the fuck?"

Milo didn't even glance at him, focusing instead on the potholed road down toward the Willis Avenue Bridge in the Bronx.

"How deep in Skinny's murder are you?"

"Deep," Milo said.

"Skinny's killing is shitcanned. I'm no threat."

"And you're not gonna be."

"The case is done, Milo. I won't touch it."

"I pulled a gun," said Milo. "Now I got to use it. Tell you what. I won't expect a tip."

"No one on top wants me to solve this fucking case, Milo. I get the message. I give up."

"Not you," sighed Milo.

"You can't murder me," said Yablonsky. "You shouldn't even have pulled a gun. Internal Affairs is tailing us."

Milo's eyes shifted out the driver's mirror. "Not anymore."

"They were on me earlier," said Yablonsky. "They saw me get into your cab."

Yablonsky felt actual physical pain sitting there. He winced, imagining the bullet already burning its way into his brain. He had to keep from freezing up.

"But why? I said I'd play ball?"

"I know you. Sooner or later you'd come back to the case. I may be small-time, but I've got to protect myself."

"What're you protecting? You could cut me in."

Milo shook his head. "You're hopeless. I've been watching you for over a month now, and you still haven't learned how to lie. Look out the fucking windshield. The reason I gotta whack you is staring you in the face."

Yablonsky stared out the windshield, at the cab's hood. "I don't see anything."

"You wouldn't," said Milo.

The car lurched forward. Yablonsky braced against the dashboard for a turn. They were under the El now, on River Avenue, not far from Yankee Stadium. Yablonsky figured Milo was driving to the industrial area near the Hutchinson River Parkway. A chill went through him. It was a good place to commit a murder.

Outside, the streets were deserted. The seasonal businesses around the stadium were shut down and gated.

"That photo with the article I found in *The Times*," Yablonsky said, "of Sully, Shelly, and Judge Dillon. You were at the table with them." Why hadn't he noticed it before?

Milo swiveled his head, smiling. "I introduced them to each other, along with Dollars."

Yablonsky stared at the road. "Don't kill me, Milo."

"Don't worry. Once the bullet's in, it doesn't hurt as much. Back in Russia I saw plenty of guys killed. The thinking about the bullet is much worse than the bullet itself."

Yablonsky glanced peripherally at the gun. It was pointed low, difficult for drivers passing by to spot. If he tried to grab it, chances were, he'd get shot in the thigh.

He did nothing.

Under the El, Milo ran a few red lights. Ahead, a huge truck slowly pulled into the intersection. The light changed. Milo slammed on the brakes and swerved, and Yablonsky threw his hands to the dashboard to brace himself. Milo's eyes darted from the truck to the road. Yablonsky slipped his left hand under the cigarette lighter. He made a show of shifting back in his seat, waiting for the lighter to pop out. Milo quickly glanced at him and returned his eyes to the road. The detective dropped his left hand and pressed the glowing lighter into the cabdriver's thigh.

Milo screamed. Yablonsky lunged to his left, snagging the gun with one hand and grinding the lighter into Milo's cheek with the other.

He screamed again. Yablonsky smashed his foot on the brake, slowing the car down, and trying to guide the car with his left hand. The cab jumped wildly. Milo lurched back and forth, as Yablonsky yanked the car to the curb, grazed a fire hydrant, and finally ground to a stop.

Yablonsky exhaled, leveled the gun on Milo. "Now the shoe is on the other foot," he said. "Give me back my gun. Slow and careful."

Milo reached into his pocket. Yablonsky, lowering his aim toward Milo's groin, took back his Glock. Then the detective backhanded him in the mouth with it and clubbed him over the head. "Talk!"

Yablonsky holstered the pistol. Cops had long since discovered that in the line of duty, the Glock was notoriously unreliable. It was much safer to use a perp's gun against him.

"I need a handkerchief," Milo gasped.

"Fuck you," said Yablonsky. "Bleed and talk."

"I don't know anything."

Yablonsky rose slightly and smashed his head with the gun. "I don't know anything either. Talk."

Milo wiped his forehead and pulled his hand away, staring in shock at the blood. "You're not this brutal, Alvin."

Yablonsky pointed the gun between Milo's legs, shot low, and missed his testicles by a couple of inches.

Milo jumped and his face turned white. He screamed, scrambling to-ward the driver's window, back as far as he could go.

"I was aiming for your leg," the detective said. "You're lucky I missed. I'm not a very good shot."

Blood dripped from Milo's skull and beaded in the corner of his mouth, dribbling down his chin. "If you're interested, you'll be one of the richest men in the city."

"I'm interested. Talk."

"I never murdered anyone. I was trying to scare you."

"Not even Skinny?" said Yablonsky. "Why'd you want to kill me?"

"What's in it for me?"

Lowering the gun, Yablonsky said, "Your balls."

Inching away, Milo said, "You can't kill me. You're a cop."

"I haven't been a cop for that long," Yablonsky said. "That fund-raiser for the Taxi and Limo commissioner who was running for office? The one where you introduced Sully, Shelly, and that judge to each other. Tell me about it."

"I was just about to get to it. Can't you drop the gun? I'm on your side now."

"The gun stays where it is. What'd the four of you cook up?"

"I told you, it's staring you in the face."

Yablonsky glanced again through the windshield at the car hood. No phony stocks. No bags of money. No inflated real estate lease statements with under-the-table kickbacks. No drugs. If Skinny was murdered to cover up the usual urban corruption, the motive was still invisible.

"Fleet owner medallions," Milo said.

"Taxi medallions? What's that, the blue-collar version of a seat on the Stock Exchange?"

"That's right. How'd you like to hook up to a market that always goes up, never goes down? What if you outlawed all sales of new stock in the stockmarket and were only allowed to buy and sell old shares? The value of those shares would skyrocket because their scarcity would make them so valuable."

"Go on." Yablonsky lit a cigarette.

Blood flecked off Milo's lower lip as he smiled. "Look, Shelly and I go way back. When I was hacking in Brooklyn, I used to run him over to the Court Street restaurants, where he'd sit in Nick and Tony's Pizzeria schmoozing with the politicians and judges. One day he went to see Dollars Dillon, and instead of taking his tip with a 'thank-you' and a smile, I followed him in and sat in their booth. Townes was shocked, but I felt like I'd come up with something that would keep me at their table. So I told them my scheme. Shelly was pissed. He said in all his years as a politician, he'd never even thought of it. He kept saying, 'It's so fucking easy.' And Dillon said, 'All great scams are essentially easy.' " Milo paused. "So while the initial idea was mine, Shelly had to put everything together."

Resting his hands on the steering wheel, he said, "You see, when the Taxi and Limousine Commission was allowed to set up its exchange and broker their commodity, it received a variance that would almost guarantee that the article of commerce would never go down in value. It would always rise."

Milo finished his story and Yablonsky sat back, stubbing out his cigarette. "How was Skinny set up?"

"Skinny was whacked on one of the weekends when the other guy was at the halfway house. All the murders were done like that."

"The other guy?"

"Shelly."

"You said *all* the murders?"

"The clerk who arranged the calendar so Judge Dillon would preside over Shelly's trial had to go. So did Dollars."

Yablonsky vaguely recalled the case. A law clerk was found in his apartment with a plastic bag over his head. Everyone had assumed it was a suicide. There'd even been a note.

"Give me the mechanics."

"They were actually two teamsters, newspaper deliverymen who drove vans, middle-aged guys associated with the Genoveses, the Mafia family that runs Jersey. They were just gangster wanna-bes, too smart to risk being picked up for illegally carrying a gun during a shakedown. Townes had to hold the gun for them, then go with them to finger each vic. After all, who's gonna pat down a white-collar criminal?"

"How'd they lure Skinny to the uptown office?"

"Two days before the murder, they called McPherson, told him that someone wanted to meet with him about his exposé on the taxi cab industry."

"What time were they supposed to meet?"

"When most reporters meet their sources, at night, around ten. They called Skinny at his apartment a few hours before to confirm the meeting. Since the uptown printing plant has a skeletal staff, the parking garage is almost always empty. They met him outside, then led him into the garage.

"We weren't pros," Milo admitted. "After we killed Skinny, everything went wrong. We stripped his clothes, his wallet, and notepad, and left them in the car to dispose of later. That was a mistake. We must've dropped him a million times on the way into the park. Luckily the storm covered our tracks. Two fucking hours covering him up in the blinding blizzard. We even screwed that up, too. The weather changed. Then you found him." Milo twisted his head away from the detective. "We got back to my cab and realized no one had locked their doors. The clothes and wallet were gone. Someone had rooted around there. They could have seen us. Who else would be out on a night like that? It had to be the homeless. Who else would steal his fat fucking clothes?"

Billy. Yablonsky looked away from his new stool pigeon. So far he had misinterpreted or misunderstood almost everything. One thing he knew: He had to find Billy first. But how?

"After we dumped Skinny, I drove to an all-night cab stand and the four of us split up."

"So Dollars wasn't with you," said Yablonsky.

"Dollars was somewhere in Florida, busy partying in his condo."

"Where'd the other men go?"

Milo paused, glanced at the gun, and told him.

"There's a guard at the halfway house," said Yablonsky. "Wouldn't he have noted the time of Shelly's entry?"

"Think about it. If security in a maximum security prison is lax enough to allow inmates, visitors, or guards to smuggle in drugs and shanks, then imagine a halfway house. All the shift guards are his friends."

"So he bribed them," said Yablonsky. "Where'd you go?"

"After we finished up with Skinny, my job was to go to his apartment, erase the incriminating tape confirming their meeting, and dispose of his Caller ID."

"Was Julie Benfield involved? How'd you get in the apartment?"

"It was unlocked. I let myself in." He paused. "But I didn't even erase the tape, and I didn't dispose of the Caller ID."

"You kept it, right? You wanted more than the one medallion they promised."

"It was my scam. They treated me like some fucking blue-collar working-class putz. They had forty medallions, I wanted ten. An equal share. If you were in my shoes, Detective, you'd have done the same."

"But I'm not in your shoes, Milo." So far the only proof that Yablonsky had was the word of this street hustler. They weren't in the precinct house, he didn't even have it on tape. "The tape and the Caller ID, where are they stashed?"

"Not in a safe deposit box," said Milo. "Somewhere out on the street."

"We'll go for it later tonight," said the detective. "If it's just your word against theirs, none of this will hold up. And you'll go down for all of it."

"But I never murdered anyone. I only did the driving. Those teamsters clipped them. I only heard about the Roth murder after the guys they contracted it to came back."

"Roth?"

"I drove you to the diner that night. I saw you meet with him."

"You drove me? What about Dollars and that clerk?"

"The judge you know about. Remember the clerk who'd shifted the calendar so that Dollars would be the presiding judge? He was dying of AIDS anyway. All they did was tie a plastic bag around his head. When they got back to the car, they called it a *homo*cide."

Yablonsky winced.

"I can prove I'm on your side. I'll show you where I hid the evidence. I'll hand it over, if you'll help me negotiate my deal."

"Sounds good," said Yablonsky. "But first drive me to the new homeless camp in Brooklyn. A source told me it's two blocks from one the cops razed last week. Billy might be there. If we can find him and he corroborates your story, it'll strengthen your deal. Is the gun still with Shelly at the halfway house?"

"As far as I know."

Yablonsky nodded. It was all coming together.

THIRTY

Firemen aimed a giant hose directly on top of the blaze's edge. Staking out a perimeter on Twelfth Avenue, they had managed to prevent the fire from spreading further into Manhattan.

Yablonsky stood next to a twenty-four-hour car wash, watching cops divert backed-up traffic down another avenue. The flames, once intense, were mostly charred embers now, but the metal cars in the city impound lot were still melting, popping like Roman candles on the Fourth of July.

Earlier, at the homeless camp in Brooklyn, someone told Yablonsky that Billy was probably staying at the West Side compound, where the homeless often slept in the cars. Yablonsky'd handed him a twenty. "Hey," he said, "the guys that were here before gave me a fifty."

Plumes of smoke from the impound lot rose to the sky. Lights flashed from squad cars and fire engines. Lines of cops and firemen stood at the impound's edge, facing the dying flames.

Yablonsky flashed his badge and had been let through. Milo, however, had been turned away and was waiting a couple of blocks over. The detective, looking away from the blaze that had destroyed an integral part of his case, peered across the river at the Jersey shoreline, where hundreds of people had lined up to watch the city battle the flames. Perched on a roof to

Yablonsky's left was the frame of a car that some hustling Chevy salesman had used to advertise his business. Yablonsky stared at the sightless head-lights.

To his right, a line of stretchers carried corpses out of the impound where the fire had finally died out. Paramedics went in as far as they could, a couple of yards, to carry out the bodies of those who had managed to flee their cars once the fire started. Caught in the open, they'd died of smoke inhalation. After the fire cooled, the medical teams would make a more complete search.

A tall, stocky white cop and a thin black patrolman detached themselves from a platoon of reporters and approached the detective. "The fire started less than an hour ago," the thin cop said. "Anyone you're looking for is toast."

"Charbroiled hamburger steak," echoed the other.

There were masses of twisted burned metal, burned ash. The car's gas tanks were still exploding. The area was scorched.

"The campfire boys in red already told me. They won't be able to go in until tomorrow. Now the best they can hope for is to contain it."

The thin black cop, staring away from Yablonsky, said, "Lot of mush-rooms still burning in there."

"Mushrooms. Marshmallows," echoed the stocky white cop.

"It's got to be arson," said Yablonsky. *He'd never find Billy now.*

"Tell us something we don't know."

Since he'd been the first cop on the scene, he'd have to be here tomorrow, too. Once the fire cooled down, they'd have to remove the rest of the bodies. Once the precinct commanders and captains pulled up and he briefed them, he slipped through the barriers, showing his shield. He walked toward Ninth Avenue, where he knew Milo would be waiting.

The atmosphere on Ninth Avenue was pure carnival. People streamed outside the clubs, drinking forties, playing the dozens, blasting their music over the blaring sirens of the fire engine. From blocks away every-one could see the red glow and columns of smoke. Parked in the alley be-hind a late-night rap club, Milo turned off the on-duty light and killed the headlights. This was where Yablonsky wanted to meet, and this was where he had to stay.

When he heard a tap on his window, he looked up, his hand moving to the steering wheel, ready to open the locked passenger door if it was the detective, or to wheel the hell out of there if it turned out to be some of the brothers.

Instead, two white guys dressed in lumber jackets. He relaxed. Cracking the window, he said, "I'm off-duty."

The tall, stocky guy with a 1950s pompadour sighed with relief. "We're stranded here. Can you take us to our hotel?"

"The Great Western on Greenpoint Avenue in Brooklyn," said the other.

"Just over the Fifty-ninth Street Bridge," the stocky guy added, touching his D.A. in the back of his head. "You're a lifesaver."

"I'm off-duty."

"We'll pay you triple the meter."

"You guys must be deaf." He rolled the window up further.

The guy in the checkerboard jacket leaned in closer. "Quadruple."

Milo rolled down the window. "Just across the river?"

"Ten minutes to the bridge, just five minutes from there."

"Not worth it." He could be there and back in twenty minutes. Yablonsky wouldn't even know he'd been gone. "Five times the meter."

They shrugged indifferently. Milo unlocked the doors. A fresh stream of limos pulled up to the after-hours club. Dozens of party-goers headed for the velvet ropes out in front. The two men sank into the car and the stocky guy turned to his friend. "See? A regular lifesaver."

As the car light briefly flickered on behind his partition, Milo no-ticed they were sweating profusely. He pulled into traffic, shooting down to Sixth where the overflow caused by the fire would lessen. They passed an all-night Smiler's. He drove uptown.

"You seen the fire?" Milo asked.

Both men had handkerchiefs out, wiping their foreheads. The tall guy nodded in a friendly, enthusiastic way. "We're from Portland. So this is quite an adventure. We really got up close."

Milo relaxed and leaned away from the wheel. "By the way, five times the meter doesn't include tip."

He glanced in the mirror, but saw no reaction. Real cornballs, he thought.

"How long you here for?" Milo asked, clicking on the radio and quickly changing channels, which zapped the meter so the fare would shoot up.

"Two weeks." The stocky guy fingered his pompadour, then his D.A.

New construction blocked off a lane. Milo pulled to the right, along with everyone else. Over the river, the giant Jehovah's Witness sign beamed "The Watchtower" in glowing red. Further away, he could see the Manhattan and Brooklyn Bridges. Further than that, leading to the Atlantic, the Verrazano.

"You must have to work really hard for a living," the skinny guy said conversationally.

At the Jackson Avenue exit, Milo made a quick left. "I'm out busting my ass every day. Who appreciates it?" He paused. "I'm glad you guys do."

"We love New York, and we love the workingman," the stocky guy said. "How much you pay for your tin on the hood?"

"My tin on the hood?"

"Yeah, you know. Your medallion?"

"I'm still paying them off," laughed Milo.

"Them?" asked the other guy. "How much tin do you own?"

"I've got two other cabs on the street."

Leaning away from the partition the skinny guy said, "I see. We thought you would have wanted to own more."

Up ahead, Milo made a left at the light, whizzing by LaGuardia Community College. The campus was deserted. Only lights on the upper levels shone. Making a right, he went by empty factories, on his way to Borden Avenue. No cars followed him.

Milo, hunched over his wheel, asked, "When are you guys going back?"

In the mirror, the stocky guy looked sad. "The end of next week. We're really gonna miss this city."

"It's so exciting," the other echoed.

"A real adventure."

Under the El, Milo made a left at Borden. "What made you decide to stay at the Great Western? It's out of the way."

"It's a real hot-sheets hotel, Milo," the skinny guy in the checkerboard jacket said. "Lots of stews from LaGuardia lay over there. We lay them."

In the distance, the driver made out the Empire State Building, lit tonight with blue and purple lights. "If you can use a guide, for you guys, I'll turn off the meter."

In the back, the thin guy smiled. "You mean you'll finally stop zapping the meter on us?"

"How the hell do you know about that?"

The skinny guy replied, "We have cabs in Brookline, too."

"I thought you said you were from Portland."

At the corner of Borden, blue rails bordered a small bridge leading to an industrial park. "Take a right here."

A small jolt of fear tore through Milo. "That's not the right way."

Tall, rusty girders jutted from the stagnant canal beneath them. A train went past, and the blue rails of the bridge shook.

Milo reached the far end of the bridge. A traffic light blinked up ahead. The skinny guy said, "Why don't you let us off here?"

"Here?"

The blue rail of the bridge led to a chain-linked fenced lot that held lines of red and yellow tour buses that said, *This Is an Official*

London Sightseeing Bus. The buses were double-deckers. Bridge after bridge, over small, narrow canals. Milo remembered watching teamsters drive Yablonsky over a bridge, then dump him in the Gowanus. Beyond the canals, hovering over an expanse of steel and water, was Battery Park City.

He stopped and the two men walked around to the driver's side. Milo's foot shot to the gas pedal, ready to wheel at the first sign of trouble.

"We're looking for girls to fuck."

Part of Milo relaxed. At night, the side streets leading to the bridge were teeming with hookers.

He rolled down the window as the checkerboard jacket produced a wad of bills. "What's the meter?"

"Fifteen sixty."

"Keep the change."

From inside the cab, Milo stared at sixteen dollars. "Five times the meter. That's another sixty dollars. Plus tip."

"What the fuck are you talking about?"

Milo kept his foot primed, ready to pump the gas. "We had a deal."

"You've made deals before, Milo. And you welshed. Now, give us the medallions."

"We were supposed to kill you—"

"But if you hand over the medallions . . ."

"We won't."

Their guns were drawn. "Why kill me?"

"Once you're gone, we get your share."

"But I'm only getting one. And it was my scam."

"But you didn't even dispose of the tape."

"Fine. I'll get rid of it now."

"Fuck the tape." The guy in the jacket gripped his gun tighter. "We want the medallions. All forty."

"I don't have them. After they deposited the bribe for the guy on the Taxi Commission, Dillon had them. The contact on the commission was his, so he wanted a bigger share."

The taller man stepped away from him. "We saw you with that cop. You rolled. Snitches get stitches."

"I wasn't with any cop. I didn't roll."

"Bullshit. You hid the tape and pressed for more tin."

"I deserved it. It was my fucking scam!"

Leaning in through the window, with both hands wrapped around his gun, the thin man shot Milo twice in the stomach. He sprawled back in his seat, motionless and moaning. The shooter strolled to the other side and opened the cab door. He fired once into Milo's head. It jerked back, then forward.

He stood and said, "Trunk music time."

His partner quickly opened the trunk. They went through Milo's pockets, emptying his wallet, deliberately tossing it next to the cab, along with the now-empty fare box.

"What do you know?" The checkerboard jacket pocketed a small roll of bills. "He had a slow night."

They tossed him in the trunk and slammed it shut.

Wheezing, the skinny guy said, "I've got to stop this moonlighting. My heart can't take the strain."

He reached through the window. The off-duty light blinked on.

THIRTY-ONE

S helly Townes took his last question from the group of psychiatrists visiting the prison.

"You were talking about the need for self-examination. How long did it take to change your perspective about your past antisocial acts?"

"Even with all the programs it's not easy," said Townes. "You constantly have to subject yourself to self-examination."

"You've made progress," answered his questioner.

"Thank you," said Townes, "but I still have a long way to go."

He moved away from the conference table and casually slipped his hands in his pockets to prevent the change from jingling. He'd already been to eight vending machines. Four more to go.

He left the classroom, heading to one of the machines by the indoor pool. Free swim ended half an hour ago.

Bending before the machine, he took out his master key, crouching so his movements would be camouflaged by his body. He was cautious even when stealing from himself.

His pockets heavy with change, he left the building, walking toward the golf cart. In two hours the detective would be here, to Q-and-A him. He planned to rabbit.

"Shelly?"

Turning, he froze. "You're not supposed to be here for two hours."

"There was a scheduling conflict," said Yablonsky. "I'll have to interrogate you now. Anything wrong with that?"

Though it was still winter, the golf course at Catskills Correctional had to be prepped so the white-collar criminals could make use of it when spring rolled around. Yablonsky watched them work. It was the closest thing to punishment he'd seen since his first visit.

One golf cart remained unused so far. As Yablonsky and the ex-borough president sat in the cart. His bungalow-mate Mel Harris and another guy swooped down from a hill, scooping up mud and flinging it at Townes.

As they drove off laughing, Harris gave Townes the finger. "That's for the last six-pack of Pepsi, Shelly!"

"Grow up, guys!" Townes said, flicking mud off his coat.

"Ignore my fan club, Detective. I can't work splattered with mud. So who did they hurt but themselves?"

The key sat untouched in the ignition. Shelly's long legs spilled out of the cart. Townes looked at the detective helplessly. "Explain to me how to do this."

"Drive?" Yablonsky asked. "Just turn the key."

He fumbled around and dropped it. Then he stood and waited on Yablonsky's side to enter. The detective shifted over, picked up the key.

Yablonsky powered the cart over a few rolling hills, working up to a speedy six miles an hour. Theoretically every time they passed a divot, Townes was supposed to order that the cart be stopped, get out, and work the divot back into the fairways and greens. Instead, Townes directed him to drive uphill. It was hard to tell if they were still on the prison grounds. There were no walls or guard towers.

Across the road were several large crater-like pits. Looking closely, the detective noticed the beginnings of a building's wooden foundation.

"A year ago, the authorities thought they'd have the prisoners construct an annex because of the increase in federal prisoners. There'd just been an election, you know. So the federal prison, right next to the state one, got a whole flotilla of new fish. But when they discovered that it was off prison grounds, they had to abandon the site for a closer one. They never got around to cleaning this place up. The pits are filled with tar. They were going to use it for the roofing, but it hasn't congealed yet, so it's like quicksand. Occasionally, inmates come up here to picnic. They make wishes and toss money in the tar pit. The cash sinks like a stone."

"The day Skinny was murdered, you weren't at Catskills Correctional. Where were you?"

"Where was I?"

"You were at the halfway house for all the killings, Shelly. You held the gun."

"Gun?"

"The teamsters you got to do the killings were gangster wanna-bes, and they couldn't risk illegally carrying guns in case of a shakedown by the cops. You went along to finger each vic."

Shelly raised his scrawny arms, as if to fend off the accusations. "I never held any gun. I never fingered anyone."

"I scanned your accounts. I know for a fact that the hundred-and-sixty-thousand-dollar bribe was spread out over a year—so your men on the Taxi and Limousine Commission and the Department of Environmental Protection wouldn't draw attention to themselves by spending it all at once. That was your idea."

Shelly trembled. "I want my attorney."

"You are an attorney. Dillon originally started out as a judge trying cases in Taxi Court. He had the contact at the Taxi and Limousine Commission. He held the medallions, but after he'd decided to keep them, you had him killed, literally laundered."

"I'm being slandered."

"You're guilty."

"Bullshit. I've been rehabilitated."

"You can't rehabilitate a cobra. You have to defang it. Talk."

"But I thought you believed me. I thought you were on my side—not like Harris. Look, there's Harris now."

The gun was half hidden under the lip of earth. A tiny two-shot pistol, different than the one used to murder McPherson. Townes reached for the gun, but Yablonsky hit him in the stomach. Townes slipped, fell over the crest and into the tar. He desperately reached for the detective's hand, and caught it. Then fumbled. Tar oozed into Shelly's mouth, muffling his screams. He sank quickly.

THIRTY-TWO

Yablonsky flashed his shield at the security guard, who asked, "What are you here for?"

"I'm on the job," said Yablonsky, moving past him. He took the stairs up one flight, then went into Shelly's room to toss it. On the walls there were photos of Shelly, posing with politicians and celebrities. Under the bed, boxes filled with counterfeit knockoffs of Sony CD players and Walkmans. And in the small refrigerator hidden behind the sink, stacks of twenty-dollar bills. Yablonsky left it where it was.

He walked into the community kitchen, checking behind the hot-plates and the pots and pans. He felt along the wall for any openings. He looked in the big refrigerator that served the floor, ignoring the cans of Pepsi and the half-eaten remains of a Payday candy bar.

Stepping into the bathroom, he searched behind the stalls and toilets, sliding off the porcelain caps and looking inside. Nothing. Paper, gum, and beer cans were scattered on the floor. One window was too encrusted with grime to move. The other screeched open. Yablonsky looked outside, his eyes darting to the windowsill. Nothing there.

He took a deep breath, standing opposite a small paper towel dispenser with no towels in it. His fingers felt around inside until he found what he was looking for. He peeled off the rows of masking tape that concealed it. Reaching into his pocket, he slipped on a pair of gloves and dropped what he'd found into the evidence bag. He put the bag in his pocket to avoid questions from security, left the building and walked to the squad car.

The detective rose as Irene approached. He was graceful for a stocky guy, she thought. "What's wrong, Irene?"

"Not a thing," she said. "I'm due for my break in five minutes." He still had the folder with the financials she had given him. "We'll go downstairs to talk. Away from the fucking security screen."

Facing him in the sub-basement next to the safe-deposit-box room, she finally asked, "Did you get any confessions with what I gave you?"

Yablonsky sat opposite her. "Only evasions."

"What did Sully have to say?"

"I interrogated him during his hunger strike at Staples's restaurant. Away from the cameras of course. He's so paranoid about the media discovering something bad about him, I think he went along with the others and had McPherson killed. When I showed Barnes that his withdrawals were made during the same time as Dollars and Townes made theirs, he maintained it proved nothing."

"How'd the Q-and-A with Shelly go?"

"Not as well as expected," Yablonsky said. "He's dead."

"Did you kill him, Alvin?"

"Self-defense. I can't report it yet, either. Once it becomes public knowledge, what I planned won't work. I'll never be able to nail his accomplices. So far, Catskills Correctional believes he's the first convict ever to escape from a minimum security facility."

"Why'd you tell me, then?"

"I trust you."

"Good. I'm taking your advice, by the way. I plan to serve Tito the papers, if I can get close enough. I want custody of my kids—but no one can penetrate his entourage."

"Don't worry. I'll get you a lawyer."

"What can you do for me? This city has you so boxed in, you can't even solve your case, even though you know who the murderers are. That homeless guy is dead. You had to kill Shelly. The administration wants you to let the case go. What the fuck do we do?"

"We do what every self-respecting detective in this city does when he reaches a dead end."

"What's that?"

"We hire our own private investigator."

Yablonsky was in his office doing paperwork when the private investigator came in and handed over his surveillance reports. He accepted the three hundred dollars Yablonsky handed him. "This guy you wanted me to sneak a peek at? He won the Nobel Peace Prize a couple of years ago, right?"

Yablonsky nodded.

"Wow." The guy whistled, then left.

The detective thumbed through the reports, which recorded Sully Barnes's meetings and nocturnal activities. Interesting.

Two detectives passed by his office. The door was open, so when he looked up, he glimpsed a *Daily News* front page. It was a photo of Milo. The three-inch-high caption under it: "Taxi Driver Found Dead in Trunk—Fifth Driver Slain This Year."

Sighing, he went back to work. There was a small package under some of the forms, from Henderson and Saunders, the precinct's garbagologists. He opened it. He sighed again, unable to go back to work. He couldn't ignore the phone's ringing, so he picked it up. His ex-wife, berating him for his inability to help her and her present husband elude their casino associate's blackmail.

"I've pleaded with you for help for months," Arlene said. "But all you seem to care about are solving murders. I read that Warhol's broad is breaking up with you, so I'm glad."

The actor had assured him, he did not have sex with that woman. "Malicious gossip," Julie had said. "We're *not* breaking up."

"Help us, Alvin. Please."

"For God's sake, Arlene. Your husband's an ex-cop. Have him dig up some dirt on his subordinate. Blackmail him back."

THIRTY-THREE

Julie and Kudos were lounging on the sofa in her apartment. They were dressed in bathrobes, sipping coffee.

Turning a blank face to Yablonsky, Officer Henderson said, "I'll leave."

"Wait outside, Wendell. You're still on duty."

The door shut. Yablonsky faced them.

"Jesus Christ, Charlie. Hours ago I saw you and Sully on TV getting arrested in Tompkins Square Park for trying to prevent squatters from being thrown out. Now you're here."

Kudos leaned back on the sofa. "You know Sully. With his contacts, all we were booked for was trespass and loitering."

"Why are you here?"

"You're the detective. Figure it out. What're you gonna do, arrest us?"

Yablonsky took out a manila envelope. "No, but I may be arresting her. Get out of here, Charlie."

Julie Benfield looked shocked. "Stay."

"I want to stay, too," said Kudos.

"I want this guy gone," said Yablonsky. "We have to talk about something important."

"Alvin, you ran out on me. That night, I needed you. Charlie stays."

"There has to be a witness present to make sure you don't steamroll her like you're doing to Sully," said Kudos. "Of course this isn't really about Sully and Julie, is it, Detective? You're jealous. This is about me."

"Believe it or not, Charlie, things in this world occur that are not actually about you." He removed the computer disk from the envelope, tossed it to Julie. "Officer Saunders found this while sifting through the *Guardian's* garbage in their sub-basement. A copy of Skinny's obit that you worked on and threw away. Dated a week before he was murdered. You don't listen to the Psychic Hotline, do you? How'd you know ahead of time that Skinny was going to die?"

Julie was about to answer. "From now on, you deal with me," said Kudos. "Someone has to take responsibility for you. You're out of control."

Turning to Julie, Yablonsky asked, "Do you usually write an obit a week before someone dies?"

"It's routine, actually. We have hundreds of obituaries of famous people on file. When they pass away, all we do is fill out the day and disease."

"I think you sold Skinny out. Sully had to call here to confirm the meeting with Skinny. So his voice would be on tape and his phone number would show up on your Caller ID, but Sully knew the tape would be erased. Not by you, though, you wanted to be as far away as possible from this apartment that night. Someone else would have to remove the evidence."

"How the hell would you know that someone else was here that night?"

"A cabdriver told me. He was supposed to visit that night, erase the tape, and toss the Caller ID to save Sully. Instead he decided to take the evidence with him and to extort a bigger share of the medallions."

Yablonsky noted she showed no surprise at hearing about the medallions. Kudos clasped Julie's hand in his, but she brushed it aside. "I know where this is coming from. You're angry because after you ran out on me, I left you."

"Why'd you write the obituary a week before he died?"

"I lived with the man, remember? He was grossly overweight, he already had diabetes, he smoked like a chimney and drank like a fish. It was a good bet he'd die young."

"That's bullshit."

"You're accusing me of being involved in Skinny's murder? Haven't I been through enough?"

"Hook up with Charlie, and you'll go through a lot more."

"You can't actually believe I helped kill Skinny."

"I've been with you enough to know you're paranoid about your physical safety. But your door was unlocked that night. Why?"

"Why'd you run out on me, Alvin?"

"I didn't run out on you."

"Who told you the door was unlocked?"

"Milo."

"The taxi driver? He's dead."

"I still know what I know."

"And I know what I feel. You were the one guy I always thought I could count on."

"You haven't answered my question yet."

"You didn't answer mine."

"Next time I question you, bring your lawyer."

He stood. Kudos followed him out. "I don't blame you for being upset," he whispered. "She gives a better blow job than most Oscar winners I know."

Yablonsky gut-punched him twice. The actor sank to the floor and gasped. "I swear I only told him not to bother you. He's an animal."

Outside in the hall, Officer Henderson turned to follow the detective to the car. "I heard a ruckus. Did you put him on his ass?"

"I'm too pissed off to answer, Wendell."

Henderson looked at the detective, hesitated. "She still didn't answer your question. Why'd she write McPherson's obit before he died?"

"She answered it."

"I heard most of their bullshit through the door. You still want me to stick around and guard her after all that?"

"Don't leave her alone . . . even for a minute."

Yablonsky crossed to the Greek luncheonette on the corner of Barrow and Hudson and sat in a booth facing Julie's apartment, munching on a cheeseburger, salad, and fries. He stopped eating when he saw Julie and Kudos skip down the brownstone's steps.

They lingered on the corner for a moment, exchanging a long kiss. Paparazzi rushed them.

"Please, no," growled Kudos, his arm circling Julie. "Can't we even share a private moment?"

"Where? Out here on the street? You're practically boning her," yelled a photographer.

The two celebrities waited patiently until it was over. Yablonsky saw them walk down Barrow Street arm in arm, toward the East Village. He left the luncheonette, walking the other way.

THIRTY-FOUR

Alvin Yablonsky stood next to Raymond Staples, out on the windy terrace of the Forty-sixth floor of his West Side office building. They stared at the Hudson River and the Jersey coastline.

"Pretty soon there won't even be a river to separate Manhattan from Jersey," Staples said. "It'll all be landfill."

"That's probably true. And you'll be responsible."

"Yeah," Staples said with a smile. "I lost, you know. Sully beat me."

"The hunger strike?"

"Food donations to his shelters start next Tuesday."

"At least the hungry will be fed. That's something."

"No one cares more about the poor than me." Staples sighed. "You don't know what it's like once Barnes's political allies start to lean on you."

"Yeah, I wouldn't know," said Yablonsky, smiling slightly to himself.

"I don't like losing," said Staples. "I'm not used to it."

"Neither am I. But before I dismiss you as a suspect, I have to know why you were with Skinny that night."

"I never was with Skinny that night."

"I visited the construction site at the Seventy-ninth Street boat basin this afternoon. After years of doing nothing, work at the sites resumed. I think you met with Skinny about the construction site. You flew into Teterboro Airport to meet with McPherson. And on the night he was murdered, offered him a bribe."

"I wasn't involved in his murder."

"No. Not his murder, but what crime were you trying to cover up?"

"No crime. Ask Shelly."

"Shelly's dead."

"Shelly?"

"He's dead. And he's implicated. If you don't want to be dragged down with him, you'd better tell me about your involvement with him and explain why you tried to bribe Skinny. And no lies."

"I never lie," said Staples. "Okay." He took a breath and gestured expansively at the rail yard beneath them. "Whenever you look at the shoreline on the West Side, there's vacant, under-used land. It's a crime. The day before construction on Riverside West was to begin, community activists stopped me with a cease and desist order. Too many apartments. Too many people for the West Side to handle. So the thinking went. We modified the sizes, and then they fought me on the composition and distribution of wealth among my future tenants and owners. Not enough diversity, not enough low incomes and middle classes in the building complex. When I went along with them on that, they tied me up on waste and disposal." He hesitated, then lowered his voice, even though they were alone. "The West Side Coalition was ready to throw the whole legal book at me. So I needed one thing from Shelly that I couldn't get on my own. I needed a variance. You know what a variance is, Detective?"

"You tell me."

"A variance is the greatest thing ever invented. It allows you to legally break the law. The law says one thing; you go to a politician and get a variance, which is a legal document that makes an exception in your case. You now have permission to break the law. Of course it's a politician who grants you permission. You understand?"

"I think so. A variance is to the law what a minimum security facility is to a real prison."

"Exactly. Even though he was kicked out of office and in jail, Shelly still controlled three votes on the City Council. Skinny and I had been meeting for drinks after hours for years. He was my major source of information on the paper. Not that he was ever aware that he was feeding me inside dope. He found out about the variance—and how it was obtained. I couldn't fire him. He'd just go to another paper. So I tried to bribe him that night at the garage—and couldn't."

"What time did you meet with him?"

"The taxi driver dropped me off at my office at seven. He must've told you that. The security staff was skeletal, since so few people really work there. Plus, there's only one security camera, and it's on the first floor. So it's the perfect place to meet with someone for a bribe."

"How long did you two meet?"

"About half an hour. He left me at around seven-thirty. I was still holding the bag, literally."

"Did you see him get together with anyone else?"

Staples shrugged. "I didn't hang around long enough to see. I had to get back to Dollars's condo fast. I had to be able to plausibly deny that I'd just tried to bribe him. I own a newspaper. Is Shelly's death public knowledge yet?"

"Don't even print one word about it."

"As long as you don't say anything about me trying to bribe my own reporter." Staples paused. "What do you want from me?"

The detective slipped the private eye's surveillance reports on Sully out of his briefcase, along with the plastic bag containing Shelly's gun.

Yablonsky talked as Staples read and listened. Beneath them, a train pulled into the ancient Pennsylvania railroad yards. "Whoever you get to do this has to know what he's doing," said Yablonsky. "His prints can't turn up on this nine."

The train's brakes screeched. "You're really going after Barnes," Staples shouted. "Not that it's hard to believe he was involved in this. I always knew that behind that peace-loving bullshit exterior he was as crooked as the rest of us. He's a former felon, right? You sure this will work, Detective?"

"If my next interrogation doesn't crack him, we'll be ready." The detective imagined the heat from Internal Affairs, knew the tickler file they had on him would probably be leaked, but he had no intention of handing out a so-called variance to Barnes for murder. "No guarantees," he said. "My idea works, but only, God forbid, if there's another murder."

At three a.m., Detective Yablonsky sped down the practically deserted Belt, exiting at Starrett City on Pennsylvania Avenue. Milo hadn't revealed where the tapes he'd hidden on Barnes were. He was guessing.

He drove past Elton, Essex, and Shepherd, the schoolyard where he'd played ball as a kid and where he used to watch helplessly as black kids were chased down by the New Lots Boys and stomped to death. Across Linden Boulevard near the El, street gangs had often rumbled with zip guns, and their predecessors, carpet guns—crossbow-like weapons that shot pieces of linoleum you aimed at your opponent's eyes. He passed the old but not yet faded graffiti he himself had sprayed over thirty years ago: "L.A.M.F., D.T.K.," the street slang of gang members in East New York. *Like A Mother Fucker, Down To Kill.* Across the street was written the acronym SPONGE, a top-secret racist gang of killers Yablonsky had refused to join, headed by some kid named DeSimone who lived across the street from him. It stood for Society for the Prevention of Negroes Getting Everything.

He reached the industrial area standing between the Belt Parkway and Linden Boulevard. Further east were tangled grassy paths leading to urban forests of junked cars, eight-foot weeds, and swamps where the Gambino and Luchese families used to dump their victims.

Wortman Street was full of rows of closed-up factories, occasionally separated by small, darkened residential houses. To his left were the train yards from the IRT line, with subway cars whose windows were filled with scratchitti.

At every other corner were luncheonettes that stopped doing business at seven in the evening: all with security gates under burned-out streetlamps.

Headlights flashed by on Linden Boulevard. At Elderts Lane, he stopped at a parking lot with floodlights surrounding it, like at a stadium during a night baseball game. He got out of his car, carrying his gym bag. The lot was surrounded by a chain-link fence, with two feet of barbed wire at the top.

No guard dogs. No security guards. Yablonsky looked for the tear in the fence, pried his way through, and was inside.

Removing a flashlight from his bag, he walked to the other side of the parking lot, making his way past broken bottles, rusty needles, and twisted condoms. More headlights whipped by. A wind blowing in from Jamaica Bay rattled the windows of a few rusted-out vans.

Four years ago, before all the murders, after Milo approached Shelly and Dillon with his idea, the Department of Environmental Protection gave the go-ahead to allow a new cab company to run a fleet with an experimental diesel engine. It'd been approved by the head of the City Council's transportation committee.

Both of these guys had been bribed by Shelly. As a result, forty medallions were added to the logbooks and were dispensed to the owners of the new company, Interboro Cab Company, for free.

When he reached the row of Checker cabs, he stopped walking. The judge had been killed so the others would get bigger shares. Had Milo lied to him? Did he actually have the medallions?

There were six cars, lined up side by side, inches from the chain-link fence. Shining the flashlight, he could see the slight indentations on the cabs' hoods, and the small bracketed holes left where Milo had removed each medallion, now that the Checkers were no longer in service.

He went around to the rear of a cab, prying the trunk open with a small crowbar. Two stacks of VCRs and tape decks, no doubt swag. But no medallions.

He moved on. Inside the next trunk he found a bag of money, which he fingered but left, certain it was counterfeit.

The next car only had a jack and a spare tire.

For a moment he stood sweating despite the winter night's weather, his coat and forehead smeared with oil. He went back to work, jimmying open the next to last Checker cab. There were no medallions. In front of the trunk, he found old clothes stained with dried brown blood. And in the rear corner, the flashlight lit up a couple of microtapes and a Caller ID machine.

He wiped his forehead with a stained handkerchief. He put the tapes, along with the Caller ID machine, into the gym bag. Not wanting any passersby to realize the trunks had been jimmied, he took out pieces of rope and secured them.

By 5:30 a.m., he was back in his apartment, asleep.

THIRTY-FIVE

S ully Barnes sailed over the sloping floors of the *Guardian*, wanting to be no more than half an hour late for this meeting.

As always, there were messages to collect from his receptionist, mostly requests for favors, interviews, or demands for his time, most of which had to be met.

The bare bulbs overhead felt as hot as spotlights. He felt dizzy. His hands trembled as he spread them before him in a too-wide arc. "Hit me with the works, Myrna. What you got for me today?"

"Nothing out of the ordinary. Just the usual six-inch pile of mail and faxes. Are you okay?"

Barnes tore at his collar. It was so fucking hot. Kaleidoscopic images whirled in front of him. Staffers moved into or rose from their chairs. They seemed to revolve around him, bits of color, quickly moving.

He stared down at his receptionist, his mouth stretched in a tight smirk. Everything was slightly distorted today. Elongated or misshapen, like an early Picasso.

"Not a thing," he said, nodding ponderously to himself, wiping his forehead. "Is Robert still there? How long have I kept him waiting?"

"Mr. Forum's been waiting patiently for almost fifty minutes." A concerned look. "Where were you?"

Moving past her, already midway through the door frame, he said, "Throwing up."

Robert Forum, the sixty-five-year-old former chairperson of the homeless coalition that Barnes now led, rose as he entered, then sat back down. "Are you okay, Sully?"

Barnes slid into his seat, interlocking his fingers, then pushing back as if the air were tangibly heavy and he could halt its inexorable progress against him. He forced himself to focus on the mighty task at hand; getting through the next five minutes. "Of course I'm okay, Bob. Why's everyone asking me that today?"

"Because you've looked better after getting worked over by cops with nightsticks at a demonstration than you do now." He paused. "It looks like you've aged ten years in the month since our last meeting." His eyes filled with emotion. "I'm not going to find out two weeks from now that you got cancer, am I? I love you too much for you to hold out on me."

Barnes sighed. "If I look shitty, it must be the strain. I don't have cancer." His head slumped lightly. "That's not what everybody's going to find out about me in two weeks."

There was a knock on the door. Barnes looked at his watch, then sat back in his chair like he'd been wounded. The detective had lied to him, and was here to take him to the precinct fifteen minutes earlier than he'd said.

But it was only an editor, Roland Stone. Barnes stared up at him, not relieved. "What is it, Roland?"

Roland stepped tentatively into his office. "I can see you're busy, Sully, but these things came up . . ."

Barnes nodded. Not since he'd taken those LSD tabs in prison had he been so unfocused. "Okay, Roland. Let's hear them."

If you were black and a militant, you'd easily classify Roland Stone as an inauthentic Afro-American, a real Oreo. But Barnes liked him. For a newspaper editor, the guy was nonaggressive and modest, as soothing to listen to as fusion music.

Stone handed him a computer printout of an article slated for publication in this week's *Guardian.* "These are figures for the latest number of homeless," Roland said. "Only they don't add up. They're inflated. Should we run it?"

"Of course they're inflated. In order to get a dime's worth of donations, we've got to hit people with a dollar's worth of hype."

"Well, in the article we claimed we made a study . . ."

"Of course it's a study. We polled our staff. Except for you, because you see moral ambiguities where there don't have to be any. What's the *Guardian's* policy concerning the wildly unreliable homeless numbers?"

"At every date, we inflate."

"Then why's this day different from any other day?"

Stone glanced unhappily at the two grinning men. "Two weeks ago, we accused a Jewish politician from Boro Park of racism toward African Americans during a town meeting up in Albany. The congressman disputed our story, claimed he didn't make any of the comments we attributed to him. This morning a young woman, one of his staffers, came to see me with a dupe of the statements we accused him of."

"So?"

"I want us to print a retraction of the article, which you co-wrote."

Barnes laughed. "We seldom print retractions, especially when we're wrong. Not while I'm on the board. Not for one of my columns."

"But if we print a retraction, the matter's dropped, Sully. Otherwise we'll get sued."

"I'm surprised at you. You're a black guy with no sense of the street. The Jew won't sue. I guarantee that. The only reason he didn't say what we claimed he said was because he knew he was going to be on tape.

Otherwise he would have said it. We don't have to report what's literally true, Roland, as long as there's *emotional* truth. Besides, over the years, this guy's always tried to slam us. Holding our paper up to ridicule during his campaigns. He deserves being classified as a racist."

"So you won't retract?"

Barnes and Forum exchanged glances. "I see that you've finally grasped my point, Roland. Anything else?"

"That's it. I'm gone."

Sully leaned back from his desk, his hand trembling as he smoked a cigarette. "You can never really go back and change things. So I never retract."

Forum spread his hands out before him. "I can see I left my coalition in good hands. I'm here because I'm about to do my memoirs with some ghostwriter. Some time next week you're going to be interviewed."

Some time next week. "So?" Barnes asked.

"Right. Remember three years ago. That committee meeting."

"Fuck, yeah."

"I'd like you to forget that night ever happened. That night goes against everything else I've accomplished."

"The night never happened," said Sully.

Forum stood. "Thanks." He smiled. "I liked the way you handled your editor just now. That's real left-wing politics."

"Anything else, Bob?"

"Yeah. What's bothering you? You look so tired."

"I'm just tired of everybody judging me." He rose and walked to the door of his cubicle, glancing through the almost opaque window. Only his receptionist was there. He and Kudos managed to prevail upon the detective to meet in a stairwell of the delivery entrance. No one would see him taken off to the precinct.

He walked to the back of his office and stepped out onto the landing. He'd often taken the delivery exit to avoid dealing with his son, who for some reason still insisted on showing up outside his office to see him. The kid wouldn't even call ahead of time for an appointment, like everyone else. In the past, Sully'd always reacted in the same way. No words, just an escape out the rear. But now if his son was sitting outside his office, he knew without question that he'd try to avoid him again.

Charlie's voice drifted up from another landing. The detective ponderously climbed the stairs, ignoring Kudos's protests. Barnes leaned back against the stairwell. He had to take all this shit from this cop now. But even if he had to wait years to turn this detective inside out, he'd do it. He'd get back at him for all this.

Yablonsky walked his suspect into the precinct through the hidden door of the basement, safe from the media.

"No press," whispered Sully. "Thanks for that."

"Once you tell me who killed McPherson and Dillon, I can do even more."

"Where are we going?"

Yablonsky didn't answer. He wanted Barnes to understand. Here he had no power. He took Sully through the forensic and chemical labs, even past Henderson and Saunders who were methodically sifting through a room of Barnes's and the *Guardian*'s refuse.

Sully walked into the interrogation room and saw dozens of giant, blown-up photos of his victims and their crime scenes. Graphic proof of what he and his accomplices had done.

On the wall opposite from where he was sitting hung computer printouts of Shelly's, Dillon's, and Sully's financial transactions over the past year. The weeks all three withdrew money to pay for the medallions were circled in red. Beneath that were forensic reports that said McPherson and Milo were murdered with the same weapon, a nine. There were no blaring newspaper headlines about the killings. This was a man who, Yablonsky knew, had murdered not for money but to prevent exposure.

Sully already knew he was due for a media lynching if the truth came out: emphasizing that might make him clam up.

"Please sit there," Yablonsky said. Barnes noticed the duffel bag on the table next to him and raised his eyebrows at the detective, who remained silent.

"Can I smoke?"

"Afraid not," said Yablonsky, lighting a cigarette.

Barnes had been given the grand tour and had been forced to face his murderous deeds.

All of the detective's suspects reacted to crime scene photos viscerally. They stared, then turned away. Sully was no different.

Yablonsky recited the day, time, and subject of his interrogation into the camcorder, then exhaled a stream of smoke. "You couldn't even begin to imagine the crimes I've seen here. Last week I had to Q-and-A a kid in his twenties who axed his own father for business reasons. Now, those photos were really full of entry and defensive wounds. Even *I* was sickened looking at them. Usually it's the other way, parents torturing, then murdering their own kids. Those little broken bodies break your heart. Whenever I see them in the morgue, that's when I remember why I'm a cop. Because, and I'm sure you'd agree, anyone who would murder a child deserves to pay."

"I agree." Sully peered back coolly. "So?"

"So this. Maybe I see the photos up on the wall different than you do because I'm a cop. But I bet we have this much in common. You believe, as I do, that the man who committed these crimes should pay?"

"Of course."

"Then we agree," said Yablonsky. "Compared with other crimes of rage, these killings are antiseptic. No overkill here. You can see it in the photos, each man was only shot. Whoever killed them must have felt remorse. There's no brutality. I know this murderer, and I can even sympathize with his dilemma. I'm sure he felt great regret. But I'm also sure that the teamsters who shoved Dollars into a double-load washer as a joke had disobeyed the orders to dispose of the judge with a nine. I'm sure that, when this man discovered how Dollars was murdered, he was shocked and saddened. Isn't this true?"

Sully was silent.

"Last year a mob guy who owned a Queens bar filled with gangster wanna-bes was sleeping with a capo's wife while the guido was imprisoned. Everyone in the family liked the sports bar owner, so he was warned to stay away. Still, he slept with his boss's wife. Parts of his body were found scattered along Woodhaven Boulevard. The details were too gruesome for the press to release, but I know from sources that he was taken to a basement in Ozone Park. They hammered spikes into his knees, and then while he was still alive, his limbs were sawed off. Every week I see this kind of shit. Believe me, Sully, the murders posted up here are at the bottom rung of the ladder. My sources tell me the guy's partners might have killed Skinny over money, but not this guy. He went along with them to protect his reputation, justifiably an exalted one. Too exalted, in fact, to be permanently stained by one mistake. Don't you agree?"

Sully nodded slightly. "Too bad the detective who's persecuting him doesn't see it that way."

"Someone has to answer for the victims."

"And you picked me. Thanks."

For a little while longer, Yablonsky had to keep humanizing the suspect to himself. He thought it ironic, assuring a Nobel Peace Prize winner that he was still in the community of men. He went on. "I'm sure you understand this guy, Sully. Of course I empathize. He takes in donations in the millions, yet because of his reputation and the I.R.S., he can't touch any of it. His daily commute goes from people living on the streets to the people owning them. The one time he fucks up and decides to take a little for himself, his subordinate finds out. It's too bad for him that in this case his underling is a reporter. He pressures the reporter to shitcan his exposé, just like everyone in the world's pressuring me to shitcan my investigation. He offers promotions, tons of money, but to no avail. The reporter's honest. What can he do but order him killed?" Yablonsky paused.

"Murder's the most serious thing there is. So I disagree with the guy who ordered these murders. I have to take a confession from him. It's my job, but I understand why he committed them. I'm sure he wishes that the day he decided to go along with those killings had never happened. I'm sure he feels real remorse. But does he feel guilt?"

Sully looked at him, but was silent.

"Imagine you're this guy, Sully. Would you feel guilty?"

Emotion flickered across his eyes, but then was gone.

"The problem, Detective, is that I'm not a motherfucking killer."

"Years ago, you started out as a petty criminal. You've won the fucking Nobel Peace Prize, Sully. You had the strength in you—and you had the weakness. When your political allies approached you with their scam, you hadn't won your prize yet."

"Bullshit."

"When you and your celebrity pals show up at a fund-raiser, you leave reams of tax-deductible contributions in your wake. You're worth millions to the Democratic Party and any Republicans you decide to help. All the money you paid out in philanthropy always went the other way, until Dollars and Shelly approached you with an idea to set up a fugazi cab company. It was a good scam. Fifty years ago the Taxi and Limousine Commission was set up. Since then the number of fleet and individual medallions have remained the same—13,700. Politicians always howl that the number of medallions should be increased, that the monopoly should be broken up."

"I have no idea what you're talking about. Where'd you get this fantasy?"

"By law, Sully, every taxi medallion in the city has to be either on a cab or at the Taxi Commissioner's office. After the D.E.P. approved the experimental diesel engine and Interboro Cab Company was granted their franchise, the books were opened up for the first time and forty new medallions were granted. Photos and registrations were taken of the cabs. Interboro Cab Company was supposed to be located in a lot on Northern Boulevard in Queens."

"Detective, since I'm lost whenever I leave Manhattan, I never leave. Who told you this?"

"The taxis were there, but they had no engines. They were shells. It was a phantom business operation, solely to procure the medallions. Others fronted for you in the beginning, but the medallions' real owners were Shelly, Dollars, and you. There are two kinds of medallions. Fleet owner's and individual. Whenever waves of immigrants hit the shore, half of them end up driving taxis. The worth of a fleet medallion never goes down."

"You still have no proof tying me to Skinny's murder."

"You were on the editorial board of his newspaper. You were his best friend, his confidant. He approached you with his latest exposé: a series of investigations of the taxi industry. What kind of reporter would go after a story even after being warned off it by a Nobel Prize winner, by the most important guy on the editorial board?"

"A dumb one."

"Or a brave one. Skinny did his research, found out that Interboro Cab was allowed to obtain the medallions. And when he visited the address, he found nothing."

"Who told you this?"

"Skinny tracked down the taxi fleet to a lot behind the auto salvage yards near Shea Stadium. Forty cabs with no tires, no experimental diesel engines, and no medallions, stuck up on cinder blocks and rusting in a field.

"And he confided in you. He told you he was going to check with a contact he had on the Taxi and Limousine Commission. He was hoping to see the logbooks with the lists of the Interboro medallion owners."

"I never knew that."

"By now, Dollars and Shelly's contact on the Taxi Commission had put in the names of the real owners—them and you. If Skinny was able to use his source and get access to the logbooks, he'd know who the medallions' real owners were."

"You're saying it's me?"

"Your business associates wanted to murder Skinny out of greed. But your motive was different—you needed to conceal your part in the crime."

"All this happened over medallions?"

"You sue the city every time it forgets to put a roll of toilet paper in a shelter. Yet here you are, without your usual phalanx of lawyers. Why?"

"I'm trapped, Detective. Once I go to my lawyers, it all comes out. The accusations alone are enough to ruin me. The lab technicians who saw me walk through here now know I'm under suspicion of murder. You've already destroyed my life."

"You surprised me."

"Surprised? Why?"

"That you went along with Dollars, Townes, and Milo. You're a bright guy. Couldn't you have guessed the scenario?"

"What scenario, Detective?"

"Your problem was that after you killed Skinny, the murders didn't stop. I could have told you they wouldn't. Guys I grew up with in Brooklyn pulled off the biggest heist in America in the 1970s. They lifted millions from Lufthansa Airlines at J.F.K. But the fight over the split killed them. I'm surprised at you, Sully, not understanding the characters of the men you were involved with. The prospect of a lot of money only makes guys that are already greedy even greedier."

"Maybe the three of them were involved in this, but not me. I wasn't anywhere near Skinny the night he was murdered."

"December twenty-third. How'd you know he was murdered at night?"

"It's speculation," said Barnes. "How do you know?"

"Sources. Look at these financials. You've never withdrawn large amounts of money, except during the weeks Shelly withdrew similar amounts."

"But the amounts are different."

"Not really. The amount deposited into Dollars's account equals what you and Shelly withdrew over the same period. Did you see Skinny at all on the day he was murdered?"

"I might've seen him in the office, but I never spoke with him."

"When was the last time you happened to see him in the office on December twenty-third?"

"Probably in the early morning. I was working on my column."

"Didn't speak with him at all after that?"

"No."

"Did you plan on meeting with him later that day?"

"Definitely not."

Reaching into the gym bag, Yablonsky pulled out a microtape, the phone machine, and the Caller ID. He plugged in the answering machine and set up the Caller ID. Both men saw Barnes's office number appear on the small screen. "I found this in one of Milo's cabs."

"Did it occur to you, Detective, that I might have called Skinny to set up a meeting on a different day?"

"It didn't occur to me, because, as this machine shows, your phone number's the last one recorded."

First Barnes heard a mechanical voice recite the day, date, and time of the call. Then he heard his own voice, confirming a meeting with McPherson for later that day.

"But I never met with him. He never showed up."

"Where were you supposed to meet?"

"At the uptown plant, where the printing goes on. I had things of a personal nature to discuss with him."

"If it was social, why choose a deserted place like that? Why not meet in a restaurant or bar?"

"I had a long night ahead at the shelter. It was easier to meet him at the uptown plant."

"Which shelter did you visit that night? How long were you there? Who saw you?"

"I never made it to the shelter, Detective. After Skinny didn't show, I went home. I was exhausted. I went to sleep."

"Which apartment did you end up in? The one you keep downtown for show? Or the uptown one you actually live in?"

"I crashed uptown, in Riverdale. I know I should have told you, but I knew that if I did, you'd pounce on it. I've known cops my entire life. You're always suspicious. You needed someone spectacular to pin Skinny's murder on, and that's me."

"With all your friends and influence, you're the last person in this city who I wanted to be the killer."

"I'm not the killer. You'll destroy my career. Show some compassion."

"Once you realized Skinny was going to be late, how long did you wait?"

"About fifteen minutes. I had no reason to worry."

"Your best friend, an investigative reporter, doesn't show, and you're not worried? Did you beep him?"

"No."

"Did you call the *Guardian?*"

"At that time, and so close to the holidays, there's barely any staff. No."

"After the twenty-third, you didn't see him. And he didn't call in. Why didn't you notify the police?"

"I thought he was on a bender. Even for an Irishman, he drank a lot."

Yablonsky grabbed the rolled-up clothes out of his gym bag and stretched them out on the table. Even encased in plastic, they stank up the room. Barnes coughed. Yablonsky ducked his head, struggling to inhale some decent air. He stretched the clothes out so Barnes would see the smears of blood at the chest. The clothes squeaked under the plastic, like upholstery.

"This was taken from Milo's cab. That night, he drove you and your teamster friends to the East Side to dump Skinny in the river; it started to sleet and rain. You didn't encase your victim in a snowy tomb in Central Park out of genius or some crazy sense of humor, like the papers said, but because Milo got a flat tire. There was a homeless guy, Billy, out puttering around that night, looking for cans. He saw what you did. So when you left Skinny's clothes in the car, he saw an opportunity. McPherson's coat would keep him warm. And that little play you performed, releasing Billy and showing him compassion after he'd tried to attack you at the homeless encampment? You only let him go was because I was there."

"I don't know what you're talking about."

"Just when I'd tracked Billy down, a fire broke out at the car impound lot. How many homeless people burned to death that night? Right after Milo rolled on you, he's murdered, just another cabbie killed on his shift."

"I don't remember that."

"I tracked down the ID machine, the phone tape, and the rest of McPherson's clothes. They were in the trunk of one of Milo's cabs."

"Are my fingerprints on them?"

"Fingerprints don't usually turn up at a crime scene, Sully. Look at the oil smears on the knees. Chemical analysis matched these two oil smudges with a pool of oil in the garage of the building where you were supposed to meet McPherson." Yablonsky dropped photos of the murder site on the table. "You set him up because you knew it was a good place to kill him."

They exchanged a glance, and the truth was revealed. It passed. "It's not a crime to be in the same building with someone while he's being murdered. Is it, Detective?"

"Don't you have a conscience?"

"Don't you?" Barnes looked at him. "Roth?"

Your people murdered Roth, the detective thought. The only thing he lacked was proof.

Barnes stood. He had no watch, but looked at his wrist anyway. "You're not charging me with anything, right? Can I go?"

Ever since the new police commissioner was appointed, cops had to be much more cautious before charging someone with a homicide. His own confession rate was 25 percent, a lot higher than most cops and detectives in the city. He rolled up the clothes inside the plastic, stuffing the roll back inside the gym bag. "You can leave."

"You aren't through with me. Any normal cop would be, but not you. Despite your superiors or your lack of evidence, you're determined to pin Skinny's murder on me. Fuck you."

"Never mind my superiors," Yablonsky said. "The evidence should have been enough."

Barnes left, moved down the hall. The detective stared at his hands folded on the table and the gym bag. Then his reflexes took over, and he followed Barnes.

Yablonsky approached him as he waited for an elevator. "If you want, uniforms can drive you uptown, escort you home."

"No, thanks," said Barnes. "Your investigation hits dead ends, your so-called witnesses die, your girlfriend leaves you to fuck your suspect's best friend. Looks to me like she's not the only one being screwed."

The elevator arrived. Barnes put a hand inside to hold it. "There are a lot more murders in this world, Detective. Someone with your skills should have no trouble solving most of them. Why don't you move on?"

"What will you be moving on to, Sully?"

"More social programs. More hunger strikes. Putting the arm on politicians for donations."

"Another award for humanitarianism?"

Barnes smiled slightly. "You know, there's no contradiction here. It's a complex world, Detective. I *am* scheduled to receive an award soon. I'm being honored by the police."

THIRTY-SIX

The next day. Late afternoon.

Irene Nuñez, sitting with her legs crossed, watched the bank's security video screen. A tall white man entered the bank. The guy took off his gloves, stuffing them in his pants pocket, causing a bulge. He brushed rain off his suede coat. The umbrella he carried went into a side pocket. But the ski mask stayed over his head.

As he moved to wait on line, Irene swung through the door, nearing the teller he was walking to, and whispered to the young woman ready to wait on him that she should take a break.

Irene flashed a dazzling smile. "May I help you?"

"Sure." A guttural voice, straight out of Brooklyn or the Bronx. He handed her a note stating that inside his pocket was a revolver and he'd shoot her if she didn't hand over money.

Be calm, she screamed to herself. "Are you a depositor here? Do you have an account with us?"

"No."

She shook her head sadly. "Sorry, but you have to have a note from the gentleman over there before I can give you any money. Only people who have an account here can rob it. Give this note to the man behind the desk. He'll be able to help you."

As the guy walked off, Nuñez pressed her foot on the silent alarm. Within minutes cops stormed the bank and arrested the would-be robber.

The reporters and photographers that spent their days tuned to the police radio band streamed in. Under prodding, the bank manager took a plaque off the wall. It delineated the achievements and life span of one of the bank's founders, but he handed it to Nuñez for bravery.

After the interviews and five spots for the local news, Irene walked out of the bank to take her delayed lunch break. She strolled through Bagel Boy and munched on a bialy with a schmear of smoked salmon cream cheese. Then the tension caught up with her.

She went home and called in sick, therefore missing three men in a white van parked in front of the bank, waiting to murder her.

Yablonsky sat at his cubicle for an hour, doing nothing but filling out police forms. The P.B.A. wanted to know if he'd be attending the three-day summer seminar in Hawaii that would detail the latest forensic techniques and DNA technology. Six months ago the detective arrested a Russian importer-exporter for murdering his accountant after being notified by the I.R.S. that it intended to audit him. Of course he'd attend. Why not? It was deductible.

He put in a call to Raymond Staples, who answered with a gruff, suspicious voice. "Who is it? Is it you?"

"Yeah," said Yablonsky. "It's me."

"This morning, one of my people visited the halfway house. The switch was made." He paused. "By the way, I've been reading about your friend Charlie Kudos. After the movie about Sully, he's set to star in some blockbuster called *Side Effects*. It's the story of a group of violent criminals who volunteer to take a new experimental drug. Needless to say, the experiment goes wrong. You've spent time with him. What's he like?"

"You'd like him," Yablonsky said. "All men are brothers, especially murderers."

Staples laughed. "I already know all about Sully. There are two kinds of people in this world, Alvin. Men like me and you, not emotionally equipped to love the world en masse, but who'll always be there for their family and friends. And the other kind, like Sully, who are kind to tons of people so they won't ever have to get close to anyone. They're cold motherfuckers. Look at their families, they're casualties."

"Maybe," said Yablonsky, hanging up.

The detective left through the precinct's rear exit, cutting down the path that led to Central Park West. At this time of night, gays moved toward the section of Central Park called the Ramble, free to enter the woods with someone of their choice. Teenagers used the paths to meet at the Esplanade, smoke grass, drink beer, and screw by the lake. Yablonsky walked along, looking to his left. The ice pyramid where he'd found Skinny was less than half a mile away.

Julie Benfield let him into her apartment, motioned for him to sit down. Crossing her pale legs, she said, "Are you still furious with me, Alvin? Can we have a safe, normal conversation?"

"Probably not. I told you I'd be back to question you."

"About Skinny's murder?"

"I'm going to keep you out of it, Julie, if I can."

"Out of Skinny's murder?"

"All the murders. I just finished with Barnes. I had to let him walk for now, but anyone who knows about the medallions had better be careful." He paused. "You did know about the phony taxi company and the medallions, didn't you?"

"I knew."

"You lied when you said Skinny was spending Christmas in Stockbridge?"

"I lied."

"Tell me about it, Julie."

"I was approached by two big guys, Alvin. They looked like football players. Really scary. They told me to erase the tape, dispose of the Caller ID. I refused." She trembled. "They threatened me."

"The door?"

"I left it unlocked. I wanted to be as far away as possible. For one week I suspected they were going to murder him. But I didn't say anything. I let him walk into that trap. And I've been slowly going crazy ever since." She reached for his hand, the surprise that he let her hold it showed in her eyes. "What's going to happen?"

"Sully doesn't know this, but we may be closing in on him." He paused. "When Barnes goes down, I'll try to keep your name out of it. If I can't and you testify, since they threatened you, you'll be okay."

"I want to get back together with you, Alvin."

"I don't think so."

"Give me one more chance. You could stay now."

He shook his head. "I'll come by at seven."

"At seven. I love you, Alvin."

On the landing, he found Wendell Henderson standing next to the chair.

"This time your voices weren't raised. I couldn't hear a thing, and I even had my ear pressed against the door. Tell me. What the fuck happened?"

Yablonsky stayed tight-lipped, still indecisive. "When does your shift end, Wendell?"

"In a few minutes. Then I go back home to Westchester."

"Who's your relief?"

"Saunders. Was Julie involved in any of it?"

"No."

"Good."

"See you tomorrow."

THIRTY-SEVEN

Julie watched Yablonsky get into a waiting taxi. She frowned. He hadn't intended to stay for long. Would he still show up at seven? She adjusted the blinds so no one could see in. Then she checked the deadbolt latch, slipping the bar lock into place and propping it against the door so no one could get in.

Lounging on the sofa in the living room, she picked popcorn out of a microwave bag, gazing at an infomercial on TV. She felt protected and safe.

"Have you tried my new ab isolator?" Tony Little screamed to an audience of millions.

Her bedroom door swung open.

"Do you want to lose weight? We have seven thousand people, and they've all lost millions of pounds!"

She started up. Two burly men smiled at her.

"The other cop, she's also outside," one of them said.

"Then she goes too."

The other man ran to the door, shot through it. Twice. There were no sounds of struggle. No return fire. He opened the door, dragging Saunders's and Henderson's bodies into the living room.

"My product is guaranteed! With proper technique, you get results!"

"Where the hell did you come from?" said Julie, trying to shrink back in the sofa.

"We came in through the bathroom window," one said.

Julie screamed. Tony Little's ponytail bobbed up and down as he shouted. "See results in minutes!"

The other guy laughed. "We came in through the fire escape. But we had to wait for the detective to leave." He spoke gently to her. "We'd like for you and these dead cops to come with us."

"Nothing will happen," said the other man. "We only want to talk."

"Nothing will happen? Look what you did to Wendell and Denise."

"We don't like cops."

As they stepped toward her, she motioned for them to stop. "I'll do what you want. You going to kill me, too?"

"No. Be nice, put on your coat, and we can leave."

"Don't hurt me, please." They made a space for her so she could stand and retrieve her coat. She lunged through the opening, trying to get to her bedroom and the fire escape. One man caught her by the shoulders, swung her toward the other, who slammed a nine-millimeter gun into her skull. She fell against the couch, knocking the bag of microwave popcorn to the carpet.

"Return it in four weeks if you're not satisfied," shouted Tony Little.

The two men gazed at the inert woman. Except for the blood trickling out of her head, she looked asleep.

"God, she's beautiful," the man who'd hit her said. "Elegant. If we weren't so pressed for time, I'd fuck her."

"While she's unconscious?" the other man said. "That's immoral."

"Bullshit. Look at her. You take a woman like this any way you can get her."

The other guy shook his head, disgusted. "You're sick. We got to get her out of here while she's still out. Then the cops. Give me a hand."

"Fucking-A," said the guy who'd smacked her. "You think the others got the broad from the bank?"

His friend tapped his pocket, which contained a cell phone. "If they did, we'd have heard from them by now. As far as I'm concerned, she's a piece of furniture. Let's move her out."

Both men held her by the shoulders. "Where we taking her?"

"To Fresh Kills Landfill. Out in Staten Island."

"Fresh Kills. That's appropriate."

The two men half carried, half led her across the living room. The guy with the nine said, "You think that cop fucked her?"

"Call us at our 800 number," screamed Tony Little. "With proper technique you will get great results!"

"Of course he fucked her." He jerked his head toward the TV screen. "Let's get out of here. That guy scares me."

At two a.m., Yablonsky sat on the wooden bench outside the Second Avenue Deli, watching the thieves' market open up as soon as the rest of the city closed down. Cars pulled up and the drivers negotiated for swag. Drunks staggered in the streets. Hookers lined up against the walls off of East Eleventh Street, johns slamming into them. Even some cops came by, confiscating goods from the street peddlers to sell for themselves.

He stood and headed for the coffee shop on Crosby Street. A van slowed, pulled up next to him. It followed for half a block, then drove off. He relaxed.

On Avenue A, Yablonsky passed a sculpture garden, a series of massive wooden towers with Santa heads, horses, metallic spheres, and rocket ships climbing upwards, soaring over the metal fence that enclosed it. Across from the sculpture garden, Vazac Hall Catering. Each streetlight had layers of posters wrapped around it. Yablonsky read, "Anti-Racist Action and Copwatch. Fight Racism! Drag March. The cops are the Squatters! Kick them out of Tompkins Square Park!" On the line of security grating, graffiti: Soul Cost. Revs. Garbage filled some of the streets, as in pre-Dickens London. Written atop of the posters along the traffic light boxes: E. Vil. Homeless Coalition: Die! Yuppie! Scum!

Beatty and Bridges, out of uniform, along with two other guys, stepped out of an alley toward him.

Four guys, three knives, one gun. "Walk with us, motherfucker!"

Yablonsky looked questioningly at Bridges. "Mark?"

"Just move, Alvin."

Yablonsky hesitated. His eyes swept the street. A couple of hookers. A few cars speeding toward the FDR Drive. The only cops on the street wanted to kill him.

He felt the point of a knife wedge into his side. The eyes of the men facing him were calm.

"Where are you taking me, Don?"

One of the other men came up close to him, dug into his pocket, removing his beeper, then went inside his overcoat, coming back with his gun.

"He doesn't carry a drop gun," Beatty said with contempt. "Walk, motherfucker."

"Right now," one of the other men whispered.

"Jesus."

"Shut the fuck up, Alvin."

"Let's go."

"Why are you doing this?"

"A favor for a friend. And for ourselves. Sooner or later you were gonna roll on us over Roth."

Bridges's hand slammed down, whacking him in the side with the gun barrel. Yablonsky grimaced and staggered along. The four men surrounded him, forming a protective shield, as if he were a politician. Across the street, groups of men streamed out of a tenement. Men, women, and kids ran north up the street. Shouts and yells, flashing lights and sirens screamed from several blocks away. A group of Hispanic teenagers jogged down the block.

"Where you guys going?" one of the men asked.

"Cops are trying to evict the squatters from Tompkins Park, but they're fighting back. Man, it's a real rumble. Eggs. Bags of shit. Tear gas. Nightsticks. Better than cable."

Beatty, walking on his left, prodded him to turn up the next block. Yablonsky strained to see if there was an opening, a chance to break away. There were a lot of dead-end streets. He knew he'd end up in one of them. Closing his eyes, he heard footsteps scrape the pavement.

More families streamed out of the tenements to watch the battle between the cops and the squatters. Across the street, Yablonsky saw lights flashing behind the small, rounded dome of a mosque in which black Muslims worshiped. One of his keepers held a knife inches away from his groin as he walked. On the corner was a black man wearing a skullcap, on the telephone. "Give me 911!"

Yablonsky felt a surge of hope. "Talk and you lose two," one of the men whispered to him.

The black guy said, "This the three-one precinct? Connect me with the desk watch. I was walking down Avenue A when I saw three men breaking into the East Village Mosque. Please come down. It's urgent." He hung up, glanced briefly, curiously at the men surrounding Yablonsky; then he crossed the street, climbed the steps, and entered the mosque.

Passing under a streetlight, the men made a right, taking him down another block. Walking toward Avenue C, they stepped over a brief patch of cobblestone. Yablonsky shut his eyes, felt himself lose his balance. The man to his right and the man behind him broke his fall. "Do what we say," the man next to him whispered sympathetically. "Be calm. Get it over with quicker."

Yablonsky looked to his left. Rows of abandoned tenements. Brick-filled lots with single-story wooden buildings that acted as Puerto Rican social clubs. To his right, three black kids hanging outside a tenement, playing cops and rappers at three a.m. One of them jabbed a realistic-looking toy gun in the air. "Up against the wall, mothafucka! Or I cap your ass now!"

The other black kid pointed his toy gun at the other two. "You ain't gonna take me out like Tupac and Biggie. Throw down, mothafucka!"

"Cute kids," the man behind Yablonsky whispered.

A group of jakes, or Jamaicans, were waiting to cross the street in front of them. Yablonsky snapped to the fact that there was no van to pick them up. They intended to kill him on the street. He knew he was five minutes away from being murdered. The group of jakes paused on the sidewalk, the two groups looking each other over. Yablonsky looked briefly to his right. He recognized this row of tenements and realized where the group of jakes had come from. Forcing himself not to think, he lunged to his right, toward the man with the knife, causing him to lose his balance. Yablonsky ran.

The men drove over the floodlit span of the Verrazano. Ahead were the beckoning lights of small, sleeping towns in Staten Island. To the left, blocks of houses, then the beach. Beyond that, the vast expanse of the ocean. To the right, the curve of Manhattan, and much farther away, the red and blue lights from the George Washington Bridge.

"What a view." The man in the passenger seat looked over the sprawling, unconscious Julie Benfield next to him.

"Fucking-A," the driver said. "How long is this going to take?"

"Forty minutes for the trip there, the deposit, and the journey back, less than two hours."

"Not bad," he said. He let out a deep breath. "Clean and antiseptic. Just the way I like it."

"Who wants to whack a woman, anyway?" said the driver. "With men, though, I actually enjoy listening to them beg. They'll offer the sun, the moon, and the stars if you let them live. And they always struggle. Soon we'll be out in the trees. I like that."

The van slowed between pay lanes, then stayed in the middle of the expressway, passing exits.

Julie stirred, her hand running through her blond hair, coming away with traces of dark, dried blood. She turned to look at the nearest man. "Why are you doing this to me?"

"Just our luck," sighed the driver. "She's up."

"Me too," the other said and chuckled.

The van drove onto the service road, then turned off on a trail that headed up a steep hill. The driver took a left, a right, then headed up a one-lane path surrounded by trees and water.

"There's no reason to murder me," Julie said. "I don't even know why I'm being killed."

"Loose ends," said the driver. The guy next to her motioned for her to be quiet. The car turned off the road, drove up a hill bordered by forests, and stopped. The driver turned the headlights off, then switched on the inside light.

Julie struggled to sit up in the seat, but she was too dazed. Glancing down, she saw a long khaki duffel bag. She shuddered. Wept. "Let me live. I'll go far away."

With a smile, the driver turned to her. "What was Andy Warhol really like?"

"Let me go. Please."

"Did he do a lot of drugs?"

"Don't," she said.

"What's it like being in an artsy, independent movie? What's it like taking your clothes off in one?"

The guy sitting beside her bent down, lifted her up slowly, and put an arm solicitously around her shoulder. Pressing her head toward him, he shot her in the ear. She recoiled violently against him. He shot her again. She didn't recoil.

First light of the morning. Mounds of landfill covered with grass stretched over the hills of trash, like felt on a pool table. They entered through an exit that was supposed to be closed and drove past the mountains of refuse. Seagulls swooped over an ocean of garbage.

"Roll up the windows, Tommy," the man in the back said.

But the stench was still overpowering. Behind them to the left, a couple of miles away, was the Staten Island Mall. They drove down to a series of piers. Fresh Kills was closed, but in reality, illegal dumping went on there all the time.

Behind the marine waste transfer stations, giant mounds of trash were already encroaching on the hills of old landfill.

"This stop, Fresh Kills," said Rocco. "Let's dispose of some garbage."

The van pulled up close to the pier. The men pulled out the three long canvas bags along with a newspaper delivery cart from the rear of the van. They stuffed the three canvas bags on the cart, wheeling it to a half-filled barge docked next to one of the piers. Then they maneuvered the three bags into the great Dumpster. Seagulls circled over their heads. The men covered their mouths and went back to the van.

The driver was up front. The other guy used the barrel of his nine to sweep up the crumbs and napkins in the back. "Boy, was she beautiful," he said. "Forgetaboutit."

The driver shrugged. "You didn't murder her. The guy who told us to murder her, murdered her. He has to live with it."

The man in back slid open the middle door, then threw himself in the front passenger seat. He looked back at the barges lined up in the harbor. One that had been slowly circling Manhattan for months came into view. "Now she'll circle around the city like a satellite around the earth. The cops, too."

"Too bad."

"Yeah."

"What do we do now?"

As he stared at the brown bag, which held his coffee and sandwich. The driver's face crinkled with disgust. "It's the opposite of *The God-father*. Dump the food. Take the gun."

Yablonsky moved quickly into the darkness, the startled men behind him. Scrambling down the steps he saw the basement's iron grated security door. Bringing his coat over his head to protect his face and arms, he crashed through one of the basement windows.

There were flickers of light from the street lamps outside. He heard the men cursing, negotiating their way through the basement and out the jagged window.

In order to survive, he couldn't allow himself to become paralyzed. He looked around, peered at the hypodermic needles pried into the steel pipes lining the ceiling, and realized where he was. Press the trip wire and the hypodermic needles, filled with the AIDS virus, would spring at your face, chest, and arms like knives.

He was in a drug den, booby-trapped to eliminate cops or other drug dealers who'd try to raid this tenement for stashes of hidden cash or additional drugs. Half a dozen firemen had been knocked off in these tenements this year alone, responding to false fire alarms called in by rival drug dealers.

"I think that's him," yelled one of the four men. "Cap the mother-fucker."

Quickly cataloguing the kinds of traps he had to avoid, he rose. Crouching under the glare of the street lamps, he headed up the steps leading to the first floor.

He was near the top of the stairs. A shot rang out, ricocheting among the steel pipes. There was a scream. Beatty sank to the ground, then pulled an AIDS-filled syringe out of his arm. He stayed where he was, staring at the syringe with horror.

Yablonsky controlled his urge to go faster. At the top of the steps, he avoided the nail-studded "Welcome" mat. Hearing footsteps behind him, he hesitated before moving into the next room. Glancing down, he saw that discarded spikes, old clothes, urine pools, and piles of feces littered the floor.

He knew what the piles of feces meant and he stopped walking. He moved up the stairs instead of entering the room, and stayed there.

"Where is he?"

"Relax. We'll get the *cafone*. He ain't packed."

Yablonsky crouched, breathing softly. He watched from halfway up the landing. Three men passed beneath him, headed into the large main room. Suddenly, a hollowed-out wall crashed open and a starving pit bull lunged at one of the men, knocking him to the ground. Another ravenous dog attacked his groin. Yablonsky grimaced and scrambled up the stairs. The dogs' vocal cords had been surgically removed, so there was no barking.

Bridges and the other guy moved up the stairs after him. There was another shot.

Yablonsky passed decoy drug stashes filled with potassium chloride and red phosphorous that would explode if touched. At the top, moving away from the stairway, he dodged a trip wire with a grenade attached. The men behind him were proceeding more cautiously now.

From his experience on the street, he knew that the walls of these booby-trapped drug dens often had balloons hidden inside them. A fire lit by rivals to destroy the drug den would therefore result in the entire building going up in flames, engulfing the competition as well.

Yablonsky headed for a small parlor room. The fire escape led to the street, but that might be rigged, too. The shooting had stopped. The man who'd been attacked by the guard dogs moaned. "Help me," he whispered.

Yablonsky moved quietly to the window. It opened easily. Definitely booby-trapped, he thought.

He crouched in the corner, hiding in the darkness, hearing the whispers and footsteps of his pursuers. They were in the other room now, methodically searching. He stopped breathing when he saw them in the doorway. One went into the room, the other walked down the corridor.

Yablonsky heard slow, soft footsteps. The man inside the room with him paused in the doorway.

"Be careful, Mark."

"Fucking-A I'll be careful."

A rush of footsteps. A scream. Sheets of fire shot out from the corridor, then an explosion. Yablonsky barreled through the doorway, knocking the guy to the floor. Scrambling over him, he leapt over Bridges's burning body and made his way to the stairway.

Midway downstairs. The man writhing on the ground gasped, "Help me!"

The pit bulls' snouts were inside his stomach, moving around in his organs, devouring the intestines. Yablonsky shuddered, sped back down the stairway to the basement. He reached the smashed window again, slammed through some glass and was in the street.

"Motherfucker," he whispered to himself. There were footsteps on the stairway behind him.

Lights wavered over the rooftops. He headed for Tompkins Square Park. There'd be cops there. Then he heard their voices. Beatty and the guy he'd knocked down were working their way through the shattered window, about twenty yards behind him. He ran across the street to the three kids playing cops and rappers in front of the stoop.

To these twelve-year-old street kids, a drug den bursting into flames wasn't news. There was no attempt to call 911. No effort to help him.

"Gonna smoke you, mothafucka," one of them said. "Throw down."

Their toy pistols looked real. Maybe Yablonsky'd be able to bluff the two men who were still after him. He handed a fifty-dollar bill to the kid who was threatening his friends. "I'll give you fifty for one of those toy guns."

The kid smirked, but handed him the weapon. He moved further down the street. The two men approached him with relieved smiles. "We saw you take the toy from the kid," one said, pointing a gun at Yablonsky. "Come with us."

"Put the fucking toy down," the other guy said. "It's not funny. Don't embarrass yourself."

The detective stepped back, reflexively pressing the trigger twice. To his shock, the gun went off. Beatty and the other guy recoiled backwards, looked at him with disbelief, then collapsed.

Yablonsky stared at the three kids. "They're *real*."

The kid stepped around the two dead bodies, putting his hand out as if he expected his weapon back. "Man, mister, you fly."

THIRTY-EIGHT

At 8:30 a.m., half an hour before the *Guardian* staff were supposed to show up, the chief of detectives of New York City, followed by an assistant, sprang up the stairs. Unshaven and tired, Detective First Grade Yablonsky trudged up behind them. Passing the newspaper bin, he noticed the most recent headline: a fight broke out between the black Muslims in an East Village mosque and the arriving police, whom Muslims claimed had broken into their building. Yablonsky had seen the fight and he stopped by the bin to fold a paper into his pocket.

From the top landing, Charlie Kudos peered down at them. He looked distressed when he saw the detectives.

Ignoring the chief of detectives, he spoke to Yablonsky. "You can't be here to arrest him. This isn't really happening."

The chief of detectives was already yards away, reaching the area where the sloping floors, out-of-date computers, and sixties posters began. As Yablonsky reached the landing, Kudos said, "It's Sully who's the real victim here."

Yablonsky passed him without an answer.

"You must've seen *Les Misérables.* You're just like that cop Javert."

"I didn't have to see the Broadway play, Charlie. I read the book. And I'm not bringing in Sully for stealing a loaf of Wonder Bread."

"Judas!"

"Actor."

Seeing Sully waiting in the small reception room off of his office, he took a deep breath. He noted to himself that Barnes had still refused to send for his lawyers. Once word of his disgrace got out, no doubt there'd be platoons of lawyers.

Yablonsky was long past the point of exhaustion. He'd reached the point where the only things that kept him going were the promises he'd made to himself. Keeping his voice emotionless and flat he said, "Sully Barnes, I'm here to arrest you for the murder of Julie Benfield, Wendell Henderson and Denise Saunders."

"Just come with us, Mr. Barnes," said the chief of detectives. "No media. No perp walk. No press conferences until they're absolutely   necessary."

Yablonsky turned to look at him with disgust.

Barnes reached for a cigarette and tried to light it. He closed his eyes briefly. Ignoring the chief of detectives, he spoke directly to Yablonsky. "I'm shocked and saddened that Julie Benfield's dead, Detective. But what has that got to do with me? I've been so exhausted from all this fucking philanthropy, I spent a good portion of last night at New World Cafe, going for a caffeine high. Then I hit the shelters. I can furnish all the witnesses in the world."

"I was with him," from Kudos.

"You have no evidence against me."

"I have your gun," said Yablonsky. "The one that murdered Julie, Henderson, and Saunders."

"I can't believe a woman like Julie, so vibrant and alive, is actually dead." Barnes smiled strangely, more to himself than the detective. Again he spoke to Yablonsky, ignoring the others. "I don't know who to feel sorrier for, Alvin, you or Charlie. I mean, Charlie fucked her too, right?"

Yablonsky started forward, then stopped. Kudos looked stunned, but took a loyal step toward Barnes. "I'm calling your lawyer."

Barnes exploded. "There's still no need for lawyers. Not yet. When was Julie Benfield shot? When were these two cops shot?"

"Some time early this morning. With your gun. How'd you know Henderson and Saunders were cops? I didn't say they were."

Barnes shook his head. "My gun is back home, inside my desk drawer. I checked it last night."

"Your gun is with the evidentiary bureau back at the precinct," said Yablonsky, "and it'll link you to this crime. So will Tommy and Rocco."

"What do you mean?"

Yablonsky found himself stepping closer to Barnes. "Once there's a trial, a lot more's going to come out. You won't be able to suppress that anymore. We have a lot more than just your gun."

"My gun, which I showed you weeks ago, is safe in my apartment in Riverdale, Detective." Suddenly comprehension lit his face. "You switched guns, didn't you?"

"Switched guns with what?" asked Yablonsky. "Our surveillance of the halfway house, where Shelly hid a gun, had to begin twelve hours ago. At five a.m., Tommy and Rocco were picked up with your gun, registered in your name, trying to re-enter the building. Unfortunately, we weren't able to prevent the last murders, only solve them."

Charlie Kudos looked at Yablonsky with hatred. "You did this to him."

"He did it to himself," replied the detective. Turning back to Barnes, he said, "Tommy and Rocco took us out to Fresh Kills one hour ago. I identified Julie, Henderson and Saunders, then called you. My partners had families, by the way. You can claim you weren't involved, but that'll have to change soon. They've already rolled on you." Yablonsky paused. "I found her in the garbage barge. That's what you fucking did to Julie."

"I see." For a moment Barnes's face seemed to collapse. Reaching into the drawer, he slipped out a tiny twenty-five-caliber, stared at it, then put it in his pocket. "After you called me this morning, Alvin, I sensed it was all over. There's a way for me to avoid a scandal. Before I'm arrested and it all becomes public knowledge, give me a moment by myself in my office."

"Out of the question," said Chief Seidleman's assistant.

Barnes ignored him, again speaking to Yablonsky as if they were the only ones present in the room. "At last you'll have your justice, Detective."

"Sully, don't," said Kudos.

Barnes looked pale, shaken. Yablonsky admired courage, even in a murderer. Why not let him go in there and kill himself? Why not let him take this way out?

"It's against regulations," he said. "No."

"It's also against regulations to break into my apartment and switch my nine with Shelly's. Look, you don't know what's in my pocket. Let me go into my office so I can call my lawyer. Give me one minute."

Seidleman and Yablonsky exchanged glances. Seidleman nodded slightly. "Give him his minute to himself, Detective."

Barnes propelled himself slowly forward, closing the door. Yablonsky, already prepared to hear the shot, waited. He took out a cigarette.

"What the fuck's going on here?" yelled Seidleman's assistant.

Kudos, clutching the desk, didn't even look at the detective. They waited. Moments went by. Yablonsky kept expecting the shot, but heard nothing. Finally he headed toward the door.

"Give him his moment," pleaded Kudos. "You promised."

He ignored the actor and opened the door. He took a deep breath. The room was empty. Running to the open window, he saw Barnes in the street.

Yablonsky drew his gun. "Stop, Sully!"

Barnes kept moving, increasing his pace.

Yablonsky thrust the gun out, gripping with both hands. No one else was on the street. He could get a shot off. His first shot missed. Yablonsky hesitated, fired again. Barnes went down. He sprawled on the sidewalk, blood seeping out. Yablonsky closed his eyes, opened them. No movement.

"You killed him!" screamed Kudos. "Why'd you kill him? He felt remorse."

From the second floor Yablonsky looked down at Barnes. "I don't," he said.

THIRTY-NINE

Standing across the street from Manhattan Mini Storage, Yablonsky watched taxis and vans pull up to the building. People pushed handcarts piled with book crates. Artists lugged canvases inside. A balding guy who appeared to be in his twenties carried in a guitar, probably to practice.

Yablonsky approached the security guard.

They exchanged smiles. "Well, look who's here," said the guard. "And it's only been five and a half years since I been on the job. I miss the action. I read about you in the papers this morning. When's the inquiry?"

"Later today."

The ex-cop wasn't concerned that the detective standing before him had killed a Nobel Prize winner. "You'll sail through it. What're you doing here?"

"Still working on my investigation."

The security guard understood. He got up, placed his keys in the bottom drawer of his desk, and left his post.

Yablonsky pocketed the keys, heading for the elevator. He already knew the floor he wanted to go to.

Passing through the long corridor, Yablonsky saw a family of four close one of the doors to an eight-by-nine storage room. It was obvious they lived there. A pair of teenagers, apparently too poor to afford a hotel room, were also just leaving. The family and the teenagers smiled at each other in a neighborly way.

Yablonsky heard the muffled sounds of a drummer from one of the rooms. After not finding the medallions in Milo's cab, he'd been going over credit card receipts and bills from Judge Dillon's still-grieving but already remarried widow. Credit card statements showed that each month she paid $242.50 in rent for a five-by-nine storage room on Manhattan's West Side. Seeing crate after crate of the judge's old law books, he had to smile to himself. There were a couple of transistor radios, stacks of paintings that looked like they'd been bought at cruise ship auctions, and metal file cabinets. The cabinets were locked. Yablonsky took out a short, thin crowbar, the kind that experienced safecrackers used for breaking into safes.

Nothing was there but old records. He looked behind the file cabinets, spotted a long, thin container and pried it open. There were two logbooks and forty medallions. Each medallion was a thin tin strip weighing only a couple of ounces. He handled them with respect. After all, men had died for them.

The halls inside the building were videotaped for security reasons, but each storage room was private. So he slipped the medallions into his overcoat pockets and left.

Yablonsky handed over the money to enter the Jacob Javits Convention Center, striding past the booths, the athletes patiently signing autographs, and the sports fans who had paid large sums of money for the privilege of receiving their signature. The number of people prowling through the main floor looking for their heroes to sign autographs or ghostwritten autobiographies was even larger than at most sporting events.

Toward the end of the main floor Irene Nuñez's husband, Tito, held court.

The former super-lightweight boxing champ and current number two contender for the crown was flanked by bodyguards. Yablonsky went to the end of the very long line and took out Irene's court papers, folding them into squares, so no legal print showed.

"Meet Tito Nuñez," signs screamed. People got a chance to exchange a couple of words, dutifully pay their money, shake hands, and get the champ's signature. For extra money, you got the opportunity to pose with the champ for a photo that he would also sign.

"I'm a big fan," said Yablonsky, thrusting forth the folded-up court paper that appeared to be blank.

The wiry champ smiled back at him mechanically. "What should I write?"

"Just sign your name, champ," said Yablonsky.

"You also want an autographed picture?"

"Maybe next time," said Yablonsky. He paid and pocketed the signed court papers, stepping up an escalator and out of the building.

Yablonsky left his car, double-parked it with all the others on West Eighty-third Street, and walked through the Central Park playground. Instead of taking the crosstown road at Seventy-Ninth, he hiked through a wooded path. This way he could enter the precinct from the rear and avoid the media horde.

Once inside, Detective Yablonsky sat down in his cubicle to do paperwork. At three, he took the elevator down to the sub-basement. A union delegate ushered him into a sparsely furnished room that served as a lounge. Except for union reps, the place was deserted.

Each of the men, including Yablonsky, had a black attaché case. The taller of the two men stood when Yablonsky entered. "Anything you want to go over before the inquiry?"

"No," said Yablonsky. "I'll go in by myself."

"Are you crazy?" the union rep asked. "I.A., the chief of detectives, and the deputy mayor are all in there, waiting. They'll murder you."

"We can't let you go in there by yourself," the other said. "Union regulations don't permit it. During your inquiry, an attorney has to be present."

Yablonsky said wearily, "This is not an inquiry. This is the pre-inquiry to decide if there's going to be an inquiry. I'll go in by myself. I'll do fine."

"They're gonna kill you. You're crazy."

"I have the right to represent myself."

"Any detective who represents himself has a fool for a client."

Taking the elevator up, Yablonsky walked down the hall toward the interrogation room. Detectives carrying newspapers still blaring headlines of Sully's violent, two-day-old death solemnly wished him luck. At least the department's foot soldiers seemed to be behind him, he thought.

The room where the rear-echelon brass chose to meet with him was familiar. He'd often conducted interrogations in it. The union reps accompanied him to the door and stood outside. "We'll be out here in the hall. Call when you need us."

Yablonsky didn't answer. Once inside, the videotape was turned on and introductions were made. Chief of Detectives Seidleman, Robert "Hey" Abbott, Michael Thornton from Internal Affairs. All sat with attaché cases in front of them. Flood, coming in late, joined them. His face was neutral. Sitting opposite was Detective Yablonsky, alone.

"Have a seat, Detective," said Robert "Hey" Abbott.

"I'm already seated," Yablonsky said.

"Where are your union reps? You're entitled to them."

"I don't need them."

"You're forgoing your rights? We're on tape here, Detective. Speak up."

"I am."

"Suit yourself."

Robert "Hey" Abbott turned to Thornton, motioning him to turn the videotape off. The deputy mayor stood. Sets of newspapers were on the table. Beneath headlines proclaiming Sully's death, on the adjoining page, blared the city's second big story: the fight in the East Village between the group of street cops and a group of black militant Muslims, who, believing they were intruders, attacked them. The article in the *Guardian* never addressed what a dozen militants were doing in the mosque at four a.m., nor did it cover the police's lengthy explanation—that they'd been summoned there by a call someone made across the street, about a burglary.

Robert "Hey" Abbott paced back and forth. "This is not the first inquiry you've been involved in, is it, Detective?"

"No, sir."

"We already know that you've lied to us about your involvement in Sterling Roth's death. Now we have yet another incident, Sully Barnes. And the Shelly Townes killing, which you allege was self-defense. Then two nights ago, you were involved in yet another incident in the East Village at 3:30 a.m. in which additional people, including two dirty patrolmen, were killed. Detectives aren't supposed to be involved in street violence. They're only supposed to record crime and try to solve murders." He paused. "I consider it a cancer, you being in this department."

Yablonsky was silent, waiting.

Deputy Mayor Abbott ruffled the police reports before him. "We have Chief of Detectives Seidleman's report. We have the assistant's statement."

"You also have my report," said Yablonsky.

"Believe me, Detective, your version doesn't help you, it condemns you. You let an accused murderer leave the arrest scene. Once inside his office, he was able to procure a weapon and escape."

Yablonsky glanced at Seidleman, who serenely returned his gaze. Yablonsky, Seidleman, and his assistant all knew that Seidleman had given Barnes permission to leave the arrest scene, not Yablonsky. Seidleman's lie didn't surprise or upset him. At least Seidleman's charge only claimed that Barnes had obtained his weapon while inside his office, not before.

Abbott, leaning his fists on the table said, "If you hadn't let Barnes enter his office, he'd still be alive. This killing, or murder, really could've been avoided. How the fuck could you have given Barnes permission to leave?"

"Off the record and the videotape, I didn't," said Yablonsky.

Abbott flushed. "You killed a man while he was fleeing a crime scene and was no danger to anyone. We have witnesses."

"You also have his gun," Yablonsky said.

"That's not the point," said Abbott. "If you'd followed proper procedure, there'd been no need to murder him."

"I resent the word 'murder,' " said Yablonsky. "I yelled a warning. I adhered to proper police procedure."

"Proper police procedure's what we say it is," said Michael Thornton from I.A., "not what you say it is. Fortunately there were witnesses. They say you never yelled a warning for Barnes to stop."

The street Barnes was running down had been deserted. "You have my report," said the detective.

"And you have ours," said Deputy Mayor Abbott.

No one wondered why Yablonsky's superior hadn't countermanded his giving permission to Barnes to leave the room. No one alluded to the fact that Seidleman and his assistant were in the room with him when he'd shouted for Barnes to stop.

"There are other charges against you as well," Deputy Mayor Abbott said, opening up his attaché case and handing Yablonsky a ream of paper. "Your tickler file, Detective. You were involved in the murder of Sterling Roth. You've stolen food and goods from vendors. You've engaged in conduct unbecoming to a detective."

The men in the room waited for Yablonsky to read the file that contained dangerous and sensitive information about him, deemed too explosive for public knowledge. The detective stood, opened his attaché case. "These are your tickler files," he said, handing a report to each of the men in the room except Flood.

The room was quiet, except for paper rustling, as the men read through the incriminating information. Yablonsky had only seen Deputy Mayor "Hey" Abbott enter the after-hours bondage club on one night, but under that one night were listed other dates. But the dates and times Yablonsky claimed the deputy mayor had been in the club didn't matter. All that mattered was that the detective knew he'd been there.

Seidleman studied his own tickler file, which not only claimed that he'd given Barnes permission to leave the room, but that he'd also allowed him to take his gun in there with him.

"This is a lie," said Seidleman.

Yablonsky took a tape out of his attaché case. "If I go before a grand jury, I'll play this tape. Do you want that?"

Seidleman looked startled. Peering at Yablonsky levelly, he said, "No."

Yablonsky put the tape, which was blank, back in his attaché case. Turning to the deputy mayor, he said, "I have access to other files detailing your nocturnal activities. Want to see those?"

The deputy mayor turned quickly to his supposed ally from I.A. Had they furnished other information that they had on him? Were there additional tapes? "No," he said.

"Two nights ago while involved in carrying out my investigation, I witnessed a black guy with a skullcap making that call to the East Village precinct, setting our cops up to be assaulted. I'm sure that no one here, but especially you, want to be subjected to additional accusations of racism. If I go to the media with this information, pressure will be put on you to launch an investigation, and that'll lead to more charges from these Muslims that you're racist." Yablonsky removed his tickler file, placing it in his attaché case. "Gentlemen, we all need a way out of our various situations. Are we going to continue this inquiry into the Barnes shooting?"

"It was completely justified." Robert "Hey" Abbott nodded.

"And the cops and teamsters who tried to murder me?"

Abbott motioned for the videotape to be turned on. "Detective Alvin Yablonsky, at 7:15 a.m. on March fifteenth, when you arrived to question Sully Barnes, did he not, at some point during the interrogation, suddenly bolt from the arrest scene, enter his office, procure a pistol, and try to escape?"

"He did," said Yablonsky.

"Is it true that before firing, you issued a warning to stop?"

"I have witnesses," Yablonsky said.

"He shouted a warning," said Seidleman.

"On the previous morning," said Abbott, "while being chased by crooked cops and teamsters, did you not fire a weapon you commandeered from an adolescent? Did you discharge this weapon to protect yourself?"

"That's correct," said Yablonsky. "I tried to protect myself."

"We find that in both of these incidents, Detective First Grade Alvin Yablonsky followed proper police procedures. What's more, the detective is to be commended for knowingly risking his life while carrying out his investigation."

The videotape was turned off. "Go back and work your street killings, Detective," from Flood.

Everyone opposite him folded his tickler file into his attaché case, where it'd be concealed from the others in the room. Yablonsky stood to leave.

"Everyone in this room is shocked and sickened by the measures you've taken to defend yourself, Detective," said Robert Abbott. "I don't ever want to see you in this office again. Everything you touch turns to shit."

Yablonsky quickly moved forward, grasping Robert "Hey" Abbott's hand to shake. The procession filed out, startling the union reps waiting in the hall.

FORTY

At Farrell's, a cop bar in Brooklyn's Park Slope, Irene Nuñez smiled when she saw him enter. The other cops stared up at the pair of TVs on either end of the bar. Today they weren't watching the ball game, but the memorial service for Sully Barnes. A couple of uniforms, noticing Yablonsky, nudged each other, raised their fists in the air in a power salute, and went back to their beers.

Yablonsky stood at the bar, staring at the photos of Henderson and Saunders that had already been placed alongside pictures of other fallen cops killed in the line of duty. He joined Nuñez at a table. "You're a celebrity now, Alvin."

"Yeah," he said sadly, thinking about Julie Benfield. Men had murdered her, had treated her body like garbage.

On the broadcast, Kudos still clutched his earring, saying wonderful things about Sully in his deep, resonant voice.

"Have a beer on us," said a cop, whose blue uniform, unlike the more experienced drinkers, was bare of medals. A rookie.

Nuñez smiled at him. "I left my computer terminal at the bank to stop a robbery, so they fired me."

"I amassed bigger tickler files on them than they had on me," said Yablonsky. "So they let me stay." He reached into his overcoat and pulled out a sheaf of legal papers. "This is for you."

"Jesus, Alvin," said Nuñez. "Were you able to get me custody of my kids, too?"

"It's in there, so you have it. Tito'll have visitation rights, though."

"It won't work," she said. "Tito's too Spanish to just accept losing his kids. He'll deny signing it. You must've made him an offer he couldn't refuse."

"Yeah. Twenty dollars an autograph. Before I go back to the precinct, I've got to go to my apartment, pick up a few things."

"You told me your landlord was going to evict you, use the apartment for himself."

"He changed his mind when I told him I also had a relative coming to stay with me. A cousin named Raskolnikov. There's a guy who knows how to handle landlords."

Safe within his cubicle, Yablonsky busied himself by looking through his large stack of priors—murder cases that were still pending. He placed one file on top of the others, a murder of a homeless person in Central Park that he'd initially tried to shitcan. He studied the investigative reports and crime scene photos.

Scattered next to the shopping cart full of cans discovered near the body were a couple of grains of rice and several purple and orange beads. Drug dealers mixed grains of rice in with cocaine to prevent the powder from congealing. The beads had probably been lost by a gang member during the struggle over the cocaine. The homeless guy had probably carried it with him inside the shopping cart. Street kids used different colors and patterns of necklaces to identify the gangs they were in.

Flood entered his cubicle, one hand lugging a two-inch TV. While that snowstorm had raged that night, Yablonsky thought, and while

Tavern on the Green diners complacently ate their food, yards away, a desperate battle over drugs had been waged.

"This is my newest red ball. I'm going back to try and solve the murder of the guy we spotted in the snow a couple of nights before Skinny."

"Not that one," Flood groaned. "Some old homeless guy attacked by some other homeless guy, probably over his share of the deposit bottles in the cart."

"Just like a struggle over taxi medallions," said Yablonsky. Reaching under his desk, he lifted a gym bag. "Open it."

Flood zipped it open and looked at Yablonsky in shock. "All the medallions? How the fuck did you find them?"

"I checked the Judge's widow's receipts, noticed credit card payments to Manhattan Mini Storage. There they were."

"You should be a detective," said Flood. "But why return them?" He paused, looking at Yablonsky as if he were certifiable. "Weren't you tempted to keep them? You have the logbooks. With a little bribery, it'd be legal."

"I want no part of them. The corruption I'd have to engage in to keep them would be too big for me. You read my tickler file. It's all small-time stuff."

"Not anymore." He paused. "So you think *I* should be the one to return them." Flood let out a breath. "Thanks. But to whom?"

Yablonsky smiled at Flood's moral dilemma. "First, tell I.A. you have them, then give all of them to Deputy Mayor Abbott. Maybe they'll murder each other over the split."

"No harm in being optimistic. You sure about this?"

"I am," said Yablonsky. "Money's not worth killing anybody over."

Flood switched on the two-inch TV, which filled with Charlie Kudos, along with many other celebrities. It was a rebroadcast of Sully's memorial service.

Flood sat on top of the desk. "Did you like Sully, Alvin?"

"At one time."

"Were you sorry you had to kill him?"

"No. He murdered Julie, Wendell, and Denise, my partners."

"You could've shitcanned the case," said Flood. "Turned the other cheek. Maybe Barnes wouldn't have had them all killed."

"If I had turned the other cheek, Barnes would have just slapped it."

"You should take a few days off."

"A few days off?"

"As a detective . . ."

"I won't get over her."

"These mistakes can't undo an entire life of doing good," said Kudos on the screen.

The two cops studied the celebrity-filled crowd. "They look almost ecstatic," said Flood.

"By committing these crimes, Barnes gave them the opportunity to forgive him," said Yablonsky.

"Sully's spirit is going to live on," continued Kudos. "Whenever a man is hungry and people refuse to feed him, he'll be there. Whenever individuals need acts of kindness, a cup of coffee, and a blanket to get them through the night, he'll be there. Whenever brutal cops use excessive force to railroad the innocent, there he'll be."

"I like watching Charlie when the screen's so small," said Flood.

Yablonsky clicked off the TV. "I have to meet with a potential source."

"I have to go, too," said Flood. "My well-connected wife's running a fund-raiser."

Outside, behind the station, the media had finally discovered the rear exit. Satellite vans parked in the woods, crawled like beetles through the bare forest behind the precinct.

Flood, walking behind him, already had a dozen microphones shoved in his face. "Can you tell us about the precinct's reaction to Sully's death?"

"A tragedy for all concerned," said Flood.

"The murder rate's creeping back up," said a reporter wearing a New York One logo. "Last weekend a dozen people were murdered in drive-bys, bar fights, and domestic disputes."

"Why don't you mention all the people in New York who *weren't* murdered last weekend?" said Flood.

"Do you think they'll rescind Sully's Nobel Peace Prize, now that he's a murderer?" one of the reporters asked Yablonsky.

Lots of murderers had already received the Peace Prize, Yablonsky thought. "I hope so."

"Did you speak to Sully at all before you killed him?"

"These are all good questions, but I've been advised by my precinct captain not to comment."

"Are you back on the job?" from Bob Anders.

"Are you interrogating me?" He paused, heading toward his double-parked car on West Eighty-third Street. "I don't like being interrogated."